WINNER OF THE 2010 W.Y. BOYD LITERARY AWARD
FOR EXCELLENCE IN MILITARY FICTION

PRAISE FOR *SEEN THE GLORY*

"John Hough catches the spirit of young enlisted men in the army, and does a splendid job of research on the Twentieth Massachusetts to get its role in the Gettysburg campaign right. It is a great read."

—James B. McPherson, author of the Pulitzer Prize–winning
Battle Cry of Freedom: The Civil War Era

"A compelling tale of friendship, family, and suspense set against the backdrop of the American Civil War, full of vivid characters, clever social commentary, and intense action."

—Stephen L. Carter, author of *Jericho's Fall* and *The Emperor of Ocean Park*

"It reads as if you were there. Hough captures the chaos, excitement, brutality and nature of the battle as well as anyone has. It is the way I think a soldier in combat saw it."

—Scott Hartwig, Gettysburg Battlefield Historian

"Hough's saga of the Chandler family of Martha's Vineyard delivers plenty of period accuracy, historical drama, and page-turning reading pleasure."

—Chuck Leddy, *The Boston Globe*

"*Seen the Glory* offers a vivid and brutal glimpse into one of America's most famous battles . . . A gripping read."

—Bob Cox, *Fort Worth Star-Telegram*

"John Hough looks at the theme of race and the battle of Gettysburg from a strikingly different angle. Join up and go to war with these boys from the Vineyard; you won't be able to catch your breath until this fast, brilliant novel is over. *Seen the Glory* is an original, profound novel, with the best dialogue of the period I have ever read."

—Lee Smith, author of *On Agate Hill*, *Fair and Tender Ladies*, and *Oral History*

"John Hough has created a true American story, truer than our collective memory has allowed until now. For that reason it deepens our understanding of the waste and tragedy of the Civil War—and the challenge for us of living out its complicated legacy."

—Lorene Cary, author of *Black Ice* and *The Price of a Child*

"Hough writes about the Civil War with a novelist's insight and a historian's eye. . . . Amid the blood and fury of battle, a tender and poignant story of idealism, love and brotherly devotion shines through."

—*Publishers Weekly*

"Hough excels at re-creating the chaos, the confusion, and the brutality of war, and his searing, authentically rendered battle scenes should satisfy Civil War enthusiasts. A heartrending family saga wrapped up in an epic clash of armies and ideals."

—*Booklist*

"Following in the footsteps of Michael Shaara's classic novel about Gettysburg, *The Killer Angels*, Hough's epic novel draws in the philosophical conundrums of a country at war and in which the lines among ideology, trust, and love can stand the barrage of battle."

—*Library Journal*

"Hough's powerful war narrative kept me spellbound throughout the course of this fine and rewarding novel. . . . [He] has an admirable ability to impart the small details that lend this narrative its heartbreaking immediacy."

—Barbara Clark, *The Barnstable (MA) Patriot*

ALSO BY JOHN HOUGH, JR.

The Last Summer

SEEN *the* GLORY

A Novel of the Battle of Gettysburg

John Hough, Jr.

Simon & Schuster Paperbacks

NEW YORK • LONDON • TORONTO • SYDNEY

Simon & Schuster Paperbacks
A Division of Simon & Schuster, Inc.
1230 Avenue of the Americas
New York, NY 10020

First Simon & Schuster trade paperback edition June 2010

SIMON & SCHUSTER PAPERBACKS and colophon are registered trademarks of Simon & Schuster, Inc.

For information about special discounts for bulk purchases, please contact Simon & Schuster Special Sales at 1-866-506-1949 or business@simonandschuster.com.

The Simon & Schuster Speakers Bureau can bring authors to your live event. For more information or to book an event, contact the Simon & Schuster Speakers Bureau at 1-866-248-3049 or visit our website at www.simonspeakers.com.

Designed by Paul Dippolito

Manufactured in the United States of America

1   3   5   7   9   10   8   6   4   2

The Library of Congress has cataloged the hardcover edition as follows:
Hough, John.
Seen the glory: a novel of the Battle of Gettysburg/John Hough, Jr.—
1st Simon & Schuster hardcover ed.
p. cm.
1. Gettysburg, Battle of, Gettysburg, Pa., 1863—Fiction.
2. Brothers—Fiction. 3. Soldiers—Fiction. I. Title.
PS3558.O84S44 2009
813'.54—dc22   2008046211

ISBN 978-1-4165-8965-5
ISBN 978-1-4165-8966-2 (pbk)
ISBN 978-1-4165-9387-4 (ebook)

For Kate, again. And for B. J. Robbins

CONTENTS

HOLMES HOLE, 1858

The stowaway, whose name was Joseph Ruffin, came ashore with young Peleg Davenport on a moonlit night in the middle of July. It was well after midnight, getting on toward one o'clock. The light of the full moon lay across the harbor with its huddled ships, its thickets of masts, booms, yards, and upslanted bowsprits. It bathed the town, glazing the dry, wagon-rutted dirt roadways, lighting the white spires of the two churches, falling liquid and faintly yellow down weathered-shingle storefronts and houses of white clapboard. Absolute silence: a ghost town. Peleg led the black man up Union Street, past Fischer Brothers Marine Hardware, past the Seamen's Bethel and Luce's Dry Goods & Groceries, then north on Main. They did not speak, Joseph trudging a little behind in his loose sack coat and denim trousers, his worn and water-stiffened brogans. They turned again, up the steep incline of Drummer Lane, and here Joseph Ruffin slowed, moving unsteadily, erratic, as if the tilt of the land disoriented him. Ahead of him Peleg Davenport stopped walking. Joseph had stopped, and Peleg sensed it. It was dark here, with lilac hedges walling both sides of the lane and the trees closing in overhead. Peleg regarded him with a worried squint, and spoke, finally, in a harsh whisper.

"You come on now. It ain't but another minute."

Joseph looked up at him from the dark of the lane and said nothing.

"You come on," Peleg said again. "We get there you can have all the damn water you want."

Joseph nodded. He fished a handkerchief out of his coat pocket and looked down at it in his hand as if someone else had placed it there and he wondered what its use might be.

"You come on now," Peleg whispered again. "I'm in trouble same as you we get caught."

He turned without waiting to see what Joseph would do, stand there contemplating his handkerchief or follow him, and went briskly, almost angrily, to the top of the lane. He crossed William Street at an angle, still not looking back, to a large white-clapboard house in the Greek revival style, its tall gable end facing front. A white picket fence set it off from the road. In the narrow front yard hung a white- and black-painted wooden sign, easily legible in the tree-filtered moonlight: *Dr. Geo A. Chandler, Phys and Surg.* Peleg let himself in through the gate then looked down-street toward Drummer Lane. Nothing. Shaking his head, he climbed the porch steps and lifted the brass knocker. Across the street, as the first tentative raps rang softly out, Joseph emerged from the lane into the lacy moonlight and came toward the doctor's house, slow, decrepit-seeming, dragging his coated and hatless shadow beside him.

Luke and Thomas Chandler, thirteen and eleven that year, woke simultaneously to the light rapping. They scrambled out of bed in their muslin union suits and knelt to look out, a boy at each window. They watched the Negro come up the street and through the gate, very thin in the loose-hanging wool coat and baggy trousers. Under the coat he wore a white shirt of cotton, no collar. His face in the moonlight was slack, haggard. The boys looked at each other wordlessly, then craned out to peer at the white man on the porch beneath them. He wore a mechanic's hat and was big and well built.

"Hey," Thomas called down.

Peleg Davenport let go of the knocker and stepped back. He looked up and found Thomas.

"What do you want?" Thomas said.

"What I want is you keep your voice down," Peleg said.

"Why?" Thomas said.

"Let us in I'll tell you."

"Go wake Rose," Luke said.

Joseph, inside the gate now, looked up at Thomas, at Luke, eyeing them with mute curiosity. After a moment he turned, slow, and sat heavily down on the bottom porch step.

"Listen," Peleg said, "I got to get this nigger off the street."

"Go wake her," Luke told Thomas.

But Rose was awake now, out of bed, they could hear her through the wall, moving about barefoot, opening and closing a drawer.

"Stay here," Luke said, getting to his feet.

Thomas rose too, as Luke had known he would, and the two of them hurried into their clothes while Rose's bedroom door opened with a snap of its iron latch and she glided down the hallway, down the stairs.

"Stay here," Luke said again, buttoning his pants.

"Why?" Thomas said, buttoning his.

Luke didn't answer, what was the use, and Thomas followed him, the two of them shoeless, thumping pell-mell down the stairs in the gauzy half light as Rose opened the front door. She had not brought a lamp or candle, there was no need.

"And what is this?" she said.

Peleg Davenport stared at her, surprise knitting his wide amiable cleanshaven face. He looked away, speechless, digesting this new development, then again at Rose.

"Evenin," he said.

"Evening."

Rose stood with her arms folded, square-shouldered and narrow-waisted, her crimson velvet robe tightly belted. Her hair was down, feathery and coal-black where the moon struck it, her skin as coffee-brown as Joseph's though she was Cape Verdean. *Rose Miranda.* Joseph twisted around finally and looked up to discover her in the doorway.

"What's all this?" Rose said.

"Look like heaven, Mr. Peleg. We done arrive among the blessed angels." The voice was low, soft, rusty, and in its lazy melody Luke imagined the South, its scented evenings and enervating summer days, its dusty roads, its bayous and swamps, its olden mystery. "A angel, sure enough," Joseph said, continuing his backward inspection of Rose.

"He ain't feelin well," Peleg explained.

Rose looked at Joseph. She looked at Peleg. "And it can't wait till morning," she said.

"Ma'am," Peleg said, "we'll come in if that's all right."

"Better tell me why, at this hour," Rose said.

"This here's a slave, run off down in Georgia," Peleg said.

"Georgia," Rose said. "A slave."

Peleg looked up and down the empty street. The trees threw their black shadows over the silk-gray road. Somewhere out behind the house an owl loosed its fluttering cry across the stillness. Peleg lifted a deep breath and began again. "I'm Peleg Davenport. Live up Manter Hill? I come back on the *Lizzie Freeman* yesterday. Captain Anson Daggett. We were all the way to Savannah, Georgia. Took on a cargo of lumber and laid over a night and while we were ashore this nigger snuck on board."

He stopped, met Rose's gaze.

"Negro," he said. "This Negro."

"Go on," Rose said.

Joseph sat with his back to them, listening.

"Nobody knows about him cep me and another boy name Charlie Swenson, lives up in North Tisbury. Charlie's the one found him. Down in the hold. Heard him movin around one night. We didn't want to send him back so we took a oath of secrecy. Charlie left it to me to come back and fetch him ashore. Said he's through with it, wasn't gonna take no more risks."

"Better come in, then," Rose said.

"His name's Joseph," Peleg said.

"He own a last name?" Rose said.

Joseph, still sitting, cleared his throat. "Ruffin," he said. "Joseph Ruffin."

"You're welcome, Mr. Ruffin," Rose said.

"I thank you." He hauled himself to his feet and Peleg took his arm and led him up the steps. "He's awful thirsty," he said. He helped him up into the house. His odor moved with him like an aura; the sweetish smell of his unwashed body, the sharp reek of sweat, of urine. Peleg took his cap off, held it with both hands.

"He run out of water, and me and Charlie couldn't always provide him," he said.

"Luke," Rose said, "fetch your father down here."

"Go get him, Thomas," Luke said.

"You go," Thomas said.

"One of you go or he'll want to know why," Rose said.

Luke jerked his chin toward the stairs and Thomas started up, then turned and looked down at the rest of them, leaning out over the banister. "Is he really a slave?" he said.

"All of em's slaves down there," Peleg said. "It's pitiful."

"We're abolitionists, aren't we, Rose?" Thomas said.

"Want me to kick you up those stairs?" Luke said.

Thomas grinned at him and was gone.

"Run fetch some water, Luke," Rose said. "Fill that white pitcher. Draw it till it flows fresh, hear?"

He came down unshaven and partially dressed in a clean white shirt without tie or collar or vest, navy trousers with braces strapping his narrow shoulders, bedroom slippers. George Chandler: a small, wiry, hunch-shouldered man in spectacles, bald on top, skin like toughened leather.

The boys stood in the hallway with Peleg Davenport. The front door had been closed and a lamp burned on a lamp rug on the hall table, its soft steady glow casting the boys in dusky silhouette in the Chippendale mirror. Rose had shown Joseph to the doctor's office and had not come back.

"Father," Thomas said, "this is Mr. Davenport."

"William Davenport's boy," Chandler said.

"Yes sir."

"I set his arm. One of my first patients."

"Yes sir."

"He'll be proud of you."

"No sir, he won't, cause I ain't gonna tell him. He thinks the slaves ought to be slaves. Way God made em."

"God didn't make them slaves," Thomas said.

"Not now, Thomas," Chandler said.

"Well He didn't," Thomas said.

"Shut up," Luke said.

Rose came through the dining room into the hall carrying a lamp, swift and silent in her belted robe. Peleg watched her come. He glanced at her bare brown feet, a slice of ankle. She put the lamp down on the table, the room brighter now, the mirror agleam.

"I don't think he understands he's on an island," she said.

"He's right ignorant," Peleg said.

"He wasn't so ignorant he couldn't find his way across the whole state of Georgia," Rose said. "Told me it took him ten days, did you know that?"

"Yes ma'am," Peleg said.

"Hiding out in the woods. Eating berries."

"Yes ma'am," Peleg said. And thought: *Didn't ever meet one like her.* He wondered if all city Negroes were as pricklesome. Talking up like that to a white man.

"He's waiting on you, Dr. Chandler," she said.

Peleg had intended to deliver Joseph Ruffin to the doctor and go home and be done with it, but here he sat, at the kitchen table with Luke and Thomas and the colored woman, eating hermits and drinking sweet milk cold from the oakwood icebox, Rose sitting elevated on a three-legged stool at the head of the table. Arms folded, bare heels propped on the rung.

"You folks got some nice things in this house," Peleg said, looking around at the icebox, the enameled Monarch stove, the shelf rows of burnished pewter plates and goblets.

"We have a Soule's Washing Machine," Thomas said.

"What does it wash?" Peleg said.

"Clothes," Thomas said, "what do you think?"

"Wipe your mouth, Thomas," Rose said.

"You like livin on the Vineyard?" Peleg said.

"Well enough," Luke said.

"How come you to leave New Bedford?" Peleg said.

"You're just full of questions, aren't you?" Rose said.

Peleg reddened, smiled, shrugged. "No ma'am."

"Father wanted a change," Thomas said. "Isn't that so, Rose?"

"Are you going to eat that hermit or leave it sit there?" Rose said.

"Eat it," Thomas said.

"I ain't never been to New Bedford," Peleg said.

"You've been to Savannah, Georgia, but not New Bedford," Rose said.

"I been to Charleston South Carolina, and up the Indian River in Florida."

"My," Rose said.

"When I'm sixteen Father's going to take us to Europe," Thomas said. "Rose, too. Isn't that right, Rose?"

"You get to sixteen and we'll see," Rose said.

"I think about shipping on a whaler," Peleg said. "A body can see the whole world that way."

"Get et by a whale," Thomas said.

"I ain't afeard of a whale," Peleg said.

A door opened off the dining room. The doctor's office was at the front of the house, adjacent to a bedroom for surgery or for patients who might need to lie down, and behind it the dining room. Rose and the boys stopped talking. The doctor stood in the kitchen doorway, at the edge of the lamp's yellow nimbus, thoughtful, eyes downcast and unseeing, as if some new thought had come crowding in and he'd forgotten the runaway slave in his office.

"How is he?" Luke said.

His father's gaze came up, found Luke. "Dehydrated," he said. "It makes you dizzy. Confused. We get some food in him, some more water, he'll be fine."

"I best heat a bath," Rose said, letting herself down off the stool. "And we better find him some clothes that don't smell like low tide."

"Wait," Dr. Chandler said. He removed his spectacles, closed his eyes and massaged them with his thumb and forefinger. He put the spectacles back on and adjusted them on his nose. "I would like all of you to come look at something," he said. "Perhaps not you, Rose."

"Look at what?" she said.

"The marks of slavery. It won't do you any good to see them."

"I might want to," Rose said.

"You might not."

"I have a right," she said.

The doctor eyed her kindly. "I suppose you do," he said.

The boys gulped the last of their milk and pushed their chairs back. Rose turned the lamp down and they followed the doctor through the dining room, where the west-hanging moon shone on the broad polished rectangle of the Hepplewhite table. Peleg eyed the table, the upholstered dining chairs and mahogany sideboard and corner cupboard whose glass door, too, mirrored the moonlight. They went through the patient's bedroom, which contained a four-poster bed, and into the doctor's office, where the Negro Joseph Ruffin sat on a Windsor chair with his soiled white-cotton shirt draped cloaklike over his shoulders, staring thoughtfully at the yellowed human skeleton that stood smiling in the corner. A lamp burned on the table beside him and another on Dr. Chandler's desk. On the table too were the white stoneware pitcher and tumbler Luke had brought. The front window curtains were drawn but the side window was uncurtained and open. They gathered before him in silent audience and Joseph looked up at them and brightened, as if they were performers, clowns, sent in to amuse him. His smell hung in the room, but it was leavened by the sweet air moving in through the open window.

"You done brung me to a good place, Mr. Peleg," he said. "Two pretty boys and a angel."

"We're abolitionists," Thomas said.

"That a fack," Joseph said.

"Father knows Frederick Douglass," Thomas said.

"He doesn't *know* him," Luke said. "He heard him speak. So did we."

"I ain't knowed him either," Joseph said. "Who is he?"

"Frederick Douglass," Thomas said. "He's famous."

"Hush," Rose said.

"Joseph?" the doctor said.

"Suh?"

"Would you show them?"

"Yes suh," Joseph said, and, rising slowly, slid the shirt from off his shoulders and turned his back to them and stood still.

"God almighty," Peleg said.

The lashes had been laid on every which way, neck to waist, the narrow back of the Negro all striped and crisscrossed with ridges that had healed gray and jagged. He'd been whipped and whipped and whipped, till the scars had crowded one another, bunching, piling up.

"Thank you, Joseph," the doctor said.

Rose turned away and put the back of her hand to her mouth as if she'd burned herself. She shot a look at the doctor, quick and savage, then shook her head as if anticipating some request from him, some command she was refusing in advance, and strode from the room.

"Rose," he called after her. And: *"Rosie."*

"She's crying," Thomas said.

"I ain't never seed it myself," Joseph said. "I guess it look right ugly."

"I'll go to her," Luke said.

"Best let her be," his father said.

"I'd like to go, Father," Luke said.

"Not now, Luke," the doctor said.

Massa, Joseph Ruffin said, done sold me to a preacher name Barfield, and that's when all the whuppins done started. Ain't been whupped but one time before that. This Barfield, he own a fine big place, bout two hundred acres, and he believe in workin his niggers long and hard and whuppin em long and hard. The first time it happen they catched me sellin liquor durin the preachin on Sunday. Massa buck me down on a barrel and beat the blood out of me. Ain't had no doctor neither, just the Missus come down out of the big house and clean me up some. Another time I done stole me a ham and a nigger name Augustus done told on me and Massa put me in the stocks this time and done whup me till I cry. Y'all know what the stocks is? They put the foots in and clamp em together, and then they got a crosspiece go right across the breast. That crosspiece, it long enough to tie the hands to it at the ends. They strip you naked and tear you up with that lash. Twenty-five lashes. Fifty of em. Massa tell you how many. Tell you before he start in. I run off after that and the patrols catched me and Massa done whup me again. He say I crazy. Say I talks crazy and do crazy. Name is Barfield. Mr. Lemuel Barfield. He say he whup me till I ain't run no more.

Luke tapped on her door and she said come in, and he did. The room smelled flower-like, the air impregnated with the compounded fragrances of cologne and facial powders and rosewater. She was sitting in her velvet chair by the window, in her velvet robe. The moon was on that side of the house and still above the treeline, and she sat in its soft bright bathe gazing down at the tree-shaded side yard and did not look at Luke, did not move. On the plank floor beside her stood an empty tumbler and a bottle with a couple of fingers of liquor left in it.

"Are you drinking whiskey, Rose?" Luke said.

"I ain't brushin my teeth with it," she said.

His father dispensed it medicinally and from time to time allowed Rose a half- or two-thirds-drunk bottle, never a full one, to take to her room because she said it helped her sleep. She'd arrived from the orphanage in New Bedford with a knowledge of spirits and a taste for them. They were strict there but Rose said the girls could sneak in and out at night if they were willing to risk a strapping. They knew their way around the city but Rose wouldn't say where she had acquired hard liquor at so young an age.

"Why are you?" Luke said.

"You sound like Thomas with your questions," she said.

Luke wanted to close the door but did not. He came in closer. "Because of what you saw," he said. "Because it upset you."

"Are you asking or telling?" she said.

"He'll be safe now," Luke said. "Father's going to take him to Gay Head in the carryall. The Indians'll take him in. They'll get him over to New Bedford. To the Railroad. He'll be in Canada in no time."

"Well, that's fine," Rose said.

"Thomas is heating him a bath," Luke said. "Father said not to bother you."

"But here you are."

"I just wanted to tell you about Joseph. I thought you'd want to know."

"I do, honey. Course I do."

He watched her, the face smooth and dark brown in the moonlight, eyes black and lustrous. *Rose,* he thought. *Rosie.* She'd been with them three years and Luke could not clearly remember their life before that, before their mother took sick and to her bed and Rose arrived from the orphanage, beautiful even then. What had the four of them talked about at the dinner table before Rose came? What had their mother said to him and Thomas as she tucked them in and bent down to kiss them? She had been pretty if not exactly beautiful, but Luke now couldn't see her face without consulting one of the ambrotypes scattered about the house.

"I'm going to give him a suit of clothes," Luke said. "Do you think he'll want a union suit?"

"What do I know about union suits?" Rose said.

Luke smiled and came closer. The room was smaller than his and Thomas's but cooler in the summertime and warmer in winter. Her bed was a four-poster with a blue-and-white-checked canopy. Feather pillows in satin cases. There was a mahogany dressing table with an oval mirror, mahogany chest of drawers, a marble-topped washstand, a wicker rocker. Silver candelabra on the mantel shelf, and on the bedside table a leatherbound *Works of Byron* and the latest number of *Godey's Lady's Book*.

"Rosie? Are you drunk?"

"You ever see me drunk?" she said.

"I don't know."

"Well I do. And you ain't."

"Why are you saying ain't?"

"Ain't there something you s'posed to do?" she said. "Something about a suit of clothes, I recollect."

"Why are you talking like that?"

"Like what?" she said.

"I know why," Luke said.

"Do you, now."

"I don't mind," he said. "I like it."

The rocking chair stood next to the bedside table with its unlit lamp and the book and magazine; Luke dragged it to the window and sat down so close to Rose that their knees nearly touched. He could smell the tang of whiskey on her breath and as well the remnant of yesterday's cologne, pleasantly faded, and the lavender soap she bathed with.

"Is that Peleg boy still here?" she said.

"He'll ride up the Highway with Father and Joseph."

"He's a hard one to get rid of, isn't he?"

"Why don't you like him?"

"I like him well enough."

Still she sat gazing down through the open window, leaning slightly forward, poised like that, motionless. "Lightning bug," she said, watching it wink, then wink again, down in the shadows.

"What's wrong, Rosie?" Luke said.

She brought up a sigh, was still a moment. "Settin here thinking, that's all."

"Thinking what?"

"Thinking I got more clothes than any white woman in this town. Got a nicer room. Eat better. Don't get whipped."

"As if," Luke said, "anyone would want to whip you."

"There's some what might."

"I'd like to see them try."

She looked at him, smiled. Below them the lightning bugs flashed white-green in the dark.

"Do you know your daddy pays me, besides? Pays me ten dollars a month, hard money."

"Why shouldn't he?" Luke said.

Then Thomas was climbing the stairs, so quiet on his bare feet that Luke wondered if he was creeping up to eavesdrop. Quiet, too, in the hall. Luke turned, watched Thomas materialize in the doorway.

"Father wants to know where those clothes are," he said.

"I'm getting them."

"It doesn't look like you are."

"Well, I am."

"Joseph's near about done bathing. Then Father says you're to hitch up the carryall."

"Why don't you hitch it up?"

"I don't like to," Thomas said. "Nancy doesn't like me."

"Baby," Luke said.

"Stop that," Rose said.

"Go on down, then," Luke told him. "I'll be down directly."

"Me too," Rose said.

"Why don't you come now?" Thomas said from the doorway.

"We will, honey," Rose said. "You go on now. Give that Joseph a nice clean bath towel."

Thomas nodded, cast a final envious look at Luke, and disappeared.

"Be nice to your brother," Rose said.

"He's bothersome," Luke said.

"You get older, he's going to need you to look out for him."

"He can look out for himself."

"Might be he can't. Might be up to you."

"Why?" Luke said.

"Just the way it is," Rose said. "You'll do it, too. I know you will."

She leaned, picked up the bottle by the neck. Bininger's Old Kentucky Bourbon. She looked down and found the tumbler.

"You shouldn't," Luke said.

"I know," Rose said.

"Father'll smell it on you."

"I've got something for that," she said.

Luke stood up. Rose placed the bottle on the chair between her thighs and uncorked it. She placed the cork on the windowsill and picked up the tumbler and bottle and poured herself an inch of whiskey. Luke stood there watching her. Her hands were almond-shaped, nails tinted red, delicate veins trickling down to smooth delicate knuckles. She capped the bottle and set it on the floor.

"What did he do to get those whippings?" she said.

"He kept running away."

"Imagine that. They whip them for wanting to live free. Just free, that's all." She tilted the glass up, took a swallow, made a face.

"Rosie," Luke said.

She looked up at him. Sad.

"You aren't going to leave us, are you?" he said.

"Why do you ask, child?"

"I don't know," Luke said.

"Where would I go?" she said.

Massa done sell my wife off to Texas, then done sell me to Mr. Lemuel Barfield. Got five hundred dollars for her. Got eight hundred for me. They make a whole heap of money sellin they niggers. My wife down in Texas, I ain't see her no more, and that's how come I run. I run three times fore I gets on that boat. Patrols catched me every time but that one. Massa say I crazy. He say it must be I likes gettin whupped.

The stable crouched behind the house to the right, unpainted, with a shed roof and a pair of sliding doors along its taller side. Next to it, directly behind the house and running some distance back to the edge of the property, was Rose's flower garden, her beds of phlox and sunflowers and tea roses and hollyhocks as tall as Luke or taller on their rigid stalks. The well stood nearby, opposite the barn, and in the early summer mornings you would hear its slow whir and squeak and after a moment a leafy splash as Rose hurled the bucket of water on the garden. Bucket after bucket in dry weather.

Luke had brought a lighted lantern and he stood a moment with the lantern held down at his side, breathing deeply of the night air, which brought the scent of honeysuckle from beyond the unpainted picket fence at the back of the property. The moon now had fallen below the tree line. He could hear the ocean on the north shore, its long sigh as it fell and moved up the beach, its inbreath as it retreated. He wondered why you could hear it at night but not in the daytime, where the trick of that resided. He wondered why, a mile uphill from the water and out of sight of it, you could hear a steamer's engine, its deep throb and hum, more loudly than if you were standing on the beach with the ship not half a mile away.

He gripped the iron ring and heaved the right-side barn door back on its roller. Nancy snorted a greeting from the pitch dark of her stall. The stable air was thick and dry. There was Nancy's rich horse smell and the not unpleasant smell of her dung. There was the warm dry fragrance of the baled hay. Luke took in these smells as he had the honeysuckle and wondered when he'd ever felt so grown-up and alive.

He set the lantern down on a barrel and took the bridle down from its peg. Nancy stamped, nickered. She was accustomed to going out at all hours and unsurprised to see Luke. He opened the stall door and got in with her. He stroked her back and held the bridle for her to smell.

"What did you do to Thomas?" he said. "Did you bite him, Nance? Did you bite that little sonofabitch?"

He slid the reins over her head and offered her the bit and she took it and he bridled her. He led her from the stall to the adjacent bay where the carryall waited and backed her between its two poles and told her to stay there. He retrieved the lantern and set it on the floor and pulled the heavy clinking harness off its rack. He threw it over her neck and back, and as he harnessed her he thought, for the first time, about what they were doing. They were breaking the law and he had not considered that, had not viewed it in that light. But they were, all of them, and now they were part of something, and Luke understood what it was to take a stand. To say to the world: No.

He led Nancy out of the barn and down the short wheel-carved drive with the yellow lantern light moving, swaying, ahead of him. The carryall creaked and rattled. He turned the mare onto William Street, the carryall swinging out wide, and stopped her at the gate and extinguished the lantern. The front door opened and his father came down the porch steps. He wore his black felt hat and had put on a silk vest and collar. He carried his frock coat over his arm and his black bag in the other hand. He placed the bag on the wagon bed and hauled himself to the driver's seat. Luke handed him the reins. The doctor swiveled around, looked up and down the street, then beckoned to the house. The door opened and Joseph emerged, with Peleg Davenport behind him. Joseph in a pair of Luke's too large cotton trousers belted above his waist, a too large red-and-white-checked shirt with the sleeves rolled. A paper sack in his hand, food put up by Rose. Peleg coatless, in his cloth cap.

"I'll take the light," Chandler said, and Luke passed him the dark lantern.

"If I knowed it was a island," Joseph said, "I find me another boat."

"Hurry up," Chandler said. "Nothing that fool Lambert would like better than to apprehend a runaway slave." Lambert was the constable. A drunken fool.

"You say these Injuns friendly," Joseph said.

"Of course," the doctor said.

"Injuns in Georgia ain't friendlies," Joseph said. "Nigger or white, don't make a bit a difference."

"They're friendly here," Luke said.

"They ain't got a choice," Peleg said.

"Hurry," the doctor said. "Cover him, Luke."

Joseph climbed into the back of the carryall with his paper sack and lay down on his side.

"Good luck," Luke said to him.

"Bless you, chile."

The tarpaulin was folded under the driver's seat. Luke shook it out and threw it over Joseph.

"Sit in back, sir?" Peleg said.

"Up here," the doctor said.

Peleg pulled himself up beside him. "Good-bye, Luke," he said.

"Good-bye, Peleg."

"Be seein you."

"I hope so," Luke said.

Dr. Chandler shook the reins and Nancy nodded and set off at a brisk walk, the carryall rattling louder under its load. Luke watched it roll away in the gray shadowy night with the darkened houses on either side, his father sitting hunched and gnomelike beside Peleg. The road bent and they disappeared, audible still, creak and rattle and the muted thump of hooves, dying away as Luke turned and saw Rose and Thomas side by side on the front porch, Rose with her arm around him.

"Rose says you and I are men now," Thomas said.

"One of us, maybe," Luke said, and looked to the southern sky. It was a molten gray now, the stars shining feebly. Luke looked to it and as if in answer a snake's tongue of dry lightning darted and vanished, darted again. The South, Luke thought. *The South.* Where somewhere the man Brown was said to be storing weapons for an insurrection he would lead. A story was being written, and they were part of it now.

"Rose says both of us," Thomas said.

Luke smiled. He went in through the gate and shut it behind him.

"Think I'll fix breakfast," Rose said, unhooking her arm from around Thomas's waist. "Anybody interested?"

"It's not morning yet," Thomas said.

"Almost is. Got fresh eggs. Got ham."

"Will you make biscuits, Rosie?" Thomas said.

"I might."

They went into the house, Thomas, then Rose, and as she stepped up onto the threshold Luke touched her elbow, whether to guide her forward as he'd seen gentlemen do with ladies or to draw her attention to himself, he could not have said. Rose turned quickly and met his eye, as surprised as he was, and Luke could only look away, wondering at himself.

Peleg Davenport, sitting silent beside the doctor, the Negro invisible under the tarpaulin, thought only of Rose. *Damn if she ain't a looker,* he thought. *Damn if she ain't as pretty as a white girl.* The doctor shook the reins and the horse sped up, trotted, hooves rhythmic on the solid dirt. They were leaving the village, climbing the gentle rise of Manter Hill.

"A mile or so," the doctor said over his shoulder, "and you can come up out of there."

"I hears you," came Joseph's muffled voice beneath the oilcloth.

"Tell me where you'll get down," the doctor said to Peleg.

"Yes sir. It ain't but a small piece from here."

Damn if she ain't, he thought.

PART I

Gather from the Plain

ONE

The land had been cleared by loggers on both sides of the river and what the loggers hadn't cut down the two armies had, leaving only the occasional tree or grove for shade. The ground was generally low along the river and in some places the river not more than five rods across, and in the evenings the pickets would come out and converse back and forth over the water. There'd been little shooting since Chancellorsville; orders to the picket details forbade firing unless fired upon, and with the river between them the men saw no point in driving one another to cover, let alone giving or taking casualties. The generals didn't like the fraternizing, but the field officers and sergeants didn't much care. No one doubted that the men would fight when the time came again.

The Union pickets came down from the heights in details of seven from each company, a sergeant or corporal and six privates. You were responsible for a mile of river and the men took turns walking the beat, two at a time, while the rest of the detail sought the shade of a willow oak, locust, or catalpa, and played cards or checkers or wrote letters or just talked. The days, eventless and reiterative under the fierce Virginia sun, dragged by slowly. The river flowed right to left, muddy, opaque, sliding noiselessly around crags of iron-gray stone. Lord it was hot.

At night the river found its voice and seemed to quicken. Now you could hear its swirl and rustle, hear the sudden splash of a fish jumping. Cool vapors rose from it, but so did the mosquitoes, and the men slapped their necks and ears and cursed them.

Damn bugs're as big as crows, they said.

Secesh bugs, they said.

Rebel bugs.

They're big as alligators.

Where'd you ever see a alligator?

They're big as seagulls, Elisha Smith said, and thought of the gulls wheeling over Lagoon Pond, and heard their tattered shrieks, wind-borne above the dark blue water. When they'd left the Vineyard—Elisha, Peleg Davenport, Bart Crowell—gulls had followed the steamer, coasting alongside her roofed deck, hovering just out from the rail, expecting or at least hoping someone would offer a scrap of bread or cold cut, reaching out for the gull to pluck it from their fingers, a trick these gulls had mastered following the side-wheelers back and forth from New Bedford. Elisha and Peleg and Bart were in their Sunday clothes, nice shirts and checked and striped trousers and polished boots, worn this day for the last time. Lieutenant Macy stood at the rail at a distance from them, dourly eyeing the birds.

A crowd had come to Union Wharf to see them off and a fat woman named Mrs. West, who taught the piano and whom Elisha had known only by reputation, had given them twenty dollars, paper notes, donated by the citizens of Holmes Hole and Edgartown, to be divided among the three of them. Elisha's family was at the front of the crowd. Mother, Father, Sarah, Katie, Georgie, Tommy. This Mrs. West had waddled halfway up the gangway of the Canonicus *and turned and summoned the boys up to present the money. Then she unfolded a piece of paper and made a speech, the crowd pressing around, shading their eyes against the morning sun, bonneted women, men in straw boaters. We will follow you in our hearts and with our prayers, she said, reading from her paper, her voice surprisingly sonorous, musical. You are to go forth to the conflict to strike for our noble cause, the great cause of human freedom. My young friends, the eagle of American liberty from her mountain aerie swoops down on spreading pinions and goes perched on your shoulders.*

Lieutenant Macy watched the gulls for a while, and the wooded shore of West Chop sliding by to port, then moved closer to them by the rail, the four of them leaning on their elbows looking out. The wind blew smartly, the golden smoky southwester, riffling the steel-blue water and putting a coppery sheen on the world.

What's the matter with this goddamn island? Macy said. I signed thirty recruits on Nantucket, did you know that?

Maybe, Peleg said, it was on account of they know you over there.

Maybe sir, Macy said.

Sir, Peleg said.

He was the oldest of the three, twenty-three or -four now, Elisha and Bart but sixteen. Peleg naturally spoke for them. The twenty dollars were in his pocket.

No, Macy said, it's because they don't listen to shit like what was being spoken back there. The eagle of liberty and so on. This war, boys, is being fought for one reason: to put the country back together again. To make it whole. You're going to hear some talk in the regiment about abolitionism and slavery and so forth, and I want you to stay clear of it. Hallowell and Holmes and Putnam and those fellows.

Who, sir? Peleg asked.

Macy looked at him. *Some of our officers. Freethinkers, utopians. They'd free every nigger if they could. Me, I wouldn't give a nickel to free a slave, and I hope you wouldn't either.*

Peleg and Elisha and Bart Crowell looked at one another. Peleg, looking away from Macy, smirked, made a face. The engine rumbled far below and they could hear the flag snapping and the great wet sweep of the wheels.

Sir, Peleg said, why not?

Why not what?

Why wouldn't you give a nickel to free a slave?

Your name again? Macy said.

Davenport, sir.

Davenport. Well, Davenport, this is just the kind of thinking I'm trying to eliminate in the regiment. This idea that we're fighting to free the slaves. Because when the shooting commences, what white man is going to risk his life to free a nigger?

The question was rhetorical, or so the boys thought. A silence followed it, during which they gazed through the smoky southwester, a hint of autumn in its textured coppery light, to the woods-shrouded slope of the Chop. They'd enlisted for three years, but no one expected the war to last that long. Lieutenant Macy doubted it himself, in spite of what had happened at Bull Run.

You boys enjoy the sail, Macy said, and went below.

Think he's right? Bart Crowell said.

About what? said Elisha.

About the nigger question.

I hear they treat em awful bad, Elisha said. You said it yourself, Peleg.

I seen it, Peleg said. Charleston, Savannah. Niggers in chains. And that runaway I helped, stowed away on the Lizzie Freeman *that time. Been whipped real awful. His back had been laid right open. Not just once, either.*

You never got in trouble for that, did you, Bart said.

Time it got around, I was to sea again. And there warn't no one gonna arrest Dr. Chandler. I'm glad I done it, too.

I'd free em, Elisha said.

You want em living alongside of you? Bart said.

Some I would, Elisha said.

We got to win the war first, Peleg said, then have this argument.

The boys thought this over.

Lieutenant's a mean sonofabitch, ain't he, Peleg said.

It was one thing they all agreed on.

Hey, Yank.

Hey yourself, Reb.

The two rebels stood on the opposite bank, wool uniforms colorless in the lilac-gray dusk. One wore a thick dark beard. They were lean, like most Rebs. They had put down their guns. The Union trio, Elisha and McNamara and a new man named Wells, put down theirs. They'd heard the Rebs talking and had come over from their outpost, which was back from the river a long stone's throw. They'd left all their gear, their accouterments, which was against regulations.

Y'all want to trade for some tobacca? the Rebel said.

Might.

Got any coffee?

Sure we got coffee. We got fresh beef, we got bacon. We got soft bread. Joe Hooker feeds us good.

Don't nobody feed us, the Reb said.

That's what I heard, McNamara said. Heard you Rebs eat your own shit.

The Rebels looked at each other and shook their heads patiently, forbear-
ingly. As if they expected as much from a Yankee.

How long y'all been in service?

Since Ball's Bluff, McNamara said.

Oh Lord, the Reb said. You had fun at that one, didn't you?

I had fun with your wife, McNamara said.

The Rebs both spat a laugh. Dumb-ass Yankee, said one.

Was you at Fredericksburg? said the other.

All of em, McNamara said.

Bet you'd like to go home, the Reb said.

Bet you would too.

Nah, we havin fun over here. Fun whippin you Yankee boys.

Elisha cleared his throat and sent his high thin voice across. You ain't
whipped us yet.

The Rebs peered at him. You a young-un, ain't you.

I been in all them battles, Elisha said.

The Reb slapped a mosquito on his ear. What regiment ya'll belong to?

McNamara spoke quietly. Don't tell him.

Why not? Wells said.

Because I tell you, McNamara said.

We're Twentieth Massachusetts, Wells said. Company I.

Massachusetts, the Reb said. Well, goddamn.

So what? Wells said.

We have heard a good deal about you Massachusetts boys.

Yes sir, we've heard right smart about you, said the other Reb.

Like what? Wells said.

Shut up, will you? McNamara said softly.

The Reb said, Do you all got nigger wives or is it just some a you?

That's why, McNamara said.

What niggers command your brigade?

Shove it up your ass, Reb, Wells said.

Tell me: Have the niggers improved the Yankee breed any?

McNamara held his tongue. He had no use for Negroes himself and
when drunk would run them down in the foulest language, not caring who
heard him. Elisha didn't know yet how James Wells felt about them.

What about that tobacco? McNamara said.

Got four hands of Niggerhead, the Reb said. I can send her over, you send us back some good coffee. Roasted, not green.

And newspapers, said the other Reb. If you got any.

We don't, McNamara said.

Yeah we do, Elisha said. We got a Frank Leslie's.

Send it over, the Reb said.

The little trading rafts were made from broken pieces of wood, planking and two-by-four, from the wrecked houses of Fredericksburg. Toy rafts, with their decks riding high and dry, rigged with sails and sometimes even rudders. Extremely clever for hayseeds who talked so lazy and crude. Or they would hollow out a three-foot log and attach an outrigger. They'd wrap the tobacco in a piece of oilcloth and weight it down with a stone. They'd give her a good shove and she'd drift out and the current would catch hold of her and you'd have to go downstream and wade in and grab her. It worked just as well in either direction.

Elisha, McNamara said, run get some coffee. All what you got in your bread bag.

What I got?

I'm a little short.

You're the one wants the tobacco.

Go on, fore they change their mind, McNamara said.

It was darker now, the heights rearing up steep in front of him as Elisha went back for the coffee. The mosquitoes went with him, whining before they landed and bit. Big as seagulls. The cookfire had burned down and Joe Merriman and Sergeant Cate had lit a candle and were seated on the ground, on their gum blankets, playing twenty-one by its light.

You boys fixin to marry those Rebs? Cate said.

Just tradin, Elisha said. Where's that Frank Leslie's Illustrated *at?*

McNamara had it, Merriman said.

Elisha found it in McNamara's knapsack. He opened his own haversack and dug out his coffee, a good couple of pounds, in a cloth bag. He considered taking McNamara's coffee but decided he'd better not.

Tell McNamara to find himself a whore if he's so lonely, Cate said.

He's lonely for some tobacco, Elisha said.

A whore would do him better, Merriman said.

He don't care for em, Elisha said.

The lightning bugs were out now, drifting and flashing over the matted trampled field all the way to the river and out over it. The lightning bugs, too, reminded Elisha of home, how they would swarm, at candle lighting, over the field running down to the lagoon, he and Georgie running barefoot to catch them, slashing through the tall grass, the white-green flashes myriad and ubiquitous in the darkness. Elisha had not been home since they'd left the island with Lieutenant Macy and had stopped thinking about returning except as a distant event, a full year away, that had no immediate relevance or meaning. Only Bart had gotten home again, minus his right leg, which he'd lost during the Seven Days. Peleg had been killed in the futile charge up Marye's Heights where so many were slaughtered and was buried just this side of the river. Elisha had been wounded at Antietam, the minnie ball entering his thigh and out again without touching bone, and they'd sent him to the hospital in Washington, D.C. He'd enjoyed a fine long rest and healed up just fine. He knew he'd been lucky and figured the next ball would kill him and wondered what the odds were of getting hit twice in one war. Small, he decided. He'd survived Fredericksburg without a scratch.

McNamara now stood alone on the riverbank, Wells having gone downstream to intercept the raft the Rebels had sent over. McNamara looming tall and broad-shouldered in the gloom, with the lightning bugs winking here, there, out over the whispering river.

You gonna share coffee with me tomorrow? Elisha said, handing him the cloth bag.

Depends what I got, McNamara said.

I ain't got any, Elisha said.

The two Rebs had sat down, cross-legged, on the dry mudflat at the water's edge. Dark, lumpy shapes in the gathering night. Without their guns they looked forbidding anyway, something wild about them, ungovernable except by their officers. Even up against their youngest boys Elisha felt young by comparison.

You got coffee, he said. You got lots.

How would you know? McNamara said.

I looked.

You stay out of my bread bag, you don't want to feel the wrath of God.

You gonna share with me?

If you shut up I might.

Some weeks later a fight broke out downriver below Fredericksburg. It begin in the morning and all day you could hear the sharpshooters potting away at each other from their hillside perches. Now and then a cannon would erupt, its percussive echo scouring the hills and then, almost simultaneous, the savage iron-flinging burst of the shell. After that the river truce became more tentative, more brittle, and the trading slowed and after a while ceased altogether.

George Macy, now a lieutenant colonel, brought the eleven fresh recruits south to the regiment in the final days of the unofficial truce along the Rappahannock. Thin-lipped, jut-jawed, humorless, Macy was the Twentieth's ablest recruiter for reasons no one could quite understand, and when his mother became ill in the days after Chancellorsville the regimental commander furloughed him home, hoping he'd bring some more of his Nantucket Islanders back to Virginia with him.

His mother had improved by the time Macy arrived. She was out of bed, in fact, causing him to wonder if his father's urgent letter hadn't been exaggerated. He lingered just long enough to pick up five recruits, gave them a date on which to meet him in New Bedford, and took sail for the Vineyard, where the towns were paying bounties in order to fill their quotas. The bounties were so high that volunteers were coming over from the mainland to enlist, and Macy wanted to get hold of a few before recruiters in Boston or New Bedford did. He stopped this time in Holmes Hole, took a room at the Mansion House, and hired a man to run an item over to Edgartown to Mr. Marchant, the editor of the *Vineyard Gazette,* with instructions to print it on the front page. TO ARMS! TO ARMS! it began, and went on, more quietly, to announce that Lieutenant Colonel George Macy of the Twentieth Massachusetts Volunteer Infantry Regiment, Army of the Potomac, would be enrolling three-year men mornings from nine to noon at the Mansion House. COME ONE, COME ALL! it concluded. GOD AND YOUR COUNTRY CALL! The results were meager enough: six recruits in three days, all but two from off-island. One had come from Dorchester, two from Cape Cod, and one from Tiverton, Rhode Island.

The two Vineyard boys were brothers, two years apart in age, for a guess. The younger one claimed to be eighteen, a transparent lie, but Macy took him anyway, marking him down as such. He was a tall reedy lad with delicate bones, not at all stupid but overly blithe, fey, a bit of a molly by the look of him. He would make a poor soldier but the Twentieth was down close to two hundred and could no longer be choosy. The older brother was a hard case, or had the illusion that he was. He said he was nineteen—another lie, to accord with his brother's fictitious eighteen—and Macy so marked him. He looked Macy in the eye and didn't blink when Macy told them—across his table in the sunny carpeted lobby with a sea breeze playing through, a couple of men lounging at the desk looking on—that the regiment was called the Bloody Twentieth and all the reasons why, beginning with Ball's Bluff. The younger brother smiled absently as Macy talked, words like *Yorktown* and *Antietam* and *casualties* no more real to him than if they'd come out of a storybook, a fairy tale. The other simply listened, unmoved, as if he knew it all already. He was no taller than his brother but packed solid in the shoulders, with sturdy legs that would be up to some marching. A man at eighteen. Macy pushed the recruitment certificates across the table and they signed. Luke Chandler, Thomas Chandler. Macy shook their hands.

"You're joining the best regiment in the best army in the world," he said. "I congratulate you."

"Thank you," Thomas Chandler said.

"Thank you *sir*," said Colonel Macy.

He gave them a week, and in early June, officer and recruits met in New Bedford and embarked on a steamer for the overnight boat ride to New York City. At New York they boarded a steamer at the Battery and crossed to Perth Amboy, New Jersey. At Perth Amboy they got on a train and rode it to Washington, where Macy, out of his own pocket, engaged rooms at a cheap hotel on E Street near the Executive Mansion, the boys sleeping two to a bed.

The brothers were given their own tiny room under the eaves on the third floor. So far they had not mingled easily with the others. Macy supposed it was their education, which showed on them like a high gloss, that set them apart, making the brothers self-conscious and the others distrustful in the way laborers and the semiliterate distrust erudition.

The mainlanders could see the molly in the younger brother, Thomas, and their manner toward him was condescending, amused, as if he were an overgrown child. It stopped short of overt ridicule because of the older brother, whose reticence and inscrutability kept you guessing. Could he use those big shoulders and his fists? The mainland boys, plenty tough themselves, had no inclination to find out. Besides, the younger boy gave no offense. Where his brother held himself back, he was friendly.

The brothers were abolitionists, as Macy had suspected. He discovered it on the last night of their journey, in his hotel room, where the older one came knocking on his door at ten P.M. Macy was sitting up, reading. He said enter and Luke Chandler stepped in from the gaslit hallway and came to the middle of the small square room and stood with his arms folded and his gaze downcast, frowning, working out what he was about to say. He wore a white shirt and collar and cravat, looking every inch the young gentleman, more appropriate to the Willard than to this fleabag. The brothers had finer clothes than the others, that was another thing

"It's rather late," Macy said. He'd been reading a worn back issue of *Harper's New Monthly,* which he now closed and set on the table by his oil lamp.

"I was wishing to speak to you about my brother, sir," Chandler said.

Macy said nothing. Waited.

"It wasn't my idea he enlist. I tried to talk him out of it. We all did."

"He's of sound mind," Macy said. "And has as much right as anybody to fight for his country."

"He doesn't know what he's in for," Chandler said.

"And you do."

"I'll stand up to it, is the point," Chandler said.

"You're certain of that," Macy said, surprising himself. Ordinarily you'd want to encourage such optimism.

"Yes sir."

"In 'sixty-one," Macy said, "all the boys who came in thought that way. The country's learned a thing or two in the meantime."

"I only meant that I expect to do my duty. I would have thought you'd be glad, sir."

"I am glad, Chandler. I'm very glad."

"Can we get back to Thomas?" Chandler said.

Macy sighed. "He will not get preferential treatment. There are a hundred thousand men in this army."

"Just one thought, sir, if I may."

Again Macy sighed. "What."

"I don't know how it works," Chandler said, "but if I can march with him. Fight beside him. I need to look out for him, you see."

"No," Macy said, "I don't see. You're a soldier, not a nanny, Chandler."

Chandler was silent, looking somberly out the window. The room was on the second story, and downstreet was the President's House. A soft light showed in a tall window here and there. Macy looked down and pictured Old Abe, who was said to be an insomniac, prowling the dark corridors and big shadowy rooms. Pondering the fix he'd gotten himself and his country into. A president beloved of niggers, Macy had concluded, and of no one else. Not even the abolitionists were for him.

"Please," Chandler said.

He didn't seem to have noticed that Macy had not asked him to sit down. He stood as he had before, arms folded, body swayed slightly sideways. Next time he would stand at attention.

"In battle," Macy said, "the stupidest thing you can do is be solicitous of the man next to you. Get yourself killed that way. We tell everybody, if your comrades fall, ignore them. That's what the stretcher bearers are for. The best way to protect them is to press on. Load and fire."

Chandler said nothing and did not look at Macy. More of that maddening unimpressionability.

"We'll shoot a man who runs," Macy said.

"He won't run if he's with me," Luke said.

"Oh Christ," Macy said, "let's go to bed, shall we? I have you both marked down for Company I. We line up with the tallest on the right, descending to the shortest at the other end. You and your brother look the same in height. Counting off, you'd be beside him or in the rank behind. In a line of battle you'd be next to him or one man away. You might even be his file partner."

"Thank you, sir."

"It's the way we do it, Chandler. Both armies. You could have saved yourself the trouble."

"It wasn't any trouble," Chandler said.

Macy watched him turn and move to the door, which seemed too small for him, as if the room had been constructed for a child.

"Chandler," he said.

"Sir?"

"Why'd you boys enlist? It couldn't have been for the bounty."

"It wasn't."

"Not to free the darkies, I hope."

Luke didn't answer him.

"That's it, isn't it?" Macy said. "Abolitionists. I thought they knew better than that on the Vineyard."

"No sir, they don't."

This sounded like impudence but not provable as such.

"Of course," Macy said, "they don't fight for their country either. They're slackers when it comes to that."

"Yes sir."

"There's a Vineyard boy in Company I," Macy said.

"Elisha Smith," Luke said.

"He's a good boy. A good soldier. I don't want you filling his head with any shit about the niggers."

"I didn't come here for that," Luke said.

"No. You came to free the slaves."

"What did you come for, sir?"

Macy looked at him awhile. Eyes a pale cold blue. "Disunion is the enemy," he said. "Disunion is treason. What they do with their niggers is their business." He smiled a thin smile. "There's some among the boys'll have a thing or two to say about your abolitionism," he said. "Try it on them and you'll learn a thing or two."

"I already have learned a thing or two," Luke said.

Macy looked at him, sharp. "Meaning what?" he said.

"Just what it says."

Macy nodded. "Dismissed," he said.

"Yes sir," Luke said, and let himself out into the ill-lit and airless hallway.

"Where'd you go?" Thomas asked him.

"Nowhere," Luke said.

"You can't go nowhere," Thomas said, "only somewhere."

They lay in bed in the pitch dark under the sloping ceiling with their backs to each other and a cotton blanket stretched taut over Luke's left and Thomas's right shoulder. The window was open and a mosquito whined somewhere overhead. The night air, city air, was moist, greasy, vaguely odorous of garbage and manure.

"I went down to the lobby," Luke said.

"What for?"

"Go to sleep."

"What for?"

"To see what I could see. Go to sleep."

"It was a good supper, wasn't it?"

"It was all right."

"What do you think of Washington?"

"Not much."

"Me either. Except for the government buildings. Boston's much finer. Remember when we went to Boston?"

"Will you please go the hell to sleep?"

"Those fellows curse a lot, don't they."

"I'm going to curse, you don't go to sleep."

"Good night, Luke."

"Good night," Luke said.

TWO

It was the lushest country they had ever seen, but the war had visited destruction everywhere. They saw almost no livestock. Brick mansions stood empty with their windows broken out, outbuildings burned to the ground. Trees had been cut down everywhere you looked, the stumps ax-hewn and gnawed-looking and overrun with brambles or newgrowth scrub. Here and there a brick chimney stood against the sky out of a heap of blackened timbers. They saw few people and most of them were Negroes, inhabitants of log and weathered clapboard houses with garden plots close by, the women wearing colorful turbans and dresses of faded cotton and staring at them, quiet and curious, as they went by.

They had come down the Potomac and up Aquia Creek on one of General Hooker's supply steamers. The army had laid a rail line from Aquia Landing to the camp at Falmouth, and after some hours of waiting the boys climbed into a couple of loaded boxcars and sat in the open doors with their legs dangling for the leisurely twenty-mile ride south.

The Twentieth Massachusetts was encamped in and about the town itself. The boys rode a freight wagon from the depot, sitting atop and amongst wooden crates of produce and barrels of flour and molasses. The teamster was a Negro, a large man and very dark, in a wide-brimmed straw hat and faded gray homespun. He drove in silence and did not look back at the white boys riding behind him. The big wagon behind its team of six mules lumbered down out of the hills and onto the lower ground where the camp began, spread on either side of the road into town, a sprawl of tents, jerry-built plank shacks, huddled canvas-arched wagons, staked mules and horses. Smoke rising here and there.

Tree stumps everywhere. A rank smell overhung it all; of manure and woodsmoke and, more faintly, human waste. Some patches of scrub and weeds, the ground otherwise featureless but for hoofprints and wagon ruts, its vegetation trampled out of existence.

It was late afternoon; the companies had been dismissed, and the men moved lazily about or sat, coatless, on hardtack boxes or plundered chairs. The near ones eyed the wagon as it passed, studying the new boys in their city clothes. A young soldier, coming toward them up a company street reading a letter as he walked, glanced at the wagon, saw Luke and Thomas, and stopped in his tracks.

"If I ain't a sonofabitch," he said.

He wore his forage cap, but his shirt was open at the neck and he wore no sack coat, like most of the men at this hour. He had flax-yellow hair and a very fine, almost white, mustache. He was tall and thin but it was a ramrod thinness, bone-hard and unfragile.

"Luke Chandler," he said.

The wagon had gone on by and Elisha stuffed the letter inside his shirt and followed at an easy, pigeon-toed trot. The wagon rattled into town on a corduroyed road past wood and brick buildings, fenced lots, an occasional surviving shade tree, and stopped in front of a tall red-brick house with a steep slate roof and a chimney at either end. A sign in dripping white paint, COMMISSARY, was nailed over the door. The building next door, also redbrick but with a front gallery, was the regimental hospital. The Negro fastened the reins and got down, and so did the eleven boys, carrying their valises. The Negro pointed the boys to the hospital and went himself into the commissary. Elisha Smith caught up, rosy from his jog.

"What the hell you doin here?" he said, grinning.

Luke and Thomas looked at each other and then again at Elisha.

"Elisha?" Luke said.

"Course it is," Elisha said. "What's wrong with you?"

"Why, you look all grown up," Thomas said. "You're tall as me now." He was more sinewy, too, but that wasn't all of it. There was the mustache, and a narrowing of the eyes.

"It don't take long," Elisha said, "not down here."

Luke proffered his hand and Elisha shook it. He shook hands with

Thomas. The other recruits stood apart from them, watching. The Negro came out of the commissary with two soldiers and the three of them began unloading the wagon, lugging the boxes inside, the Negro carrying two at a time stacked against his chest, the soldiers one.

"Macy must of brung you," Elisha said. "Same sonofabitch what brung me."

Thomas looked at Luke, surprised to hear Elisha talk so.

"Me and Bart and poor ol Peleg," Elisha said. "You seen Bart on the island?"

"Father looked after his leg when he came home. It was troublesome for a while. Leaking and hurting him. Heard you were wounded yourself."

"Antietam," Elisha said. "Took one in the leg. Wasn't but a scratch. What company you in?"

"Your company. I."

"I thought so. They put all the island boys in I. Vineyard and Nantucket both. You been up to Head of the Pond of late?"

"I went with Rose a couple times this spring," Luke said. "Bought eggs, some spring vegetables."

"Rose," Elisha said. "She still with you?"

"Why wouldn't she be?"

"Still make that upside-down cake?" Elisha said.

"Sure. Apple cobbler. Indian pudding."

"And that bread pudding," Elisha said.

The men came out of the commissary. "We could use some help here," one of them said.

"They got to take their examination," Elisha said. "Anyways, they ain't in the army yet."

"Enjoy it while you can, you lazy sonsabitches," said the soldier.

Elisha seemed not to hear him. An officer came out of the hospital. Elisha rose to attention and touched his forehead. "Where's Dr. Perry at, sir?" he said. "Got some new boys here."

The officer paused at the edge of the gallery and looked down the street. "I don't know," he said, and went down the steps and down the street toward the river.

"Let's us sit down," Elisha said. "Might be you got to wait awhile."

They sat down on the gallery steps, in the warm shade. The others drifted up past them and sat or stood behind them. One of the Nantucketers, an older fellow named Riggs, asked Elisha where he might take a piss, and Elisha told him around back of the building. He said the sink, if he needed it, would be farther down, toward the trees. Several sauntered around the house to relieve themselves. The rest sat down with their backs against the wall and listened to Elisha and the Chandlers talk.

"First thing," Elisha said, "the surgeon'll examine you. Then Macy swears you in, then you go to the quartermaster, draw your gear. Tomorrow they'll drill the hell out of you. Teach you the formations, manual of arms, all that."

"Is it difficult?"

"It ain't if you know left from right. Some boys don't, you know. Instructor'll tie a piece of hay to their left foot, piece of straw to their right. Hay foot, straw foot, stead of left right. If them boys can learn, you can."

Riggs and the others had come back from pissing. They sat down against the wall.

"When's the fightin start?" one of them said.

Elisha glanced at him over his shoulder. "Soon enough to suit you, I bet. The cavalry was upriver a couple days ago, got in a big fight with Jeb Stuart. They come back and said Lee's whole army is movin out. We'll go after em, and one day all hell'll break loose."

They sat awhile, Elisha long-backed, bony, long wrists hanging off his knees. Muslin shirt yellow with wear and age, sky-blue pants with the dark blue infantry stripe down the legs. Square-toed leather brogans, cracked and heelworn.

"Our company commander's a regular sonofabitch," he said. "Name of Paine. One a them Harvard College boys. Likes to throw fellows in the guardhouse, hang em up by their thumbs. Mean as cat piss."

"You got a lot to say, ain't you?" said one of the men behind them, the fellow from Rhode Island. His name was Delaney and he had orange hair and blue eyes so pale they looked bleached.

Elisha twisted around and eyed him a moment. He spat past his shoulder into the dust by his feet. "You will too, you been here awhile."

The men had finished unloading the supply wagon. The Negro

climbed up onto his seat, picked up his whip, shook the reins, and swung the team in a wide circle and away down the street. The mules had shat while they waited, and flies were gathering. On the blue cloudless sky a hawk circled, coasting.

"How many battles you been in?" Delaney said.

"A smart of em," Elisha said.

Thomas, turning to look at Delaney, said, "He was wounded at the Battle of Antietam."

"I'd say he has a right to talk," one of the Nantucketers said.

"Never said he didn't," Delaney said.

Elisha nodded, spat again. "You two'll be in our mess, a course," he said. "And, hell, you might as well tent with me and my friend Mac till we break camp. You boys'll get shelter halfs—dogtents, we call em— what you button together to make one, but for now we got a wedge, sleeps four comfortable, and there ain't but us two in it. Ain't neither of us got graybacks, by the way. Not at the moment."

"What's graybacks?" Delaney said.

"Lice," Elisha said. "Hope you ain't allergic."

"Well I am," Delaney said.

"I won't stand for them," Luke said.

"They ain't so bad," Elisha said. "You'll see."

"Lice," Luke said. "By God."

Thomas let a few moments pass. "We sure were sorry about Peleg," he said.

"He talked about you boys," Elisha said. "He never did forget the night you helped that runaway."

I wronged him, she said, when the news came. Sitting in the dark by the low fire wrapped in a wool shawl with the bottle at her feet.

You didn't know he'd be killed, Luke said. They spoke very softly, so as not to wake Thomas.

When he came back I was going to say something to him. Make it right.

Luke sat down on the floor close to the fire.

You had nothing to make right, he said. You know what he said? He said it was a grand night, all the way around.

She was quiet awhile. It was January, cold, and she sat huddled in her shawl, gazing sad and lovely and perhaps slightly drunk into the fire. He would hear her get out of bed, unable to sleep, waking as if he listened for her in his sleep, had learned to do that, and would get up without waking Thomas and pull on some clothes and creep out and tap on her door. It was then that she opened up to him, about her life in the orphanage and her vanished parents and the burden of living colored in a white world.

How'd he die? she said. Did it say?

Gunshot, I guess. It said he died instantly.

They always say that, she said.

"He come out against slavery," Elisha said. "Surprised some people."

"I got a speech from Captain Macy," Luke said. "Said I best never mind about slavery."

"We all get that one," Elisha said, "specially now. Was a lot of abolitionists amongst the officers could offset Macy, but most all of em been wounded. Captain Babo. Lieutenant Putnam lost a arm at Ball's Bluff. Hallowell and Holmes got shot bad at Antietam. Like the Rebs could pick em out."

Two riders came up the street from the direction of the river, an officer on a horse and behind him a Negro on a mule, hooves loud in the quiet. The officer wore a kepi and frock coat with a double row of brass buttons.

"Get up, boys," Elisha said, rising.

The surgeon looked at them as he slowed his horse. He turned it toward the corner of the building and disappeared around it

"Anybody ever fail these examinations?" asked the Nantucketer Riggs.

"You was half dead you'd pass," Elisha said over his shoulder.

THREE

___

In the autumn of 1859 the Eastville School failed to open for lack of a schoolmaster, and Elisha, of his own volition, attended the Centre Street Academy in Holmes Hole, where Luke and Thomas Chandler were enrolled. He made the better part of the journey by water, rowing the family skiff down Lagoon Pond and around Little Neck and down the inlet to Bass Creek, a pull of nearly two miles. He would drag the skiff up onto the sand and walk Beach Road to Main Street, and then over to Centre Street, another mile. He would leave in the dark without a lantern, swishing through the knee-high grass of the field and rowing by the vague light of the stars, of silvery winter moonlight when there was a moon. Dawn would be breaking by the time he reached the town.

Elisha was Luke's age, fourteen, and the two of them studied some of the same lessons. Luke was the bigger of the two, and much the quicker at lessons. Elisha's summer tan had faded, and he was very thin and looked undernourished, and yet he had a resilient physical strength, a stubborn vitality instilled by life on a farm, perhaps, or perhaps, as Luke thought, because being poor, even undereating, toughens you in some mysterious way. That Elisha could row all that way with those puny shoulders annoyed rather than endeared him to his schoolmates, as though he were behaving above his station, while the rowing itself confirmed the abnormality of this pale, quiet, plainly dressed boy from the wind-beleaguered farm at Head of the Pond.

The school day began at eight o'clock, when the master, Mr. Pease, came out and struck a rope-hung steel triangle with a hammer. There were two front doors side by side, left door for the girls, right for the boys. Elisha would be standing apart in the long yard in front of the building, watching other children play tag or quoits or, before it got cold, base ball. The triangle would clang, and Elisha would pick up his dinner pail and join the file of boys entering the building and go directly to his desk.

All day he bent to his lessons, reading and copying and doing sums, silent and oblivious-seeming of everyone but Mr. Pease, who was a kindly man and coaxed him along very gently. At noon Mr. Pease put on his coat and top hat and dismissed everyone for dinner. All went home except Elisha, who ate alone in the school building, or on the front steps if the day was warm.

"No one talks to him," Thomas said at supper one night.

"He doesn't care," Luke said.

"How do you know?" Thomas said.

Luke shrugged, eating.

"Sit up straight, Luke," their father said.

Rose, seated opposite him at the long table, smiled her languid smile, watching Luke. Her eyes black in the candlelight, watchful.

"I don't think he washes," Thomas said. "Everyone says he doesn't."

"Wellwater's precious on a farm," their father said. "That's an almighty barren place out there. I'm surprised they can raise what they do on it."

"Who is it says he doesn't wash?" Luke said.

"Ben Howland. Ty Luce. Why?"

"I'll tan their hides for them, that's why."

"You'll do no such thing," his father said. "You might, however, invite him home for dinner. As a daily event, I mean."

The boys paused with their forks halfway up and looked at him. "Elisha Smith?" Luke said.

"Who else are we talking about?" Rose said.

"I don't think he'll come," Luke said.

"If you're tactful he might," said his father. "If you give him his dignity."

"Thomas has to stay out of it," Luke said.

"Why?" Thomas said.

"Let your brother handle it," Rose said. "It don't need two of you."

The doctor glanced at her but did not comment on her grammar.

"Thank you, Rose," Luke said, with a look at Thomas.

"You do it nicely, hear?" Rose said.

Next day at noontime they waited till the building had emptied and the students' voices had scattered out of hearing on the thin cool November air. Elisha had sat down on the wooden bench along the back wall and was digging his cheesecloth-wrapped dinner out of his pail. He did not look surprised as Luke approached but his face did open a bit, his thin mouth tugging sideways in the hint of a smile. Thomas stood across the room, watching.

"Hidy," Luke said.

"Hidy," said Elisha.

"What you got there?" Luke said.

Elisha placed his dinner on his lap and peeled back the edges of the cheesecloth. "Cornbread, it looks like. A portion of ham. A cold potato."

Luke squared up his shoulders, gave his trousers an upward tug. "Say. Whyn't you come eat dinner at our house. Seeing how you can't go home, I mean."

Elisha eyed him mildly, not saying yes and not saying no.

"My pa wants you to come," Luke said. "It's not like it was just me saying it."

"Rose does too," Thomas said.

Elisha's gaze shifted over to him. Luke glanced at him irritably but said nothing.

"Rose does the cooking," Luke explained.

"I heard about her," Elisha said.

"Our ma's dead," Thomas said.

"I know that," Elisha said.

"You don't have to come again, you don't like it," Luke said.

Elisha rewrapped his cornbread and ham slice and potato in the cheesecloth. He returned the little bundle to his dinner pail.

"I'll like it," he said.

William Street was leaf-strewn, and the cool air held their burnt smell and an acrid-sweet touch of woodsmoke from the brick chimneys. The sky was a sunless glossy mother-of-pearl, the tree trunks rising black above the pitched shingled roofs. The roadways were dry. It had not rained in a while.

"What was it took your ma?" Elisha asked.

"You know what pneumonia is?" Luke said.

"I heard of it," Elisha said.

"It's quick," Luke said. "Couple of weeks."

"Rose came before she died," Thomas said, "to help take care of her. Then she just stayed."

"She stayed because Father asked her to," Luke said.

"Well, of course," Thomas said.

"I've heard a good deal about her," Elisha said.

"She's the beatenest cook," Thomas said. "You like chicken chowder?"

"I ain't never ate it," Elisha said.

"Bet you'll like it," Thomas said.

"I bet so, too," Elisha said.

FOUR

The uniform, save the shirt, was of wool. Heavy; you could feel its weight when you draped the various pieces over your arm. Heavy and coarse.

"Them coats is a hell trip in the hot months," Elisha said. "The manual says you got to button em to the neck. The boys'll button the top button, wear it open rest of the way down, and most officers don't say nothin. I wouldn't try it with Lieutenant Paine, though."

"I wouldn't either," said Corporal Dugan.

"Nor I," said the quartermaster, whose name was Folsom. He was slightly built and wore a pair of spectacles low on his nose. He'd taken over an inn near the destroyed bridge over to Fredericksburg and was dispensing uniforms and equipment across the tavern bar. He would measure each recruit briefly with his eye, then rummage in a box or along a shelf.

"If it doesn't fit," he said, "you'll have to swap around."

"They never do fit," Elisha said.

"As I always say, this isn't Brooks Brothers," Folsom said. He placed a new pair of brogans on the bar, and another. "You boys want to be careful of these shoes or somebody's likely to steal them. I have men in the regiment who haven't been shoed since March. Some are practically barefoot."

"And a campaign coming up," said the corporal.

"It's no fault of mine," Folsom said.

"These shoes is both the same," one of the Nantucketers said. Chase was his name. "Nor right, nor left."

"That's right," Folsom said.

44

"Wear em awhile, they sort theirselves," Elisha said. "Just remember which shoe is which, left and right."

Ordnance was in a back room which might have been a dining room or parlor, it was hard to tell, the furniture all looted to feed campfires, wainscoting stripped, mantel shelf pulled down. Folsom distributed black leather cartridge and cap boxes and gave each man a handful of caps and paper cartridges. He pried the lids off two crates of brand-new Springfield rifles packed in oiled cotton batting and let the men help themselves, which they did with gingerly deliberation, looking the guns up and down, hefting them, beginning now to smile. Folsom watched them. It was always the same, even with boys who'd grown up in the far north hunting deer or squirrels but who had never seen a gun so well made, so perfectly designed for murder. They began lifting the muskets to their shoulders, tentative at first.

"You boys're lucky," Elisha said. "Everybody wants a Springfield."

Luke and Thomas had claimed theirs last. Neither had ever held a gun and as Luke grasped his and lifted it he knew he'd crossed another of those lines, those Rubicons, which had been his destiny this last month. The musket seemed more compact, more wieldy, than the old black-ened Revolutionary War pieces he'd seen in antique shops and attics and hung decoratively under mantel shelves. It had a kind of lethal beauty, all shiny steel and finished hardwood, its weight and length and balance promising a terrible and satisfying efficiency. Thomas drew his up out of its crate, hefted it with both hands, and looked at Luke.

"What," Luke said, pausing with the rifle halfway to his shoulder.

Around them now a chorus of double clicks and sudden sharp *clack*s as the others cocked and pulled the trigger.

"It's heavy," Thomas said.

"You get used to her," Elisha said. "And say, she'll knock a man down at better'n a quarter of a mile. *Half* a mile, if you're any good."

Thomas still held his gun uncertainly, as if its purpose were a puzzle to him. He watched as Luke raised his, thumbing the hammer back through half cock to cock, two soft bright clicks, and sighted down the barrel at the far wall. "Get you a Reb," Elisha said, and Luke squeezed the trigger and the hammer fell, *clack*, and Luke knew he would, would shoot men dead before this was over, and without remorse.

Then they met John McNamara.

Supper call had been drummed and fires were blossoming in make-shift tin cookstoves and the men gathering around them with their cups and plates. The new men were in uniform now, buttoned up and belted, strapped and hung with knapsack, haversack, canvas shelter half, canteen, tin cup, bayonet. They wore their forage caps variously, perched to one side or the other, jaunty, with the white felt trefoil, badge of the Second Corps, emblazoned on the sloping hat tops.

Elisha had left Luke and Thomas at the quartermaster's, giving them directions to the wedge tent he shared with McNamara, and they found it halfway down the dirt street of Company I, Elisha standing in front with his hands on his hips, waiting for them, McNamara seated on a weather-damaged mahogany and velvet chair, drawing on a pipe. The smell of woodsmoke was strong now, and there was still that nagging trace of shit and urine.

"This here's Luke and Thomas," Elisha said.

"Hidy," Thomas said.

"Look at them slick new uniforms," McNamara said.

"Mine's big on me," Thomas said.

"Springfields," McNamara said, eyeing the boys' new muskets. He took the pipe out of his mouth. "Which one a you wants to swap for my Enfield?"

"Whyn't you say hello, Mac," Elisha said.

"I just did," McNamara said.

"Pleased to meet you," Luke said.

"Likewise," McNamara said.

"Should they call you Mac or John?" Elisha said.

"I don't care what they call me, just so it ain't late for dinner."

Thomas looked at Elisha then grinned uncertainly. Luke stared at McNamara and did not smile.

"You boys seen any snakes yet?" McNamara said. "Rattlers? Water moccasins?"

"Rattlers," Thomas said.

"No one ever sees em," Elisha said.

"They just get bit by em," McNamara said.

"I never heard a one and you ain't either," Elisha said.

"Who wants to swap me their gun?" McNamara said. He looked up at Thomas with the pipe again in his mouth and spoke past it. "I think you do."

"No he doesn't," Luke said.

"Is that right," McNamara said. "And how the hell would you know?"

"Mac," Elisha said. "These boys're my friends, remember?"

"Shoes, then," McNamara said. "Swap shoes with me."

"Gonna tent with us, Mac."

"Maybe not," Luke said.

"Mac don't mean it," Elisha said.

"What's the other gun like?" Thomas said. "The Enfield."

"You don't want a Enfield," Elisha said. "She's heavier, for one thing. For another, she's a bitch to keep shiny. Got all them brass fittings."

"It shoots straighter'n the Springfield," McNamara said.

"No it don't," Elisha said.

"Let's go pitch our tent, Thomas," Luke said.

But Elisha grasped his arm. "Wait," he said. "Mac, you go on to mess, we'll come after."

"Go when I want to, Elisha."

"Just go on," Elisha said.

McNamara stood up, stooped, and went in through the open A of the tent front. The brothers looked at Elisha, who smiled and lifted his thin shoulders in an apologetic shrug. McNamara emerged with his mess equipment, metal plate and cup and utensils.

"Either a you boys ever been shot at?" he said.

"Go on, Mac," Elisha said.

"Tell em who's boss a the tent, Elisha. That's the main thing."

He threw Luke a scowl and walked past the tent to the open ground behind it where the men were gathering around the scattered fires.

"Why'd he want to know if we've been shot at?" Thomas said.

"He knows you ain't," Elisha said. "He's a little peculiar. Says odd things."

"Why do you live with him?" Luke said.

"No one else would, I guess."

"That's no reason."

"He don't mean half a what he says. Listen: Him and Peleg was friends. They was shelter partners on campaign. He was alongside of Peleg when he was hit."

"I don't want to live with him," Luke said.

"It's just a few days. Then we'll be movin."

"We can do it, Luke," Thomas said.

"Course you can," Elisha said. "Now get them knapsacks off and store em. Take your coats off. Better wrap your muskets in your blankets, you don't want to come back and find someone swapped em for a Enfield after all."

"I'm awful hungry," Thomas said, unshouldering his knapsack.

"We're havin baked beans," Elisha said. "Fellow in our mess cooks em special. Puts em in a hole with the fire over em like a oven and cooks em all day. Plenty a pork and molasses. Wait'll you see."

It was warm in the tent, the air thick with the day's accumulated heat and smells of wool and leather and human habitation. They stashed their knapsacks, haversacks, blankets, shelter halves, cartridge and cap boxes, guns, and scabbarded bayonets under the eave.

"Don't forget your table furniture," Elisha called in to them.

They gathered it up, metal knives and forks and spoons, metal cups, new and shiny, and rejoined Elisha outside.

"I'm real glad you boys are here," Elisha said.

"I might could get home," Elisha said, "if she was to let up."

"Sleep here," Thomas said. "We'll have the grandest time."

"As long as your folks won't worry," Rose said.

"I guess they'll figure it out where I am," Elisha said.

At three o'clock the snow still fell, and Rose said she wanted to see what the harbor looked like, and if the ships were holding and how high the sea was.

"Who's coming with me?" she said.

"You want to, Elisha?" Thomas said.

"I wouldn't mind."

Luke went to find a pair of boots to lend him.

"I don't like it, Rose," the doctor said. He was reading by the fire in the back parlor, vestless now and in his bedroom slippers.

"Why don't you come, Dr. Chandler?" she said.

"You can lose your way in a snow like this. People have frozen to death, going from barn to house."

"We're smack in the middle of town," Rose said. "You sure you won't come?"

"No thank you. And be careful, you hear?"

Luke went first, breaking a trail for them. The snow had risen knee-deep, with drifts waist-high and in their lee sudden wind-scoured places where the ground was nearly bare. There was no one else out; the town was muffled up, buried, as if in hibernation, though in some downstairs windows you could see the low glow of a lamp. Rose came behind Luke and reached to lean on him from time to time, losing her balance in the snow. She wore a wool cloak with a hood, sable-trimmed, and kid leather boots. She'd removed her petticoat and crinoline, and the skirt of her dress slipped weightlessly over the snow. Luke plowed his way across William Street and into the protected corridor of Drummer Lane, where the snow whispered in the lilac hedges.

"What if someone sees you like that?" Thomas called from behind.

"Like what?" Rose said.

"Without a hoop."

"Damn cages," Rose said, loud enough to be heard inside the house they were passing. "I've half a mind to take up bloomers."

"I'd like to see *that*," Luke said over his shoulder.

"Could be you will, smart boy," she said.

Main Street was filling, losing all definition. The snow had buried the board sidewalks and drifted up against doors and shop windows. The linden tree was frosted on every candelabra limb, and the fountain had disappeared under a drift. They turned down the alley between the drugstore and Thomas Bradley & Sons and filed downhill across a field of beach grass to the crescent shore, which the wind had kept clean.

"Snow's thinning," Luke said, looking out.

"Not for long," Elisha said. "A northeaster like this'll blow all night."

"I hope it does," Thomas said. "I hope it blows all weekend."

The anchored ships tossed restlessly, all aligned to the north, the wind overruling the flood tide. Snow clung to the riggings, tracing slanted ice-white spider webs above the white-shrouded decks and deck houses. Beyond, clear of the windbreak of West Chop, the Sound was as dark as blued steel, writhing and heaving and coughing whitecaps.

"I want to be a bird," Rose said. "Fly up on that wind and see the world all spread out white below me."

"No bird could fly in this," Thomas said.

"You get above the wind," Rose said, "and ride it. That's how you do."

Luke had turned around, sensing something, and the others saw him and turned too. Three men or boys, traveling single file, were coming down the field, down the path Luke had cut through the drifts. They wore heavy coats, fur-lined hats with ear flaps. They came out onto the beach and peered through the snow to see whom they'd been following.

"Life is aboundin in disappointments," Ben Howland said. With him were Jared Cromwell and Peter Daggett. All of them were fifteen or sixteen. Ben attended the Centre Street Academy, but Jared and Peter had quit, Peter to work at the shipyard, Jared to crew for his uncle Ned ferrying passengers from Woods Hole. They came closer. The wind whistled along the beach, worrying Rose's skirt.

"What were you expecting?" Luke said.

"Pirates," Ben said. "Marauders come ashore to take advantage of our women."

"Ain't it pretty?" Thomas said, gesturing at West Chop and the harbor.

"Cold, is what it is," Jared said.

"Cold as a witch's tit in January," Ben said, watching Rose out of the corner of his eye. They all were watching her. They knew well who she was, but Rose with her skirt dragging and blowing, Rose out in the snow with the three boys, was not the aloof and genteel and beautiful Negress they would see on Main Street with a shopping basket on her arm. Had she been, Ben Howland would not have talked so.

"What're you folks doin out here in all this storm?" Jared said.

"Same as you," Luke said.

"What's Smith doin here?"

"Same as you," Luke said again.

"He's stopping over with us," Thomas said.

"Bet you like that, don't you, Smith?" Jared said.

"Sure I do," Elisha said. "Who wouldn't?"

"Bet you eat good."

"Eat good enough," Elisha said.

"Coloreds is good cooks," Jared said. "Wish we had us one."

"Shut your mouth," Luke said.

"That ain't a insult."

"What else are we good at?" Rose said, and right away wished she hadn't.

"Nothin," Jared said.

"You don't have to take that off a her," said Peter Daggett, who had not yet spoken. "That's a white man you're talkin to, miss."

"Shut your mouth," Luke said.

"Luke," Rose said, and took his arm.

With that the wind seemed to redouble, the snow to thicken and fly harder. Rose's skirt whipped, pulled at her knees.

"We're going home now," she said, and moved Luke away by the arm, not up the path through the snow but along the beach toward Water Street, toward the wharf. They would go up Union Street to Main, and over.

Behind them Peter Daggett called through the keen and shudder of the wind. "Good at music," he said. "Good at makin babies."

Luke stopped dead but she had his arm still and pulled, hard, and Luke let himself be led on. The three boys stood watching them, he knew that, but he did not look back.

"Isn't anything you can do with their sort," Rose said.

"They're bigger than you, Luke," Thomas said, moving up beside him.

"It's my fault," Rose said. "Got to open my mouth, don't I."

Thomas looked at her, looked again. "You're crying, Rosie," he said.

"No I ain't," she said.

Later Luke would ask her and she would deny it still. Of course my eyes were leaking, she would say, with all that cold wind at them. Would I allow such an ignorant fool to cause me tears?

They struggled up Union Street in silence, Luke again leading the way, and down Main and up Drummer Lane still without a word being spoken. Their old tracks were nearly gone, wind-obliterated as much as filled in. The front gate was stuck fast in the snow—Luke wondered why they'd closed it—and he climbed it and then gave his hand to Rose and helped her over.

It was cold in the front hall. They hung their snowy coats and hats and Rose's cloak and sat down to remove their boots.

"I don't want anyone telling the doctor what happened," Rose said.

The three boys looked at her, bent down to their bootlaces.

"Why not?" Thomas said.

"It'll do no good and will only discomfort him."

"Father could speak to their parents," Thomas said.

"Did you hear her?" Luke said.

"I heard her."

She made Indian pudding that night, and they drowned it in thick cream and ate and ate and ate. Elisha had never eaten as he did that year at the Chandlers', and never would again. The snow still peppered the mullioned windows and shook the sashes in their frames. The boys drew pots of water—there was a cistern under the kitchen—and heated them for Rose to wash the dishes in and tossed the used water out into the snow for her. She sang to them as she worked, the boys sitting now at the pine table waiting for more water to heat. She sang "Listen to the Mockingbird." She sang "Come Where My Love Lies Dreaming." In the back parlor George Chandler put his magazine aside and looked into the fire, listening. They'd brought Elizabeth's Steinway from New Bedford and put it in the front parlor, and Rose had eyed it awhile and then said she'd like to learn to play, and he'd sent her to Miss Thomasina West for lessons. Her playing was adequate but her voice was good, a mezzo, Chandler thought. Miss West had taught her "Come Where My Love Lies Dreaming." She would teach her the new songs, as they were published.

Elisha slept on a straw mattress on the floor between Luke and Thomas. The snow had stopped quite abruptly, and now a half moon shone mistily from behind blowing shreds of cloud. He had thought it would storm all night and Elisha's heart sank with knowing he'd be going home tomorrow. Luke and Thomas would help him shovel out the skiff and he would pull home and wade the drifts covering the field. The house would be very cold, with wood to be carried and water, and his father behind on watering and feeding the stock. They'd probably lost some chickens. Find em in a week or two, froze solid.

"She sings pretty, don't she?" he said. He was lying on his back, warm under the blankets and the air cold on his face.

"I wish Father would marry her," Thomas said.

Elisha turned his head, looked up at him. "A colored woman?"

"It's happened lots of times," Thomas said.

"It has?" Elisha said.

"Father's too old to marry her," Luke said.

"How old *is* she, then?" Elisha said.

"We don't know," Thomas said.

"No one does," Luke said. "The orphanage didn't have a record of it."

"She must know, about," Elisha said.

"She won't say," Thomas said.

"Why not?"

"She just won't."

"She doesn't *know*," Luke said.

"You could ask the orphanage what age she looked like when she come in."

"What for?" Luke said.

"Ain't you curious?"

"I'd say she's twenty," Thomas said. "Twenty, twenty-one."

"Younger," Luke said. "Eighteen or so."

They were quiet awhile.

"That Peter Daggett shouldn't of talked to her so, never mind her age," Elisha said.

"I'm going to settle up with him," Luke said.

Thomas sat up. "When?" he said.

"I don't know," Luke said.

"I could help you, Luke," Elisha said.

"Two to one wouldn't be fair," Luke said.

"Who cares if it's fair?" Elisha said.

"I do," Luke said.

Again they were silent. Moonlight fell on Elisha, intermittent through the scudding clouds. He thought about Rose, a colored woman, marrying Dr. Chandler. It would beat all. *But if I was the doc,* he thought. *Good at makin babies* . . . And Elisha thought of the picture Ty Luce, one of the older boys, had brought to school one day, a daguerreotype glued to cardboard of a girl lying on a couch with her dress pulled all the way up around her waist and nothing on underneath. Ty had led several of the boys around the corner of the building during recess and shown them the picture at no charge. Elisha had followed uninvited and Ty had not objected. He'd feigned nonchalance as he took his turn and did not look long, but afterward the white thighs and triangle between them had dogged his thoughts like a waking dream.

Now, suddenly, he wanted to see Rose that way, like the girl in the daguerreotype, and he longed to hear her sing again, and to speak her name.

"Rose," he said. "It's a pretty name, ain't it?"

He wondered what Luke would say to this, if he would read the thoughts that prompted it, but Luke hadn't heard it. Thomas, too, was asleep.

SIX

Even after hearing Elisha and McNamara, Thomas was surprised by the cursing.

"That goddamn Bobby Lee, what's he up to?"

"And that sonofabitch Stuart."

"We'll see how goddamn good they are without Jackson."

"Good enough to steal the march on us. Most of em's up in Maryland, you know."

"No, I don't know, and you don't either."

"They're gone, is the point, while we set here."

"What the hell's Hooker waitin on?"

"Sonofabitch ain't been right since Chancellorsville. Since that roof fell on him. You boys all know that."

"It warn't a roof. Shell hit a column next to where he was standin. Affected his brain someways."

"Is that the way of it?"

"What I heard."

There were seven or eight of them seated around a campfire, some on the ground, some on ladderback chairs and wooden supply boxes, Luke and Thomas sitting tailor-fashion on the ground between Elisha and McNamara, who had a chair, and speaking only when spoken to. The five recruits from Nantucket had also been enrolled in Company I, but they'd found men they knew from home in another mess and had joined them.

"These beans're good, Stonewall," Elisha told the man who'd cooked them, a Roxbury farmer who bore the same name, Thomas Jackson, as the Confederate general who'd been mortally wounded at Chancellors-ville by his own pickets. The only good to come of that terrible day.

"Everyone be fartin all night," said the drummer boy, Willie Davis, a rank-smelling little Boston tough who cursed as filthily as any of the men, who encouraged it for their amusement.

"Watch your mouth, boy," McNamara said.

"Sure," the boy said, "I'll watch my goddamn mouth," and there was a chorus of laughter.

"Well," said a man who had not yet spoken, "we'll be marching soon, for sure. Any day, I speck."

It silenced them, like the melancholy toll of a bell. They looked into the fire, looked down at their plates of syrupy beans. There was white bread, too, and slices of dried apple.

"There's gonna be a big fight," the man said. He was hatless, and his hair was chestnut-brown and he wore a long handlebar mustache. Eyes quiet, and as dark and deep as wells. "The biggest yet," he said.

"Where at, Henry Wilcox?"

"Hooker's got to get between Lee and Washington, d'you see? Lee's behind the Blue Ridge, reason he got away so clean, and by the time he turns east he'll be clear to Pennsylvania. That's where we'll be fightin, boys."

"Pennsylvania," someone said. "By Christ."

It was getting dark. Voices rose around the other fires, short bursts of laughter. A soft evening breeze brought a foul smell from the company sink, an evil shit-piled trench hardly two feet deep, a middling walk from the rearmost row of tents.

"Lee gets up there, he'll go clear to Harrisburg," someone said.

"Could be," said Wilcox.

At a fire not far distant a fiddle struck up, slow, inexpert, sawing a plaintive, weepy "Lorena." The fiddler, or perhaps another, added his voice, a reedy tenor.

"Someone tell them boys that's a goddamn Reb song." The speaker had a narrow shriveled-looking face, squint-eyed and feral as some mean little animal, rat or weasel, with thin shoulders and long snarls of black hair and an untrimmed mustache.

"So what if it is?" said Tom Jackson.

The sun's low down the sky, Lorena,
The frost gleams where the flow'rs have been.

Luke looked at his brother in the firelight. Thomas was looking out into the distance. His mouth was full but he wasn't chewing. In the past year Rose had been singing "Lorena" and often playing it on the front parlor piano. She'd gotten the sheet music from Miss West.

"What's the matter with him?" someone said.

"He's tired," Luke said. "The day's been a long one."

"He'll see ones longer."

"That's a pretty fiddle," Thomas said softly, as if to himself.

"Isaac Brophy," someone said. "Dumbest bastard in the regiment."

"He can fiddle, though."

"Thomas," Luke said, "eat your supper."

"You homesicky, little girl?" It was the unkempt squint-eyed little man.

"Hey," Luke said.

"Hey yourself."

"What's your name?" Luke said.

"Jake Rivers, and what's that to you?"

"I'll lick you, you don't shut up," Luke said.

"Will you, now," Rivers said.

"Try lickin *me* and see what happens," another, larger, man said.

The music had broken off.

"Let's not go to lickin each other," Wilcox said. "Let's save it for the Rebs."

"These two're my friends from home," Elisha said. "They're Mac's friends too. What if he *is* homesicky? What of it?"

"He ain't even been here a day."

"That don't matter," Elisha said.

"What's their names, Elisha?"

"I done told you their names."

"Well tell em again."

"Luke and Thomas Chandler. They're brothers."

The fiddler began again. "Lorena."

"They talk intelligent, both of em."

"They come from education," Elisha said. "Their pa's a surgeon."

"You boys know Latin and Greek?"

"Some," Luke said.

"Thomas, is it?"

"How many times you need tellin?" Elisha said.

"How old're you, Thomas?"

Thomas smiled wanly. "Eighteen," he said.

"You ain't either."

"He's sixteen," Luke said.

"Lie to the recruiter, did you?"

Thomas nodded.

"Colonel Macy," Elisha said.

"That sonofabitch would of took you anyways," said the big man who'd challenged Luke. His name was Merriman and, the challenge done with, his broad fair face was open and genial, of a fit with his name. He was another Roxbury man, a stonecutter. "He'd of took you at fourteen. You get a bounty?"

"We didn't join for the bounty," Luke said.

"Sure you didn't," said Rivers.

"They didn't," Elisha said. "Didn't I tell you their pa's a surgeon? They got all the money they need."

It quieted them momentarily. "Lorena" played on.

"If that's so," said one, "you're either foolish or crazy, one."

"They're both," McNamara said.

"Takes one to know one, Mac," Merriman said.

"They come to help us whip the Rebs," Elisha said. "It ain't no more complicated than that."

"Hell. Can't argue with that," said Wilcox.

"Just next time don't get so hot, big brother," said Merriman. "There's some boys in this regiment you don't want to tangle with."

"He was standin up for his brother, Joe," said Tom Jackson. "Who can fault him that?"

"I ain't faultin him," Merriman said. "Gimme your hand, Luke. I like a man'll stand up for his own."

Luke put his plate down and Merriman laid his aside, and they leaned toward each other and shook hands.

"You go on eat your beans, Tommy," said Henry Wilcox. "Won't be any baked beans where we're goin."

Thomas managed another smile. He nodded, and dug a spoonful of beans.

"They're awful good," he said.

"Ain't they?" said Tom Jackson.

"It's a pretty song, even if it is secesh," Henry said.

They weren't alone together until an hour or so after taps, when Thomas got up and went out behind the tent to pee and Luke followed him. Neither had slept yet. They'd lain quiet, side by side, listening to McNamara snore, grabbing at invisible mosquitoes. The night air was warm, soft. Somewhere in the distance a mule brayed. Somewhere closer a whippoorwill called softly.

"Hear that?" Thomas said.

"Yeah."

"Didn't know they had them down here."

"What's wrong, Thomas?" Luke said, just above a whisper.

"Nothing."

"It isn't nothing."

"It's the music. It makes a body sad."

"You'll be glad of it by and by," Luke said, and thought *I told you so, didn't I? Didn't I tell you to stay home?*

Thomas had finished and now Luke stood spread-legged, peeing.

"How do I look in my uniform?" Thomas said.

"Fine. Like a soldier."

"I feel like I'm going to a costume party."

"So do I," Luke said.

"Do you wish Mariah could see you?"

"No."

"Why not? She might change her mind if she could see you now."

"I wouldn't want her to."

"Why not?"

Luke had finished and was buttoning up. "Let's go to sleep," he said.

"Do you think Henry's right about a big battle in Pennsylvania?" Thomas said.

"Probably."

"It'll come soon, won't it," Thomas said.

"Thomas, listen to me. Don't look ahead. Live in the present, like each day was a complete thing—like your life was one day long. That's what the soldiers do. I can already see it. You'd have thought Elisha had never had baked beans before, and in a way he hadn't."

Thomas nodded. He was looking at the ground, standing very still. Again Luke thought *I told you so* but he did not say it. Nor did he, ever, in all the difficulty to come.

SEVEN

He'd settled up with Peter Daggett sooner than he expected. The Academy had reopened four days after the storm, and when the boys came back from dinner, traipsing through the snow, Luke had found a piece of ruled paper where he'd left the bookmark in his Latin grammar. A question, pencil-written, the script bunched but tidy: *Is yr Old Man screwing that collored girl???* Luke closed the book on it and looked at Ben Howland, who sat a couple of rows in front of him. The children were arriving, peeling off their coats and hats. Mr. Pease stood up front, watching everybody settle in. Howland looked back over his shoulder, met Luke's eye and smiled.

Luke opened the grammar again. He picked up the note and rose from his desk and went forward and handed it wordlessly to Mr. Pease. Mr. Pease took it, a questioning smile on his benign pink face, and peered at it through his double spectacles. Luke turned, went quickly but without any show of haste to Ben Howland, who was now bent studiously over an open book, and hit him hard in the face.

Some of the older girls screamed. Howland leaned back in his desk and stared up at Luke in slack-jawed confusion. Luke hit him again and the girls loosed another scream. Howland tried to get up—the little desks were bolted to the floor—and Luke hit him a third time and he fell back into his seat and sought to grasp Luke's wrists and now Mr. Pease's arms were around Luke's middle, wrestling him away in a stumbling backward dance.

"Luke," he said. "*Luke.*"

Luke stopped struggling. He didn't say anything. Mr. Pease let him go. The children were all on their feet, staring, eyes wide and fearful, even Thomas's, even Elisha's. The woodstove muttered and seethed in the sudden quiet. Ben Howland had gotten up but made no move toward Luke. There were vivid pink blooms on his jaw and forehead, and his lip had been split.

"You're dead meat, Chandler," he said.

"Not another word," Mr. Pease said. "Not one."

"He bushwhacked me, Mr. Pease."

"I know what happened, Ben. Luke, I wish to speak to you outside, then to you, Ben."

"Me?"

"Ty, fetch some snow in the bucket. Put it to your mouth, Ben."

Luke glanced at Thomas on his way out, and at Elisha. They looked at him questioningly. All eyes were on him, and Luke could feel the reproach in them, censorious and vaguely horrified. Mr. Pease followed him out and closed the door. He had not put on his greatcoat. They stood on the top step. The snow here had been tramped down hard and flat and icy. Mr. Pease pushed his hands into the pockets of his frock coat.

"I understand your anger," he said.

It was well known that Mr. Pease was an abolitionist.

"There was more to it," Luke said.

"I'm sure there was."

"They hate her because she's a Negro."

"I don't think they hate her, Luke. I think it's more complicated than that."

"Do you know Rose, Mr. Pease?"

"I think everyone's aware of her," Mr. Pease said. "She cuts quite a figure, you know."

"Her and my father aren't . . ."

"*She* and my father. No, I'm sure they aren't."

"You going to punish me, Mr. Pease?" Punishment at Centre Street was copying and memorizing and staying after school. Mr. Pease had no use for the rod or strap.

"You, nor Ben. Nor do I intend to tell your father."

"I appreciate that, sir."

"But if Ben's father comes to me, I'll have to tell the whole of it."

"Yes sir."

"Luke?"

"Sir?"

"If you hadn't beaten him, I could have punished Ben."

"I know."

"It's no solution, Luke."

"With respect, Mr. Pease, you might feel different if you were a Negro."

Mr. Pease smiled. "I might indeed."

"What are you going to say to Ben?"

"I suppose I'm going to tell him to keep such thoughts to himself, if he must have them."

"That's all?"

"I think he might say the same about this conversation, could he hear it."

"I had cause, Mr. Pease."

"But you're not listening to me, Luke."

"I'm listening," Luke said.

The next day Peter Daggett was waiting for him on the corner of Centre and William Streets, by the cemetery. There was a trodden path down the middle of Centre Street; Luke, Thomas, and Elisha walked it single file, Thomas bringing up the rear. Luke had described Ben Howland's note to both him and Elisha and made them promise not to speak of it. Daggett came up the path to meet them and stood blocking Luke's way.

"You bushwhackin sonofabitch," he said, and swung, hitting Luke a painless glancing leather-mittened blow on the side of his head.

Both boys were bundled up in their winter coats and fur-lined hats and so they swung at each other's faces but at arm's length, the blows grazing or missing altogether. Luke's right hand was bruised and sore from yesterday but he forgot about that now. It was hard to fight in overcoats in the snow and Daggett caught his heel and fell backward into a drift and Luke was on him instantly with his knee on his chest. He raised up and slugged him, and slugged him again, and it was over.

Ben Howland had arrived in time to see it. Daggett's nose was pouring blood and swelling had begun already under his left eye. Howland didn't say anything. Luke got up and brushed himself off. Elisha handed him his books and he gestured with his head for Elisha to follow him and Thomas down William Street. They went a block and stopped. In the distance they could see Daggett, on his feet now, holding a mittenful of snow to his nose while Howland stood watching him.

"What I want to say," Luke said, "is if you hear anybody else talk about Father and Rose that way, you make them quit or you tell me."

Elisha and Thomas looked at each other.

"What?" Luke said.

"You can't stop it, Luke," Elisha said.

"What do you mean?" Luke said.

"There's been such talk," Elisha said. "Me and Tommy've both heard it."

"Where?"

"This place and that. It don't matter where."

"Yes it does. In school?"

"In school, a bit."

"Why didn't you tell me?" Luke said.

"Didn't want to upset you more than you already was," Elisha said.

"You, Thomas. Why didn't *you*?"

Thomas said nothing.

At the end of the street Daggett and Howland had begun to move, down Centre toward Main, slow. Daggett was holding a fresh scoop of snow to his nose.

"I'll whip anybody says it," Luke said.

"You can't whip growed men," Elisha said.

"What men?"

"I just hear things, Luke. It don't matter who from."

"Goddamn it, Elisha."

"They don't say it to her face, so what do you care?"

"I'll whip their goddamn asses."

"Then your pa would hear of it. And Rose would."

"You got to stand up, is all I'm saying."

"Well," Elisha said, "if I got to boilin every time someone spoke disrespectful of the Smiths, I'd be fightin the whole island."

"I don't know how you stand it," Luke said.

"It ain't true, that's how I stand it."

To which Luke made no reply. He knew what he had to do, must do, true or not.

"What'd you do to your hand, sugar?"

"Nothing," he said.

"You've been fighting, haven't you?"

"Maybe."

"Who with, Luke?"

"Never mind."

"What was it about?"

Luke made no answer.

"Someone bothering Thomas," Rose guessed.

She'd noticed the swollen hand at supper and had sat up reading till ten and then gone down to use the kitchen privy and Luke had heard her, as she'd known he would, and after a short diplomatic wait had come into her room to talk awhile. A candle burned on her bedside table. She sat up and wrapped herself in a shawl. Luke in the rocker, in his union suit and trousers and unbuttoned untucked shirt. The fire had burned down and there was the steady whisper of a last smoldering log.

"It wasn't Thomas," Luke said.

Rose studied him some more. "There's a reason you don't want to tell me," she said.

Luke looked at the floor between his knees and said nothing.

"Know what I think?" she said. "I think it concerns me. And if it does, that's reason to tell it, not reason to hide it."

Luke thought this over and saw the truth in it. And so he told her. The vile note, the two fights.

Rose surprised him by smiling. "That's what they all think, honey. How else I be earnin these fine clothes, place at a white man's table? Ain't for my brilliant conversation."

"Don't talk that way, Rosie."

"I thought you liked me to."

"Sometimes I do."

"The older you get, Luke, the more you're going to hear it."

"Does Father hear it?"

"If he did he wouldn't care. Rise above it, he'd say."

"I'll whip anybody I hear say it."

"You be careful, hear? You can't whip the whole island."

"You sound like Elisha," he said.

"He's a wise boy, well as a sweet one."

"I don't care, Rosie. I won't stand for it."

It earned him another smile. "Come here, Luke," she said.

He rose and approached the bed. She reached and took his shoulder and drew him down and kissed his cheek. She smelled sharply sweet, like a hothouse flower.

"Don't judge your father hard," she said.

"I don't," he said.

"Nor Thomas, nor Elisha."

"I don't."

"Good night, then."

"Good night," he said.

EIGHT

Reveille was drummed at five and the men would emerge in semidress sleepy and quiet and form up for roll call. Elisha nudged Luke and Thomas into place the first morning, and showed them how to stand. Breakfast call was a half hour later, and after breakfast the eleven recruits went off with Sergeant Cate to a well-trampled meadow east of the town and learned the commands and how to execute them.

Fall in by height, count off by twos, left face, front, right dress, guide right, by the right oblique: by such orders a single line of men became two lines, and the two became a marching column four abreast, or a line of battle two deep, and all you had to do was worry about yourself, turn where you were told or step where you were told, and the maneuver resolved itself crisply and perfectly, as if by the wave of a magic wand. They learned to march, the rapid steady rhythm of it, the economy, and the controlled speed of the doublequick. They learned the Manual of Arms; shoulder arms, secure arms, right shoulder shift, support arms, trail arms, carry at will. With blank cartridges they learned how to use their muskets, load in nine times, load in four, fire by rank, fire by files, fire at will. The black powder when you bit open the paper cartridge had a bitter charcoal and sulfur taste but Elisha said you didn't notice it in a fight. Their arms ached from handling musket and ramrod. They sweated in their wool uniforms, and the sun burned their necks and faces.

Elisha asked them if Sergeant Cate had told them to leave the spent cap on the nipple until *after* they'd reloaded and explained how, if you didn't, air could rush into the barrel and ignite any embers that might have been left after firing. He told them how hot the barrel would get and showed them how to use the leather sling to avoid touching it if you couldn't wrap it in a rag. There's things, he said, they don't think to teach you.

"Does your shoulder hurt?" Luke asked Thomas the second night, rubbing his.

"I'll allow I do ache," Thomas said.

They were sitting on hardtack boxes in front of the tent waiting for supper call. Luke, Thomas, Elisha. McNamara was inside, working on a bottle of whiskey he'd won in a game of draw poker from a soldier in Company D who had purchased it during the truce off a Reb picket in trade across the river.

"Feels like that goddamn rifle sawed into the bone," Luke said.

"She'll kick harder," Elisha said, "you got a live round in her."

"Maybe you ain't as hard as you think," McNamara said from inside the tent.

"Luke's plenty hard," Elisha said.

"Harder'n Lieutenant Paine?" McNamara said.

"Why don't you come out here, you want to talk?" Luke said.

"In a fair fight, easy," Elisha said.

"Harder'n Hancock?"

"He ain't gonna fight Hancock, Mac. It's a stupid conversation."

"Him and his shirts," McNamara said. "Looks like a damn fairy."

"Well, I'm glad we got him," Elisha said.

"Glad we got a fairy for our corps commander? I guess you would be."

"He'll be drunk, they don't call supper soon," Elisha said quietly.

"What does he mean about Hancock's shirts?" Luke said.

"Always got a clean white one on. Fancy ones, with frills and such. Middle of a battle."

"Must take about ten niggers to keep them shirts clean," McNamara said.

"Mac," Elisha said, "get up out of that tent and quit fore one of the sergeants sees you stumblin around."

"How's your feet, Tommy?" McNamara said.

"Raw."

"I got blisters on my blisters," Luke said.

"I think your brother's tougher'n you are," McNamara said.

"Cork the bottle, Mac," Elisha said.

"God I miss ol Peleg. Peleg didn't nag me so."

"Cork the bottle, will you?" Elisha said.

The musket with a live load kicked your shoulder hard and the explosion blew a hole in the air and went careering across country in a wild and antic echo. Blank cartridges were nothing in comparison: live ones in miniature. The Army was thrifty of its ordnance and the recruits were permitted to fire two rounds and no more until they should encounter the enemy, and, all being anxious to try it, they got to it on the third day of drilling. Sergeant Cate supervised each shot, the men stepping forward in turn while the others watched. They were well acquainted with one another now and there was some good-natured joshing.

"Bet you can't hit that thing, Chase."

"Pretend it's Jeff Davis."

"Pretend it's that boy to home been attendin to your wife."

The target was a weathered plank leaned up against a tree and Luke and Thomas were surprised at how distant it was. Rods and rods. Elisha had said you could hit a man at a quarter of a mile and this was something less than that, but it seemed a long way for a ball to carry and still be accurate, and lethal. A man wouldn't know who'd killed him.

"Aim low," Cate said. "You boys remember it when the time comes. It's a natural tendency to shoot high, get anxious and fire before you bring the gun down level. Anyways, hit a man in the knees and you good as killed him."

"Hit him in the balls, Sergeant."

"That'll answer," Cate said.

The plank actually made a generous target and Luke hit it with both rounds, saw the ball gouge the wood and send splinters flying almost simultaneous with the kick of the stock against his shoulder and the deafening blow to his eardrum. Thomas took so long aiming that Cate barked at him, "Fire, damn it!" He did fire, and missed and said *Shit*. He missed again, but the new men had softened toward him, as the veterans had, and their jibes were friendly.

"Where's his spectacles at?"

"It's all right, Tommy. There's plenty a Rebs blind as you are."

That night Thomas asked Elisha how many men he'd killed. Elisha said he didn't know, but guessed it was a right good number. He said it was hard to know, exactly.

"They come at you so thick," he said, "it's hard to make em out individual. In a charge they'll go down three four at a time, who's to say who hit em or if they're dead or wounded? And then there's the smoke, pretty soon you're shootin at shadows. Aim low, is the thing. You aim low, you *got* to hit somebody. If they're behind a wall, like they was at Marye's Heights, you're tryin to get at em so desperate you rush your shot and don't know where it goes."

"Is it hard to shoot at somebody?" Thomas said. "To kill a man?"

Elisha looked away. He thought awhile. "I guess you want me to say yes," he said.

"I didn't say that," Thomas said.

"I couldn't do it on the Vineyard," Elisha said, "Reb or no."

"I know you couldn't."

"Down here," Elisha said, "it ain't no choice. Everybody's shootin, both sides. When the time comes, you just do it, that's all."

You just do it.

"It's what we come for," Elisha said.

"You think I don't know that?"

"Best not to think on it," Elisha said.

They'd been in camp four days when a peddler came through, an elderly black man in a frock coat and threadbare gray silk vest and stovepipe hat carrying a wicker basket loaded with pies. He walked slowly, swayingly, the basket hung in the crook of his arm. It was an hour before supper and as he came up the company street, first one, then another called to him to wait and went into their tents for money.

"How bout it, Elisha," McNamara said.

"How bout what?" Elisha said. He and Thomas were sitting on Elisha's gum blanket and Elisha was teaching him the rudiments of poker. The cards belonged to McNamara.

"I'm broke," McNamara said. He was on his chair, smoking his pipe, polishing the buttons of his sack coat. He would spit on one, rub it, spit and rub again.

"That there's a full house," Elisha said. "Three and two. Beats everything but a flush and four of a kind."

"I forget what a flush is."

"Straight and royal. Remember?"

"What do you want to learn poker for?" Luke said. He was reading a story called "The Lady Passenger; or, After the Train Robbers" in an old *New York Ledger* of Elisha's.

"It passes the time," Thomas said.

"Separate you from your money, is what it'll do," Luke said. *At last,* he read, *two were dead and one dying, when the other flung up his hands in token of submission.* The officers, he'd heard, had books. Dickens, Eliot, Fenimore Cooper.

"You rich boys," McNamara said. "Separate that nigger from a few pies and we'll enjoy em later."

"What do they cost?" Luke said.

"How much you got?" McNamara said.

"A double eagle," Thomas said.

McNamara took the pipe out of his mouth. "A double eagle?" he said.

"It's his, Mac," Elisha said.

"Hey," McNamara called. "Sambo. Get your ass over here."

The peddler had just concluded a transaction with two of their neighbors in the adjacent tent, veteran Nantucket men named Stackpole and Murphy. He pocketed a coin, touched his hat in thanks, and came slowly toward McNamara on his varnish-peeling mahogany and velvet chair.

"Can you change for a double eagle?" McNamara said.

"Wish I could, suh."

"Shit," McNamara said.

"Yes suh, I agrees."

"Where'd you get that hat, you steal it?"

"No suh. Done found it."

"*Found* it?"

"Yes suh."

"Them pies still run twenty-five cent?" Elisha said.

"Yes suh."

Elisha put down his cards and picked himself up off the blanket. "I'll take a couple," he said. "You got peach?"

"Got apple and blueberry, suh."

"Thomas," Luke said, "go get a couple of those silver quarters."

"Silver quarters?" McNamara said. "How much you boys got?"

Elisha's money—some greenbacks, some coins, left from last payday—was in a cigar box under his blankets. Luke and Thomas kept theirs in a cloth bag, the bag rolled in Luke's red wool blanket. Thomas knelt and felt for the bag while Elisha found his cigar box.

"What you aim to do with them twenty-dollar pieces?" Elisha said.

"I don't know. Father gave them to us for when we'd need them."

"Need em for what?"

"I don't know."

The pies were wrapped individually in newspaper, the *Richmond Examiner*. Luke took the money from Thomas and paid the peddler, who dropped the coins in his coat pocket and lifted two apple pies from the basket in their oil-stained wrappings. Luke had never seen pies so flat and heavy. Elisha bought an apple and a blueberry.

"I thanks you both," the peddler said.

"Same," Luke said.

"You stole that hat out a your master's house, what I think," McNamara said. "You better hope he don't come back."

"Whyn't you leave him alone, Mac," Elisha said.

The peddler removed the hat, the tall stovepipe, and looked thoughtfully into its deep interior. "Abe Lincoln done freed me, suh," he said, and put the hat on again.

"That's just for the war. After the war, you're a slave again, didn't you know that?"

"That's just some foolishness," Luke said. "You're a free man, now and forever."

"Such was my understandin, suh." The peddler moved on, slow, down the dusty footworn company street.

"Abolitionists," McNamara said. "Well, I ain't surprised."

"Elisha's one," Thomas said.

"Who listens to Elisha?" McNamara said.

"Peleg become a abolitionist," Elisha said.

"Peleg just liked to argue," McNamara said.

"Peleg had cause," Thomas said. "Didn't he, Luke?"

"He had a heart," Luke said.

"And I don't," McNamara said.

"Sure you do," Elisha said, and sent Luke an anxious look that quieted him.

At supper McNamara waved his fork at the Chandlers—onions and potatoes tonight, boiled beef; Hooker's superb organizing and logistics—and said, swallowing, "Boys, meet the new abolitionists in the regiment."

"There's always a few, ain't there," said the weaselly Rivers.

"You say a few," said Henry Wilcox, "but how bout Howard's corps? Howard, Schurz. It's solid abolitionist."

"Goddamn Dutchmen," Rivers said. "They can't fight, but they all want to free the niggers."

"You notice Howard got all them contrabands waitin on him?" said another. "Seems like there's more of em every day."

"Revere got em," Rivers said.

Colonel Paul Revere was the current commander of the regiment. He was the grandson of the night rider of '75.

"He got *one*," Henry said.

"Meade, Sickles, all of em got em," Rivers said. "Them niggers eat better'n we do. They get better grub, and they got a chaplain and a surgeon ready to jump when they say so. It's the nigger first, then the mule, then the white man."

"Ay-men," someone said.

"Henry Wilcox," McNamara said, "you with us on this?"

Wilcox smiled mordantly into the fire. Eyes large and dark and gentle.

"Henry's right up there with Sumner and Chase and Old Abe, ain't you, Henry?"

"Human bondage," Henry said. "You boys want to stick up for it, God forgive you."

"Is a nigger human?" McNamara said.

"Half human, I'd say," said Rivers.

Thomas looked at Luke. Luke's eyes were downcast, brooding.

"The Southron ones, anyway," said another. "You boys"—addressing Luke and Thomas—"wait till you see some of em. Lazy sonsabitches, and ugly as sin. And dirty? Oh, Lord."

"This is wicked talk," Thomas said.

Everyone looked at him. The fire seethed, crackled.

"Go ahead argue with em, Tommy," Elisha said. "They won't bite you."

Merriman, the stonecutter, was the first to smile. "Hell," he said, "we don't bite Henry Wilcox we won't bite you. Nor Luke."

"I've seen em scarred from head to foot," said Wilcox, "and so have you. Seen em with their ears cut off. Right up here at Lacy House"— sweeping an arm at the heights to the west—"was a stocks, ball and chain, handcuffs, whips. Are you boys Christians?"

There was silence, as often there was after Henry had spoken.

"No need to throw the baby out with the bathwater," said Merriman.

"What the hell does that mean?" McNamara said.

"Means you can have em and not torture em."

"You got to discipline em, they act up."

"That don't mean you cut a man's ear off," Merriman said.

"They behave theirselves, you won't have to."

It was dark and they were boiling water for coffee in a blackened quart tin can to which a wire loop had been attached. Around them other low fires, other profane, bantering conversations. Luke wondered if the officers talked this way, and how these same men comported themselves in civilian life.

"Sumner and Chase and them sonsabitches," said Rivers. "Ought to give em a musket, let em come down here, they want to free the niggers so bad."

"It was Abe Lincoln freed em," said Tom Jackson.

"Give him one too."

"What are we fightin this war for, boys?"

"Damn if I know."

"That water boilin yet?"

"Close."

"We're fightin to save the Union, and you know it," said Joe Merriman.

"Hell with the Union."

"Hell with the niggers."

"And fuck Bobby Lee up the ass," sang out Merriman.

"Ain't you boys glad you joined up?" said Tom Jackson.

Elisha answered for Luke and Thomas. "You ain't gonna discourage em," he said. "Not these two."

Falmouth, Virginia
June 13, 1863

Dear Rose,

We did not think to bring pen & paper & it is for this reason you have not heard from us & I ache to think how long this missive will take to reach you. Today a delegation of the Christian Commission came through with a "coffee wagon" bringing besides soap & towels & other sundries paper & envelopes ready-stamped as you can see. They are good people, ladies & men both. They told me they were from Philadelphia. Now I will be able to write frequent & they say that the chaplains will provide writing materiel when we are marching, and altho our Regt has no chaplain plenty of other regts do. But to continue, we will be moving any day now as Lee's Army is gone.

Rosie it is 9 PM & I am outside the tent whch we share with Elisha Smith & a man named John McNamara employing my knapsack as a writing desk & by the light of a candle stuck in my bayonet whch is stuck in the ground. Thomas wrote Father—a short one, I think—& is inside with Elisha & Mac playing or I should say learning to play draw poker. He is picking up some bad habits down here—learning to curse as bad as I do! Elisha was on hand to greet us the first day & has been our true friend ever since, as for instance not letting the veterans stick us with fatigue duty when it isn't our turn or twit us too much. I know you always liked Elisha & it is strange to see him here a soldier & not at our table enjoying your upside-down cake.

Anyway Rosie we are soldiers ourselves now. The sgt who trained us said so. We have taken part in a division drill up the hill in back

*of Lacy House which was formerly a slave plantation & is now a
hospital. They say Geo Washington spent the night there one time &
for a fact Abe Lincoln did back before the big fight at Fredericksburg.
The slave houses are still there, they are brick with dirt floors &
no windows except on one side & those without panes, & I think of
all the people that had to live their whole lives there & toil without
recompense with no end to it & I know this War is just. We did not
get inside the mansion but the boys say it has been torn up for wood
for fires & winter huts & is bloody as a shambles from the surgeons
amputating. Fredericksburg was a terrible loss for our side &
Chancellorsville too but the boys are in good spirits notwithstanding.
It was the generals' fault, not theirs, & if we had someone like Genl
Hancock over us, he is our Corp Cmmdr, or Genl Reynolds of the 1st
Corps, we cd whip anybody.*

*Anyway the drill was grand. Imagine in your Mind's Eye 15,000
men in lines stretching 1/2 mile (for a guess) moving in perfect
precision. The orders go somewhat as follows: RIGHT FACE!
FORWARD MARCH! COMPANIES ONTO LINE, MARCH! BY
FILE RIGHT, MARCH! BY THE LEFT FLANK, MARCH! The
flags are snapping very colorful, and how the guns do gleam in the
sunlight! Thomas has stood up to it very well so far. He is stronger
than I thought.*

*One thing Rosie, not everyone in this Army is against slavery, far
from it. It is just like on the Vineyard where people are prejudiced
against Negroes without knowing any. Some are afraid that when
the slaves are free they will all come up North & take their jobs at
lower wages. There are a lot of Negroes around the camp, they come
around selling things and some poor souls to pick through the garbage
and some of the boys go pretty hard on them & insult them by
disrespectful & indecent language, men & women. The curious thing
is why they are fighting. Putting aside the genls they say no army
ever fought better than this one. They will say they won't lift a finger
to free a "darkie" but Elisha swears the ground below Marye's Hghts
was so thick with Union dead you cd not walk without stepping on
one. They never retreated until ordered to tho it meant almost certain
death. Peleg Davenport died there as you may remember.*

Rosie it is nearly 10 & I must stop before taps. But you must write
Rosie & tell me how you and Father are. You are allowed to send
things—did you know that? Use a shoe case or soap box they say.
Food wd be welcome, & butter & condensed milk, & Elisha says put
in some wool socks for the march. Also Rosie I wd love a book for the
march, just one, for there is a great deal to carry. Dickens or Eliot or
Scott, one I hvn't read. Father can tell you. Order it from N. Bedford.
A sutler name of Lamb sells newspapers all through the Army incl the
Bost Transcript and NY Herald but there will be no reading matl
once we are under weigh.

I miss you Rosie. What I wd give for 5 minutes in yr company!
There are whippoorwills here just as on the Vineyard & it is
like seeing Elisha here, an innocent creature in a land of war &
desolation. Maybe the impending battle—one OUTSIDE of Va. on
our own soil—will end the War as some of the boys are saying & I
will come home to you and Father & slavery a thing of the Past. In
the meantime give my love to Father & I remain

Yr devoted
Luke

In the late afternoon of the final day they built fires and commenced to
traipse back and forth from their tents with chairs, stools, plank table-
tops, and wooden boxes, which they cast on the fires, the flames leaping
higher than a man's head and the smoke tumbling white into the cobalt
sky. They burned their accumulated newspapers, they burned books.
Elisha burned his *New York Ledger*s and McNamara's *Frank Leslie's
Illustrated*s and he burned his letters from home.

"But why?" Thomas said.

"You don't want to carry nothin you don't have to," Elisha said.
"You'll see."

"But they're just paper."

"I don't want no Reb readin em off my dead body."

Then they fell in and marched, company by company, to the commissary, where they drew their marching rations, and it was during the
wait in line that Luke had his first serious words with McNamara. The

corduroyed road was strewn with broken barrels and boxes, empty bur-
lap sacks, and snowlike drifts of sugar, salt, and rice. Two Negroes were
performing this destruction, one lugging the provender out of the building, the other slashing open the sacks with a knife and smashing the
barrels and boxes with an axe. They went about it methodically and with
deliberate efficiency, as if they'd done such work before and had no feeling about it, one way or the other. The men of Company I watched them
sourly, standing coatless under the hot sun, the men on the porch making room as the sweating black man went in and out.

"Ought to throw it in the river you don't want the Rebs to get it,"
someone said.

"Rebs won't get it," said Jake Rivers. "These niggers here'll lick it up
soon's we're gone, ain't that right?"

The Negro wielding the axe looked blandly at him.

"Why not give it to them?" Thomas said.

"They'll be comin with us," McNamara said. "Freeloadin off the U.S.
Army. A whole army a freeloadin niggers."

"They work for it, Mac," Elisha said.

"I've yet to see a nigger work," McNamara said.

"You're an ignorant bastard," Luke said.

"Suck my ass."

Elisha stepped between them and put his hand to Luke's chest.
McNamara smiled, as if Luke were acting as he'd hoped and expected.

"You quit it too, Mac," Elisha said.

"Yes ma'am," McNamara said.

Other men, turning to watch, smiled and shook their heads, indul-
gent, as if McNamara were indeed a little off and needed pitying.

They moved inside and received their rations, unpackaged. Salt pork,
coffee, hardtack, blocks of brown sugar, soap, cubes of desiccated vegetables. Elisha had instructed them to find rags or handkerchiefs to wrap
their food in if they could not buy poke bags from the sutler. The hardtack amazed Luke and Thomas, for all they'd heard about it; Luke tried
to break a cracker in two with his strong hands and could not.

Elisha grinned. "Ol tooth dullers."

"How do you eat them?" Thomas said.

"Dip em in coffee. I seen ones you had to beat on with your rifle butt. At least these ones here ain't got weevils in em."

"Weevils?" Luke said.

"Weevils. Worms. Worm palaces, the boys call em."

Supper was pork fried in deep grease, fried onions, soft bread. Afterward they built up the fires and fried their salt pork and wrapped it in cloth or newspaper and stashed it in their haversacks. Then they got to the cakes and cookies and pies they'd bought in a final orgy of spending in the sutler's tent, many using the last of their money. Thomas had broken his double eagle and bought food and extra soap and a second toothbrush and razor and a mending kit and had a little over eleven dollars left. The sweets were shared generously, and at every fire there was a bottle or two of whiskey, some of it stolen from the commissary, some of it looted when they'd cleaned out the town months ago, some acquired in the river trade. The men drank it openly and the sergeants allowed it and even took a drink themselves. No officers came down from their hillside quarters to interfere.

The drummer boy, Willie Davis, was at their fire tonight and they were giving him whiskey and laughing as it began to affect him. Luke and Thomas had tasted wine and claret but never hard liquor, and both poured some into their coffee when the bottle came around. Its smell made Luke think of Rose, and how she'd sit in the dark so still and sad with a bottle at her feet, and the lavender smell of her, and the fragrant womansmell of her bedroom. The whiskey was a tongue of flame in his coffee and he could feel its warmth as it went down. Thomas sniffed his, sipped it, and grimaced.

"What's the matter, Tommy?" said Merriman.

"Drink it," said the Nantucket man Stackpole, who had joined their mess tonight. "It'll put hair on your chest."

Thomas sniffed again and tried another sip. "Burn my goddamn mouth out," he said.

Everyone laughed. Luke smiled. He drank again.

"I'm a fight this time," said the boy, Davis. "I'm a kill me a Reb."

"We get to a river," said Merriman, "first thing I'm gonna do is throw you in. Boy don't wash. He smells like he been dead awhile."

"And you smell like a rose, I suppose," said Tom Jackson.

"More like a gardenia," Merriman said.

The talk around the other fires was as boisterous, as noisy with laughter.

"Wonder where the others are," Stackpole said. Nearly half the army, three of its seven corps, had left a day ago.

"Somewhere near Manassas," Henry Wilcox said.

Silence.

"Godamighty," Rivers said. "Ain't that place seen enough fightin?"

"You won't fight there," Henry said. "Lee's way north of it, I told you that. But we'll go through it. I can tell you the whole route. Cross the Potomac at Edwards Ferry."

"That's near Ball's Bluff, ain't it."

"Right upriver of it," Henry said.

"Ball's Bluff," Stackpole said, thoughtful. There was an air of education about him, if not gentility. He'd been a typesetter at the Nantucket newspaper, *The Mirror*, and had aspirations to journalism. "It was worse than Chancellorsville some ways," he said.

Rivers took a sip of whiskey from his metal cup and stared into the fire. "God we've took some whippins," he said. "I can't remember the last time we won a fight."

"We ain't won any," McNamara said.

"Antietam," said Wilcox.

"You call that winnin?" Rivers said.

"Well we damn sure got whipped at Chancellorsville."

"We'd of been all right if them Dutchmen hadn't of run," McNamara said.

"You'd of run too you got hit like that," said Wilcox.

"No I wouldn't."

"They're all cowards," Rivers said. "Cowards and nigger-fuckers."

"It's a good army," said Jackson, "Dutchmen or no."

"Rebs don't whip us, they whip our generals."

"I'm glad we got Hancock."

"Reynolds is the best of em."

"Hancock or Reynolds, one."

"Let's get that who-hit-john goin around again."

The bottle was going from hand to hand. Luke's coffee was gone but he took another drink, straight. Thomas added a very small amount to his coffee.

"No more for Davis," Merriman said.

"I ain't drunk," Davis said.

"Give him a drop, no more."

"Davis, you got a girl?"

"I don't like em," Davis said.

"You like to fuck em?"

"Sure I like to fuck em."

It brought a raucous laugh. Luke smiled.

"Won't be no women for a while, boys."

"Hell, they ain't any here."

"Use to be," Merriman said. "Recall that laundress use to come around? Wore them plaid skirts and hoops?"

"Her name was Jennie," Stackpole said. "Wanted three dollars a jump."

"Was worth every penny," Merriman said.

"It's all you think about, ain't it Joe?" Tom Jackson, not entirely disapproving.

"You're lucky you ain't sick with the clap," McNamara said.

"Be worth it if I was."

"I never did know what happened to her," Stackpole said.

"Officers found her out. That pissant Paine. Told Colonel Hall about her and the colonel run her off."

"I'm surprised Paine didn't shoot her," Stackpole said.

"He might of."

"More I see a them Harvard men," said Rivers, "the gladder I am I ain't there."

"I don't think you have to worry bout bein at Harvard, Jake."

"Where's that bottle?"

"She's comin."

"What time is it gettin to be?"

"Never mind the time. Come tomorrow, it's all marchin and fightin."

At another fire a song began, two or three voices, slow at first, dirgelike, and then, as more and more joined in, growing not just in volume but in tempo, exuberance, gaiety.

> *Yes we'll rally round the flag, boys, we'll rally once again,*
> *shouting the battle cry of freedom.*

"Let's do her, boys," said Henry Wilcox.

> *We will rally from the hillside, we'll gather from the plain . . .*

Wilcox sang, and Merriman, and now McNamara, whose voice was a smooth true baritone that seemed to gather in and meld the other two.

> *The Union forever, hurrah, boys, hurrah!*
> *Down with the traitor, up with the star . . .*

Luke was singing now, and Thomas. They all were. Willie Davis sang, his silky young voice inaudible in the raw din of male voices, which now overrode McNamara's fine baritone. Singing, Luke and Thomas looked at each other and smiled.

> *We are springing to the call of our brothers gone before,*
> *Shouting the battle cry of freedom,*
> *And we'll fill the vacant ranks with a million freemen more . . .*

Other groupings at other fires had taken it up, the night reverberant, aroar with voices. Luke could not hear himself, it was so loud. With a start of surprise he realized he was drunk. He tried to remember how much whiskey he'd had and could not. Beside him Thomas sang with a will, and they looked at each other again, and Luke took his brother's hand and held it, and the men saw it, and said nothing.

NINE

They left at dawn, the thousands of men funneling like sands through hourglasses onto the several primitive roads threading northeast. Every column on every road stretched for miles, serpentine, shouldered guns bristling aslant in the air like innumerable glinting quills. Leaving Falmouth the brigade bands tootled "Garryowen," "The Girl I Left Behind Me," "The Campbells Are Coming," and other lively tunes, until the churned-up dust powdered their lips and instruments and put an end to it. The baggage and supply trains followed their respective corps, and at the end of each column came the artillery, yet another mile or so of horses, guns, limbers, caissons, mule teams, and wagons. The Second Corps moved out last, Colonel Hall's brigade bringing up the rear, and so the two hundred forty-three men of the Twentieth Massachusetts were among the very last to take the road north. The commander of the Twentieth, Colonel Revere, was fever-weakened and lame at the hip with rheumatism, and began the trip in an ambulance.

Elisha was in the rank in front of Luke and Thomas, who marched side by side as Macy had predicted they would, while McNamara was a couple of ranks behind them. He spoke often, his big voice audible above the thick dull mutter of tramping feet, the rattle and clink of accouterments.

"Anyone know why we're in such a goddamn hurry?" he said. They'd been marching three hours without rest. It was very hot.

"Your wife's waitin on us, that's why," someone said.

"Mac ain't got a wife nor ever will."

"We let Lee get away from us," McNamara said. "That goddamn Hooker sittin there enjoyin his whores while Lee runs all over Pennsylvania."

"Shut up, Mac."

"You shut up," McNamara said.

"All of you shut up," said Sergeant Cate, who had come up alongside, and they did, and went on silently, the dark-blue river of the column ahead of them vanishing in the clouds of white-gold dust. Woods pressed in dense on either side of the road, a sylvan tunnel of scrub oak and jack pine and catalpa, the trees creeper-clad, bedecked up and down with white flowers. There were flowers everywhere, mountain laurel and honeysuckle and lady's slippers and Queen Anne's lace. White dogwood bloomed, and wild roses. The air hot and still. Hawks circling, a buzzard.

Another hour passed, and another, and it grew hotter still. The dark blue sack coats were like ovens. Heat built too under the rolled gum blankets and shelter halves slung across their upper bodies. The full knapsacks were heavy on their backs, and the leather straps chafed and cut. The smell of sweat was as ubiquitous now as the roiling dust, like some sour taint on the air they marched through.

"Are you all right?" Luke asked Thomas.

"Stop looking at me. I'm not a baby."

"Take some water."

"Take some yourself."

It was hilly country. The hills were long and often steep, the road riding them straight up, carved into the earth like streambeds by wear and erosion, the column flowing up and disappearing into the sky between the trees. The sun climbed and men began to break rank, stumbling and sitting down semiconscious in the roadside weeds and flowers, their faces dry and flushed pink, aburn with heatstroke. They would sit there dazed, their muskets lying forgotten beside them. Some of them unslung their knapsacks, some seemed not to remember they wore them. Some lay down and closed their eyes as if to compose themselves for sleep. The officers and noncoms whose job it was to harry stragglers back into line would lean over these men and look into their eyes and feel their foreheads and leave them. Pretty soon an ambulance would stop and the men would jump down and give them water and help or lift them bodily into the hot shade under the canopy. Some in the ranks did not stagger away but claimed they had to relieve themselves and disappeared among the trees and did not come back.

Midday, and under the white sun men began lightening their loads, littering the roadside with knapsacks, blankets, tents, clothing, utensils.

"Look there, Luke," Elisha said over his shoulder.

A set of books had been tossed away. Luke had received no book yet from Rose, and the thought of Dickens, of Eliot or Scott or Thackeray, had become a craving in him.

"Go on get em," Elisha said.

Luke looked up and down, saw no officers or noncoms through the dust, and darted back to where the books lay in the trampled bluegrass. They were bound in dark cloth and were the size of pocket Bibles, which perhaps they were intended to resemble. *The Marriage Bed. The Lustful Turk. Prostitution in Paris. The Libertine Enchantress.* Luke smiled, shook his head, and rejoined his rank.

"Erotica," he said.

"What say?" Merriman said.

"Lewd stories," said Matthew Stackpole. "Lots of screwing and such. How many you got, Luke?"

"None," Luke said. "I left them."

"*Left* them?" Merriman said, and was gone.

One of the sergeants hollered at him as he knelt to the books, and he scooped three and crammed them into his haversack, running to catch up.

Then McNamara went into the woods to relieve himself, with permission, and found a revolver, stepping on it in some poison ivy. It was a Remington forty-four, well blued, with a brass trigger guard. Five loads, the top chamber empty. McNamara squeezed the gun into his full knapsack and rejoined the column.

"Some officer dropped it," Stackpole said, when McNamara had told it. "You'll catch hell."

"It wasn't dropped," McNamara said, "it was throwed. Someone got tired a carryin it."

"You be careful of it you don't shoot anybody," Stackpole said.

"I'll shoot *you,*" McNamara said, "you step on my heel again."

A good half of all dwellings were empty, the brick houses shuttered, the log and plank houses with their shake roofs doorless often and window-broken. Fields of corn and cotton and tobacco were choked with pokeweed and nettles. Rail fences had been pulled over or had vanished altogether.

"Where is everybody?" someone said.

"Richmond. They know Hooker ain't gonna bother em there."

"The niggers ain't in Richmond."

"They're up north takin your job," McNamara said.

Then they did see Negroes, sometime after the noon hour of that first long day, gathered beside the road below a long hill on the summit of which sat a plantation house of sand-brown limestone with a red tile roof and two-story portico. There were perhaps thirty of them, come from somewhere behind the untenanted house of their once-master. Young women in cotton dresses, some with infants cradled against them, men both young and very old. Some children, shirtless and barefoot, some boys and girls in their pubescent teens. The men had removed their hats in solemn deference, porkpies and straw planter's hats and a few Rebel forage caps. There was no way of knowing how long they'd been stand-ing there, watching the army pass.

The soldiers grew strangely quiet as they went by. They eyed the Negroes only briefly but when they did a sudden sobriety came over them, an air of solemn purpose, and they went on by with their guns at right shoulder shift, long barrels in perfect vertical alignment.

"Hallelujah!" said an old man suddenly—a preacher, to judge by his dress and oaken voice.

"Ay-men," came a young woman's voice.

"Bless the Lord," said the preacher, for he was started now, some-thing pent up in him finding release. "Trumpets blowin, walls comin down," he said.

"Oh yes," someone answered, "oh *yes.*"

"Comin *down,*" said another.

The answering voices at first were of women and old men, but the young men too began to call out, and finally the children, in reedy mimicry or echo of their elders.

"Walls of Jericho."

"Oh yes."

"Comin *down.*"

"Down!"

"Abe Lincoln comin . . ."

"Comin sure enough."

"Comin sure."

"Comin wid his chariot," said the preacher.

"Chariot a-comin, oh yes."

"I sees it!"

Swaying now, their words more sung than spoken.

"Massa gone, Abe Lincoln comin," sang the preacher.

"Massa gone, oh yes."

"Ol Massa wid his mustache."

"He gone."

"Abe Lincoln, he a *mighty* warrior."

"Mighty, oh yes."

"Oh *yes.*"

"Abe Lincoln comin . . ."

"I sees him."

"River Jordan runnin, runnin . . ."

Singing now, high sweet women's voices, the frailer voices of the girls, the solid collective baritone of the men, rising with the skyward-tending dust.

> *River Jordan runnin, runnin,*
> *Million soldiers passin o'er.*
> *Glory, glory, hallelujah!*
> *Bless the Lord forever more.*

And Private Jake Rivers, Company I, Twentieth Massachusetts, beyond them now, the Negroes lost in the dust but not their song, which rose in the distance full-bodied as a cheer, shook his head and smiled a grim half smile.

"Sonsabitches can sing, I'll say that for em," he said.

"They sing beautiful," said Henry Wilcox, tears filling the deep wells of his eyes.

They covered nearly twenty miles that first day with one halt lasting a little more than an hour. The halt—for the Twentieth, at any rate—was in deep woods, and the men threw themselves down on fern and wild garlic in the muggy shade and began immediately swatting blackflies and cursing them. Some of the men had water left but most did not and Colonel Revere, in his ambulance, ordered company details to look for a stream or brook, but those they found had all gone dry. There was talk of rattlers, copperheads, and moccasins, but as usual no snakes were seen. They chewed some salt pork, some hardtack, but did not make coffee. Some slept, and the flies bit without waking them. A few of the men, when the order came to fall in, groaned and shook their heads and did not move. Officers and sergeants went around prodding and kicking them, and when they did not get up cursed and left them.

The sun was dropping toward the Blue Ridge when the Second Corps halted for the night on open ground rising gradually from the muddy flats along Aquia Creek, which Luke and Thomas would have called a river. The road, which followed the river as it twisted north and west, had been planked and corduroyed by the army. Trees grew along the river flats but higher, to the west of the road, only stumps remained of the copses and tree belts that had marked off these fields before the army had come. War rolls over everything, Luke thought. Isn't anything safe from it.

They encamped division by division, the order traveling back from Hancock to the division commanders, a staff officer at the gallop, dust-begrimed and sweating, his gelding's hooves thumping the hard-packed roadside dirt, pulling up and saluting, being saluted in turn. Division commanders informed brigade commanders, and they informed the regimental colonels, and as the order proceeded rearward the column dispersed, spilling right and left over the treeless countryside in either direction.

The lead division, Caldwell's, had found wood and was building its fires by the time the men of the Twentieth got the godsent order to break ranks. Luke and Thomas followed Elisha, who followed McNamara, who went toward the river, swishing through the shaggy grasses, the nettles and poke. He stopped perhaps six rods from the trees curtaining the river flats and dropped his musket. He unshouldered his knapsack and his rolled shelter half and gum blanket and dropped them and sat down. He took off his forage cap and wiped his dust-smeared face with his sleeve and slumped forward.

"Elisha," he said, "stack them guns."

"Goddamn it to hell," Luke said.

"It's all right, Luke," Elisha said. "Mac, gimme your bayonet."

McNamara leaned sideways and drew his bayonet from its leather scabbard. Elisha took it and picked up McNamara's musket and fixed the bayonet. He fixed his own, and Thomas, and finally Luke, scowling, fixed theirs, and they stacked the rifles. McNamara unrolled his gum blanket and moved over on top of it. He peeled off his coat. The others took off theirs. The coats were damp with sweat. Around them men stacked arms, spread blankets. There was a general weary movement toward the river.

"We gonna pitch our shelter?" Elisha said.

"The hell with it," McNamara said.

"We won't pitch ours," Luke said.

"You boys go on down to the river," McNamara said, "fill the canteens. There'll be wood down there too."

"You'll come with us," Luke said.

"I got to hold our place," McNamara said.

"Against what?" Luke said.

"He's right," Elisha said.

Luke cursed but he went with Thomas and Elisha, the three of them picking their way around men collapsed on their blankets, two or three asleep already. Faces sun-blistered and thick with dust. None were pitching tents. They went on through the trees and scrub and across the muddy shelf where men were undressing, sitting and pulling off their brogans, stepping out of their pants. Their bodies were very white below their brick-red necks and faces. The water glittered under the westering sun. Luke and Thomas and Elisha undressed wordlessly and strode together into the river and fell backward into the warm still water, which was pale brown in color, and sat chest-deep on the pebbly bottom. They scooped water into their parched mouths and splashed their faces with it.

"Lord that feels good."

They drank the silt-tasting water. They drank and drank. More and more men came wading in. They sat, splashed, drank, wallowed.

"Why do you let him order you around so?" Luke said.

"Let who," Elisha said.

"You know who."

"I don't mind him," Thomas said.

"He's a little off, is all," Elisha said. "Don't this bath feel good?"

"He isn't off, he's a bastard," Luke said.

"I got to stay friends with him, and that's all there is to it," Elisha said. "You boys do what you want."

"I'm beginning to think all three of you are crazy," Luke said, looking at Thomas.

Henry Wilcox came wading up to them thigh deep, naked, grinning under his mustache. He fell backward into the water.

"Oh my achin bones," he said. He ducked under, came up with his face streaming. "You baptize these children yet, Elisha?" he said.

"They're atheists," Elisha said. "Wouldn't do a speck a good."

"It's a unchristian army," Wilcox said. "You hear about them books Joe Merriman picked up?"

Wilcox and Tom Jackson had begun a fire not far from the spot McNamara had chosen, and most of the old mess had gravitated there. There'd been plenty of dead wood among the trees and along the river, plenty of rail fences on the other side of the road, and campfires burned as far as you could see in the darkness, and the men boiled coffee and crumbled their hardtack in it and ate their salt pork cold.

"When I go out on picket I'm gonna get me some real food," said Rivers.

"Get you some shoes while you're at it," McNamara said.

Rivers's brogans had come apart and he'd left them and gone on barefoot. His feet were sooted with dust and grime but he didn't appear to have cut them. "I told that sonofabitch Folsom them shoes wouldn't get me far as the Mason-Dixon," he said.

"There's others barefoot."

"What kind a army is this?"

"It ain't the quartermasters' fault," Wilcox said. "Not the regimental ones, anyways."

"It's somebody's," McNamara said.

"Everything is."

"I'll find me some shoes," Rivers said.

"You'll find Mosby and his guerillas you go wanderin around."

"I ain't afeard a Mosby."

"You're stupid if you ain't."

"Anybody seen Willie Davis of late?"

"Boy got the heat stroke. Ambulance picked him up."

"Goddamn Hancock. He'll kill more of us'n Lee will."

"Look what I got, boys," said Rivers, reaching into his haversack. It was a quart bottle of tinted bluish glass with a hand-lettered label stuck on, BLACKBERRY BRANDY. It was more than half full. "Better'n shoes," Rivers said.

"Where'd you get that, Jake?"

"Never you mind where I got it," Rivers said. He uncorked the bottle and took a swig and passed it to Matthew Stackpole, who accepted a cautious sip.

"Men'll throw away their necessaries," Wilcox said, "and go to carryin pistols, bottles a liquor, dirty books—anything heavy, so long as it's sinful."

"Speakin a them books, Joe, where are they?"

"Don't worry, I got em."

"I know you got em. That's my point."

"Whyn't you fetch em, read us a story."

"Go on."

The bottle had reached him and Merriman took a drink of brandy. He passed it on and rose and went off into the fire-tinted night. The bottle came to Elisha and he took a pull on it, against his better judgment.

He'd never drunk alcohol before joining the army and any small amount operated on his mood, waking in him a longing for a thing or things he didn't understand but which probably came down to simple loneliness. Often he thought of home when he drank, the dry coarse winter field transformed to velvety gray in the starlight, or teeming with fireflies on a summer night, he and the others running to catch them, and the warm fragrant smell of it by day, the clover blooming, the lazy murmurous hum of a thousand honeybees. He thought of his brothers and sisters and how few friends any of them had, living as they did out at Head of the Pond, and the way they'd all looked at him, even little Katie, when he came back from Edgartown and said he'd enlisted. Their love he'd always taken for granted but here it was, pronounced and eloquent in their softened speechless gazes. Their brother leaving the island, going off to war. The immensity of it, the thrilling sadness. The apple- and ginger-smelling kitchen, a moth fluttering at the lamp glass, Elisha's dinner awaiting him, the family all gathered. His father finally had broken the silence that had greeted Elisha's announcement. *You'll eat good, Elisha. They don't let a body go hungry in the army, one thing I do know.* Down in the field the whippoorwill called.

Merriman came back with the books, and this was another thing that preyed on Elisha, drunk and sober, but worse drunk. Girls, women. The female body, the prospect of fucking, as the boys would say. Some of them had pictures, acquired by mail from New York City, *cartes de visite* or tiny ones set in innocent-looking stickpins which were anything but innocent when you put one to your eye. A naked woman stepping out of a bath. Men and women doing it lying down, doing it sitting upright on tasseled velvet chairs. In one, a woman lay on her back with her knees drawn up and a swan between her legs. Elisha would look only when others did, Joe Merriman or Matthew Stackpole sharing their illicit treasures with an air of proprietorship and condescension, as if the girls were real and belonged to them, as if they'd actually fucked them. Elisha would take his turn and act only mildly interested, as if he were merely curious, but later, while McNamara slept soundly beside him in the dark, he would summon the women to his mind's eye, their soft white bodies, their brazen smiles, and reach down and go to work on himself, taking care not to shoot it on his blankets where McNamara might see it.

Afterward shame came on him and he lay in the dark disliking himself and despising his weakness. As if he were the only soldier in the Army of the Potomac who masturbated, and when reveille sounded the desire was gone and he would pull on his clothes and head for roll call resolved never to touch himself again.

"I ain't a very good reader," Merriman said. He'd sat down Indian fashion with the books in his lap.

"What'd you pick em up for if you can't read em?"

"I can read em. Just not fast."

"What if they call assembly tonight?" Elisha said. "Us all with liquor on our breath."

"They won't. Not after a march like that."

"Hell, half the regiment's down the road somewheres. Be all night fore most of em get here."

"Give them books to Luke you want em read good," said Rivers.

"I'll read them," Thomas said.

"Little Tommy?" Merriman said.

"Why not?" Thomas said.

"Give them here," Luke said.

"Don't want to mislearn his little brother, ain't that right, Luke?"

"Give them here," Luke said again. Merriman handed them over. Luke tilted one after another to the fire. *The Lustful Turk,*" he read. *"Secret Passions. The Libertine Enchantress."*

"What's that mean, libertine?" Rivers said.

"A libertine's a fallen woman," Wilcox said. "Like you boys're lookin to be."

"Whyn't you leave, you ain't enjoyin yourself," McNamara said.

"Where would you lost lambs be if I was to leave? Anyway, it's Stonewall's and my's fire."

"Read that one about the fallen woman," Rivers said.

Luke opened *The Libertine Enchantress* and bent down over it. No author was listed. He turned the page. "This first part's called 'The Love Feast.' It's a poem." He cleared his throat. The fire whispered and snapped. A murmur of voices stretched toward the trees above the river and back toward the road and beyond it. A half-moon was pasted to the blueblack sky.

> *The feast was over, the guests were gone*
> *And youthful Frank was all my own. . . .*

Luke looked up. "You sure you want to hear this?"

"Go on read or else I will," Stackpole said.

Luke bent again to the page.

> *We gave the rein to ardent lust*
> *He praised my dainty legs and bust.*

"What's her bust?" Merriman said.

"Her titties," Stackpole said.

"Shut up and let him read," Rivers said.

The fires were burning down and men rose and moved apart in the darkness. No tents had been pitched and clearly none would be. They were all too tired, the night was too warm. McNamara was asleep already and Luke, Thomas, and Elisha slung on their haversacks and went down to the river. They stripped once more and waded in and washed their faces and necks and underarms with bars of soap. The moon cast a soft pewter sheen on the water and here and there men splashed themselves or filled canteens and bottles. The boys dipped their toothbrushes in the river and brushed their teeth. They filled their canteens.

"I'm stiff all over," Luke said.

"Was a hell march," Elisha said. "You boys done good."

"And another one tomorrow," Luke said.

"I speck so," Elisha said.

"Did that poem make you horny?" Thomas said.

They looked at him in the thin light of the moon. He scooped some water and drank it.

"No," Luke said.

"It did me," Thomas said.

"It's foolishness," Luke said. "Don't pay any mind to it."

Thomas and Elisha looked at each other but didn't say anything. The three of them rose out of the water and came ashore. They donned shirts and trousers and sat down and pulled on their socks, their shoes. There was a breeze on the river and the mosquitoes weren't biting.

"It warn't a *terrible* poem," Elisha said.

"The words were slick," Thomas said. "The way the rhymes came out."

"Well," Luke said, "it isn't like that."

"What isn't?" Thomas said.

"Screwing," Luke said.

The boys looked at each other again.

"How do you know?" Thomas said.

"I have common sense, that's how I know." He picked up his canteen and haversack and got to his feet and went up the long shelf in the moonlight toward the trees. Elisha and Thomas watched him disappear into the darkness.

"Did we aggravate him?" Elisha said.

"He likes to act superior, is all."

Elisha nodded. The two boys sat side by side, looking out over the moon-glimmering water. Here and there men were still washing themselves, conversing quietly. The water mirrored their voices distinctly and Elisha thought of the oystermen on Lagoon Pond on a still day, and how their voices carried on the water, their idle conversations clearly audible onshore. They wouldn't know you could hear them.

"Tommy," he said.

"What."

"You ever done it?"

"Hell, no."

"I didn't think you had."

"I ain't but sixteen," Thomas said.

"I'm eighteen and I ain't done it."

"Eighteen ain't old," Thomas said.

"I know boys eighteen have done it."

"They *say* they have."

"Yeah. They say they have." Elisha looked out at the opposite shore. It was black and ragged with trees and high thickets. There were pickets over there somewhere and he wondered how they'd gotten across the river. "What about Luke?" he said.

"I don't think so," Thomas said.

"He acts like he done it."

"He acts like he's done everything."

"He must of sparked some girls," Elisha said.

"Mariah Look, mainly," Thomas said.

"Mariah Look?"

"He sparked her about a year and then she threw him over. I think that's why he enlisted."

"Mariah Look," Elisha said. "My Lord."

"Father said she looked like a goddess. Rose said she had thick ankles."

"I wonder did Luke see them ankles."

"He kissed her, I know that," Thomas said.

Elisha looked at him. His narrow chin and tapered jaw, palely visible, wore a fuzz of whiskers, very fine. The whiskers of a boy. Put cream on em, let the cat lick em off. And yet Elisha felt more Tommy's age than Luke's, even after two years of army life and all the fighting he'd seen and a man's mustache on his face and his body a sinewy man's body, his hands big-knuckled and strong.

"I keep thinkin," he said, "what if I was to get killed and didn't never do it."

"Maybe you ought to have gone with that prostitute they were talking about."

"I'm shy to."

"Why?"

"I wouldn't know what to do."

"She'd have shown you."

"I s'pose she would."

"That's what you're paying her for," Thomas said.

"Well, I might try it if I get a chance," Elisha said.

"I bet you'll get one."

"Whyn't you come with me?"

"Come with you where?"

"If it's a house, I mean. A brothel. I don't think I'd care to go in alone."

"Where we going to find a brothel?" Thomas said.

"The towns all have em. We bivouac near one, we might could get a pass some night and go in. In case we get killed, you see. There wouldn't be no rush otherwise."

"They might not let me in, young as I am."

"They wouldn't never say no to a soldier."

"Then I will," Thomas said.

"Shake on it?"

"Shake on it," Thomas said.

Near Aquia Creek, Virginia
June 15, 1863

Dear Rose,

We have left Falmouth & will not see it again I firmly believe. A terrible hard march today, hot as you-know-what & boys dropping by the way side with the heat stroke and I am told that men actually died & were left where they fell in shallow graves. I write this by candle as before. It is not late, Taps has not been blown, but the boys are half dead from marching & the campfires have burnt down to glowing embers twinkling or seething I shd say like orange stars scattered far & wide in the darkness, & the men almost all asleep already on their rubber blankets. The little breeze we had is gone & with the fires dying and their smoke too the mosquitoes have commenced to nibble.

I do not know when this letter will go out nor when mail will reach us but it will be soon I think. I shd add that Thomas did not succumb to the heat today as I thought he might. I am watching him you will be glad to know & will not desert him if he shd falter. Elisha I think cd march forever, he is tireless & in good spirits always. If you are wondering about Rebels we have seen none but their Cavalry are not far off I believe. Genl Lee is well ahead of us & on the other side of the Blue Ridge Mts. & his cavalry shielding him whilst we are playing catch up.

The boys talk awful dirty & I know you wd laugh to hear them.

*Father wd not & as I know he will be reading this I will spare you
both the details wch wd make even you blush Rosie. Except to say that
there was some erotic books at our camp fire tonight & the fellows all
begged me to read one aloud whch I did & it was quite comical to see
how the younger boys took on. Afterwards I told Thomas & Elisha it
was rubbish & inaccurate & I think they believed me. There is lots
of such stuff around, books & pictures etc., the provost officers don't
catch most of it coming in but the boys say they will find liquor in
a minute. Anyway to hear them talk sometimes you wd think the
whole Army of the Potomac has Sex on the brain & it is strange to
think that these men with all their quirks & faults are on History's
great stage & that the deeds of such callow youths & Lumpkins will be
remembered thro long centuries of Time.*

*We passed some Negroes along the road. They were slaves, I
am sure, but are slaves no more, and they gathered by the road to
watch us pass, and called out and sang to us. Up the hill stood the
plantation mansion, abandoned by its owner, & how sullen & out-
of-sorts it looked, as if it knew that it wd never more be kept in high
style by the sweat of human chattels. Rosie—Father—we must win
this War lest it ever be again.*

Write me.

*Yr devoted
Luke*

*That night the drummer boy, Willie Davis, crawled out of the ambulance
where he'd been left to sleep or die, whichever, and slung on his drum and
haversack and, swigging warm water from the full canteen an assistant
surgeon had left him, began the search for his regiment. The fires had died
to little mounds of glowing coals. The men slept like the dead and the half-
moon lit them dully, and Willie chose his way among them, looking for
familiar faces or the red wool blankets of the Twentieth Massachusetts.*

*Willie was not the only one who rejoined his unit under that waxing
summer moon. Heat stroke sufferers, stragglers, quitters, had had second thoughts—some had thought of Mosby's guerillas, some had decided
that they had more walking in them after all—and had picked themselves*

up and strapped on their knapsacks and shouldered their muskets and trudged on as the afternoon faded and the fierce heat let up. Hundreds of them, thousands, moving fitfully in the direction of their army.

Dusk fell, and their pace quickened. The stars wheeled up the sky. The air held the sweet smell of bloom and fern instead of choking dust. Those with blistered feet took their shoes off and tied the laces together and hung them around their necks and went on, and the road felt good to their bare feet, powdery and cool and faintly moist with dew. There'd be plenty of water, they knew, where the army was. Owls trilled from high perches in the ink-dark woods. Whippoorwills piped up in the rank neglected fields. The Big Dipper hung in the sky ahead of them and they remembered that they were heading north, leaving Virginia, going home. All night they trickled into the camps along Aquia Creek and when roll was called at eight A.M. the sergeants could report nearly all present and accounted for.

TEN

Dr. Chandler had intended to hire a boy to feed and brush Nancy and muck out her stall, but Rose said she would do it. Said she wanted to.

"I'm not such a lady I can't clean out a stable," she said.

"You're every bit a lady," he said. "I only thought to save you a disagreeable task."

"If I get tired of it," she said, "I'll tell you."

She would rise at dawn, which came, on these early-summer days, around half past four o'clock, and put on an old cotton house dress and creep out noiselessly. The door of the boys' room was ajar and the silence within seemed sepulchral and terribly final and she thought about them as she passed, thought of Luke on Union Wharf, standing apart from the others, from Thomas even, his hands thrust down in his trouser pockets, gazing out past West Chop with a steely and remote intensity, as if he could see all the way to Virginia with its smoke and carnage. *Lord God,* she thought, one more time, *what have I gone and done? Why'd I preach so hard?*

She padded silently down the stairs, down the hallway past the parlor and dining room and through the kitchen to the mudroom, where she sat down and pulled on an old pair of Blucher boots that had belonged to Thomas. The boots were big on her; she laced them on snug and went out into the pearly morning. Robin's egg sky, birds twittering in the apple tree, dew on the grass, the flowers in her garden charged with color. Yellow tea roses, violet-pink hollyhocks, snowy phlox. She heaved the barn door back and smelled its hay and dung and horse sweat. Nancy nickered, stamped. Rose spoke to her.

"Morning, sweetheart. How y'all this fine morning?"

She opened the stall door and touched the mare's neck, her face, crooning conversation to her, then lifted down the halter and lead rope and slipped the halter on and attached the rope and led her out into the narrow bay and tied her. She filled the grain bucket and set it down for her then took the shovel and scraped up Nancy's droppings and dumped them into the wheelbarrow and pretty soon was singing.

Swing low, sweet chariot

She sang it softly, keeping it back in her throat, a sweet airy purr. Nancy, munching, swung her head around and looked at her. Rose smiled.

Comin for to carry me home

She leaned the shovel against the wall and gripped the wheelbarrow and trundled it out into the sweet air and clear light, down the hard dirt garden path to the manure pile, and upended it, throwing all her weight into the effort.

I looked over Jordan, and what did I see?
Comin for to carry me home
A band of angels comin after me

Nancy was eating the last of her grain, her head tucked down in the oaken bucket. Rose forked hay into the hay rack. She took the metal bucket out to the well and filled it and brought it back, lugging it with both hands, and hung it in the stall. She took the brush and comb off their ledge. Nancy withdrew her head from the bucket. She eyed Rose. Blinked. Rose smiled.

If you get to Heaven before I do

Brushing Nancy's smooth hard back.

Comin for to . . .

She stopped, leaned sideways, and looked Nancy in the eye. "Why I singin that?" she said. Nancy stared at her. "Sad song like that, why I want to sing that today?"

She resumed brushing.

> *Jus tell all my friends I'm comin there too*
> *Comin for to . . .*

"It's pretty, that's why. Ain't it pretty, Nancy?"

> *Comin for to carry me home.*

She finished brushing and combed the mane and tail, then led Nancy back into her stall and removed the rope and halter. She shut the half door and latched it.

"You got everything you need, Miss Queen of the Universe?" she said.

The mare had seen the hay and pulled an ample mouthful from the rack. Rose stood watching her.

"What do you think Luke and Thomas are doing now?" she said. "Right this very minute, what do you think?"

> *Swing low . . .*

The song followed her into the house, would not be still in her heart.

> *Sometimes I'm up, sometimes I'm down . . .*

She sang very softly now, almost under her breath. Dr. Chandler slept badly, as she did, and Rose was careful to let him sleep when he could.

> *Comin for to . . .*

In summer she bathed in cold water, usually twice a day. It was another of the ways Dr. Chandler spoiled her; most years the kitchen cistern went dry by August. Now, as quietly as she could, she pumped the kitchen bucket full and emptied it into the tin washtub. It took five bucketfuls to make a bath. She closed the door and took off the house dress and her chemise and stepped into the water and stood, washing herself with a sponge and a bar of lavender soap.

We spied on you a couple of times, he said.

You did what?

Spied on you. Me and Thomas. Once in New Bedford, once on the Vineyard. You left the door open. We heard you splashing and sneaked up.

You were nothing but little boys. What did you want to see a naked lady for?

The second time I was thirteen.

Then you were old enough to know better.

I guess I did know better.

Luke Chandler, she said.

The funny thing was, we didn't talk about it afterwards. Either time. I think we were afraid to. I think we were afraid to admit what we were feeling.

You gettin awful fancy describin what was nothin but a couple a horny little boys.

Are you angry?

I ought to pitch a fit. Right this minute I ought to.

It's too late now, Luke said.

You think so.

I do, Luke said.

Dr. Chandler had gotten up. She could hear him moving around in the room above. She finished washing herself and reached for the bath towel. Ham and eggs for breakfast, bean porridge. Biscuits. The way that little man could eat and never get heavy while she had already added an overlay of soft flesh to her stomach and bottom. *Still,* she thought, and ran a hand down over her right breast, her rib cage, stomach, hip, thigh. *There's worse. Yes there is.* She stepped out of the bath, toweling herself, and was singing again, louder now, for Dr. Chandler loved to hear her sing.

ELEVEN

———————

They were almost a hundred thousand officers and enlisted men, with nearly four thousand wagons drawn by some twenty-one thousand horses and mules. A marching column, comprised of a corps and its supply train, could stretch ten miles. And so, of necessity, they took different roads, parallel and sometimes convergent, to Pennsylvania. It was said that the Army of the Potomac, had it moved as a body on one road only, would have measured eighty-five miles from end to end.

Thomas gave out late in the afternoon of the third day. The heat had not let up and veterans said it was the worst weather they'd ever known, and the hardest march. Many now went in socks or barefoot with their brogans hanging from their necks, and some had cut ferns and tied them to their caps to keep the sun off their necks and foreheads. That morning they'd crossed a bridgeless stream, wading thigh deep, the water delightfully cool with a vigorous current tugging at their legs. A supply wagon marked with the cross of the Sixth Corps had lost a wheel on the stream bank and staggered into the water, where one of its mules had been pulled under and drowned before the harness could be cut. The crippled wagon and dead mule lay there still but the men drank the water anyway. They ladled it up in their caps and poured it over their heads, necks, faces. They filled their canteens. Luke thought this would sustain Thomas until nightfall but some hours later, with the heat unabating though the sun was well over in the west, he fell out of march step and began to shake his head as if to clear it. The man behind him gave him a gentle push and Thomas reeled against Luke, who took his arm and swung him to the right, out of the column.

"Elisha," he said.

Elisha looked back and dodged out of line and took Thomas's other arm. Thomas had dropped his musket. Elisha picked it up and he and Luke moved Thomas up a short embankment and sat him down in the shade of a pine tree.

"I lost my gun," Thomas said. He looked around in bewilderment. "Where is it?"

The country here was mostly open. Snake rail fences ran along either side of the road with fields beyond them. Trees here and there in the distance, a distant white farmhouse and outbuildings. The men passing looked at the three of them but said nothing.

"Ambulance'll pick him up," Elisha said.

"I'm not leaving him," Luke said.

"The provost guard'll arrest you, Luke."

"I'm not leaving him."

Elisha looked up and down the column. You couldn't see more than a few rods for the dust. Colonel Revere was still traveling at the front of the regiment in his ambulance. The sergeants and corporals, on the wings, had gone on ahead. Lieutenant Paine, at the rear of the company, would be along any moment.

"Get him over this fence, then," Elisha said. "Lay down in that grass and won't nobody see you."

They hauled Thomas to his feet and helped him over the fence. Luke scrambled over it and Elisha tossed the two muskets across.

"When you come on, stick to the road," he said. "Just because you ain't seen Mosby don't mean he ain't around."

Luke had picked up both guns and was steering Thomas away from the road. There was a copse of swamp maples in the middle distance, gathered, surely, about a water pocket of some sort. The dry grass rose above their knees and grasshoppers sprang from it as they advanced.

"Mosby'll shoot you he catches you," Elisha called after them.

Luke turned and waved and lowered Thomas into the high grass and crouched down with him out of sight of the road. He worked the knapsack from Thomas's shoulders. He untied his rolled gum blanket and shelter half and freed him, then uncapped his canteen.

"I don't think I can drink," Thomas said.

"You have to."

His dust-grimed face was dry and very warm to the touch. Luke held the canteen to his lips and tilted it and Thomas swallowed a large gulp of water.

"Go on," Luke said, and Thomas drank again.

They could hear the column passing, a river-like shuffle and mutter of tramping feet and the never-ending musical rattle of canteens and cups. It went on a long time and then the supply train passed, wagons creaking and jolting, mule hooves thumping so multitudinously that the ground seemed to shake. Finally came the artillery, limbers and caissons and guns, horse hooves now, beating the road less solidly than the mule teams had. Thomas had closed his eyes and Luke had pushed a blanket under his head. He drank some water and urged more on Thomas, who rose on an elbow and held the canteen himself and emptied it.

"What are we going to do, Luke?" he said.

"I don't know," he said.

The column was moving on down the road in its dust and after an interval came the Negro camp followers, a straggling migration of refugees dogging the army for protection and in the hope that it would lead them to freedom, safety, some nameless promised land that would be the fruit of all this upheaval. Luke took off his cap and raised himself and peered across the field. Creaking wagons with mountainous loads covered with tarpaulins. Some were mule-drawn, some were pulled by oxen, the animals gaunt, weary-looking. A few skinny horses, rump-branded CSA or USA. Women and small children sat atop the tarpaulins. Men drove the wagons or walked alongside. Older children sat astride harnessed mules and yoked oxen, swaying in long lazy arcs to the animals' rhythmic plod. Luke had heard the Negroes were back there, but the order of march was rotated each day and Hall's brigade had been toward the front of the column after the first day, so this was his first look at them. They traveled in silence, even the children, and Luke could see the apprehension in their faces, the cloud over their dawning hope. He wondered what would happen to them.

The last of them straggled by. A boy driving a two-wheeled oxcart, a young couple with sacks on their backs, bent forward as if the dust were a hard wind driving against them. Luke got up and shouldered his knapsack. He helped Thomas to his feet and Thomas leaned over and vomited, spewing his bellyful of water and with it yellowish gobs of hardtack and undigested desiccated vegetables, colorful shreds of carrot, cabbage, turnip, parsnip. The vomit came in two surges. Luke held his arm. Thomas wiped his mouth with the back of his hand.

"We're going to have to find more water," Luke said.

"I can't drink it."

"You have to."

"I ain't going to make it, water or no," Thomas said.

"You want Mosby to shoot you?"

They jettisoned their tent, Luke's half and Thomas's, and Luke shouldered both muskets. He linked his other arm in Thomas's and they set out for the trees, scattering grasshoppers before them. They went very slowly, like invalids. Thomas's legs had no strength in them and the weight of his knapsack and blankets would have pulled him to the ground if Luke hadn't held on to him. The two rifles rested with a bruising weight on Luke's other shoulder.

"We'll likely miss that tent," Thomas said.

"We should have put it in the baggage wagon. I don't know why Elisha didn't insist."

"It ain't fair to blame Elisha. He ain't in charge of us."

"Stop saying *ain't*," Luke said.

The maples grew around a pond, all right, but the drought had burned it down to mud. At its edge, in the shade, sat two soldiers, stripped to their drawers. Both had their uniforms in their laps and were inspecting them minutely, inch by inch. One of the men was Jake Rivers. Luke and Thomas had never seen the other, or could not remember doing.

"Hidy, Jake," Luke said.

Rivers stared at the two of them, Thomas still leaning on Luke's arm. "Hidy," he said, and went back to work on his trousers. His mustache drooped villainously past his mouth and his hair was tangled and greasy-looking. The other man gave Luke and Thomas a friendly half smile.

"This here's Tinker," Rivers said.

"Blair Tinker," the stranger said, "Fourteenth Vermont."

Luke introduced himself and Thomas. "You wouldn't happen to have any water I suppose," he said.

"Shit," Rivers said, without looking at him.

"We're bone-dry," Tinker said. He was fairer than Rivers and rounder of face, clean-shaven and clearly older.

Luke eased Thomas to the ground and helped him shuck his knapsack. Luke shucked his and sat down. "What is that you're doing?" he said.

"Nittin," Rivers said.

Luke looked at Tinker. "Killing graybacks," he said, picking one and crushing it between his thumb and finger.

"Ain't you got em yet?" Rivers said.

"There appears to have been an outbreak," Tinker said.

"My brother has to have water," Luke said.

"I spose you think we don't," Rivers said. He found and killed another louse.

Thomas lay down on his back and closed his eyes. "I'm played out, Luke," he said. "You'd best go on."

"Say that again, I will leave you," Luke said.

Rivers looked at him. "Leave your brother?"

"What the hell do you think," Luke said.

"Don't fret him then. He got the heat stroke?"

Luke laid his hand on Thomas's forehead. It felt less hot. "You aren't deserting, are you, Jake?" he said.

"Got the flux," Rivers said. "Been shittin every half hour since mornin."

"I'm just tired," Tinker said.

"You Vermont boys tire easy," Rivers said.

"There's a log house yonder," Tinker said. He'd laid his uniform aside.

"There's a big farm right here across the road," Luke said.

"I don't like all that open country in the daytime," Tinker said. "There's woods back here. We had to make a stand, we could."

"A stand," Rivers said, "against Mosby's whole band."

"I heard you say you weren't afraid of Mosby," Luke said.

"I could catch that fucker alone I wouldn't be afraid a him," Rivers said.

"Let's get our clothes on, Jake," Tinker said.

"I ain't finished dee-lousin," Rivers said.

"This boy's in need," Tinker said. "The graybacks'll wait."

"Sure they'll wait. Eat me alive while they're doin it."

He got up nevertheless and he and Tinker began pulling on their clothes. They put their hats on, shouldered their knapsacks, slung their blankets and shelter halves and haversacks. Rivers still had no shoes. His bony high-arched feet were scabbed and filthy.

"Can you get up, Thomas?" Luke said.

He and Tinker each took an arm and pulled Thomas to his feet.

"If one of you could carry his musket," Luke said, "I'll take his knapsack."

"Give me the knapsack," Tinker said, "and you attend to your brother."

"You boys go on," Rivers said. "I got to squat again."

"We'll wait for you," Luke said.

"You wait nearby you'll be sorry," Rivers said.

The log house was not half a mile away. It faced a white scar of a road that came downhill through woods to the east and curved past it south. It was made of bark-sheathed logs chinked with mud, an off-plumb box no more than twenty feet square with a shake roof and mud-and-sticks chimney built up its outside. A sagging shed barn, chicken coop, privy, well, a garden patch of withering half-grown corn and another of what looked like potatoes. Smoke rose, dark and thin, from the chimney. The four men—Rivers had caught up with them—looked at one another.

"Watch yourselves," Tinker said.

"It ain't nothin but some poor niggers," Rivers said.

"Just go slow," Tinker said.

The dooryard was hard-packed ginger-brown dirt with a few parched thistles growing out of it. A decrepit wooden wheelbarrow, an upended washtub. The men stood aside from the half-open door, two and two.

"Hello in there," Tinker said.

A white man appeared in the doorway, hardly taller than Rivers and as unkempt, matted beard and hair to his shoulders. He wore a blue-checked cotton shirt, overlarge cotton trousers, and braces.

"Shitgod*damn*," he said. The voice nasal, sourly musical, like a reed instrument out of tune. The four of them moved over in front of him, Luke still supporting Thomas. The man eyed them.

"We'd like the use of your well," Tinker said.

"You gawn pay for it?"

"By God," Rivers said, "I'll put a hole in you."

"Sir," Luke said, "if I could bring my brother inside to rest a bit, I'll pay you."

Tinker and Rivers looked at him. "You dumb bastard," Rivers said.

"Greenbacks or hard money?" the man said. "Cause them greenbacks a your'n ain't worth a shit."

"Hard money," Luke said. "I'll want water, too."

"You dumb bastard."

"Quit it, Jake," Tinker said.

"Come on bring him in, then," the man said.

Luke had never seen such poverty. There was a paneless window on either side of the cabin but it was dark, even with the westering sun shining through unobstructed. The dirt floor had been so compressed that it shone like polished ebony and the stirless air seemed inviolate with its captive smells of woodsmoke and bacon grease and unwashed bodies. A haggard woman knelt by the open fire, poking slabs of meat in a big flame-blackened fry pan deep in bubbling fat. Four children with mute vacant faces, a girl and three boys, sat along a bench at a trestle table set for supper. They'd been shorn almost bald, even the girl. There was a maple bed in the corner. Plank shelves holding some pots and crockery. Chairs with their backs broken off. A loft with a homemade ladder leaning against it.

They dropped their equipment by the door. Thomas sat down on one of the backless chairs. The children eyed him in silence. The woman continued to push the frying meat around. Tinker had gone out for water and now the well creaked out back.

"Y'all deserters?" the man said.

"No sir," Luke said.

"Looks like it to me."

"We'll be going back," Luke said.

"You won't be goin nowhere, them partisans git you."

Luke looked at him but said nothing. Tinker came in lugging a wooden bucket with water slopping over its edges. Rivers stood in the doorway, watching out. Luke took the bucket and held it while Thomas ladled water up in his tin cup.

"You all right?" Luke said.

Thomas nodded, drinking.

"What's he got?" the man said.

"Nothing," Luke said. "He's just tired."

Thomas drank on, dipper after dipper. Luke felt his forehead. It was cooler.

"Why ain't you in the army?" Rivers said.

The man stepped closer to the fire and spat into it. "Wouldn't take me," he said.

"Why wouldn't they?"

"Don't know."

Thomas put the cup down and smiled.

"All right?" Luke said.

"Yeah."

"That side meat smells good," Rivers said.

"It ain't enough for y'all," the man said.

"I'd like to buy some for my brother," Luke said. "And a couple of chickens and some potatoes. I've got a double eagle in my knapsack."

"You got *what*?" Rivers said.

The man studied Luke. "Show her to me," he said.

"You're crazy, Luke," Rivers said. "Why, we can take them chickens. This here's the enemy."

"He's right, Luke," Tinker said.

Luke had knelt down and was unbuckling his knapsack. The double eagle was in a sock at the very bottom. He dug it out and held it out on the palm of his hand. The coin was a luminous gold in the smokelike murk of the cabin.

"What else have you got?" Luke said.

The man was eyeing the coin. "Got some taters," he said.

"You got any shoes that would fit this man?" Luke said.

"Do I look like I got extra shoes?"

The woman stood up with the fry pan and set it on the table. The children in turn pushed their metal plates forward and she forked a side of pork onto each. Then she went to the shelves and found a chipped china bowl and served Thomas. No fork or knife seemed to be forthcoming so he picked up the hot grease-dripping meat and took a gingerly nibble.

"The shoes you're wearing," Luke said. "I'll pay extra for them."

The man looked down at his shoes. "These ones?"

The soles were coming off both of them. The leather was worn almost white.

"It's a kindly thought," Rivers said, "but my feet's newer'n them things."

"How much you offerin?" the man said.

"He ain't offerin nothin," Rivers said.

"I ain't talkin to you," the man said.

"Jake?" Luke said.

"It's kindly, Luke, but don't waste your money."

The man shrugged, giving up. "Kill you a chicken, then," he said.

"Two," Rivers said.

Tinker followed him out with the well bucket. Thomas gnawed at his meat. Its warm grease ran down his dirty whiskered chin. The well whirred and creaked and then came a panicked flutter and squawk as Rivers wrung a chicken's neck. The woman had sat down at the end of the table.

"What's your name?" Luke said.

"Buford," the man said. "Calvin Buford."

"Ma'am?" Luke said.

She brushed a wisp of graying hair back from her face. "Belle," she said.

"It's a pretty name," Luke said.

"You reckon?" she said.

"This war been right hard on us," Buford said.

"I'm sorry," Luke said.

"What y'all want to come down here for, fret us bout our niggers?"

Then Rivers hissed *sonofabitch* and he and Tinker came in fast, moving doubled over.

"Riders," Rivers said, and slammed the door.

Luke sprang to the window. The riders were still very small in the distance. There appeared to be a dozen, perhaps fifteen of them. They were coming across the fields where Luke and the others had walked, following the beaten trail. Tinker came to the window for a look, and Rivers.

"They seen you, sure," Buford said.

"You shut up," Rivers said.

"I don't think so," Tinker said, "but they're coming, all right."

"Load your guns, boys," Rivers said.

"Y'all wait a damn minute," Buford said.

But all of them except Thomas had seized their muskets. Thomas rose from the chair but only stood there with a look of alarm on his face. The others bit the ends off the paper cartridges and began loading. The rammers went in with a steely slither.

"You go on outside and fight," Buford said.

"Hell if I will," Rivers said.

"They'll fire my goddamn house," Buford said.

The children were eating. The two older ones had forks, the younger two ate with their hands. They ate and watched. Belle Buford watched and said nothing.

"Talk to them," Luke said. He rammed the ball down and fitted a percussion cap on its nipple. "Send them away," he said. "That'll be part of the double eagle."

"Y'all pay me then."

"After," Luke said.

"Shit," Buford said.

Luke took another look out the window. The riders had seen the cabin and were coming on through the tall yellow-green grass at an easy canter. They wore Confederate cavalry shell jackets but were otherwise without uniforms.

"Tell them we went back the way we came," Luke said, "why there's only one trail. Tell them we went on after the army. You do this, we'll stop at one chicken."

"No taters," Buford said.

"All right," Luke said.

"Ain't you a greedy sonofabitch," Rivers said.

"Thomas," Luke said, "load your gun."

Thomas nodded. His rifle stood against the wall. He bit the end off a cartridge and spat it out. His hand shook as he poured the powder down the muzzle.

"Ma'am," Tinker said, "maybe you and the children ought to get down on the floor."

"Go on do like he says," Buford said, and went slowly to the door.

"Hallo the house," called one of the riders.

Buford glanced back over his shoulder and spat on the floor and opened the door and stepped out into the brassy light of the evening sun, which hung above the distant Blue Ridge. There were closer to twenty than a dozen riders. Except for their cavalry jackets and slouch hats they were dressed like farmers in denim and homespun flannel and cotton. They carried neither sabers nor carbines, just big Colt and Remington pistols stuck in their belts.

"Howdy," Buford said, shielding his eyes against the sun. He'd left the door ajar.

The men sat their horses, studying him. "Y'all got some guests, I reckon," one said.

The horses snorted, stamped.

"Did have," Buford said.

"Yankee infantry, and they still in there, I believe."

"Niggers," Buford said.

"Say what?"

"Gang a niggers. They was followin the Yankee army and cut over here lookin for water. Like to of scared the piss outta my wife and childs. I run em off."

"Run em off, did you."

"Y'all think I'd let a nigger inside a my house? They went right back over yonder, way they come. I'm surprise y'all didn't come up on em."

"Kill that chicken did they?" another rider said.

The neck-wrung chicken lay where Rivers had dropped it.

"Yes sir," Buford said, "but they won't eat it."

"Nigger killed my chicken, I'd shoot him."

"Well, I almost done."

"We catch up to em, we'll shoot em for you."

"I wish you would," Buford said.

The first rider nodded and touched his hat brim and wheeled his horse, and the others wheeled theirs and followed him back across the field. Buford watched them into the middle distance then went back inside. He sat heavily down and let out his breath.

"Godamighty," he said.

"We thank you for that," Luke said.

"Where's my money at?" Buford said.

"You'll get it when we leave," Luke said.

"I done risk my life, you sonofabitch."

"You'll get your money," Luke said.

Thomas sat down on the floor with his back against the log wall and heaved a sigh. Belle and the children had risen from the floor and sat down again to their supper.

"Y'all get on outta here," Buford said.

"When it's dark," Luke said. "We'll eat in the meantime."

"They gawn come back they don't find no niggers."

"Maybe they will find some," Tinker said.

Luke looked at him. He hadn't thought of that.

"Anyways," Rivers said, "you shut your mouth. I ain't above confiscatin that twenty dollar piece to my own use."

"Luke," Thomas said. "I could use some more water."

"Take your gun," Tinker said.

"They're out to the road already," Luke said.

"Take it anyway," Tinker said.

But there was no further trouble and after dark, before the moon had risen clear of the wooded hills to the east, they took leave of the Bufords.

"We thank you for your trouble," Luke said, and pressed the double eagle into Buford's soiled and callused palm.

"You're lucky it was Luke come along," Rivers said. "I wouldn't of paid you, nor put up with your sass."

"You'll git more'n sass, them partisans come up on you."

"Good-bye, Mrs. Buford," Luke said.

She smiled at him wanly from her place at the table. The four children stared, mute and expressionless to the end.

"They don't ride much at night," Buford said. "You might get on, you step lively."

"Good luck to you," Blair Tinker said.

"Good-bye, you greedy sonofabitch," Rivers said.

Thomas could walk comfortably now. They recrossed the two fields in the moonlight and took the road north after the army.

"By God you got a soft heart, Luke," Rivers said.

"They were pitiful," Luke said.

"It was a kindly thought about the shoes."

"How're your bowels?" Luke said.

"Quiet," Rivers said, "and I thank you for askin."

The night was the coolest since they'd left Falmouth. The air was sweet and dustless and Luke filled his lungs with it and felt a thrill of validation. The courage he'd discovered today was gathered inside him solid and immovable and part of who he was forever. His scalp had begun to itch and he supposed the graybacks had found him, but he guessed he could stand a few bugs.

TWELVE

Sangster's Station, Virginia
June 18, 1863

My dearest Rosie,

Well Rosie there is naught but good news today as the mail wagon caught up with us bringing yr letters & box & the hot weather has finally lifted & Thomas & I after getting lost or I shd say falling by the way side—Thomas, not I, I only get stronger as our hardships increase—have rejoined our regiment unscathed. Thomas has written Father about it so I will not repeat, only to say you once told me to look after my brother & by God I am. We have been 2 nights at this place & will move on tomorrow much rested & restored in spirit etc.

Thomas & I both enjoyed yr letters & Father's & we are glad you are both well & that Father's practice is busy. I am not glad he is coughing but he is a Dr. & I suppose knows how to take care of himself. Please make him rest Rosie & not be called out at night so often, I think people take advantage of him altho I don't guess the women can wait till morning to have their babies.

It might surprise you to know that all the food you sent is eaten, even the pickles. You see, some of the boys will be selfish with a box from home. "Send for a box yrself if you want one," they will say, while others share. We let Elisha dig in—he still loves to eat!—and McNamara dug in w/out being asked & a fellow named Merriman came along, he always seems to be in the right place at the right time, & we gave some cheese & ham to Jake Rivers & snuck some of that excellent chocolate to Henry Wilcox, who is an abolitionist & willing to say so. Of course we kept the socks, paper, envelopes, postage stamps, etc., whatever cd not be eaten. The boys praised yr cake up to the Heavens, you might like to know.

Thomas has written a good account of our adventure in Dixie's Land, for once he has taken the time to do so, & I will only add a few observations of my own wch seem to have escaped him. First, the poor people with whom we hid out disliked Negroes as much as any Slave Driver & I can only conclude that looking down on another Race is how such unfortunates maintain their self respect. Slavery is of no use to them & in fact if there were no slavery this fellow might find remunerative employment on a wealthy plantation or as a teamster or drover but he is blinded by his ignorance. Rosie do you think white people are born despising Negroes or does Life instill it in them? I cannot decide.

Now, there is a fellow named Rivers here, Thomas writes of him in his acct of our adventure, a foul mouthed & dirty little man who says the vilest things about Negroes and you will wonder how came we to share the food with him as above mentioned. It is like this: when I was dickering with the man in the cabin I asked if I might purchase some shoes for Rivers whose Army issue brogans wore out on him & who has been marching barefoot almost since we left Falmouth. The man had no decent shoes to sell but Rivers was strongly affected by my attempt in his behalf & has since been as devoted to me in his silent & surly way as a loyal mongrel dog. Clearly he has received few kindnesses in his life & if you are cruel to a dog it snarls & bites in turn. I almost came to blows with him our 1st night in camp, you know me, Rosie!, but I do not think I cd bear to hurt him now tho he says the awfulest things.

Rosie, I told Thomas not to mention the lice but he had written already & said he was not about to write another letter for the sake of that & besides, said he, Father's a Dr. I did not see what that had to do with it but Thomas was stubborn & said it was his letter wch it was, so now you know. One of the corporals has borrowed a kettle out of the supply wagon & we will boil our clothes tonight wch the boys say sometimes does the trick tho perhaps not for long. Anyway Rosie do not worry, graybacks, as the boys dub them, are the least of the dangers we face.

Lastly, I thank you for Wuthering Heights. *It was not one I thought of but as it is a particular favorite of yrs I look forward to reading it & will think of you when I take it up. I wonder now when I will find time to read it but it is a treasure anyway tho heavy in my knapsack, a link so to speak with the world of Home, Culture, & Decency. I hold it thinking that yr hands held it not so long ago & that perhaps you perused some of its pages & my heart warms. Good night Rosie, & do not worry about us. Elisha says Thomas and I will come to believing in God by & by & while I doubt that I do feel that there is a Providence guiding us all & protecting the 3 of us, who will be forever bound in friendship.*

Yr devoted
Luke

PS—Another package wd be much appreciated.

They'd eaten dinner and she was clearing away the dishes when Dr. Chandler proposed that they take a walk. "I don't get out of doors enough," he said, and coughed the short dry cough that had been stuck in his chest for some weeks now. "I don't take enough exercise."

Rose put the platter back down, a fine pork loin purchased this morning fresh at Smith, Bodfish, Swift, and roasted in the oven of the big Monarch, whose radiant heat had turned the kitchen itself into an oven, and drew herself up and looked thoughtfully at the doctor.

"What is it?" he said.

"Dr. Chandler . . ."

"I wonder," he said, "if it isn't time for you to begin calling me George."

Rose smiled. "I don't know that I can."

"But I'm asking you to."

"It's been Dr. Chandler a long time."

"Too long," he said.

She smiled. "George," she said.

The doctor returned the smile. His smile pinched his eyes but not merrily. There was always a wince in it, an abiding sadness.

"Well done," he said.

It was a sunlit evening, with shadows now welling up in the large silent rooms. In the hallway the Seth Thomas clock tick-tocked with a querulous insistence, as if it resented the smothering quiet. Standing in the mote-swarming dusk Rose felt the devilment rise in her, that ungovernable buoyancy that would come over her.

"George," she said. "George Washington. King George the Third."

The doctor's smile had turned uncertain. Was she teasing him? Mocking?

"George Eliot," she said. "George McClellan."

"Good God, not McClellan," the doctor said.

"Just thinking how many Georges I could name."

"Go put your walking dress on," the doctor said.

But Rose did not move. For two weeks she and the doctor had dined alone, dinner and supper, conversing as equals, as would a husband and wife. She dressed for dinner as would a wife. They'd gone out once together, to a lyceum debate, "Ought This Island to Be Exempt from Military Duty?" A tie vote when it was over, to Rose's disgust.

"What do you suppose folks'll think, they hear me call you George?"

"I doubt they'll think about it at all," Chandler said.

"Dr. Chandler . . ."

"George."

"George." She sat down opposite him, her crinoline rustling, bunching beneath her. "There's talk," she said.

"Talk?"

"About you and me."

The doctor frowned. "I see."

"It's been going on awhile," she said.

"It's only natural that I employ a woman to keep house. What would they have me do?"

"You treat me better than a housekeeper, George. You dress me up pretty. You buy me things. And then you're an abolitionist, and you know what I am, and you know what kind of talk that breeds."

"I see," the doctor said again, looking down at his hands.

"I don't mind for myself," Rose said. "It don't trouble me what some ignorant fool says."

"I don't mind either," he said.

"I mind for you," she said.

"Dear Rose," he said.

"I do."

"Well," he said, "we can mind for each other, and that'll be the end of it."

"I'm not so sure. It's going to get worse, you see. Without Luke, I mean."

"Luke?"

"Luke sort of kept it in check. He once beat two boys who made some unpleasantness. Bigger boys. Beat em bad. Didn't anyone ever forget it."

"Why did nobody tell me this?"

"To spare you."

The doctor smiled unhappily. It was getting darker in the room. A wagon passed out front, swaying and rattling. "I think I could have withstood the truth," he said.

"You don't know what meanness there is."

"And you have no faith in my ability to protect you from it."

"It isn't that," she said.

"What, then? What are you proposing?"

She looked down, away from him, and a gray, desolate wind blew through her. "I don't know," she said.

"To leave me," he said.

She looked at him. He would release her without reproach, she knew that. He would give her money. She could try New Bedford, Boston, even New York City. She could study music.

"I wouldn't do that," she said.

"But you'd like to."

"No. I wouldn't."

"What, then? More freedom? Is there a young man you fancy?"

Rose's cheeks warmed. "You're forgetting I'm colored. Who around here would I fancy?"

"You're a beautiful woman, Rosie."

It did not surprise her. He had never touched her, in his occasional doctoring, except to take her pulse or feel her forehead for a fever, and Rose knew the reason for this fastidiousness and respected him for it, loved him.

"This wasn't a very good place to bring you, was it?" he said.

"It's a fine place," Rose said.

"In New Bedford there are educated Negroes. Merchants. Writers."

"Your wife was there," Rose said. "She wouldn't rest till you left."

The doctor's gaze lifted, fixed itself on her. "Perhaps that's changed," he said. "Perhaps we could go back."

"Don't even think of it," she said.

"But why?"

"Are we going to take that walk, or aren't we?"

The doctor looked at her. He put his fist to his mouth and coughed. "It isn't necessary," he said.

"Let's do," she said. "It's a fine evening."

"I wouldn't force you, Rosie."

"Don't you think I know that?" she said.

Thoroughfare Gap, Virginia
June 22, 1863

My beloved Rose,

We left Centreville yesterday morning, having camped to the north of the town where there were some good springs. Centreville is nothing but a dirt road much rutted & defaced & some dilapidated wood buildings & a stone church & the people very few and those few unfriendly to us & our Cause. You do not see many men, they are all away fighting, & the women greet us with stony stares & will not give us water if we ask. They are thin and pinched of countenance & their children shabby & in poor health & I cannot but wonder why they wd sacrifice so much for a war to preserve an institution that will never benefit them.

We passed some abandoned Rebel fortifications, earthworks & barriers of stones & sticks & what was most interesting, logs laid in the openings to resemble cannon. Are the Rebels running out of guns?

*The boys say McClellan fell for such tricks & I believe we are well rid
of him, tho not all the boys think so.*

*From Centreville we marched west & soon crossed the Bull Run
Battlefield & what a sight there met our eyes! I will never forget it
as long as I live. The fields around Bull Run are broken by clusters
of magnificent green forests & the fields cd be imagined as thick
with grain & corn & rolling pristine & beautiful to the forest verge
but not now, after two visitations by the God of War. Rosie they did
not it appears bury any of their dead mules & horses after the 2nd
engagement last Aug. & the carcasses lay all about with their hides
shriveling on their bones & the poor creatures' teeth bared in the most
hideous spectral whinnies & their eyes naught but hollow sockets. But
worse, Rosie, there were human bones everywhere, the rains having
excavated the poor fellows from their shallow graves & I suppose wild
hogs & buzzards did the rest, separating & strewing them hither &
yon. We saw skulls lying about and all manner of leg pieces and arm
bones & in some instances bones protruding from the ground, as for
instance knee bones sticking up and in one case a wrist bone & hand
reaching up & the hand actually open palm up & some of the boys
joked that the poor b—— only wanted to be paid before he left this
World. The bones were bleached very white, they were white as fish
bones & not sallow like the skeleton in Father's office.*

*There were as well on this Terrible Field many 100's of discarded
articles of equipment & clothing, I do not understand why so much was
left behind. We saw: canteens, rotting blankets, rotting shoes, belt buckles,
cap boxes, cartridge boxes, & even some rusting muskets. Also limbers
& caissons stood brokenly about, they had lost a wheel or been blasted
by an exploding shell & cd hobble no further. There are farmhouses at
spacious intervals, stone & wood, and these were badly scarred & pocked
by balls & shell fragments. The inhabitants have mostly fled & their
livestock with them or eaten. It was truly a place of Horror.*

*Rosie you said you wanted to hear all & and so I give it to you. We
have stopped in this beautiful place where Broad Run cuts thro the
Bull Run Mts. with the Blue Ridge beyond & all is green & idyllic tho
there has been fighting here too. We are getting some rest but still no
food beyond the usual hard tack & salt pork & desiccated vegetables*

wch the boys call "desecrated vegetables." There has been some
"foraging" on the sly, a nice word for "stealing," but we have not yet
enjoyed the opportunity.

We have boiled our clothes & for the moment are free of graybacks.
Thomas has the runs.

Yr devoted
Luke

Luke woke dreaming it was Rose's hand on his shoulder, then smelled the
smoke of the almost-dead campfires and knew it was the tentative hand of
his brother. He rolled over and Thomas spoke to him in a half whisper.

"Where's your sanitary paper?" he said.

Luke stared at him. "Sanitary paper. For the sake of Christ, Thomas."

"I need it," Thomas said. "Mine's run out."

Then Luke saw the fear in his eyes and suddenly Thomas looked as
young and vulnerable as he could ever remember him. "All right," he
said, and threw off his blanket.

Elisha and McNamara had pitched their dogtent. Some had, some
hadn't. The night was overcast and the little tents looked fleece-white in
the sullen darkness. Luke unbuckled his knapsack and found the thin
wad of soft paper. He'd bought it from the sutler in Falmouth and it was
nearly gone. Most of the boys didn't bother with sanitary paper.

"I think I have dysentery," Thomas said.

"It's diarrhea," Luke said. "Half the army has it."

"It weakens a body so."

"Go on do your business," Luke said. "I'll wait for you."

Thomas stood up, barefoot in his shirt and trousers, his braces hanging. He went off into the darkness among the sleeping men and tiny
wedge-shaped tents toward the malodorous sink now two nights old. The
encampment sprawled across a sloping field with the river called Broad
Run below. The river came through Thoroughfare Gap, falling in a magnificent silvery cataract. You could see the gap in the middle distance,
wide and irregular, with trees shrouding the two mountainsides and the
Blue Ridge looming darkly beyond.

Thomas was gone a long time. Rivers still was similarly afflicted and had been to the regimental surgeon, whom he reviled as a jackass and ignoramus. "He give me salts," he said, "and then a powder that like to of turned my fuckin stomach inside out. Time before that he give me a mix of whiskey and quinine and painkiller and I ain't never tasted nothin as odious. Didn't work, besides. None of em did."

Thomas reappeared, quiet as a phantom. He lay down next to Luke and pulled his wool blanket up. All around them men breathed, snored, stirred, and slept on.

"Luke."

"What."

"When I close my eyes I see those bones."

"Then don't close them."

"Don't sleep?"

"Lie with your eyes open, is what I mean, and suddenly you're asleep."

"I dreamed about them," Thomas said.

Luke didn't say anything. He lay with his back to Thomas.

"They rose up," Thomas said in his ear, "and came chasing me. A whole army of skeletons."

"They were just bones," Luke said. "Leg bones, ribs. All separated."

"Not in the dream. They were whole, like the one in Father's office. Thousands of them."

"Go to sleep."

"I miss Rose," Thomas said.

"So do I. And Father."

"Those bones did give me a turn. All those poor fellows, all that's left of them."

He was quiet awhile, his breathing regular. Luke thought he'd nodded off.

"Luke?"

Luke did not turn, but spoke to Thomas over his shoulder. "Get up close to me," he said. "Spoon."

"Yeah."

Thomas was knobby and warm, curled fetally against his back. Luke held still and pretty soon Thomas's breathing steadied, slowed, and he fell gradually back from Luke, and slept fretlessly.

THIRTEEN

They lived in a small whitewashed plank house on the southern edge of town which she rented from Abraham Bryan, whose several farm buildings huddled uphill of her on the near side of Cemetery Ridge, house and barn and crib whitewashed too but sturdier than her leaky shack, of more permanence. Delia Wilkes and her son Floyd, born out of wedlock. Abraham Bryan the farmer was freeborn and prospered growing hay and grain and keeping a peach and apple orchard. He had a wife named Elizabeth. Children. Delia was freeborn too but one night—two years before the War, it was—as she walked home from her work a slavecatcher from down South and two men she knew by sight, Mr. Aaron Riddle and Mr. Luther Schultz, young idlers and no accounts both, attacked her right on Baltimore Street intending to bind and gag and load her like a piece of stovewood into the slavecatcher's spider phaeton for a nighttime dash to the Line, where he could slow down and continue to Virginia leisurely by day. This was the first of the events, though he did not witness it, that turned Floyd Wilkes, who was naturally gentle, into a hater of slavery and the South, which was to have its fateful consequences five years later. Floyd, at this time, was thirteen.

It was summertime and the leaves were out and it was in the shadow of a big old elm or sycamore that they tried to take Delia. It was past eleven o'clock and the brick rowhouses along Baltimore Street were dark and asleep. Luther Schultz caught her from behind with an arm locked around her neck; Aaron Riddle then joined in, attempting clumsily to lash her wrists together, the two oafs knocking into one another and pouring curses into Delia's ears as she struggled, thinking of Floyd at home and what he'd do if she disappeared, and now she noticed the slavecatcher, crossing

*Baltimore Street, strolling with his hands in his pockets and his coattails
pushed back, thinking his accomplices would do the work of subduing and
silencing Delia. What he'd paid them for.*

*They did not take into account Delia's physical strength, her vigor. And
yet wasn't that why the slavecatcher had selected her, for the good price
that strength would bring? She was tall, angular, with wide shoulders
like a man's and a man's strong hands. The two fools now were pulling
her backward across the street, Aaron Riddle having given up trying to
bind her wrists for the time being. Delia saw the phaeton, two night-black
horses waiting quietly, indifferent to this human ruckus. Delia had not
spoken or screamed. She ceased struggling and let them move her out of the
tree shadow into the paler darkness of midstreet and then wrenched herself around so violently that the two men lost their grip and when Luther
Schultz stepped forward—pig-pink face knitted in dismay and perplexity,
this wasn't happening like it should—Delia kicked him between his legs.*

*She'd been cooking dinner and afterward doing the weekly laundry for
a white family over on Chambersburg Street and was wearing soft-leather
lace shoes but the kick even so buckled Luther Schultz's knees and hunched
him down with his eyes wide open, cradling his privates in both hands.
Delia spun back to face Aaron Riddle and kick him too but Aaron had hesitated, looking at the slavecatcher as if he, Aaron, had run out of answers
for the moment.*

*The slavecatcher was a short soft-looking man but no witless fool like
these boys. As Aaron and Delia watched he went to the phaeton, calm as
could be, and reached under the seat and came out with a pistol big as an
army pistol, so blueblack it gleamed in the darkness. He came halfway
back and leveled it at Delia, who looked into the black hole of its muzzle as
he cocked it, the quiet double-click cutting an icy nick in the stillness and
freezing Delia where she stood.*

*Stand still, girl, he said, the voice Southern-sugary, easy. You scream,
I'll blow your black head off.*

*His soft round face was a blur to her. What she saw now was that ter-
rifying black hole.*

*I wonder, he said, still eyeing Delia down the barrel of his pistol, if you
two circus clowns could tie this nigger's hands if she was to stand still for
y'all.*

Luther Schultz half straightened, releasing his privates. He drew a deep breath. Goddamn, he said.

I thought you boys was hard men, the slavecatcher said, faintly smiling. Ain't that what you told me?

I'm a kick her in the cunt, said Aaron Riddle.

No you ain't, said the slavecatcher. You gawn tie her up and be quick about it, too.

I gots a child to home, Delia said huskily.

That a fact, said the slavecatcher.

And that is when the sound of Dr. Duffy's carryall reached them, the doctor returning from visiting a patient at one of the farms in the valley, rattling home weary and abstracted, the reins slack in his hands, the mare knowing her way. At the sound the slavecatcher lowered his revolver and held it, still cocked, at his side.

If I lose this nigger, he said, you boys're shit outta luck far as any money goes.

Delia's heart pounded in her chest. She had not known that anything could fright her as that gun did. She could only wait for whoever was coming and pray he was righteous. The slavecatcher let the hammer down and pushed his coat back and shoved the pistol into his belt, outside of his vest. The wagon rattled closer and in the thin darkness Delia made out Dr. Duffy's mare and the doctor on the box with his round shoulders collapsed forward, asleep up there, it looked like. But the sight of the four of them woke him—Delia in her fright, the two bumpkins standing there in uncertainty and self-doubt, the bland unruffled slavecatcher in his morning coat and silk vest and gray trousers—and Dr. Duffy reined up and looked at Delia, at Luther, at Aaron, at the slavecatcher.

What's this? he said.

Luther glanced at the slavecatcher, who was studying Dr. Duffy.

Girl here kicked me, Doctor, Luther said.

Kicked you, eh, Dr. Duffy said.

Yes sir. In my balls. Like to of broke em.

You, sir, said the doctor. Are you part of this?

He a slavecatcher, Dr. Duffy, Delia said. Her courage was returning, a savage disregard of her own safety. She would be glad to kick somebody again. He tryin to carry me down South, and these two fools helpin him.

I got papers, sir, said the slavecatcher. This girl belongs to a gentleman name of Carter Lord. Lives in Page County, Virginia.

Bosh, said Dr. Duffy.

You required, said the slavecatcher, to assist me, sir. Accordin to the Fugitive Slave Law.

She's no more a slave than you are, Dr. Duffy said. He turned to Luther and Aaron. You boys surprise me, I swear.

He done threaten us into helpin him, Luther said.

Threaten to pay em, thas what he threaten, Delia said.

Done both, Luther said.

Why ain't you tell the truth? Delia said.

The game was up and the slavecatcher knew it. He was used to this; sometimes you succeeded, sometimes you didn't. Even when a nigger really was a runaway there were white people who would lay obstacles in your way, so long as it didn't involve risk to themselves. And of course the niggers helped one another and were clever about it, too.

You'd better climb up, Delia, Dr. Duffy said, let me drive you home.

It ain't far, she said.

I know how far it is. Luther and Aaron, I'll say no more about this— unless some darky turns up missing from this town. Then I'll make it warm for you.

Yes sir.

Yes sir.

Get on home, both of you.

Yes sir.

And you, sir, Dr. Duffy said, had best skedaddle. We want none of your sort in Gettysburg.

Reckon I'll take me a lodgin in the hotel yonder.

Well, it's a free country, Dr. Duffy said, already wheeling the horse around, the carryall, as if disdaining to look at the slavecatcher any longer.

It was, last time I heard, the slavecatcher called after him.

Delia turned for one more look at him. The two fools for hire had disappeared. The slavecatcher stood in the middle of Baltimore Street dim and half real in the soundless night, watching her ride away to her freedom. It was the first of two times she was nearly taken, twice saved by white folks.

After all that hurry—hurry that had killed more than a few of them—they stayed four nights in the gentle hills east of Thoroughfare Gap, where life turned leisurely, pleasant. Mail and newspapers came down under cavalry escort from the new supply base at Alexandria. Evenings, the brigade bands performed under the stars. "Katy Darling," "Annie Laurie," "Old Folks at Home," "My Old Kentucky Home." Soldier-fiddlers like Isaac Brophy entertained by the campfires and the men sang unashamedly. "Home, Sweet Home," "Weeping Sad and Lonely," "Come Where My Love Lies Dreaming." There was liquor, bottles passing surreptitiously from hand to hand around the fires, but Luke and Thomas did not know how Rivers, Merriman, McNamara, and their like came by it with no Rebs to trade with. Half of Company I by now had spent some time alone with Merriman's books, and a trove of *cartes de visite* had sneaked in by mail—*London and Paris Voluptuaries, The Mysteries and Delights of Naked Female Beauty, Bedroom Photographs for Gentlemen Only*—from companies in New York City that catered to the lonely soldier. The pictures made the rounds and one night Elisha sneaked one into his tent.

They washed their clothes and themselves, and shaved and brushed their teeth, in Broad Run. They filled their canteens and cookpots and tin cans for boiling coffee. They boiled their clothes and the dead graybacks floated to the surface, and a day later a live one would appear on your neck or crotch or could be felt tickling your scalp, and in no time there was a new regiment of them acrawl in your clothes and hair.

They were still receiving no rations but hardtack and salt pork, and the hardtack they were drawing now was half of it weevil-infested or worm-ridden. You'd break it into boiling coffee and presently the surface in the cup or can would be swimming with dead worms or bugs and you'd skim them off and drink the coffee and it tasted as usual, and so did the hardtack. Elisha said he'd come to like the taste of hardtack, and Luke and Thomas ate it and the stringy salt pork willingly enough, which surprised Elisha, who could not forget Rose's cooking.

But after a couple of days their diet improved. The war had not come down hard on the farms hereabouts, and now the Second Corps did. Wagons went out, Negro-driven, with foraging details which broke into barns, smokehouses, and corncribs while girls and women shrieked at them, raining imprecations on their Yankee heads, or wept helplessly, or stood by silently, in a kind of stoic fury. One night about an hour after taps Sergeant Cate woke Jake Rivers and Merriman, and the three of them took up their muskets and went off into the night and returned at dawn with two turkeys and five chickens whose throats had been cut with a penknife. They died quiet, Rivers said. Didn't nobody hear a thing. Who didn't? Elisha said. Never you mind, Rivers said, because the raid had been unauthorized, and Sergeant Cate could have lost his chevrons for it. The next night they roasted the turkeys and chickens and collected the fat and fried their hardtack in it, and Thomas said it was better than gravy bread, and Elisha agreed. If that bastard Paine was to of caught us . . . Rivers said, with the grease shining down his chin.

That bastard Paine, that sonofabitch Paine. Now that they weren't marching all day Paine was after them constantly, nosing into their business, haranguing them at assembly or roll call for disrespect or rowdiness or sloppiness in line. Elisha said he was worse than Macy when Macy had been company commander. The sonofabitch was hardly more than Luke's age and acted like he was Hancock or Hooker himself. *Is this a goddamn ladies' sewing circle? Is this a goddamn quilting party? You. Private. Get your goddamn chin up where it belongs.* Handsome, the girls would have said. His hair was wavy and light brown and took on a honeyed luster in the bright sun. He had a shapely bowlike mouth and was as big as Luke and as well built. *It sounded like a bunch of goddamn monkeys around those fires last night.* Everybody knew that his great-grandfather had put his name to the Declaration of Independence and no one cared a bucket of piss for it. Elisha told Luke and Thomas how, just this spring, the men had gotten up a petition to Governor Andrew asking him to remove the stuck-up Harvard sonofabitch for pulling a pistol on a private named Donovan, not to mention putting good soldiers in the stocks and hanging them from tree limbs by their wrists and locking them in the guardhouse for as small a thing as spitting on the ground. It was a grand petition, Elisha said, but nothing came of it.

On the third morning at Thoroughfare Gap it was Company I's turn to go out on picket duty. Lieutenant Paine lined them up and ordered them into column and put them in motion roughly southeast, away from Broad Run. The morning was mild, the heat of the march a memory. They marched at route step with arms at will, and the farther they got from the campsite the more easy and casual it became, taking on the feel of a country outing, a picnic, even the officers relaxing a little, Paine at the head of the column, the noncoms on the wings. They followed the trodden route of the previous guard, through woods, over weed-choked fields, past a prosperous-looking farm that they steered well clear of, and finally picking up a narrow road through virgin forest, in whose humid shade the blackflies rose to attack them.

"Which is worse, blackflies or mosquitoes?"

"They're both of em a plague."

"We ain't got blackflies on Martha's Vineyard," said Elisha.

"Well ain't you special," someone said.

"Got deerflies," Elisha said. "They ain't as bad, but they're bad."

"How long we gonna be out here?"

"Company E been out two days."

"That's us, then."

"Naw," said Henry Wilcox, "the army'll be movin tomorrow."

"Was you ever wrong about anything, Henry?"

"Not ever," Tom Jackson answered for him.

The road came out of the woods and in front of them the land fell away in a wide deep valley with wooded hills rising beyond, and here, along the forest edge, Company E of their regiment had formed its rear line, the men idling in the shade, arms stacked and the morning cook-fires still smoking. Paine gave the order to break ranks and the men scattered, disencumbering themselves of their knapsacks and blankets, and struck up conversations with the men of E while the officers conferred in the formal unsmiling way of officers on duty.

Elisha and McNamara found an acquaintance named McAlister, a lank infantryman with a wry smile who said that Mosby's guerillas were in the area and had captured a couple of commissary sergeants from Harrow's brigade.

"These two boys here seen em," Elisha said.

"Seen Mosby?" McAlister said.

"It was just some partisans," Luke said. "Didn't even have rifles on them."

"Them partisans're trash," McAlister said. "Won't fight nobody fair."

"Mosby's trash too," McNamara said. "Got any pipe tobacco?"

McAlister opened his haversack and dug around for some. "Down that valley where the road splits off," he said, "there's some nigger cabins and this one nice house where lives a couple a white girls, own the niggers. The white girls're twin sisters. Can't tell em one from the other. Their pa had a tannery down there, but he's in the army or dead, one. Them girls're randy-lookin things. Might give somebody a good time, I wouldn't be surprised."

"I ain't seen a pretty woman down here yet," McNamara said.

"You got to look for em," McAlister said. "There's no men down there, white or black. I believe the Rebs killed the nigger men. That, or pressed em into labor. Them girls is randy-lookin. I'd a give em some business, I'd a had a chance."

"Business?" Thomas said.

"How you think they're keepin theirselves?" McAlister said.

Then E's drummer boy sounded the general, and McAlister winked them good-bye and went for his knapsack and musket.

Right off, Lieutenant Paine sent Luke and Thomas down on post with Elisha and McNamara, among other veterans, under the command of Sergeant Holland, the Englishman. The road ran twisting down the long belly of the hill and at the bottom of the valley split right and left, as McAlister had said. The house and cabins stood along both branches of the road with the land rising behind them, open at first, then wooded. The sentinels were to watch the road in either direction and the woods beyond the buildings, though the trees were thick and the hillside rugged with stone outcroppings and it was doubtful any Rebels would come at them that way.

The girls' house was a two-story brick, not large, with a chimney at either end and a pillared verandah with a balcony on top. The big tannery building, unpainted and barnlike, stood well to the back, its sliding door padlocked. There was a shed barn. Chickens scratched and pecked around the yard, and on the rise beyond the house a couple of jersey cows grazed. The slave cabins were poor things of clay-chinked logs. Smoke rose from all the chimneys, a peaceful sight, somehow.

The two sisters had come out onto the balcony to watch the sentinels and outpost change over. McAlister was right, you couldn't tell one from the other. They stood there, leaning on the balustrade, frowning, watching the men of Company E recede up the hill, the men of I come on and take their places.

"They build em skinny down here," Merriman said. "Pale and skinny. Chew tobacca, half of em."

They were standing uphill of the road, across from the house. Nine of them, and Sergeant Holland. McNamara and the Rhode Islander Delaney and the Nantucketer Riggs had gone down to take first sentinel. McNamara looked up at the women and went on around the house without speaking to them. Riggs and Delaney separated in either direction to picket the road. The twins were still on the balcony.

"They ain't wearin hoops," observed Merriman.

"They ain't so skinny," Elisha said, watching them.

"Skinny ain't the worst thing," Merriman said. "I definitely would fuck em."

"There'll be none of that, lads," said Sergeant Holland.

They spread out in the tall summer grass, bent flat here and there by the previous pickets, and sat down and kept a casual watch on the road. The twins had gone inside. A Negro woman, slender and pretty, came out of one of the log cabins. She wore a red bandanna on her head. She looked at Delaney, who was watching down the road with his back to her, then shaded her eyes and gazed uphill at the men on post. She went around behind the cabin and was lost to view. A bobwhite called from somewhere deep in the grass. A red-tailed hawk wheeled and coasted. Just like on the Vineyard, Elisha thought. Hawks, bobwhites. All of em in our field, and the whippoorwill at candle lighting.

After an hour Sergeant Holland sent Luke and Thomas and Elisha down to relieve the three sentinels. Elisha told Thomas to go a short ways uphill beyond the house and make sure he was within calling distance of him and Luke.

"What if somebody comes?" Thomas said.

"They ain't gonna come that way," Elisha said.

"What if they do?"

"Shoot one of em and run like hell. If there's one on a horse, shoot him."

Thomas nodded and went past the house, the backyard well, with his heart overpumping and his hands perspiring where they held the Springfield. McNamara was standing at a rail fence with his gun resting on the top log.

"Take a nap, Tommy," he said. "There ain't a Reb for twenty miles a here."

"There's Mosby," Thomas said, "and I know there's partisans because I've seen them."

"I'd like to see em. Put a ball in em."

"Well I wouldn't," Thomas said.

McNamara snapped him a mordant grin, then shouldered his musket and swung away, past the house and across the white road. Thomas's mouth had gone spitless. He could see Elisha, small down the road, but not Luke, who was hidden by the little cabins. He looked at the well, looked uphill at the two placid cows and the dense woods. His canteen was better than half full but the water in it very warm and he looked again at the well and thought of cold well water and the clean taste of granite stone and went to it and set his musket down and cranked the oaken bucket downward. Down it went, down and down, and struck the water and bounced, tipped, and went under.

"And just what y'all think you're doin?"

Thomas turned, holding on to the crank. The girls stood side by side and it was like seeing double. They were skinny, all right, with long sallow faces and yellow hair squeezed into buns. They wore plum-gray cotton dresses with lace collars, pointy women's boots. No hoops, as Merriman had observed, but corsets, so that their breasts stood up prominent.

"What does it look like I'm doing?" Thomas said, and resumed cranking. The bucket came up and he unhooked it and lowered it to the ground. He unslung his canteen and emptied it. The girls had come closer.

"Cost you twenty-five cent," one of them said.

"For water?" Thomas said. He'd submerged his canteen and the water was entering it in gulps. It was cold and delicious feeling on his hands and wrists.

"You Yankees gawn drink it dry. How we gawn make out we ain't got water?"

"There's plenty of water," Thomas said. He raised his canteen and drank. Delicious.

"Twenty-five cent."

He drank again and stoppered his canteen and wiped his mouth with his sleeve. "My money's in my knapsack over there across the road," he said.

"Y'all go fetch it, then."

"I can't. I'm on sentry."

"Some sentry, ain't you. If General Jackson was to come down that mountain he'd cut your head off fore you saw him."

Thomas slung his canteen. "General Jackson's dead," he said.

The girls looked at each other. "He ain't neither."

"He was shot at Chancellorsville," Thomas said. "Lost an arm and died of it."

"You goddamn Yankees."

"It was his own men shot him," Thomas said. "By mistake in the dark."

"He's lyin," said one of the girls.

Thomas shrugged. He took up his musket. "I'll send your two bits down with my relief," he said, and turned away.

"How much money you got?"

Thomas stopped. He turned. They were thin, yes, but there was a softness about them, a malleable fleshiness, over their womanly bones. They were, he realized, full as tall as he.

"I got quite a bit," he said.

"You look like it."

"Don't he?"

"Looks like a rich boy from way up North. New York, I'd say."

"Massachusetts," Thomas said. He looked back at the hillside, the woods. Nothing.

"Nice clean boy, too. How old're y'all?"

"Eighteen."

"No you ain't."

A smirk, identical, had begun to change the shape of each girl's long face.

"You're right," Thomas said, and smiled. His heartbeat picked up again, but not from fear.

"You got four dollars?"

"Why?" Thomas said.

"Listen. You ever done it with two girls at once?"

Thomas looked at them. The one, then the other. "Not at once," he said.

"Y'all come back down tonight and bring four dollars. Two for each girl, you see."

Thomas swallowed. He roused himself and looked again at the woods and decided there was no one up there. In these easeful days at Thorough Gap his bowels had quieted, and he knew at least that he did not have dysentery.

"I guess he ain't interested," one of the girls said.

"I might be," Thomas said.

"Might be don't feed the bulldog."

"Can I bring a friend?"

"You do, y'all bring eight dollars."

"If we each go with one of you, I mean."

The girls looked at each other again. The smirks widened, cutting upward.

"Listen at him tryin to cheat us."

"No I ain't," Thomas said.

"We don't go alone."

"Why not?"

"We just don't."

"I want to bring him anyway."

"Bring him or don't, that's your business. Y'all come to the front door, whichever, and knock three times, wait, and knock two."

"The sentinel'll see us."

"Don't come, then."

"I *might* come," Thomas said. "Depends if I can sneak away."

"Y'all knock three times, then two, else we won't open it."

"I guess I can remember that," Thomas said, and turned and headed for the rail fence and this time kept going.

"Hey. Is General Jackson dead truly?"

"I swear," Thomas said over his shoulder.

"Y'all oughta be ashamed," the girl called after him.

"Well I ain't," Thomas said, now unafraid of the thick woods in front of him, and what might, theoretically, come boiling out of them.

"Have you lost your senses?" Luke said.

"My senses are fine," Thomas said.

"They might cut your throats. You think of that?"

"I'd like to see em try."

"You'll get the clap," Luke said.

"These girls aren't like that. They're just temporary whores."

"Temporary. Next thing you'll tell me they're virgins."

They'd rotated up the hill to the third line, where now the fires were dying and the men bedding down on their gum blankets. Lieutenant Paine too would sleep under the moon like everybody else but apart from the enlisted men, with a fire of his own.

"If you get caught you're in trouble," Luke said.

"Elisha says not. He says they'll need every man when the Rebs hit us and it's going to be forgive and forget for a while."

"You better hope so."

"Why don't you come, Luke."

"Don't even ask."

"You've done it, haven't you? Or else you'd come."

Luke didn't say anything.

"You have, haven't you?"

"Maybe."

"With Mariah."

Luke was silent. They'd come into the woods together and it was very dark here but the road wasn't far away, winding velvety-gray through the moon-filtered forest night. Mosquitoes bit them.

"Why didn't you tell me about it?" Thomas said.

"I don't tell you everything."

"What else haven't you told me?"

"Nothing," Luke said. "You be careful. Take your guns."

"There's men all around."

"Take them," Luke said.

They waited a long time, waited and waited and finally rose on their elbows and looked at each other and nodded and sat up and pulled on their shoes and got up. They put on their sack coats and hats. They buckled on their cap and cartridge belts and slung their haversacks and went diagonally down the hill in the moonlight, away from the direct line of the road, carrying their unloaded muskets. No lights burned in the brick house. The grass was wet, soaking their trousers as they kicked through it. A whippoorwill called out softly. In his haversack Thomas had brought his money, eleven dollars, a half eagle and the rest greenbacks. Elisha had four dollars in greenbacks. By luck they'd boiled the graybacks out of their clothes this very morning and fire-dried them and washed themselves in Broad Run.

They circled wide of the second line of pickets—wide but not too, for there was another picket detail off that way—and struck the road perhaps a half mile below the house. To their right, dark woods. They stopped and listened. A bullfrog spoke distantly, a thick glottal twang, and another answered. An owl cried, shrill and tremulous, high up. Thomas's heartbeat was a steady solid throb in his chest but his hands were dry and he was not afraid. Elisha nodded and they set off, pushing pale stunted moonshadows before them.

The sentinel was sitting in the grass beside the road with his musket across his lap. He bolted to his feet, cocked his musket and put it to his shoulder.

"Stop right there, you sonsabitches," he said.

Thomas and Elisha froze.

"What regiment?" the sentinel said.

It was Tom Jackson.

"It's only us, Stonewall," Elisha said. "Elisha and Thomas."

"Shit fire," Jackson said, lowering the gun and easing the hammer down. "What you want to scare me for?"

Elisha and Thomas came on, carrying their muskets by their sides.

"The hell you boys up to?" Jackson said.

"Gonna buy some eggs from them two twins," Elisha said.

"Eggs," Jackson said. "It's almost midnight."

"They ain't got many. They wanted to sell em private so didn't everybody come pilin in on em."

"You ain't buyin no eggs," Jackson said.

"Never mind about that," Elisha said. "Who's down the road?"

"Henry."

"Shit."

"Henry ain't a tattle."

"He ain't gonna approve, either."

"Henry thinks he'll be kilt next fight. It's his own soul he's worryin about, not yours. You boys go on now fore somebody sees us. And just remember: I ain't seen you."

"We ain't seen you either," Elisha said.

They went down the road and climbed the steps onto the verandah. They could see Henry Wilcox down beyond the cabins, standing, not sitting, with his back to them. Thomas knocked three times, then twice, and Henry turned around, sharp. Elisha waved to him and Henry studied the two of them then shook his head and turned and resumed watching the road. Thomas knocked again, thrice and twice. Footsteps within, and then a light flared in the window and a lock turned and a bolt shot back and the door opened and one of the twins stood stiff and unsmiling, holding a candle in a brass stick. Her hair was down about her shoulders and she wore a chemise and pantalettes and that was all, and in the candlelight her eyes appeared very large and solemn with her yellow hair framing her face, and her skin was more milky than sallow. Was she pretty? Thomas would ask himself that in the days to come and think yes sometimes, and sometimes no. She stood aside and he and Elisha walked in still carrying their muskets. They took off their caps. The girl closed the door and double-locked it.

"I'm Lilac," she said.

"Thomas."

"Elisha."

"Elisha? What kinda name is that?"

"Don't know," Elisha said. He was having trouble looking at her.

"It's a Bible name," Thomas said.

"Well ain't we fancy," Lilac said.

"Yes ma'am," Elisha said.

"Put them guns down," Lilac said.

"They aren't loaded," Thomas said.

"Well the bed won't fit em, loaded or not."

Thomas and Elisha looked at each other, shrugged, and leaned their muskets against the wall then followed Lilac up the stairs, watching the movement of her thin bottom under the cotton chemise and drawers and, alternately, her white calves and ankles. The house smelled of lye or wood ash or both. It smelled of damp wool. The walls were papered and wainscoted. It was a nice house and Thomas wondered how people so ignorant had come by it. Lilac led them into a bedroom with a four-poster on which her sister sat in the same state of undress, combing her hair. A candle burned on a bedside table. There was a brick fireplace, a chest of drawers, and nothing to sit on. Elisha and Thomas stood with their caps in their hands.

"This here's Iris," Lilac said.

"Pleased, I'm sure," Iris said.

The boys introduced themselves.

"Ain't Elisha a peculiar name?" Lilac said.

"Right peculiar," Iris said, and set the comb down on the table.

Lilac had placed her candle on the mantel shelf and moved to the bed. She sat down beside her sister. The windows were open and moths danced about the candle flames.

"Now then," Lilac said. "Who's goin first?"

"Who's goin first *after* somebody ponies up four dollars, she means," Iris said.

Thomas cleared his throat. "We were wanting to do it separate," he said. "One with each of you."

"Now what did I tell you bout that?" said Lilac.

"But why?" Thomas said.

The twins looked at each other. "Go on tell him," Iris said.

"All right, then. So's we can look out for each other."

"We wouldn't hurt you," Thomas said.

"So you say."

No one spoke then. The girls sat back with their arms propping them, watching Thomas and Elisha, patient, mildly curious, not judging of them. It was dawning on Thomas that they were as young as he was and he knew, quite suddenly, that all they knew of fornication had been learned whoring, in this room, and that it might be a vast knowledge and it might not, but it was a bargain with the Devil either way and the Devil would always be in the bed with them, always, when they lay down with a man. For that, he pitied them.

"Elisha," he said, "you go first."

Elisha brought a hand up and wiped his mouth with the back of his wrist. He'd gone white under his deep suntan. "We should flip for it, Tommy."

"You're the oldest," Thomas said.

"That don't signify."

"I want you to."

"Be four dollars," Iris said, "hard money."

"I only got greenbacks," Elisha said.

"What about you?" Iris said.

"Got a half eagle you can have," Thomas said.

"Tommy," Elisha said.

"You can give me greenbacks for it," Thomas said. He opened his haversack, found the money sock and untied it, and took out the half eagle. He stepped forward and handed it to Iris.

"I cain't break this," she said.

"It's the only coin I got," Thomas said.

"You won't get your turn," Elisha said, alarmed now.

"Never mind that," Thomas said.

"You cain't watch," Iris said. She'd pushed the coin under the mattress.

"I don't want to," Thomas said.

"Wait," Elisha said.

"You scairt?" Lilac said, but not unkindly.

"Where you goin, Tommy?"

"Ain't nothin to be scairt about."

"Just down the stairs," Thomas said.

"Don't be scairt, Elisha. We gawn have fun."

Elisha looked back at Thomas. "This ain't right, Tommy."

"He's scairt."

"No I ain't," Elisha said.

"I wonder might I have a candle," Thomas said.

"One on the mantel," Lilac said. "They's some fresh hoecake in the kitchen. Go on help yourself."

Elisha had no idea what to do now. He stood rooted, as weak in his legs as he'd been at Ball's Bluff, his first action, the regiment getting shot to pieces all around him. He could feel his cheeks warm, as he'd felt the bloodless pallor in them before.

"Well?" Lilac said. He knew it was Lilac because she was on the left.

"Cat got his tongue," Iris said.

"Y'all take your coat off and them belts and come on over here."

He obeyed and they slid apart to make room for him and he sat down between them. It was dark in the room with just the one candle. Lilac put her arm around him and kissed his cheek. Iris laid a hand on his privates and Elisha felt a stiffening down there and a tightness in his chest making breathing difficult, sensations such as the illicit pictures caused him, the naked women on their couches and canopy beds like this one. Lilac was on the floor now, kneeling, untying his brogans. Iris pulled his braces down his shoulders. She unbuttoned his shirt.

"You want us both, or one?" Lilac said. She was up beside him again. His shirt was gone. Iris had peeled it off and he'd let her.

"I couldn't say," Elisha said.

"Want us both naked, I mean. Some don't."

"I don't think he ever done it before, Lilac."

"You ever done it, Elisha?"

"Ain't that obvious?"

"It ain't nothin to be anxious about," Lilac said.

"I ain't anxious."

"I can see you ain't. Feel of that, Iris."

It seemed to get bigger when she touched it. Elisha couldn't look at either girl. Like he'd turn to stone if he did.

"This un's a sweetie," Lilac said.

"And him a Yankee," Iris said.

"We had us some rough ones. Why we keep together."

"This un ain't rough," Iris said.

"Nor smells," Lilac said.

"I believe I could do him alone."

"I believe I could too," Lilac said.

"Maybe we ought to flip that half eagle for it. Like they was gawn do."

"You go on, you said it first," Lilac said, rising from the bed. She looked at Elisha. "Unless you got a objection."

"No objection," Elisha said.

"Well then," Lilac said.

Elisha watched her go out, barefoot in her chemise and drawers. Heels like giant pearls. The door closed softly. Iris put her arm around his shoulders. He didn't dare move.

"You gawn be gentle, ain't you?" she said.

"Why a course," he said, surprised.

Iris loosened the drawstring of her chemise. "You ain't never seen a naked lady have you?"

"I guess that ain't no secret," he said.

"Here goes then," she said, rising, and in the same motion lifting the chemise up over her head.

Elisha looked at her in the candlelight. He watched as she stepped out of her pantalettes. "Skinny, ain't I?" she said.

"You ain't a bit skinny," he said.

Thomas was sitting on the second stair from the bottom with the candle beside him. He heard the door open and close and rose and looked up into the darkness where in a moment Lilac materialized, descending slow and ladylike with a hand on the banister.

"Sit down," she said. "It ain't nothin wrong."

She sat down on the stair and Thomas did too.

"She wanted to do him alone," Lilac said. "Took a shine to him, I guess. You didn't want hoecake?"

Thomas shook his head. "Which one are you?" he said.

"Why, Lilac. You cain't tell by now?"

"How could I?"

"There's ways." She looked at him for a moment. "Was nice a you, lettin your friend at us and you not."

"He's older."

"That ain't why you done it." She stole another look at him. "You can still do me, you care to."

Thomas made no answer.

"Y'all don't want to?"

"I don't have four dollars hard money."

"You done paid. Two for each girl."

Thomas didn't say anything.

"You don't like me," Lilac said.

"Yes I do."

"Think I'm ugly."

"No."

"What, then?"

"I don't know," Thomas said.

"Well hold my hand, anyways."

Thomas took it. Her palm was warm, moist. The hand pale. Clean.

"How long have you been doing this?" Thomas said.

"Whorin, you mean."

"If you want to call it that."

"What else you gawn call it?"

"Taking care of yourselves."

"One way a sayin it. Been doin it since the war. Our pa died a couple a months after Sumter, just fell over dead one day. He was sixty-seven, you see. Too old to serve. He done real good with his tannery, business come from Leesburg, Warrenton, all over. Had three niggers to work it, come with the place when he bought it, but with Pa gone wasn't nobody to run the niggers and then some partisans come through and somethin happened, some argument, I guess, and next thing happened they hung one of em and took the other two off with em. They'd got right troublesome with no one to run em but what happened was pitiful, and we warn't no party to it. They hung the one nigger and left him, and Iris and me helped his woman get him down and bury him. It wasn't no call to hang him."

Thomas sat in silence. The candle held them, within the darkness, in its soft sad light.

"You a abolitionist?" Lilac said.

"Why I joined up. Elisha too."

"Well," Lilac said, "y'all gawn get your way, I reckon. Me and Iris freed ours, you might say. Cain't feed em, you see, and it ain't fair to make em work for you if you cain't. We told em to look out for theirselves any which way they could."

"You ought to tell them they can leave."

"I wouldn't have no objection if they did. But tell me: Where would they go?"

"Where they want."

"Where's that?"

"I don't know."

"What's your Mister Lincoln gawn do with round about a million free niggers?"

"He'll figure it out," Thomas said.

Lilac smiled sadly and shook her head. She had not let go of his hand nor did he want her to. "Your name was Robert, ain't it?"

"Thomas."

"Thomas. You want to screw me, Thomas?"

"I don't know," Thomas said truthfully.

"Don't *know*?"

"I've never done it, you see."

"That ain't no reason not to want to."

"I wouldn't want to do it in the same room with Elisha."

"Did I say we had to?"

"I just assumed."

"Assumed? Problem is, you don't think I'm purty enough."

"You're more than pretty enough," Thomas said.

"Truly?"

"Truly."

"Tell you somethin," Lilac said. "My daddy treated em good. The niggers, I mean. Worked right alongside of em. Never whipped a one. Me and Iris weren't no party to that hangin, neither."

"I know you weren't," Thomas said.

"We argued with them partisans a good deal. Told em that nigger was ours and they hadn't no right to hang him, but they said it was a war goin on, and the times called for it."

"Bastards," Thomas said.

Iris turned to look at him, still holding his hand. "Such talk," she said.

"I mean it."

"I know you do, Thomas. And they was. They was bastards. But that ain't no cause not to screw me if you wanted to."

"I do want to," Thomas said.

"Pick up that candle, then, and let's us go into the parlor."

Their last name was Purdy. Rhymes with purty, they said. They told Thomas and Elisha good-bye at the front door wearing robes and nothing under them. "Y'all could come back tomorrow night, you wanted," Lilac said.

"I don't think we can," Thomas said. "They say the army's moving tomorrow."

"After the war's over, then."

The twins' hair was tumbled about their shoulders in identical fashion, but Elisha knew Iris now, and not only by the color of her robe.

"Come to Martha's Vineyard," he said.

"Now how we gawn find Martha's Vineyard?" Iris said.

"We ain't never been north a the Mason-Dixon," Lilac said, "and that ain't but a few miles from here."

"We'll come back, won't we, Tommy?"

"Sure we will," Thomas said. "And it'll all be the same country then."

"Come back even if it ain't," Iris said.

"We will," Elisha said.

"Give us a kiss," Iris said.

"Kiss," Lilac told Thomas.

They kissed with their eyes closed, holding the girls and smelling the fleshy sweetness of them until Thomas broke away and took up his musket. "Be daylight any minute," he said.

"Good-bye, Iris," Elisha said.

"Y'all come back," she said.

"Y'all do," said Lilac.

The boys looked at them one more time then let themselves out and crept down the verandah steps and went down the moonlit road without speaking. The new sentry was sitting down as Tom Jackson had been.

"Elisha Smith, Company I," Elisha called to him, and he jumped up gripping his musket, whirling around, and saw the two of them and lowered the gun. Isaac Brophy. They couldn't have asked for better.

"Good Lord," Isaac said.

"You gonna let us pass?" Elisha said.

"Sure I am, but you better not say I did."

The boys came on.

"You boys find what you were looking for?" Isaac said.

"Maybe," Elisha said.

"Was she white or dark?" Isaac said.

"Ain't none a your business," Elisha said.

They went on, until Isaac was lost behind them around a bend in the road, and turned up the hill the way they'd come.

"Tommy."

"What."

They were walking in the tall grass, climbing the long hill. Guns on their shoulders.

"Was it like you expected?"

"Not really."

"There's more to it than I thought," Elisha said.

"Me too."

"Iris said I done all right for my first time."

"So did Lilac."

"She done me again," Elisha said.

"So did Lilac."

"It gets better each one."

"I thought so too," Thomas said.

They went along, climbing, wading up through the high grasses.

"The kissin's nice too," Elisha said. "I never knowed it was so much to it. It ain't like kissin your mother, is it."

"I'd say we did some learning tonight," Thomas said.

"Screwin. Kissin. Wish I could get about a week of it," Elisha said.

"You come back here you will."

"I will come back, by God. And I'll pay you my share a the five dollars."

"I ain't even thinking about that," Thomas said.

"I owe you," Elisha said.

"You don't owe me anything."

"You're a good friend, Tommy," Elisha said. "By God you are."

When reveille woke them Luke followed him into the woods. The day had broken cool and gray.

"Well, they didn't cut our throats and they didn't steal our money," Thomas said.

"Were they clean?"

"Hell yes they were clean. Why do you push it so?"

"I don't want you to catch anything."

"If I do it's my lookout."

"And mine. And the surgeon's. And Father's, when you come home with it."

"Maybe I won't be going home."

"What's got into you?" Luke said.

"You think everybody here is going home?"

"Of course not."

The men were drifting back to the campsite.

"If I die, it won't matter if I have the clap," Thomas said.

"You aren't going to die," Luke said.

"I don't have the clap, either," Thomas said.

FOURTEEN

They arrived in Chambersburg just before midnight, pounding through the town like a thunderous seething river and dispersing by regiment to hasty bivouacs in corn and wheatfields and the yards of unlucky farmers to the north of town. At dawn the bugle cry of reveille rang out from field to field and by the time the sun had risen these lean Confederate horsemen were scouring the countryside for livestock, clothes, food, hay, and Negroes.

Many Negroes, former slaves and freemen alike, had fled days ago, when rumor came of the invasion. Some had loaded wagons with food and valuables and driven north toward Harrisburg. Some, having no stomach for a journey so long and uncertain, had provisioned themselves and found hiding places in cellars and lofts and woods, hoping for the best. Still others hid in farmers' fields and the majority of these were flushed out and ridden down and brought in with their wrists bound behind them.

Late that morning Sally Creedon answered a knock on the door of her brick rowhouse on Loudon Street. Sally had locked her doors when the Rebel cavalry had woken her last night. This morning, peering from the curtained window of the front room upstairs, she'd seen riders go up and down the street singly and in small groups, moving at an urgent canter. The men looked battle-hardened, she thought, and hardened too by hunger and fatigue and life in the saddle. They looked impervious to all hardship and indifferent to their own deaths. Their uniforms, shell jackets and yellow-striped pants, were torn and patched and had been bled by age and exposure to a blanched gray or watery butternut. Some had replaced their army issue with plundered denim or cotton trousers, muslin or cot-

ton shirts of various colors, so that they looked like ruined farmers turned to outlawry. Their hair fell tangled to their shoulders and many wore thick mufflike beards and some rode barefoot. They wore feathers and plumes in their slouch hats, even so, and rode with the ease, the naturalness, of trick riders in a circus, whom you could imagine sitting a galloping horse sound asleep, their thin bodies glued in place, lithe and slouched and weightless.

Why, William, she said. You shouldn't be out in all this.

William Stumpel was eighteen and had a clubfoot and was said to be simpleminded. Sally wasn't sure about that. Sally's husband had employed William in his law office as an errand boy before the war. Now he did odd jobs when he could find them. Sally often paid him to weed and water her little vegetable garden.

They've done took Delia, he said. She's down to the Diamond.

Delia? Sally said. Delia Wilkes?

Yes'm. They've took all the darkies. Got about a hunderd of em down to the Diamond. Gonna carry em down South, it looks like.

Delia Wilkes? Sally said again.

I seed her.

Delia had come here on foot from Gettysburg a week ago and taken lodging with her first cousin, Miss May Stevens, Sally Creedon's longtime cook and laundress. Miss May was ailing and sent Delia to work in her place, to which Sally readily agreed, though she knew Delia Wilkes was—no way to gild the lily—a prostitute. She'd gotten herself into some trouble over it and had removed herself to Chambersburg until things should blow over.

William waited downstairs while Sally wetted her neck with French perfume and painted her lips in front of her bedroom mirror. She came back down and fitted and tied her black-dyed Scotch straw hat. She chose a parasol.

You needn't come with me, she said. The gallant cavaliers of the South would never harm a lady.

I'd feel better to come, William said.

The sun was halfway to noontime and Sally wished she'd worn her sun hat instead of the Scotch hat and wondered why she hadn't and knew why: the Scotch gave her a jaunty and rakish look, a look—she hoped—of high spirit and command. It also revealed more of her golden hair. She opened her parasol. The street was dusty and white in the sun, and nicked all over with Confederate hoofprints. In the near distance, from the direction of the Diamond, a commotion rose on the warm still air, shouts and hoofbeats and the rattle of wagons.

They say General Lee ain't far behind these riders, William said. He walked lurchingly beside her, swinging his bad foot. Him and his whole dang army.

I wonder what General Lee thinks of these goings-on, Sally said.

Maybe he don't know, William said.

It's his business to know, Sally said.

The Rebels had put the Negroes facedown on the brick pavement in front of the courthouse. There were twenty-five or thirty Negroes, all but a few of them women and children. Soldiers stood over them with their small-ish breech-loading rifles resting on their shoulders and their limp slouch hats shading their faces. Horses were tied in bunches to all the hitching rails and soldiers stood holding the reins of others. The horses stood quiet, unrestive, now and then switching their tails at the flies. White brands, CSA, on their bony rumps. Droppings everywhere you looked, their odor slicking the air.

Pardon me, Sally said. The sun was behind her and she held her parasol almost horizontal on her shoulder. William stood behind her.

Ma'am, the soldier said, and smiled vaguely and without impudence. He had a short beard the color and texture of dirty straw. Sally could smell him now, sweat and black earth and the sour smell of his horse. He unshouldered his rifle and held it inconspicuously by his side.

Could you explain to me please what you men are doing here?

The soldier wiped his mouth with the back of his hand, gaining some time, perhaps. His face grew serious. His teeth were yellow-brown. These here is contrabands, ma'am. We gawn take em back down where they belong.

Contrabands, Sally said.

Slaves, ma'am. Runaways, else stole from us by the Yankee army.

Another soldier had come over, lank like the first. A small red feather in his hatband. A cardinal feather. Sally by now had located Delia, prone in a blue cotton dress, her face hidden in her folded arms.

Not all of these Negroes were slaves, Sally said. Some of them were born here.

I got my orders, ma'am.

A two-horse carryall came into the square with soldiers riding before and behind it. The wagon was crammed with Negroes, women and children, two men. The driver was a soldier. His horse was tied to the back of the carryall. He stopped it, and one of the riders snapped out an order and the Negroes got down, slow, looking around them as if the place were alien, as puzzling to them as a dream can be puzzling, as grotesque and chaotic. Two of the children had to be lifted down by their mothers.

And do you intend to abduct the children? Sally said.

They's contrabands, ma'am.

Y'all favor niggers over your own kind, said the second soldier. It ain't natural.

The new arrivals were ordered to lie down on the pavement. They had brought no valises, no belongings.

Who is your commanding officer? Sally said.

The soldiers looked at each other. General Jenkins, the first one said.

It ain't none a her affair, said the second.

Where would I find him? Sally said.

That boy your'n? The second soldier nodded at William Stumpel.

Where would I find General Jenkins? Sally said.

Why ain't you in the army, boy?

He got a lame leg, the first soldier said. I seen him gimp along.

Get shot, did you? said the second.

I ain't got shot, William said.

Why ain't you?

Don't know, William said.

Over yonder's the general's headquarters, the first soldier said, indicating a large, square, gray-painted brick house facing the square. The residence of Charles Montgomery, president of the Bank of Chambersburg.

I thank you, Sally said, and I hope you rejoice in the work you're doing today.

It's our orders, ma'am.

There were two sentries at the Montgomerys' front door. They both looked very young and their uniforms were relatively new, the gray in them still fresh, velvety. They told Sally and William to move back from the door out of the shadow of the building and wait there while one of them took her request inside. While he was gone another wagon rattled into the Diamond with another cargo of Negroes. The sentry came back out and motioned with his head and held the door open for her. She told William he might go home if he wished but he said no, he felt bound to wait for her. Sally closed her parasol and climbed the stone steps.

General Jenkins was in the front bedroom upstairs. The general had put on his coat and sword to receive her and she wondered if it was military etiquette or if he thought to cow her with these trappings of his rank and profession. There were two rows of brass buttons down his coatfront and a gold sash around his waist. The general had the longest beard she'd ever seen, waist-long almost, pouring off his face like a cascade of knitted black yarn. He was standing when she came in. Two officers stood at the window looking down into the square. The canopy bed had been slept in and the carpet was tracked with dirt. The room smelled of sweat and leather and cigar smoke. She wondered where Charlie Montgomery and his family had gone.

General Jenkins gave her a slight, formal bow. He had a mournful brooding face above all that beard and Sally knew that her Scotch hat and French perfume and whatever other weapons she possessed would be useless here.

General Jenkins, said the general. Brigade commander under General Stuart. And you are . . . ?

Mrs. Whitney Creedon.

Husband in the army, I imagine.

Seventy-second Pennsylvania. You may run into him one of these days.

I would like that.

The two officers at the window had turned and were appraising her. They looked at each other and one of them raised his eyebrows and smiled. They were young men, sun-bronzed, with crescent mustaches.

Of course, Sally said, you may be too busy abducting Negroes to do much fighting.

Again the two officers looked at her. They looked at Jenkins, who was watching Sally, standing now with his hands clasped behind his back.

I would ask you to sit down, he said, but I have work to attend to. What is it you wished to say to me?

Sally told him about Delia Wilkes. That she was freeborn, over in Get-
tysburg, and was stoppng with her cousin for a time. Had a son in Gettys-
burg, highly educated, would make something of himself one day.

You have no right to take her, Sally said.

We have a right to take every nigger ever ran away from us.

She didn't run away from you.

Her father did. Or her grandfather.

And so she must become a slave.

So she must, if we can help it.

There are little children out there, Sally said.

And their mothers. Would you have us separate them?

Good God.

Where are all the bucks? Jenkins said.

The what?

The buck niggers. The men. They're so human and brave, why'd they
run off and leave their women and children?

Maybe they supposed you wouldn't harm them. That men would hunt
men, not women and children.

We harm no one, Jenkins said. We're returning them to their natural
condition, for which God made them.

Sally felt her chest tighten. She felt a torrent coming—of revulsion,
anger, sharp words. She closed her eyes, took a breath.

What will you do with them? she said quietly.

Sell them, Jenkins said.

Sell them, Sally said.

Unless the owners claim them.

You will burn in hell, Sally Creedon said.

General Jenkins didn't blush or flinch. He watched her, sad coal-dark
eyes above the beard. The two young officers watched her too, stiff now and
formal, the affability gone from their faces, the roguish interest in her.

Captain Fitzhugh, Jenkins said over his shoulder.

Sir.

Take her down and give her her nigger.

She isn't mine, Sally said.

Just the one, Captain.

Yes sir.

Do not expect me to thank you, Sally said.

I expect nothing of the sort, General Jenkins said. Just the one, Captain, hear?

She had no protector now. And while the doctor was esteemed for his kindliness and valued for his professional skills and generosity in plying them, he was a known abolitionist, and he bore without knowing it the disdain and bitter resentment that those sentiments provoked. People didn't fear an abolitionist unless he was John Brown, and even Frederick Douglass had distanced himself from old Brown's bloody deeds. Abolitionists were Unitarians, Quakers, philosophers, Concord transcendentalists, learned women like Mrs. Stowe. Harmless, aside from their ideas. In Holmes Hole they were the doctor, the meek schoolmaster, Mr. Pease, and Mr. Benjamin Crowell, the coal merchant, whose son had lost his leg in Virginia. Who else? Nobody! No chapter of the Antislavery Society in any of the towns.

Oh, this island! This narrow-minded and unfeeling island! *In regard to the slavery question, some of us think there is no great harm in it if thereby we can enlighten their dark and benighted minds and improve their moral condition. Indeed, we think it would be no great trouble for us to find several texts of Scripture to support this view.* This, just the other day in *The Vineyard Gazette,* where such letters appeared regularly, with seldom a voice to oppose them. What scripture? Rose thought. What texts? Whose dark and benighted mind? The writer had signed his name Spindle Shanks, no different in his anonymity from the faceless coward who throws a brick through the window in the dead of night, gone by the time you find a light and throw the door open. Nantucket had sent dozens of boys to the war, maybe not all abolitionists as Luke explained but they'd spilled their blood anyway all up and down Virginia and would again and again and no end to it, Rose sometimes thought. But where was Martha's Vineyard in all of this? There were some Vineyard boys with the occupying army in the Georgia and Carolina islands, and a few others with the army out West, but in the whole Army of the Potomac, the army that must fight General Lee to the death no matter how long it took, there were only Luke, Thomas, and Elisha Smith from the Vineyard. Peleg Davenport dead, credit him. She'd have prayed for his soul if she believed in prayer or God or any of it. And Bart Crowell, home with a leg cut off above the knee. Credit him, too. But the young manhood of Martha's Vineyard otherwise were shirkers and Negro-haters, like that Peter Daggett, whom Luke had beaten all those years ago for his meanness.

Peter was full grown now, still working at the shipyard, by trade a caulker. A big strong boy (not as strong as Luke, nor ever would be) whom the young slackers of Holmes Hole looked to for ideas and the bravery they lacked themselves. There was no Sons of Temperance chapter in Edgartown, and nights these village rowdies—and that's all they were, *village* rowdies, bumpkins; why, the toughs of New Bedford would knock their heads together and laugh about it—traveled there and drank illegally, bought spirits and roamed about making noise and harassing girls and ladies in the streets.

The Daggetts lived close to the center of town, up from the shore a ways near Frog Alley, and as he grew older Peter could be seen on Main Street, loitering about the barbershop or drugstore or on Union Wharf, outside the fish market or alongside the lading schooners, the sidewheelers as they discharged or took on passengers. Bothering acquaintances and nonacquaintances alike with ignorant remarks and small talk.

After Luke had beaten him he had taken to ignoring Rose when they happened to meet in town, and this shunning had passed, over time, from stage to stage. It was, at first, an embarrassed averting of the eyes, as a body would expect after such a humiliation. Then—Rose looked right at him, she observed the changes—there was feigned indifference to her presence, a lack of interest, as if she weren't worth notice. It made Rose smile to herself, this hauteur. Finally, quite recently, had come an aggressive kind of ignoring, a loudening of his voice in street corner conversation as she passed by (what a talker he was), a discernible rearrangement of his limbs and body when he saw her coming out of the corner of his eye, drawing into himself, as if he breathed it, a truculence, a swagger. Striking a pose. Rose smiled at this too, thinking of how Luke had beaten him and would again if Peter bothered her.

Now Luke was gone, and Peter looked at her. Hadn't he always? Because he couldn't act like she wasn't there if he didn't *look* at her first.

And looking at her as he had years ago in the snowstorm, and then the remark about making babies, Rose had not forgotten. Now it was in the open again, a keen and predatory light in his eye as he looked at her, the light composed not just of lust or desire but the memory of his beating, the shame it must have brought him. Wanting to have and hurt her, both.

Every morning at ten o'clock she walked out to do her shopping, in a summer dress, Leghorn straw hat with a black velvet bow, silk shawl, kid gloves, Balmoral boots, French parasol of ivory silk, crocheted silk purse. The finery won her no good feeling, especially among the women, but she dressed so anyway, not to spite them but in obedience to her own nature, a call from within herself to cut a vivid swath in the world because she was born to. *It's who I am,* she thought, *and ain't no tired old righteous-talkin white woman gonna rob me of myself.* And so she set out on those late-June mornings with her basket on her arm and the parasol on her shoulder, a familiar sight in the village, and the men eyed her and thought wistful uneasy thoughts and wondered about her and Dr. Chandler, and the women looked at her petulantly and wondered too.

Down Drummer Lane she went, to Main, which lay wide and pale under the high sun, a slight bend to it, the huddled stores nocking the deep-blue sky with their peaked gray-shingle roofs. Linden tree, as old as the Revolution, shading the hot dusty street all those years. Cast-iron fountain, cool to the touch, ice-cold spring water rising into its basin in a steady trickle. A miracle, Rose always thought, the water never stopping. Her boot heels tapped hollowly on the board sidewalk. She went into the drugstore, which smelled of cigars and tobacco, and closed her parasol.

"Top of the morning, Rose," said Mr. Daley, glad to see her, for all the confusion she bred in his mind, or perhaps because of it.

"Good morning," Rose said, nodding to Mr. Daley and to Mrs. Lawrence, who was just leaving.

Mrs. Lawrence returned the nod, gave a stiff smile, and went out with her basket on her arm.

"Any news of the boys?" Mr. Daley said.

"Army's still moving north," Rose said. "I'd like a box of stationery, please."

"I hear General Grant's got Vicksburg surrounded," Mr. Daley said. "They say the war's over if Vicksburg goes."

"The war won't be over till General Lee is beaten."

"He's a fox, isn't he," Mr. Daley said.

"More a wolf, I'd say."

"Smart, I mean."

"We'll see how smart," Rose said. "You advertised in the *Gazette* you had some bonbons."

"Stuyler's," Mr. Daley said, turning. "The very best. Sweets for the sweet." He would not have talked like this had someone else been in the store.

Mrs. Davenport came in, Peleg's mother. Stick-thin and graying, her cotton dress belling out enormously over her crinoline. A hard little woman, looking hard at Rose. Didn't know her son had helped a slave to freedom.

"How do you do," Rose said, smiling sweetly.

"Very good, thank you," said Mrs. Davenport.

"I'm glad," Rose said.

The bonbons came in a pale-blue satin-covered box. They cost steep at forty-five cents. The stationery went for fifteen.

"My, we're eatin handsome today," Mrs. Davenport said.

Another sweet smile from Rose. "Ain't we?" she said.

"Tell Doc I've a new shipment of silver nitrate," Mr. Daley called after her, as if to check Rose in her stroll to the door.

"I will indeed," she said over her shoulder.

Next stop was Smith, Bodfish, Swift, down on Water Street. A long dim room with oiled hardwood flooring, a restful smell of sawdust and feed. Cuts of meat under glass, shelves to the ceiling of canned food, crates and bushel baskets full of early-summer produce. Rose had Mr. Bodfish cut her two sirloin steaks, a side of ham, a side of bacon. The store was busy and Mr. Bodfish, always dour, glanced moodily at her as he worked behind the counter and did not offer to converse with her. Rose waited, motionless with her purse and basket, smiling a contented smile while the usual notice was taken of her. She bought peas, a head of lettuce, a bouquet of radishes pulled from the earth this morning. Greenbacks had arrived on the Vineyard but the merchants distrusted them and Rose paid in banknotes and hard money.

"That's a pretty shawl," Mr. Bodfish said, not looking at her, as he took her money. No one had heard him: he spoke that quietly.

"Grenadine silk," Rose said.

"It becomes you," he said, with his gaze still downcast.

Outside, in the dazzle of the seafront, she was hailed from across Union Street by Mr. Thomas Bradley, the wealthiest man in Holmes Hole, or so he was reputed.

"Miss Miranda," he said.

Rose's first impulse was to go to him but in another instant she thought *no* and waited right where she was. Mr. Bradley nodded as if granting her that choice and came across the street in his frock coat, face ruddy and damp, warm from the heat and coat.

"Good morning, sir," Rose said.

"You're looking spruce today," he said.

"Well thank you. I was sorry to hear of your whale ship." A lie. She wasn't sorry at all, though it was the *Alabama* that had sunk her, doing the despicable work of the Confederacy on the high seas.

"Do you know," he said, "they'd just killed a sperm whale. They'd stopped, of course, to cut it in. If they hadn't, that raider would never have come upon them."

"Maybe another would have."

Mr. Bradley looked at her, studying her for her meaning, for any intent of disrespect.

"It's a wonder any of them come home safe," she said. "I read in one of the newspapers . . ."

"Miss Miranda."

"Sir." She eyed him mildly, tolerant of the interruption.

"Is Dr. Chandler well?"

"A slight cough, is all. Is there a reason you ask?"

"I sent him a note last Saturday by my Betsy, inviting him to dinner. He declined, but gave no reason."

"He didn't have one to give."

"It wasn't the cough, then."

"No sir."

"I don't take it as an insult. I was only concerned as to his health."

"He prefers to keep to himself since the boys went off to the war."

"He was unsociable long before the war, Miss Miranda."

"His family's his comfort. That, and his work."

"Misses his wife, does he?"

"A whole lot."

"She was a Shaw, I hear."

"Yes sir."

"Wealthy."

"So they say."

"I don't suppose he'll remarry," Mr. Bradley said.

"I doubt it," Rose said.

"A pity."

"Oh, I don't know," Rose said, with just the hint of a smile. *Let them think it. I want them to. They want to think it, and they don't want to. Don't know what they want.* Then she saw, over Mr. Bradley's shoulder, Peter Daggett, and her smile vanished and she was glad suddenly of Mr. Bradley's presence. He, Peter, had come out of Fischer Brothers carrying a sealed can of paint. He was dressed for work, denims and a pullover shirt. Mechanic's cap set at a tilt on his shaggy head. He saw Rose and stopped. He shifted the heavy can from one hand to the other.

"Shall we walk along?" Rose said.

"I was going this way," Mr. Bradley said, nodding toward Water Street.

"Well, then," Rose said. "Good day."

"Good day, Miss Miranda."

She did not look back and did not know he'd been following her until she was halfway up Drummer Lane and he called to her from the bottom of the incline.

"Hey there."

Rose stopped. It would have been easy now to run on home and beat him there but she did not. She let some seconds go by in which her unfear of him—if unfear it was—would proclaim itself, then turned, with her parasol and basket.

"What is it," she said.

"I was just wonderin if you hear aught a Luke and Thomas." He had not brought the paint can.

"I believe you know the answer to that."

"Imagine you do hear from em."

"There's going to be a big battle," Rose said. "The biggest ever. They'll be in it. They and Elisha Smith."

Daggett grinned. "That little goober, Smith. Who'd of thought he'd be a fighter?"

"Surprising, who goes and who doesn't," Rose said.

A cloud crossed Daggett's face. "I'll go when I'm called," he said.

"Why wait?"

Daggett raised both hands to his cloth cap and readjusted it. "Cause I'm smart, that's why."

Rose smiled.

"You best not put on them airs with me," he said.

"I'll write to Luke, tell him you were asking after him."

"Take that fuckin look off your face."

"Oh my."

"I was tryin to be friendly."

"I'll tell Luke you were."

"Tell him I hope he don't get shot."

"Don't follow me anymore, Peter Daggett."

Daggett's grin resurfaced. "I told you: I was bein friendly."

"Don't follow me," she said and turned, faster than she wanted to, and went on up the lane, trying not to hurry.

"I've been practicing it," she said that night.

"You sing it beautifully."

"Oh, if these island boys would listen to it," she said. "It might shame them."

She had left the supper dishes for now and they'd adjourned to the back parlor and were drinking port. Rose had downed a glass and poured herself another while the doctor watched her with his worried smile. Rain smeared the mullioned window and whispered in the towering side-yard elm. Rose was tipsy halfway through the second glass and the voice inside her seemed to belong to someone else, a woman older and wiser than she, a woman blacker, more long-suffering. *Don't rile that Peter Daggett, Rosie. No more'n you would a snake that wasn't tryin to bite you. Maybe if you be, civil to him he'll think he's gettin enough of you to satisfy him. Remember: Luke isn't here.*

"Rose," Dr. Chandler said. Not Dr. Chandler; George. She was learning to say it. He sat in his easy chair to the side of the cold fireplace, cupping his wineglass in his small knotty hands. Rose sat opposite him. "If we should lose the war," he said, "you must, *must* go on living."

"I ain't gonna curl up and die."

"You know what I mean."

The song, sheet music from Ditson & Co. in Boston, from whom she ordered regularly, was taken up by that inner voice that was hers but not hers. *Mine eyes have seen the glory of the coming of the Lord. He is trampling out the vintage where the grapes of wrath are stored.*

"'He has loosed the fateful lightning,'" she said, "'of His terrible swift sword.'"

George smiled wanly. "If there *is* a God," he said. "If there *were* one."

"God is justice," Rose said. "The army is its weapon. Mr. Lincoln's army. You want to hear?"

"I know some of it, but go on."

"It's righteous," she said. "I'll speak it, so's you can get the words."

"Go on."

"'I have read a fiery gospel writ in burnished rows of steel,'" she said. "Fiery gospel! The god of justice doesn't play patty-cake, George."

"'. . . burnished rows of steel,'" he said. "'as you deal with my condemners . . .'"

"Con*tem*ners," Rose corrected.

"Ah."

"What are they?" she said. "Con*tem*ners."

"To contemn is to despise."

"Good. My despisers."

"Then?"

"'So with you my grace shall deal. Let the hero born of woman crush the serpent with his heel.'"

The doctor nodded thoughtfully. No, the god of justice did not play patty-cake. He remembered the glass in his lap and took a sip.

Rose drank too. The port was thick and sweet. It didn't burn going down like whiskey did. "Glory, glory, hallelujah," she said.

"Yes," he said, "glory hallelujah."

"The last verse is the best," Rose said.

"Sing it."

She lifted her glass. It was empty. How had that happened? Getting drunk. How did that last verse go, the best one? She remembered something else. "George," she said, "whyn't you go to dinner at Mr. Bradley's house when he invited you?"

"Don't start that," he said.

"You ought to, you know."

He'd finished his port. The decanter stood on the tea table in front of Rose. The doctor eyed it.

"Go on," she said. "We're drinking to the death of slavery."

"In that case, I will." He leaned forward, reached, grasped the decanter by its neck. The rain whispered down. He poured and then Rose took it from him and refilled her glass. She set the glass stopper in its neck.

"Mr. Bradley was wanting to know this morning. He spoke to me very politely."

"I told him I was indisposed."

"Indisposed could be anything."

The doctor lifted his glass and drank. "What I should have said is, I don't live alone."

Rose took his meaning and lowered her eyes.

"Or I should have said, we'd be delighted to come. Rose and I would be delighted."

"It would only make trouble," she said, and drank, hiding behind the uptilted glass.

"I don't care."

She set the glass down but did not look at him.

"Rosie . . ."

"You can't change what is."

"Yes you can. What's this war about otherwise?"

"Justice."

"See?"

"Not in Holmes Hole," she said.

"For you, I mean. As my friend. As . . ."

He broke off, looking down into the dark red circle of port. Dark red, like new blood. Rose doubted he could say it, prayed he wouldn't.

"I'm fifty-one years old," he said, circling around it. "As you know."

She wanted to laugh and kiss him on the cheek for his shyness, his delicacy. And now here came the hymn again, the verse she thought she'd forgotten, spoken by that wise colored woman's voice inside her that knew all there was to know about her. *In the beauty of the lilies Christ was born across the sea. . . .* That was it. In the beauty of the lilies.

"Elizabeth was younger than I," the doctor was saying. He still couldn't look at her. The gray twilight flashed dully on his spectacles. "A girl, really, though I never thought of her as such."

The voice was her own now, rising unstoppable, her fine mezzo-soprano, Rose could hear it before she began.

"She must have been a fine lady," she said. *In the beauty of the lilies . . .*

"She was. And so are you."

"Not a lady," she said.

He took some port, coughed, reached and set the glass down on the table, and coughed again. "I've told you you're a lady. How many times must I say it?"

"I remember it now," Rose said, and straightened, lifting her diaphragm, stretching and opening her throat, and sang.

> *In the beauty of the lilies Christ was born across the sea,*
> *With a glory in his bosom that transfigures you and me.*
> *As he died to make men holy, let us die to make men free*
> *While God is marching on . . .*

The doctor was watching her now, knobby face radiant with love and port, but at *let us die to make men free* his smile faltered, his brown eyes shifted behind their spectacles. Rose sang the verse out, her voice silvering the dimming air, even after she'd finished.

"Glory hallelujah," she said. The words had made her heart swell and harden.

"They must die, mustn't they?" the doctor said.

"Some."

"Luke and Thomas."

"No."

"Perhaps," he said.

"Perhaps nothing. God has other plans for Luke and Thomas."

"There was no stopping Thomas, was there?"

"You know there wasn't," she said.

"I suppose if I were another sort of father I could have."

"George, you listen to me. Our boys aren't going to die."

"Who can know?"

"I can."

"Perhaps you can. There *is* a power in you, Rosie."

"Witchery. Black witchery."

"Well," he said, "glory hallelujah."

"Glory, *glory* hallelujah," Rose said, and got up to see to the dishes, thinking *I'll break em I'm so drunk.*

FIFTEEN

Delia Wilkes stayed hidden in Mrs. Creedon's cellar until the Southrons moved on. Then William Stumpel drove her, in the night, to Gettysburg, where they intended to collect Floyd and head farther north, to Wrightsville, where Mrs. Creedon's sister lived. News of the abductions in Chambersburg had spread town to town, and most of Gettysburg's Africans had already fled, freeborn and runaway alike. They took to the dusty roads as refugees, some driving creaky wagons while others walked lugging blanket-gathered loads on their backs as big as feather mattresses, which bent them over almost double. Children stumbled along in the hoof- and foot-churned dust. Old men plodded, shuffled. Old women.

Most had left, but not all. Floyd Wilkes would not, for all his mother's pleadings. Floyd had a remunerative job as a waiter and dishwasher at the Globe Inn and the Globe's owner, Mr. Charles Will, had said he would protect his colored employees from the Rebels, should they come into Gettysburg.

How that Mr. Will gonna proteck you from General Lee?

I'm a free man, Momma, Floyd said, and I intend to act like one.

I a free woman and look what happen. Happen twice.

You got to speak up, Momma. Stand on your rights.

What rights?

William Stumpel had come inside and the three of them were sitting in the back room in the cool blue-gray light of the breaking dawn. William sat silently drinking a glass of buttermilk, eyes shifting gravely back and forth from Delia to Floyd, as each spoke. You could not tell what he was thinking, if anything. Being inside a colored house, clearly, in no way bothered him.

*Their residence at this time was on Long Lane, a narrow tiny wood-
frame building with a roofed front porch and a backyard garden for growing vegetables. Farmers' fields all around, the cemetery on its leafy hill in
the middle distance to the east.*

Why'd you go so sudden to Chambersburg? Floyd said.

See May Stevens and you know it. She poorly.

Trig said you got run off by some white ladies.

That Trig a black fool ain't know nothin.

You didn't know Cousin Stevens was poorly time you went.

I know now.

Oh, Momma, Floyd said.

*He was nineteen and had earned his diploma at the colored school, a
quick learner and a pious boy who read his Bible and attended the AME
Zion Church, which forbade dancing, attending circuses, and other such
frivolities. Floyd, though, had his flighty side: he wrote poetry, odes and
elegies full of summer flowers and rippling brooks and mantles of snow
and the like. Swans. Doves. Ladies with parasols.*

*Please come with us, son, Delia said. Your Bible learnin ain't matter
to them Southrons.*

I spit on them, Momma.

You spit on General Lee, see what happen.

*William Stumpel had finished his buttermilk. It had left him a butter-
milk mustache. General Lee ain't God, he said.*

Floyd and Delia looked at him. Floyd smiled. You see, Momma?

*Delia brought up a sigh. William Stumpel a fine boy, but he ain't know
much.*

Know General Lee ain't God, William said.

You're damn right he's not, Floyd said.

Please, Son.

Better eat some breakfast, Momma. You've got a journey ahead of you.

To the west, in the narrow gaps cleaving the Blue Ridge, the cavalry
were running at each other, fighting on each side to prevent reconnais-
sance and keep secret the whereabouts of its main army. Marching north
from Thoroughfare Gap the men of the Twentieth could hear the shoot-

ing in the distance, and sometimes the thunderlike bellowing of cannon. It put the new men on edge, but the veterans said it was just cavalry and to pay it no mind.

"Chicken thieves," Elisha said. "Rob a barn, and away they go."

"Think about it," said Matt Stackpole. "Where was the cavalry at Fredericksburg? Where were they at Chancellorsville? They aren't anywhere there's real fightin."

"They're out scoutin is where they are."

"Scoutin barns and cribs. They eat good, them boys."

"What I hate," Merriman said, "you got to get out a their way, how they come gallivantin by, kickin up the dust or mud or whatever. Like they was all officers."

The dirt road traversed the usual weed-grown fields and deep woods. The sky was overcast, a flat sodden gray. The cavalry fighting rattled on, swaying closer and then back again, and after a while it was behind them and then out of hearing.

In the afternoon the rain began, and they unrolled their gum blankets and cloaked themselves, tying the blankets in front, and went on. The road began to muck up, clinging to their shoes, then turned glutinous, a yellow-brown paste that gave under their weight, sucking at their feet as they trudged, staggering sometimes in the deep-sliced ruts of the wagons that had gone before.

"Ain't this fun," McNamara said.

"Sit in the sun three days and march in the rain," someone said.

The rain pattered on their knapsacks and the stiff rubber blankets and drowned out all sounds but the jostle of canteens and cups, which clinked with a dull and sullen persistence. Once Thomas had to run into the woods and squat; Luke wanted to wait with him but Thomas said no with so much vehemence that Luke shrugged and remained with the column, wondering if Eros had put some backbone in Thomas.

They passed through a huddled town—the sign said Middleburg—the wide road all mud now and cut with watery ruts. It was a handsome town that the war hadn't scarred, redbrick and fieldstone residences, white-shingle stores with second stories and balconies, two churches. Not a soul to be seen in the steady rain. The column went right on through and just beyond, on the porch of a redbrick farmhouse and spilling out across its front yard, were some two score wounded troopers. Those in the yard were on litters of straw. Some lay fetally under a cloak or blanket, asleep or unconscious or unmindful of the rain on their faces. Others sat, wrapped in cloaks or blankets, staring sullenly at the passing column. Some wore straw hats, some forage caps. You could not see their wounds unless it was a leg or arm and then only the blood that had soaked through, copious and almost black in this wet gray light. The house door was open and in both front windows glowed the thin light of candles.

"You boys cheer up," Merriman called out to them. "You're goin home."

Below a window lay a scattering of amputated arms and legs. A few of the legs, taken off high, wore a pant leg and boot. The rest, arms and legs, were naked and white in their blood, and they looked alive, on the point of writhing and squirming, as if presently the legs would right themselves and hop, the slack hands open and grip.

"Don't look," Luke said, but Thomas already had.

"You get used to it," Elisha said. "Then all you think is, you're glad it ain't you."

They were past the farmhouse now, moving out into open country.

"I guess *those* cavalry fought," Luke said.

"I guess they did," Elisha said.

After another mile they came on a group of Rebel prisoners who had perhaps stopped and gotten out of the way as the army had overtaken them. They stood ranged along the road like spectators at a parade, weaponless of course, some in gray wool cloaks with yellow cavalry piping, some without even shell jackets against the rain. A guard of cavalry stood by with drawn carbines, supervising this parade watch as if they'd brought the Rebels here for just that purpose. The Rebs, thin and bedraggled and wet as they were, spoke boldly to the soldiers passing.

"God*damn* it's a big army."

"Won't be so big after Marse Robert gets aholt of em."

"Abolitionist sonsabitches."

"Nigger fuckers."

When they'd left them behind, Luke said, "Bastards."

"Our men talk as bad," Thomas said.

"Not all of them."

"Jake does. Mac. Lots of them."

"It's different," Luke said.

"How?"

"Mac don't go in for whippin em," Elisha said.

"Some he might," Merriman said. "Them uppity ones."

"That's ignorant talk, Joe," Luke said.

"Well, I never said I was no Greek philosopher," Merriman said.

The rain came down harder. It soaked the wild meadows and cultivated fields, the bottle-green forests. The farm fields here were marked off by walls of jagged black stone. They passed an undamaged field of ripening corn but no one broke rank to steal an ear, as if the weather somehow precluded it. In the distance rose the silhouette of the Blue Ridge, indistinct and ghostly in the veil of the rain, with Robert E. Lee moving somewhere behind it.

Gum Springs, Virginia
June 25, 1863

My dearest Rosie,

I write to you lying on my belly in Elisha's & J. McNamara's shelter tent wch they have graciously allowed for a time tho Mac says No more than 20 minutes. It is raining you see & Thomas & I have no tent having unwisely abandoned ours when Thomas got the heat stroke altho I don't know what else we could have done at the time. It is dark but I have a candle & my knapsack for a writing desk & how the rain does beat on the sides of this tiny tent! Thomas & I will have to sleep out in it if it doesn't let up, think of that!

We marched today & in the afternoon passed some wounded cavalry hurt, they say, when Jeb Stuart's horse artillery surprised them. They looked very young & forlorn sitting & lying outside in the rain & watched us pass with little or no interest, like they'd gone over into another world & none of this mattered to them anymore.

It was a terrible long march today. Some of the boys say 25 mi
& most of it in the rain wch tho disagreeable was far better than the
heat wch laid so many low. We are all muddy to the knees & our shoes
soggy & some of the boys' falling apart as tho made of cardboard.
Thomas stood the march very well. He is growing up I think.

Rosie I don't have much time but I wanted to write a few words
as I don't know when the next mail will go out, we never do know, &
it can be damned annoying. Tomorrow we are expected to cross the
Potomac R. at a place called Edwards Ferry & the boys are much
excited at the prospect of being Home in the Union again & not to
have to look any more at these surly Virginians & be subject to their
taunts & vitriol & hateful stares. Even I feel the excitement for altho
it has been but a few weeks since we arrived in Va. it feels like years.
All the boys say Wait till Bobby Lee fights us on our own ground, he
will find out what we are truly made of. There is some puzzlement
among us, we do not know where we are going nor why & the boys
don't think much of Genl Hooker any more, but they are confident
in themselves & that is what matters. They say Genl Ewell is near
Harrisburg, where the citizens are building fortifications & arming
themselves & and that only makes the boys madder. Anyway Rosie
there will be a fight soon & I thank God—I am feeling religious of
late—that I will have—

"Hey. Twenty minutes."

It was McNamara, on his knees at the tent entrance. The candle lit
his wet stubbled face. He was wrapped in his gum blanket and the rain
ran off his forage cap.

"Lemme in," he said.

"Five more minutes," Luke said.

"You writin a damn book? Lemme in."

"All right," Luke said.

But then Elisha leaned down over McNamara's shoulder. "Let him
finish, Mac."

"I didn't say he couldn't finish."

"He can't write with you right up next to him."

"Five minutes," Luke said.

"What'll you give me?"

"Nothin," Elisha said.

"Half a ration a coffee," McNamara said.

"Shit, Mac," Elisha said.

"All right," Luke said. "Half a ration of coffee."

"Why do you act so?" Elisha said, straightening.

"It's my goddamn dogtent," McNamara said. He stood up, and he and Elisha were lost to sight. "Who's he writin to, anyway?"

"Never you mind."

"Got a pigeon to home, I suppose."

"Never mind," Elisha said.

—a hand in crushing the Rebellion, Luke wrote.

We saw Hancock up close today. Well I have seen him of course but not close up & today he rode down the column in the rain—he was wrapped in a cloak & and wore a slouch hat pulled down low—with his various staff members, adjutant & aide-de-camp & the like, & he is made to command a Corps if anyone ever was, sitting erect & Godlike on his jetblack horse & with yet a very human light in his fierce eyes that lets you know he approves of & loves his men tho he drives us hard. They say he is as brave as Agamemnon & uses the foulest language in the heat of battle & makes no apology later. Of all the Corps cmdrs he is the best except perhaps for Genl Reynolds of the 1st Corps who is more gentlemanly in his demeanor & not so lionlike as Hancock. With Genls like Hancock & Reynolds we will come through just grand I have no doubt.

Rosie I must close now. How we are going to sleep in this rain I don't know. The land hereabouts is low & swampy & Thomas & I will be practically under water. Thomas is still plagued by the aforementioned problem but 1/2 the Army is I think. Nobody cares to go to a surgeon with this complaint as it is embarrassing & the remedy invariably calomel, turpentine, castor oil or the like wch they say is a torture worse than the runs. I myself have never been healthier.

You are in our thoughts constantly.

Yr devoted
Luke

The rain stopped, miraculously, it seemed, a few minutes before taps, and Luke and Thomas lay down side by side on their rubber blankets, stripped to their drawers, under their rain-soaked wool blankets. There was a stream close by and along it graceful trees with waxy starlike leaves which Henry Wilcox said were gum trees, and they could hear the purl and rustle of the swollen stream and the rainwater dripping from the trees. They could hear snoring from inside the little shelter tents. There'd been no dry wood to be found, and so no fires. The invisible moon thinned the darkness faintly.

"Luke."

"What."

"Did you tell Rose about the arms and legs?"

"No, nor the Rebel prisoners."

"I'm afraid I'm going to dream about arms and legs. Like I did the bones."

"Think about Violet."

"Lilac."

"Think about *her* legs."

"She had pretty ones."

"Not too skinny?"

"Not too."

They lay awhile, listening to the wet sounds.

"She doesn't hate Negroes," Thomas said.

"Who doesn't?"

"Lilac."

"What did she have slaves for?"

"Her father had them. Then she and Iris let them go."

"That's something, I guess," Luke said.

"She's a nice girl," Thomas said. "Just ignorant, like you say."

"All right."

"Maybe that's all it ever is," Thomas said. "Ignorance."

"If that's all it was we wouldn't need this war."

Thomas didn't say anything.

"It's beyond ignorance to own a human being," Luke said. "To whip them. Brand them. Cut off their ears. Sell them away from their families. You think General Lee is ignorant?"

"He doesn't do those things."

"He tolerates them. Fights those trying to stop it."

"I know," Thomas said softly.

"I wish it *was* just ignorance," Luke said.

"I wish so too," Thomas said.

They crossed the river in the light of a three-quarter moon, raising cheers as they stepped from the corduroyed bridge ramp onto Maryland soil, hoarse frothy outbursts that carried back across the moon-glittering water like the sounds from some great match or game or horse race. Bonfires had been built on the riverbanks to help light the column across the bridge. On the Virginia side, stretching up from the bank, was the enormous fleet of wagons that had brought the pontoons and timbers, their hundreds of mules, their army of Negro teamsters. Many of the teamsters stood along the road in the dark, watching the army pass with the wordless inscrutable interest that puzzled so many of the white men, irritated so many.

"It's the one thing this army does right, is build a bridge," Merriman said, out in the middle of the river.

"Ain't this somethin?" Elisha said.

The bridge swayed heavily beneath them, the pontoons shifting this way and that on the slippery surface of the river. But the bridge was solid, all right. The planking had been covered with straw, and it deadened the noise of their measured tramp, route step, decreed by a guard of engineers as they went up the abutment onto the bridge, the order repeated as each new company passed.

"Be some good boys alive today if we'd had a bridge at Ball's Bluff," Stackpole said.

The Bluff, and Harrison's Island, were a couple of miles downriver. Elisha looked in that direction and shook his head. He'd been sixteen. Peleg still alive, blasphemous and comical as ever, and Bart Crowell with both his legs.

"We crossed in scows and rowboats," Stackpole said. "I'll let you imagine how we got back under fire, Luke."

"We read about it," Luke said.

Elisha remembered a scow, overloaded and sitting low in the water, and an officer standing in her square end with his revolver drawn promising to shoot any man who tried to lift himself aboard. And boys swimming for it, the current running them downriver, their shouts for help before they drowned. He and Bart and Peleg and Mac had gotten across in a rowboat, Mac cussing a blue streak all the way.

"This goddamn army," McNamara said behind them. "Every order was gave that day was stupid."

"Well, we'll be home in a minute," Elisha said. "Listen to them cheers."

The bank was low all along the Maryland side and thickly wooded, the trees black against the sky. The fires near the bridge leapt and snapped and sent their sparks flying up the sky. Colonel Hall sat on his horse watching the column stream off the bridge and onto the road through the woods. They went down the ramp and, stepping on the riverbank, which was flat as a beach and covered in little stones, Luke felt the solidity of the Union underfoot, where a Negro could live free and where slavery found the opprobrium that was its due. They were cheering now, roaring *Hurraaaah,* and Luke too opened his throat and yelled till it burned, and knew he was part of this army now.

The road was pale gray through the woods and still wet from yesterday's rain, and the men and wagons going before had churned it to mortar. The cheer died and another rose behind them and they marched on in the sticky mud, the darkness between the trees.

"We'll see us some pretty girls now, boys," Merriman said. "No more a them Southron beanpoles."

"They aren't all beanpoles, are they, Elisha?" said Stackpole.

Laughter in the ranks ahead and behind. Luke smiled. It had gotten around about Lilac and Iris but there'd been no chaffing until now. Now they were in the mood.

"Thomas," Stackpole said, "what was the girls' names?"

"Never you mind," Thomas said.

"Them girls was beanpoles, for sure," Merriman said, "but they warn't bad to look at."

"I never saw em," Stackpole said.

"They was hard-lookin girls," Merriman said. "If Elisha and Tommy hadn't of jumped em, them girls would of jumped *them*."

Luke looked at Thomas in the dark and found he was smiling.

"They're jealous, Thomas," he said.

"Damn right I'm jealous," Stackpole said. "I'm a horny sonofabitch. You still got them books, Joe?"

"They're gone," Merriman said. "I got tired of em, way you do of a woman."

"I misdoubt you ever had a woman long enough to get tired of her."

"Sure I did. I had a smart chance of em."

"Bullshit you did."

"It's good to be home, ain't it, boys?" Merriman said.

They bivouacked a mile from the river and Sergeant Cate took six privates back to the shore on picket, including Luke, Thomas, and Elisha, who had volunteered when Cate called Thomas forward. Jake Rivers was another. They loaded their muskets and went back down the gummy road, which was empty now, all three corps having come across. Night birds called softly in the woods. An owl cried. No one had slept much on the wet night previous and Elisha felt a delicious physical lightness, a bit like drunkenness but without the dullness in his mind. He felt alert, in fact, attuned to the night sounds and the warm sweet forest air, which he breathed like perfume. He was happy and not happy, a peculiar combination of contentment and yearning that he had known before but never to such a strong degree. He was *alive,* and he felt it keenly.

The engineers were dismantling the bridge, assisted by the teamsters, lugging timbers on their shoulders with a man at either end, while others hauled up the anchors of the pontoon boats and poled the boats to the Maryland shore. Their voices, instructing one another or cursing the weight of an anchor or timber, traveled on the water and Elisha thought again of the voices on Lagoon Pond and wondered what the science of it was.

Sergeant Cate led the detail away from the bridge and along the riverbank, the stones crunching and skritching underfoot. Rivers was shoeless still but didn't seem to mind the stones. The Virginia shore was higher now, dark and rolling. They could not see any houses. After a mile Cate stopped them and ordered Luke and William Crocker, the Cape Codder who'd come down with him and Thomas, to walk the first beat. The rest of them retreated to the edge of the forest and hunted around for wood and built a fire. Cate had brought a tin can with a bail and they scooped water out of the Potomac and threw some coffee into it and boiled it.

"I got some playing cards if any of you girls are interested," Cate said.

"What stakes?" Rivers said. "I got exactly one dollar two cents to my name."

"Penny a hand."

"Half a penny," Rivers said.

"All right."

The card game began. Elisha had declined to play and he and Thomas drifted down to the river, bringing their rifles. They found a grayed log that had been thrown ashore in some flood and sat down on it with their guns leaning beside them.

"Remember that thing's loaded," Elisha said.

"I don't guess it'll go off by itself."

"No, but you got to be mindful," Elisha said.

They sat awhile. They could hear the card players behind them, Sergeant Cate making wry remarks and laughing, Rivers cursing. Another of them, a boy named Ditchfield, cursed nearly as prolifically as Rivers.

"You think about Lilac any?" Elisha said.

"Sure I do," Thomas said.

"I been thinkin on Iris from the time we come ashore here. She ain't been out of my thoughts. It's why I volunteered for picket. I wanted to come back down here and look across to where she's at." He looked at Thomas. "You feel that way?"

"Kind of."

"No you don't," Elisha said.

"I do."

"For a time I thought it was just screwin and it could of been anybody. Then I started thinkin about her, and not the screwin. The things she said, and what she looked like. Told me if all abolitionists was as nice as me then she was on the wrong side of the war."

Thomas smiled.

"I been imaginin," Elisha said, "what it'd be like to desert, go back and work that tannery for em."

"You'd be hanged in about two days," Thomas said.

"I know. It's just imaginin."

"After the war you can go back."

"You said you was comin with me."

"I'll come."

"I don't know I'd want to travel that far alone."

"It'll be different from wartime," Thomas said. "No partisans. You could ride a train straight down to Alexandria or Fredericksburg."

"Bring em home on the train," Elisha said. "Get a steamboat over from New Bedford." He saw the girls on the deck of the *Canonicus*, ladylike in bonnets and dresses and button boots. French parasols to shade their faces. In this waking dream, which was not new, he and Thomas were dressed like gentlemen, vests and checked trousers, cuff links and shirt studs and watch chains, starched collars. (Elisha had never worn a collar.) Bowler or derby hats. It was summertime, a fine day, the island jewel-green and the sea and sky their own soft blues and utterly tranquil. Home.

"If we married em," he said, "you and me'd be kin."

Thomas smiled. "Let's don't jump ahead to marrying."

"It's just imaginin," Elisha said.

SIXTEEN

When Jubal Early came to Gettysburg the first time, which was four days before the battle, his cavalry arrived in advance, pouring into town on Chambersburg Street, whooping and hollering and discharging revolvers into the air like celebrants heralding a parade. There'd been distant shooting earlier, the Twenty-sixth Pennsylvania Militia having been called out to try their luck against this substantial segment of Lee's army, then a pregnant silence of an hour or more, and now a sound like the rumble of thunder on the horizon.

The girls at the Young Ladies' Seminary were at their literary exercises. It was three and a quarter in the afternoon. Mrs. Eyster heard the great noise and her eyes grew round and without a word she made for the door, with the girls piling after her, all gathering on the front portico, from which they could see, up the hill near the Theological Seminary, the dark, seething, hard-charging mass of the Rebel cavalry.

Mrs. Eyster clapped her hands. Run home! she said. As fast as ever you can, children!

And they did, not even pausing to collect their slates and schoolbooks, scampering this way and that, and now the pistol shots erupted behind them, staccato, like strings of fireworks on the Fourth of July. East on High Street ran Tillie McCurdy, then south on Baltimore. The streets were still damp from the rain and soft and pliant underfoot. There was no dust. Her father was shuttering his butcher shop and he came out and locked the door and pocketed the key and he and Tillie hurried into their house on the corner of Baltimore and Breckenridge, breathless. The door was unlocked and her father left it so.

It will only make them suspicious, he said. As if we had something to hide.

Tillie's mother and sister had shuttered the sitting room and gone back to the kitchen.

Thank God, her mother said, laying her hand over her heart.

Feeling safe now with Mr. McCurdy home the family went to the sitting room, which was dim and very warm with the shutters drawn, and James McCurdy peeked out through a crack. A mud-deadened pounding of hooves, and then a string of riders floated quickly by, like ragged dun-colored ghosts.

Where are the militia? said Margaret McCurdy.

Scattered, I imagine, said James.

Well that's just fine, isn't it.

This is Lee's army, Margaret. The Army of Northern Virginia.

Well, what do we have a militia for?

James made no answer. He was still watching through the sun-filled gap between the shutters. A final horseman cantered past. James turned from the window. It was quiet now on Baltimore Street but they could hear hoofbeats on other blocks, distant yelling, a pistol shot.

Young Floyd Wilkes is under our porch, he said.

Margaret McCurdy looked at him. What on earth is he doing there? she said.

I've hidden him. He was walking to the Globe. He works there, you know. I told him he'd never make it before the Rebels came into the Diamond.

And what of that? Margaret said.

You know what's been happening.

It's none of our concern, said Margaret.

Floyd's a nice boy, James said.

His mother's a you-know-what.

What? Annie said.

I know what, Tillie said.

Hush the both of you, their mother said.

Well I think Floyd's nice even if he is a darky, Tillie said.

He's a good pious boy, James said. Be a shame if they took him.

I don't believe those stories, Margaret said. I don't believe they're taking any but runaways.

It's wicked even so, Tillie said.

It's Mr. Will ought to be worrying about it, not us, Margaret said. He wants to hire darkies, let him protect them.

He's only under our porch, Margaret. We can deny we knew anything about it.

And so we will, Margaret said.

General Early arrived a half hour later with the two thousand men of General Gordon's brigade. The bulk of them stopped on Chambersburg Street and General Early came into the Diamond with his aides and a guard and a regimental band and sent a couple of riders to the courthouse with a demand that the mayor come right away to negotiate the surrender of the town. It was David Kendlehart who came, accompanied by Swinton Kesey. They walked up Baltimore Street in the waning heat of the afternoon and found General Early on the verandah of the Gettysburg Hotel, rocking and fanning himself with his plumed hat. The band, seven or eight men, was arrayed in the middle of the square playing "The Bonnie Blue Flag," drums and fifes and a blatting cornet. The Rebels had run their flag up the Diamond flagpole. There were horses tied all about, and soldiers on the lookout. The soldiers were lean and dirty and grim-faced, with a slouching grace about them and a light in their eye both fearless and cold, and Kendlehart wondered if the Union army could stand up to them. He wondered if any army could. He and Kesey climbed the steps to the verandah. General Early did not get up, nor did any in his entourage of officers. He did not invite the two men to sit down. General Early in his ash-gray uniform and gold braid. Jubal Early in Gettysburg.

Mr. Mayor, he said.

I'm David Kendlehart, president of the city council, and this is Swinton Kesey, a council member. Mayor Martin is out of town.

Out of town.

Yes sir.

The mayor.

Yes sir.

The general leaned and spat. Y'all got yourself a goddamn poltroon for a mayor, ain't you.

He's away on business, sir.

Shit, said the general.

Kendlehart and Kesey looked at each other and both shrugged. The Rebel band had stopped playing, but Kendlehart did not remember when. General Early was thickset, with a graying bushy beard and a stoop to his shoulders that seemed to pain him when he moved.

Well, he said, reaching beside him without looking, here's what I want. An officer put a piece of paper in his gloved hand. General Early handed the list to Kendlehart, who had to step forward to take it. It was quiet as he read it, Kesey reading too over his shoulder. The wicker rockers went back and forth, gnawing softly at the wooden flooring. General Early fanned himself.

Good God, Kendlehart said.

Pardon? said the general.

We can't possibly provide all of this. We don't have it.

There aren't seven thousand pounds of bacon in the whole county, Kesey said. Nor a thousand pounds of sugar. Nor any of it.

That a fact? said the general. Well, I'll tell you what, then. Y'all open them fat Yankee banks of yours and pony up—let's see—say five thousand dollars.

Again the two councilmen looked at each other. We can't, Kendlehart said.

Well you better. I'm in the mood to burn this goddamn town.

The banks have all moved the bulk of their monies. To Baltimore, mostly. Some to Philadelphia. They knew you were coming, General.

Early looked at the officer beside him, a major wearing a forage cap. Seems like they're afraid of us up here, don't it.

Seems like it, sir.

Well, Mr. Kindlinwood, what idea have you got that might dissuade me from burnin Gettysburg, Pennsylvania, to the goddamn ground?

We'll open our stores to you, Kendlehart said. Take or buy, it's up to you.

General Early considered it, squinting across at the redbrick dry goods store of John Schick, who had, as David Kendlehart knew, shipped most of his inventory to Philadelphia. It wasn't just the bankers who had anticipated the Rebel invasion.

Well shit, the general said. Be the easiest thing, under the circumstances.

*Kendlehart and Kesey exchanged another look. You agree, then, Kendle-
hart said.*

I do.

*Very good, sir, said Kendlehart. I only hope you'll give us some time to
explain to everybody.*

Time to hide things, you mean.

No sir.

We'll be along right quick, said the general. And Mr. Kindlinwood—

Sir?

I find any runaway niggers I'll take em or shoot em, one.

All the niggers here are freeborn.

How many you got?

*Couple hundred. Most of them have left town. There's a few work at the
Globe Inn, back of this hotel. They're good boys. Don't bother anybody.*

They got manumission papers?

They were born here, sir.

*General Early nodded dubiously and reached inside his coat and
brought out a gold watch on its chain. I'll be sendin details in an hour.
Foragers. Y'all be ready to welcome em with Christian benevolence.*

*Floyd Wilkes, in his little hiding place, heard the talk in the street as word
spread from block to block that the stores were to be opened to the Southerners. He heard Mr. McCurdy unlock the butcher shop and leave it unlocked.*

Floyd, he said.

Yes sir, Floyd said, down in the dark.

You stay put now. They'll be all over here in just a few minutes.

Hi, Floyd, Tillie said.

Hello, Miss Tillie.

*They went into the house and pretty soon Floyd heard the shuffle of foot-
steps and the clink of equipment and the ribald-sounding voices of the soldiers as they moved from shop to shop, helping themselves. He heard them
go into the butcher shop and come tramping out again laden, he pictured,
with whole haunches of beef and mutton, whole hams. There were cracks
in the stone foundation—Mr. McCurdy had removed a rock to let Floyd in
and jammed it back in place—letting in shards of white daylight but none
large enough to peer out of.*

We gawn eat good tonight, someone said.

Officers gawn take the most of it, said another.

No they ain't.

The alien voices—Mississippi, Alabama, Louisiana; who knew?—seemed to strike at Floyd's lower vitals and the result was a terrific need to urinate. It grew and he slid over in the dark and, lying on his side, unbuttoned and relieved himself in the powdery dirt. He slid back again but the odor followed him and at that moment, with his bladder comfortable again and the smell of his own urine in his nose, Floyd recalled his decision to remain in Gettysburg and the defiance behind it, and now he saw the ignominy of what he was doing, hiding under a house like a runaway slave with a reward on his head when he was a free man, educated, Bible-read, and well known to God. The Southerners were capturing free men, it was true, but those would be the helpless ones, his own mother an example, the ignorant and the docile who in fact spoke the broken English of slaves and could be passed off as such when it came time to sell them. They could not make a slave of Floyd Wilkes. He would die first.

It grew dark, pitch-black under the porch, and Floyd lay there and once nearly went to sleep before a passing wagon woke him. Then Mr. McCurdy came out and knelt down and pried the rock free and Floyd crawled out powdered with the strange gray-brown dirt that never saw rain or daylight.

I thank you, Mr. McCurdy, he said, and commenced to slap the dust off himself.

They never searched our house, Mr. McCurdy said. If I'd known that . . .

I've no complaint, Floyd said.

The militia ran like rabbits, apparently. A boy was killed. Shot in the back as he ran. Others were captured.

The Army of the Potomac won't run, Floyd said.

I wonder where they'll fight, Mr. McCurdy said.

Mrs. McCurdy stood in the doorway, in its screen of pale gold light. James, she said.

Evening, Mrs. McCurdy, Floyd said.

Good evening, she said.

You'd best go on, Floyd, Mr. McCurdy said. Be careful, though. There may be soldiers still about.

All right, Floyd said, but listen. I'm going to enlist.

They stared at him.

Enlist? Mrs. McCurdy said. Enlist how?

There are Negro regiments now, Margaret, her husband said.

Negro regiments?

Yes ma'am, Floyd said. Several of them.

Heavens, she said.

And then, Floyd said, I'm going to further my education. Might be I'll go to divinity school.

That's quite a plan, Mr. McCurdy said.

I formed it under the porch.

You hear that, Margaret? Under our own porch.

James, I do wish you'd come inside to your supper.

Good night, Floyd, Mr. McCurdy said. You watch out, now. They haven't gone far.

I'm not afraid of them, Floyd said.

Maryland was a slave state but here, suddenly, the white people were glad to see them and the Negroes no more than curious, studying their faces as the column passed, as if trying to divine some hidden purpose in their marching here, some agenda that did not meet the eye and that might not be entirely beneficial to colored people. No hymns were offered as the army rolled by, no cries went up of "Jubilo."

It was the whites who called out to them, who smiled and waved. In Poolesville and Barnsville, country towns huddled along dusty tree-shaded thoroughfares, American flags hung from second-story windows and pretty girls leaned out, smiling and fluttering handkerchiefs. Full rain barrels had been dragged to the roadside for the men to dip out of or fill their canteens. Girls handed out sandwiches and pies, the men taking them up in their dirty hands and wolfing them down as they marched. In the towns the brigade bands struck up, and if you were in earshot of the music, as Luke and Thomas sometimes were, you could feel your heart lift, could feel it fill with optimism and love of country. Schoolchildren stood in neat rows, waving tiny American flags and watching with such respect and wonder it might have been a procession of storybook heroes passing in front of them, knights from King Arthur or the demigods from their child's Homer.

"It warn't like this last time we was up here," Elisha said.

"They weren't scared of the Rebs," Stackpole said. "Now they got the sense to appreciate us."

"What's wrong with the niggers, they ain't glad to see us?"

"They ain't been freed, that's what's wrong with em. Old Abe's proclamation don't apply to em."

"It will," Luke said.

Then McNamara went too far, he pushed Luke beyond where Luke was going to stand for it. Maybe he thought he was entitled to say what he would, now they were home in their own free country, or maybe the reticence written in the quiet faces of these Maryland Negroes stirred something in him. Some need to be caustic. They'd put Barnsville behind them, were in the country again.

"When the war's over," Luke said, "there won't be slavery anywhere."

"Luke's gonna marry one," McNamara said, marching two ranks behind Luke and Thomas. "Marry him a black wench can't read nor write."

"Luke ain't that far gone," Merriman said.

"I bet so," Mac said. "Have him a good time, won't you, Luke? A nigger woman'll do you all day long, I hear."

Luke spun out of line without a word, dropping his musket, shedding his knapsack, and took McNamara by the collar of his sack coat, and swung him over into the roadside weeds, and while he staggered, off balance and weighted by his knapsack, Luke hit him. McNamara doubled over and turned away and Luke threw himself on him and drove him to the ground, McNamara still harnessed to the knapsack, and Luke punched him in the face, punched him again, and then Sergeant Cate swung his musket and the world slewed and went dark and Luke woke up in the grass and thistles, blind, trying to make out what was being said over him.

McNamara had clambered to his feet and was being held by Elisha and Merriman and Thomas. Luke's punches had bruised his jaw and scraped his chin and forehead bloody. Cate grabbed Luke's arm and hauled him to his feet.

"You stupid bastard," he said.

Luke shook his head, trying to see. The back of his skull was vibrating like a bell.

"Get back in column," Cate said.

It was a disciplined army and it kept moving, the men staring as they passed, taking it in without comment.

"Smith," Cate said, "Merriman. Move. You too, Tommy. Quick, you sonsabitches, before the lieutenant comes up."

The three snatched up their muskets and ran to catch up to their ranks. Cate lifted Luke's knapsack and helped him shoulder it. Luke could see now but his head was throbbing. He felt it: a lump rising. Cate put his musket in his hand. McNamara touched the raw places on his face and looked at the blood on his fingers.

"Get in column," Cate said. "If there's any more of it I'll arrest you."

"You'll pay, you sonofabitch," McNamara said.

"He already did," Cate said. "Now *git*."

A pair of officers was coming, Paine and Captain Abbott, at the tail of the regiment. The blow to his head had killed Luke's rage and he understood the jeopardy he was in and took off forward at a jog. McNamara ran ahead of him.

"Sergeant Cate," Paine said.

"Sir," Cate said, turning.

"What was all that?"

"A little fracas, sir. It's over."

They were moving, route step, Cate to the right of Lieutenant Paine with his musket shouldered.

"Chandler and McNamara," Paine said.

Abbott laughed.

"I don't know how it started, sir," Cate said.

"If it starts again I'll buck and gag both of them."

"Yes sir."

"I'd enjoy doing it. I hear Chandler's quite the abolitionist."

"Sir, I haven't discussed it with him."

"You tell those two idiots what'll happen if they fight again."

"I will sir."

"Go on tell them right now," Paine said.

South Mountain now imprinted the sky to the west, rising distantly, smoke-blue, gently rolling. Lee behind it somewhere, there was no doubt of that now. The Maryland roads were good. The farms of course were undamaged, and fields of grain and corn and tobacco stretched out amber and gem-green. Cattle grazed on the hillsides and smoke rose peacefully from farmhouses of red- and white-painted brick.

Luke marched in silence the rest of that day. Thomas, beside him, said nothing. Nor did Elisha, in front. The unfairness of their reproachful silence, if that's what it was, irritated Luke but his head hurt and he knew talking would aggravate it, and anyway if they didn't like what he'd done they could both go to hell.

They broke ranks to rest and fill their canteens from a stream, and Luke sat apart from Elisha and Thomas and didn't look their way. He filled his hat and let the cold water rinse the lump on his head and it froze the pain a little. He ate a hard cracker. No one spoke to him. He wondered why and then thought of Rose and imagined her sitting beside him, lifting her skirt perhaps to put her slender feet in the water, and wondered what she would say about John McNamara.

They made camp in farm country beside the winding Monocacy River with the spires and steeples of a town or city poking up above the treetops lower down to the west. At roll call Paine told them that they had marching orders for four in the morning. They built fires but the march today had been a hard one and, as so often happened, very few bothered to pitch their tents.

Thomas was speaking to Luke now but did not mention McNamara until they went to the river at twilight to wash. They stripped off their shirts and knelt and splashed themselves. They'd used the last of their soap and the sutlers had been sent away so there was no way to buy more. With a sopping rag Luke gingerly mopped the back of his head. Around them men bathed, soaked and wrung out shirts, talked quietly.

Luke and Thomas sat down and inspected their shirts for graybacks.

"He doesn't mean it," Thomas said.

"Who doesn't?" Luke said.

"Mac. It's just talk. Trying to get your goat."

"Why do you take up for him?" Luke said.

"You take up for Jake."

"Jake doesn't know any better."

"Neither does Mac."

Elisha came down the riverbank. There were willows along it, and grazing cattle had kept the ground unthicketed and parklike. Elisha sat down and took off his shoes. He unbuttoned his shirt.

"How's your head, Luke?"

"He could have hit me harder, I guess."

"Joe said Cate did you a favor," Thomas said. "Said Paine would've arrested you sure if he'd seen it."

"I hope I don't get too many more favors from Cate," Luke said.

Elisha grinned. He was stepping out of his pants, his drawers. They watched him mince, naked, into the water.

"Colder'n hell," he said.

"Does Mac want to fight me?" Luke said.

Elisha sat down in the water, grimacing. "Damn that's cold," he said.

"Does he?" Luke said.

"Hell," Elisha said. "He's afeard of you, Luke. Don't you know that?"

Luke stared at him. He looked away, downriver.

Jake Rivers came down the bank, barefoot still, after all these days and miles. His feet looked like a Negro's, they were so begrimed and sunburned. He sat down.

"Hear Cate almost took your head off," he said.

"He gave it a good tap," Luke said.

"I can see he did. You ask me, it's about time somebody took care a that sonofabitch McNamara."

"He ain't a sonofabitch," Elisha said.

"He ain't? I swear, Elisha. If you hadn't of fucked that girl down at Thoroughfare Gap I'd worry over you."

"Who says I fucked her," Elisha said.

"Well did you or didn't you?"

"He did," Thomas said.

"By God I hope so," Rivers said. "Mac still got that pistol? You best watch your back, Luke."

"Mac ain't gonna shoot nobody," Elisha said.

Rivers shrugged. He took off his battered and blackened forage cap and looked at it. "General Early was over to York, Pennsylvania," he said. "Laid tribute on em. Sergeant Holland was tellin it. Took everythin. Stock, money. York ain't far from here. It's comin, boys."

"How many days, do you think?" Thomas said.

"Two. Three."

"Be a hell of a one this time," Rivers said.

"When ain't it?" Elisha said.

"Well, that's so," Rivers said.

"You better take a wash, Jake," Luke said. "Your odor doesn't improve the air."

"Listen," Rivers said. "There's a town over yonder two three miles. Name of Frederick, Maryland. Me and Joe are goin in there tonight. Find us some liquor. Some girls. You boys're welcome to join us. Do you some good."

Elisha had come out of the water. He was drying himself with his shirt. "I already got a girl," he said.

"That girl's your *girl?*" Rivers said.

"She is if I can help it," Elisha said. He sat down in his drawers and began looking for graybacks in his clothes. He found and killed one.

"You know what time we're marching tomorrow?" Luke said.

"I know what time," Rivers said. "I know where we're goin, too. Why I want to have some fun."

"How you gonna get passes?" Elisha said.

"We ain't," Rivers said.

There was a noise, a stir, running through the acres of campfires and humanity. Shouts. Close by, a drum rolled. Their boy, Willie Davis.

"I wonder what all that's about," Rivers said.

_____

Near Monocacy Junction, Maryland
June 28, 1863

My dearest Rose,

The news came just a little while ago: HOOKER IS GONE.
He has been replaced by Genl Meade & most of the boys are highly
pleased tho they wonder why Genls Reynolds or Hancock did not
receive the appt. They call him the Snapping Turtle & in truth he
looks like one with bulging mirthless eyes & a hard little mouth not
made for smiling & appears always in ill humor. I do not know where
he stands on Abolition but suspect the worst or there wd be grumbling
here & there as there is of Genls Howard & Schurz of the 11th Corps
who are staunch abolitionists. Rosie there is ignorance & prejudice
everywhere in this Army but they will do their duty to a man & in
victory the terrible blight will be lifted from this Country at last &
all men will see. But back to Genl Meade, he will have to fight Bobby
Lee soon (as the boys call him) & one can only sympathize with him
in his new position. They say Lee has never lost a battle unless you
count Antietam & the boys who fought there say if that is Victory we
might as well pack up & go home because we cd not stand many more
of them.

Rosie this will I am certain be my last letter to you until after the
Battle. Mail goes out every day now we are on Maryland soil but we
move before dawn tomorrow & will I believe keep moving hard until
we strike Lee or he strikes us. I will write Father as well so you can
consider this yrs alone. We will have fought by the time you read this
& if you have heard nothing of me & Thomas fear not because we will
come through it. I have decided or I shd say seen that there is logic
to everything incl War & therefore I will come back to you. I must.
Elisha confirms this, he says a fellow senses when his time has come
& that is when they give away their valuables & pin their names to
their shirts etc. They have felt the logic of it, you see. There is a man
in our Company, Henry Wilcox, who fears he will not survive this
time. The boys chaff him some but only to relieve the dread of Henry's
premonition by making light of it.

I have come to believe there is a God Rosie, perhaps to be found

*in the Church perhaps not. He is a Just God, there is no other kind,
& I can feel His presence among us & know He will be present in all
the din & turmoil of battle. A loss this time wd mean loss of the War,
so Victory is ordained & the names of the dead already written. Not
mine, not Thomas's, not Elisha Smith's.*

*Now in all of this folderol I forgot to mention the hermits & cheeses
& cake etc. wch arrived our 1st night in M'land & went very fast as
you might imagine. We are too generous, especially Thomas. Send
more if you are so inclined.*

*I had a row today with John McNamara & was able to knock some
sense into him before Sgt Cate curtailed the argument by using my
head for a base ball. Mac is sulking in his tent like Achilles & Thomas
& Elisha say I must make it right with him as it is bad luck & bad
war to go into battle with a grudge against a fellow soldier. I don't
want to but they say I must & admittedly you don't want a man
fighting alongside you who is yr enemy, there will be enemies enough
wearing the Gray.*

*Rosie I must do that & write Father if I can & so Good Night
to you. You once said you wd enlist if you were a man & you will
be fighting beside me & never shirking & yr heart as brave as any
man's.*

*Ever yr devoted
Luke*

"Go on, Luke," Elisha said, "get her done with."

"Go on," Thomas said.

"What if he was to get kilt and you ain't made it right with him,"
Elisha said. "How would you feel?"

"I don't know," Luke answered truthfully.

"That's just it," Elisha said. "Why find out when it ain't nothin you
can do to change it?"

Luke cursed under his breath and got up and made his way across
the campground to the dogtent. McNamara was sitting in its dark interior sachem-like with his legs folded, smoking his pipe. The tent flaps
were open, but even with the big moon it was hard to read his face. The

air was thick with sweetish pipesmoke and a stink of sweat. Luke knelt, looking in.

"Shake hands, Mac," he said.

"Go get fucked."

"I ambushed you. It wasn't fair."

"I'll ambush you, you sonofabitch." Sitting placidly, almost ceremonial, with his elbow on his leg, the pipe in his upraised hand. Now Luke could make out the raw marks he'd left on Mac's face.

"Mac," Luke said again.

McNamara did not look at him, sitting aloof and very composed. Luke sat down on his haunches. Thomas and Elisha, sitting at their mess fire, kept glancing over. Everyone around the fire did.

"Deep down you don't like slavery any more than I do," Luke said.

"Hell I don't."

"Elisha says you're as brave as any man in the regiment. He says you fight like a sonofabitch. You're slavery's worst enemy, Mac."

McNamara drew on his pipe. The embers brightened in the dark.

"You're Bobby Lee's worst nightmare," Luke said.

McNamara smoked and said nothing. Luke shifted, got more comfortable. The long grass under him had been flattened to a soft mat. At another fire Isaac Brophy played his fiddle. "Aura Lea."

"How many battles has that fiddle seen?" Luke said.

"Two."

"Chancellorsville," Luke said.

"And Fredericksburg. We didn't get much into it at Chancellorsville. Only one we didn't."

They were silent a moment, listening. The words spoke themselves in the melody across the darkness.

> *Aura Lea, Aura Lea,*
> *Maid of golden hair;*
> *Sunshine came along with thee,*
> *And swallows in the air . . .*

"Do you like the songs?" Luke said.

"Some of em."

"Do you like this one?"

McNamara made no answer.

> *When the mistletoe was green,*
> *'Midst the summer air . . .*

"How do you think Thomas'll do when the fight comes?" Luke said.

"He'll do all right. He's a good boy."

> *Aura Lea, Aura Lea,*
> *Take my golden ring . . .*

"If I was to get shot," Luke said, "I'd like to know you were seeing to him."

McNamara took the pipe out of his mouth and looked at Luke for the first time.

"I'd feel content to know it," Luke said.

"I like Tommy," McNamara said.

"I know it's a deal to ask," Luke said.

"Not for Tommy. He wouldn't bushwhack a man."

"No," Luke said, "he wouldn't."

Love and light return with thee . . .

"Will you see to Thomas?" Luke said.

"I might do."

"I'm sorry, Mac," he said, and left him.

SEVENTEEN

She harnessed Nancy to the carryall and led her down the drive and around the corner and stopped her in the elmshade in front of the house. She looped the rein around a picket and went inside and down the cool hallway to the kitchen and opened the icebox and completed the loading of her basket with a quart pail of blueberry ice cream she'd cranked not an hour ago. She swaddled the pail in a cotton towel. In the basket also were a jar of her applesauce, a bottle of her currant wine, and an upside-down cake. She covered the basket with a blue napkin and hooked it on her arm.

It was Sunday morning and George Chandler was relaxing in the sunny front parlor with the week's accumulation of newspapers that came over in sporadic fashion from New Bedford and Woods Hole. The *Morning Mercury, Boston Transcript,* Garrison's *Liberator.* He would read the war news as soon as a paper arrived and save the rest for Sunday, on which day he never ventured out of doors except when summoned to deliver a baby or set a bone or stitch a cut.

"They'll wonder why you didn't come," Rose said, stopping in the doorway.

"I can't cure rheumatism, Rose."

"You could look in on her."

"You're doing that. And much better than I could."

She'd run into Elisha Smith's father on Main Street two days ago. He'd tipped his hat and been deferential to her. They'd exchanged news of the boys and Rose had asked after his wife and Mr. Smith had hesitated, then admitted she was down with the rheumatism. Rose had insisted he come to the office and the doctor had given him a bottle of Vita Oil and not charged him. It was Rose's idea to call with a food basket. Elisha's upside-down cake, she still called it.

"We'll have a cold dinner if that's all right," she said.

The doctor smiled at her. "Don't ask me; tell me."

"That's what I was doing," she said.

Again he smiled. "My best to the Smiths," he said.

Nancy watched her come down the porch steps past the heaven-blue hydrangeas and shut the gate behind her.

"Don't you give me no trouble today," Rose said. "I ain't gentle like the doctor."

Nancy watched her. She pricked her ears.

"I'll take a switch to you, girl."

She placed the basket on the floor behind the seat. She took the reins and sprang lightly up. Her crinoline resisted as she sat down on it, springy beneath her. She tied her straw hat under her chin—the Leghorn with the black velvet bow—shook the reins, and Nancy set off at a reluctant-seeming plod.

The sun had crept above the treetops. Up William Street they went, past the Greek revival houses glowing chalk-white in the lucid air of the June morning. Tea roses swarmed on white picket fences, red and pink and yellow, the colors of the summer dawn. She passed their neighbor, Captain Ephraim Harding, the whaler, out for a stroll, and he touched his hat and watched her go by with mild interest. The carryall creaked and rattled. Nancy's hooves thumped the dirt in slow patient rhythm and Rose decided there was no reason to hurry on such a day.

"You just take your time, girl," she said. "I b'lieve I'll be drunk on this air time we arrive."

At the graveyard she swung the wagon downhill on Center Street and then right on Main, the shorter way but a mistake, because Peter Daggett and another boy or young man were loafing on the bench in front of the Mansion House. They wore Sunday clothes, starched collars, silk vests, wool trousers, Peter a derby hat and the other a bowler. The one she didn't know—he could not have lived in Holmes Hole—was whittling on a stick. Rose saw them first and looked quickly away, up the highway where she was going, and then Peter called to her.

"Hey. Missy."

Missy, she thought, and gave the reins a shake. Nancy quickened her gait but the incline worked against her and they caught up, laughing breathlessly, like frolicsome schoolboys, and Peter took Nancy's bridle and halted her.

"Get your damn hands off her," Rose said.

There were houses along here but the Sunday stillness pressed down on them and no one stirred in any dooryard or widow's walk or open window. Some perhaps were at church but in any case Rose knew she could expect little help from these Lamberts and Luces and Dexters, not against a Daggett, whose family went back as theirs did to the dawn of the island's history. White history, she should say.

"We only want a lift," Peter said, still holding the bridle. He was catching his breath. He had high cheekbones and bright hazel eyes and would have been handsome if not for the disdainful set of his mouth and the malicious glint those bright eyes gave out. "We're trying to get to Edgartown," he said.

"I'm not going there," Rose said.

"You might could take us partway," he said. "I'll be truthful, Rose. I'm in dutch with my parents. They won't let me borrow the rig."

"I can't say I'm surprised," she said.

Peter grinned up at her. He still held fast to the bridle. "I bet you ain't," he said.

His companion was on the heavy side, flushed from the run. His plumpness and joviality, his Sunday attire, gave him the look of a prosperous, if very young, businessman—a merchant or banker or underwriter of clipper voyages. Rose wondered what he was doing in the company of Peter Daggett.

"What did you want in Edgartown?" she said.

"A bottle," Peter said.

"Well, well," Rose said.

"You goin up island or t'other way?" Peter said.

She considered the lie but rejected it as risky. "I'm going to Head of the Pond," she said.

"See them Smiths, are you."

"Give them some comfort, if I can. The boys'll be in a big battle any day now. Might have fought it already."

"There you go again with the war," Peter said. Still grinning.

Rose had been looking him in the eye, steady, but now she turned to his friend. "What's your name?" she said.

"Oliver Shiverick, ma'am. It *would* be a help if you'd drive us."

She looked up the Highway, pale and dusty in the shade of the great trees that had been left to grow old beside it. Nancy snorted and abruptly nodded, and Peter let go of the bridle.

"All right," Rose said. "But I want the both of you to sit in back."

"That's fine," said Shiverick.

They climbed up and she started Nancy.

"What's in the basket?" Peter said behind her.

"Never you mind," Rose said over her shoulder.

But he bent down and she heard the basket slide out from under the seat. "What's this?" He'd found the pail, unswaddled and opened it. "Oh Lord. Ice cream."

"You cover that back up, you hear?" she said.

"What kind a ice cream is it?"

"Looks like blueberry," Shiverick said.

"It's meltin," Peter said.

Rose twisted around to glare but Peter, sitting with his back to her, had pressed the lid back on and she turned front again.

"You wrap that pail," she said.

"Feisty, ain't she," Peter said, and returned the pail to the basket.

They went on up the highway, past the Widow Cromwell's house and the cemetery, and were in the country, woods and scrub, here and there a sheep-pastured field set off by a crude stone wall. She turned Nancy left onto the Edgartown Road, which was narrow and well worn and sandy, like a trough carved through the scrub, the fields choked with wild huckleberry, blueberry, bayberry. The road was hard and white with grass growing in scraggy patches up its middle. The sun climbed higher and Rose felt its weight on her shoulders.

She would have liked to speak to Nancy, and she would have liked to sing. She had not thought of that. Nor, when she told them both to sit behind her, had she reckoned on the unease it caused her, the exchanged looks she suspected, the sign language. Better, she saw, to have one beside her where she could keep an eye on him. They'd fallen silent back there and she wished they'd speak, even if it was to be insolent.

"Where are you from, Mr.—"

"Shiverick. Sandwich, ma'am."

"He come over last night," Peter said. "Put up at the Mansion House."

"Where do you get a bottle on a Sunday?" she said.

"Wouldn't you like to know," Peter said.

"I wouldn't, but the Sons of Temperance would."

The boys spat laughter behind her. "Them old farts," Peter said.

"We got them in Sandwich," Shiverick said. "Think they're the law, but they aren't."

"Say. Whyn't you come with us to Edgartown?"

A moment, then Shiverick threw off the veil and let the truth come dancing out into the light of day. "You'd ride into town with a nigger?" he asked Peter Daggett.

It froze her blood. He was why she'd consented to this. His manners, the bland look of him.

"This one I would," Peter said. "Anyways, she ain't a nigger, she's Cape Verdean. There's a difference."

"What kind of difference?"

"Well, a big one."

"I don't see it."

They rattled briskly downhill, Nancy hurried by the weight of the wagon, into a wide swale choked with ferns and berry bushes. It was a good mile still to Head of the Pond. Nothing but dense scrub in between. There could be a traveler on the road, but not likely on a Sunday morning. Nancy labored up out of the swale and there was movement in back, Peter getting into the basket again.

"This here ice cream's naught but soup," he said.

"Did you wrap it like I said?"

"Could be I forgot."

"Well wrap it now."

"It ain't but soup. I say we put her out of her misery."

She stopped Nancy, pulling hard, angrily, and wrapped the rein around the whipstock and turned. Peter, bending over with his back to her, had pried the lid off the pail. He straightened, turned halfway around.

"Here's to you," he said, and raised the pail with both hands and drank.

"Damn you," Rose said, and grabbed at the pail. But Peter sprang away, passing the pail to Shiverick. Rose climbed over the seat. Peter had turned and now stood face-to-face with her, purplish ice cream mustache, derby hat cocked forward, so close to her she could smell the camphor in his vest and the sweat darkening his underarms. He was smiling, but it was a nervous smile, as much uncertainty in it as savor, and Rose knew there was a particle of fear in him, of her and all her race.

Oliver Shiverick, still sitting on the back seat, was drinking the ice cream down.

"Lord, that's good," he said.

"You get off," Rose said. "The both of you."

"There you go again," Peter said. "You just *got* to put on them airs, ain't you."

"Get off," she said.

"What else you got in there?" Shiverick said. "We could have us a picnic."

"Big upside-down cake," Peter said. "Bottle a wine."

"Get off," Rose said.

"After our picnic we might."

Rose shoved him hard. He flailed his arms for balance and fell anyway and his back hit the edge of the back seat and the pain of it flashed across his face.

"Sonofa*bitch*," he said.

Shiverick giggled, an airy whinny like a girl's.

"You get off," Rose said. "*Off.*"

Peter got a knee under him and stood up. His face had gone crimson. The light in his eyes had hardened. Rose stepped back from him involuntarily and he slapped her. He slapped her again and she tried to grab his wrists and he shoved her and she sat down hard on the wagon seat with her straw hat pushed back on her head. Her left cheek burned and she tried to clear her mind, tried to think.

"Let's fuck her," Shiverick said.

Rose thought *Oh God* and looked around for a weapon and found nothing.

"Fuck her here?" Peter said.

"In the woods, you dumbass."

Rose sat still. Readying herself. Her cheek felt soft and pulpy and aburn where he'd slapped her.

"She'll tattle," Peter said.

"No she won't. She wants us to."

Rose looked up at them, squinting through the white sunlight. "Luke Chandler'll kill you you lay another hand on me."

"Who's he?" Shiverick said.

"One a the family she works for. Thinks he's a hard man. He's away at the war."

"Time he gets back, he won't be in any condition to kill us," Shiverick said. "*If* he gets back."

"I thought you didn't want to go to town with a nigger," Peter said. A note of uncertainty, of hesitation: perhaps he lacked the heart for this. It was her one hope now.

"I don't, but fuckin em is different. You afraid of this Luke fellow?"

"Hell no."

"He'll beat you, Peter Daggett," Rose said. "You know he will."

"Don't you threaten me, you black bitch."

"This nigger pushed you down, in case you forgot that," Shiverick said.

"I ain't forgot it."

"Let's get to it, then."

She fought them harder than she'd ever fought anybody—girls at the orphanage, three boys who'd dragged her into an alley for money she'd earned apprenticing at the Chandlers', the policeman who had gotten her in the orphanage carriage shed. She knew to punch rather than slap or scratch, and to use her elbows and knees, and both assailants had pink marks on their faces and their clothes were in disarray by the time they'd separated her from the carryall. They locked her arms behind her and drove her stumbling and tripping into the scrub, through brush, between stunted oaks whose low branches caught at her face and arms. When they thought they'd come far enough they forced her to the ground on her back and she struck at them with her fists and they cursed her and slapped her face and finally pinned her down with Peter lying athwart her heavy and strong-smelling as a horse, crushing the breath out of her, while Shiverick got under her skirt and in among her undergarments, scrabbling at her crinoline, unhooking it, sliding it petticoat and all down her kicking thrashing legs and over her ankles, her boots, and off. Her drawers. She kicked with her bare legs. He dropped to his knees, wrapped an arm around each of her legs, his naked thighs warm and greasy with his sweat against hers, Rose now immobile, trussed, there was nothing to do but close her eyes and pray vengeance and endure the pain and wait for him to be done.

He was quick about it. Like that policeman. When he left her she lay still, weeping quietly. Peter Daggett, still sprawled across her, unpeeled himself and rolled away. He scrambled to his feet. Shiverick was fussing with his trousers.

"Take a turn," he said.

"I don't want no more of it," Peter said.

"You took all this trouble you ought to fuck her," Shiverick said.

"I ain't in the mood."

"Well aren't you something. You're the one began it all."

"I wouldn't of if she hadn't of pushed me."

"Pushed you right down on your ass. Got sassy. Ordering us around. Tried to throw us off her wagon like we were niggers ourselves."

"I did warn her about it."

"I heard you. Now let's find our hats, shall we?"

She lay in the fetal position and listened to them move away through the brush. A deerfly landed and bit her shoulder—her dress had come down on one side—and she slapped at it too late. The bite itched, burned. The flies pestered her and she lay there slapping at them, killing some, till long after the rustling movement had died away. She sat up finally, blinking to clear her vision. Her jaw hurt, she could feel a swelling over the cheekbone. The sun had climbed to the top of the cloudless sky. The air was warm and thick and held the gin smell of bayberry. Rose pulled her dress up her shoulder and climbed slowly to her feet. A rawness between her legs. She'd been badly bruised on each thigh. Her drawers were still down around her ankles. The crinoline was undamaged, the hook and eye unbroken. She stepped into it and pulled it up her legs, up under her corset, and hooked it. She worked the petticoat up and fastened it. Her hat lay nearby—had they torn it off her?—and she put it on and tied it.

She would not have known which way the road lay but for the crease they'd made in the low bushes pushing her in front of them. She was surprised at how close it was; she was there in hardly more than a minute. Nancy had moved to the roadside and was cropping weeds and grass. She lifted her head, eyed Rose with unsurprise. The basket sat on the wagon bed and Rose looked into it and saw that half the cake was gone. They'd torn it with their hands. The wine bottle was gone, the applesauce had been opened and partly eaten. Rose threw it into the scrub, jar and all. She upended the cake pan and tapped it and the cake released and plopped into the tall grass. Nancy had gone back to grazing. What good is a horse, Rose thought, if it can let this happen?

She pulled herself up onto the box. The two boys, she had reason to hope, had gone on toward Edgartown. If not, and if she should overtake them on the road home, she doubted they'd trouble her further and anyway there was no choice about it. She unwrapped the reins and put Nancy forward until they came to a rise where there was grass on either side and the road not so sunken and there was room to turn, and so started back under the high sun toward the village. She did not pass Peter Daggett and the devil Shiverick.

He'd fallen asleep in his chair with the *Morning Mercury* open across his chest like a blanket and had not heard Nancy's hooves or the wagon clattering in the driveway. Rose felt a spasm of anger to see him so peaceful, so oblivious of the violence, the outrage, that hung in the air like the taste of sulfur. She crept on past the door and up the stairs and came down with her douche bag and a change of clothes. The doctor still slept. She shut herself in the kitchen and filled the washtub without taking time to heat the water and stripped and sat down with a shudder in the cold cistern water and douched. She still felt raw down there but she could not see any blood. Her thighs were discolored and sore to the touch, as if she'd been hit there by a bat, a club. She was bathing with lavender soap when the doctor tapped on the door.

"You wait for me in the parlor," she said.

"Rose," he said.

"You wait for me," she said.

"What happened?"

"Are you listening to me?"

"All right," he said, and padded down the hall in his slippers.

She finished her bath and dressed herself in clean drawers and petticoat, no crinoline, and a simple dimity housedress. Barefoot, she dragged the tub to the door and tipped the water into the dooryard. Her torn visiting dress was a fine one of pale green cambric; Rose bunched it and pushed it into the stove for burning. She pushed her violated drawers in, and the violated petticoat, and hid them behind crumpled newspaper.

The doctor watched her come into the front parlor with a look of ashen alarm on his face. Eyes squinted in that perpetual grimace. How small he was, how tentative in all his dealings. Rose sat down opposite him. The sun was above the house but the parlor still swam in its goldenness.

"Some boys met me on the road," she said. "They stole the food so I came home."

"What boys?"

"I never saw them before."

"What did they look like? We'll go to the constable with it."

"No," she said.

"Whyever not?"

"An upside-down cake. Some ice cream. That's all it was." Her gaze was downcast. She sat very still.

"They struck you, didn't they."

"No they did not."

"You've some swelling under your eye."

"A yellowjacket stung me. They were nested in the ground where I turned the wagon and Nancy tromped on them."

"I see."

"It was just the one flew up."

"And it bruised you, did it."

Rose said nothing.

"Tell me," he said, "why did you bathe?"

"I just felt like it."

"What really happened, Rosie?"

"I told you what happened." She stood up. "I wonder could you look after yourself for dinner. There's cold leg of lamb in the icebox. There's that blueberry pie."

"Of course," he said.

"Nancy'll need stabling," she said. "I gave her some hay and left her tied."

"I'll attend to it right now."

She had not looked at him since entering the room and did not look at him as she left it. She climbed the stairs, the worn scuffed pine boards warm against the balls of her feet. Her bedroom never got the sun direct and was always cool. She did not close the door. The whiskey bottle was in a corner of her closet floor. There was plenty in it. There was water in the ewer, and the tumbler she'd used last night was still on the bed-side table. She filled it halfway, topped it with water, and sat down in her wine-red velvet chair with its window view of the side yard, the driveway, the great elm.

It's white men, she thought. *Got to hurt what they want but lower themselves by wantin it. Got to have it but only can they hurt it too. Only can they break it. If I gave it to em gentle they'd hurt me anyway. Kill me if they could, to cover up what they did. Cover up wantin me.*

She drank, and the rawness between her legs diminished, and the day's events took on a quality of logic and inevitability, as necessary as the final act would be. Luke would about kill Peter Daggett. Rose imagined him breaking one of Peter's arms, one of his legs. The whole island would know why and would remember it for years and years, how the wrath of God fell on two white boys who raped a colored girl and thought not to ruffle anybody by it, thought no law would bother them. But Luke would be the law, home from the war, home from giving General Lee his whipping.

Nor was she forgetting Oliver Shiverick. Luke would find him. Sand-wich, that shouldn't be too hard. Or beat his whereabouts out of Peter Daggett. Peter could keep from getting both arms broken by telling it.

Shiverick with that duplicitous sunny grin greeting a stranger. Do I know Rose Miranda? Don't recollect that I do. Luke would beat him worse than he beat Peter, Rose would tell him to. Terrible swift sword, fiery gospel, burnished rows of steel . . . *All the people in this country that are right now waitin on their judgment, Robert E. Lee and Jeff Davis and that General Longstreet all the way on down to Mr. Oliver Shiverick. It will come, oh yes it will.*

She drank another bourbon and the sun moved over and the light dwindled. Her time of month had ended two days ago and she did not think she'd get a child out of this. That way, at least, she'd been lucky. The policeman in the orphanage carriage shed had pulled his billy and rapped her on the head, stunning and scaring her both, and she'd stopped fighting him. She'd sneaked out that night to go walking with a Portuguese boy from the Catholic orphanage whom she'd met at the annual picnic and the policeman had caught them in Fort Taber Park with a bottle of watered sherry the boy had brought. He'd run the boy off and walked Rose home. He'd said he could pinch her for what she'd done and she believed him. She was sixteen. It was past midnight and she did not scream when he took her arm and hustled her toward the carriage shed because she could not yet imagine that a policeman would have anything very terrible in mind for her whereas the matron would have strapped the tops of her hands bloody for sneaking out. She was a virgin and bled badly but did not get with child and did not know why.

The pendulum clock in the downstairs hall whirred and struck three and a few minutes later the doctor climbed the stairs in his slippers and stood in her doorway.

"Rosie," he said.

She did not answer, did not look at him. Tears rolled down, her first since she'd lain in the brush alone, with the deerflies nattering at her.

"You must tell me," he said, and came in and stood with his back to the fireplace.

She shook her head, weeping, gazing out the window. The bottle and empty tumbler were on the floor at her feet. He'd seen them, of course.

"Were you attacked, Rosie?"

"I told you what happened," she said.

"Why did you bathe?"

"I told you."

The silence seemed dense, tactile, gathering in against her. She kept her face averted to the window, but she could feel the doctor's twiggy presence like the sliver of a shadow visible in the corner of her eye. The shadow came nearer. She heard the rocker drag and he sat down opposite her, as Luke used to, though not quite so close.

"I'll not press you anymore," he said.

Rose nodded.

"But if you're injured, Rosie . . ."

"I'm not injured."

A breeze stirred in the leaves of the elm. A pair of girls' voices went by on William Street, speaking in the low excited way of children sharing a secret.

"Will you come downstairs?" the doctor said.

"Fix supper, you mean."

"Rosie," he said, and the hurt in it did finally touch her stone heart, and she remembered that he had not made this world and would never harm a soul in it, white or black.

"I don't mind fixing supper," she said.

"I didn't mean that."

"I know."

"Is there nothing I can do for you?" he said.

She was weeping again, the tears sliding down. "Not refer to this anymore. That's what you can do."

"That's asking a lot," he said.

"I know that, too," she said. "It's why I dare to ask it." She found a smile for him, blinked away some last tears. "You go on down, hear? Give me a minute to wash my face and I'll come down and we'll have us a nice supper."

He nodded slowly, it was the best he could hope for and he knew it, and stood up. Rose watched him go out, diminutive in his clean white shirt and braces, fragile, and yet with a knotty obduracy about him, quietly doing life his way. He might cling on a long time, she thought, cough or no. He descended the stairs and his whispered slippered footsteps died away in the Sunday stillness, the thick dead air of these unused rooms. *I must fix us some supper,* she thought. *Oh, God, but I must.*

PART II

Carry Me Home

ONE

General Lee had been conferring with two of his corps commanders, Long-street and Hill, and had dismissed them, and now Longstreet was back alone, wishing a word in private. The tent flaps had been tied back and he stood in the broad wedge of lingering daylight in his black slouch hat, his cigar tucked in the corner of his mouth. He had a thick black beard much like General Stuart's, luxuriant and assiduously combed, but Longstreet's eyes above all that dark thatch did not sparkle like Stuart's, did not dart about.

Sir, he said.

Come in, General, Lee said.

He was sitting on his cot in the act of removing his coat. All spring there'd been a recurring prick of pain deep in his chest whose cause he could not guess but which had to do, he knew, with his chronic fatigue. Lately he'd been assailed by diarrhea, further inconveniencing and wearying him. He peeled the coat back, half rose and shucked it, and sat back down in his dove-gray vest and white shirt.

Longstreet had stepped inside the tent. The light here was mellow, buttermilky, for the sun still shone on the western tent wall, sinking toward the mountains. Longstreet removed his hat and General Lee nodded him to the canvas chair. Longstreet unbuckled his sword and sat down with the bright silver scabbard leaning against the chair between his legs.

I wonder, Lee said, if the fight will come Fourth of July.

It might do, Longstreet said, speaking past the cigar.

Be ironic, wouldn't it?

Highly.

Our own Independence Day.

We'll have to win the war first, sir.

We can win it here, General Longstreet. It's why we came.

Around them, through the tent walls, came the sounds of evening camp. Officers' voices, bantering and convivial, the day's march done, and a good day without any shooting. A horse went by, musical chink of sword and spurs. In the distance somebody plucked clear sweet notes on a banjo.

General, said Lee.

Sir.

You wanted to say something.

Longstreet picked the cigar from his mouth. He looked at it. *I've been thinking about the contrabands, sir.*

Lee didn't say anything. No one had brought this up yet and he had thought they wouldn't. He had hoped not. Longstreet, though, would be the one.

I was wondering if we ought not to turn them loose.

To what end? Lee said.

Ties up some good manpower, for one thing. Got to guard them, feed them, see they don't make mischief. We're going to need every man when this fight comes.

They'll all be in Virginia soon. The Negroes, I mean.

Not before we fight.

General Jenkins has transported some already. Upward of a hundred, I believe.

Couple hundred still left.

We can accommodate them.

There's also the political question. We don't want to turn anybody against us we don't have to.

Aren't you warm in that coat? Lee said.

I'm tolerable, sir.

I'm warm looking at you.

Longstreet took a pull on his cigar. Its odor reminded Lee of the smell of cherrywood, that odd astringent sweetness. Longstreet again removed it from his mouth.

There's some, he said, *who might say these abductions don't fit with your general order.*

Don't call them abductions, General.

Removals.

These are stolen property. Runaways.

Not all of them, sir.

You sound like some Boston abolitionist.

I'm trying to think practically, sir.

Then do it. I can restrain the men from destroying private property, molesting women, bullying civilians, setting fires. The things all soldiers do. But if I forbid the seizure of a runaway slave I put their loyalty to me in some jeopardy. The Negro is the cause of this war, and the men know it, and I can't stanch the rage they feel. I'm not sure I'd want to. It makes them terrible fighters. There's nothing these men can't do. There's never been such an army.

It's a point, Longstreet admitted.

You say three hundred Negroes have been taken.

About that.

How many men did we lose, killed, at Sharpsburg?

About three thousand.

Gives you some perspective, doesn't it.

Yes sir, it does.

It seemed to Lee now that he was winning the argument, as he had won it with himself. He had learned of General Jenkins's roundup of Negroes almost a week after it was begun, and Lee had known right away he must let it continue. The argument with himself was after the fact.

It was a Northern general, Lee said, who invented the term contrabands for our Negroes, wasn't it.

That sonofabitch Butler.

The idea was to induce them to cross the lines. Put them to work for his army.

Yes sir.

A theft of our property.

Point taken, sir.

There's more to worry about than a handful of Negroes, General.

I won't argue with you, Longstreet said.

————

Reveille was drummed before dawn and they formed up as the sky was beginning to pale and the almost full moon to blanch on its low perch above South Mountain. Rows and rows of men standing silent in regimental formation across the fields and hills between the river and Frederick and more rows to the north of the city, more thousands of men and mules and horses and wagons and limbers and caissons and guns. A circular had gone out, penned by Meade and copied by the clerks at corps headquarters and distributed by mounted couriers to every regiment, to be read at roll call. Colonel Revere disliked these addresses, their mawkishness and grandiosity, and so he ordered Lieutenant Colonel Macy to read it to the Twentieth Massachusetts. Twenty-five rods away Colonel Ward read it to the Fifteenth, his voice rising in monotone and jaded-sounding reiteration of Macy's more ringing exhortation.

Afterward the men all said it fell flat alongside of McClellan's speeches. Some said they couldn't understand all of it, it got so tangled. *The enemy are on our soil. The whole country now looks anxiously to this army to deliver it from the presence of the foe. Homes, firesides, and domestic altars are involved.* The usual shit, McNamara said, except for the closing, which struck a different note altogether. *Corps and other commanders are authorized to order the instant death of any soldier who fails in his duty at this hour.*

Thomas Chandler's heart froze when he heard it. It brought back the bones on the field at Bull Run, the arms and legs beneath the farmhouse window outside of Middleburg, macabre intrusions on this carefree life of marching and camaraderie and girls and camping under the stars. Live each day as if your life were one day long, Luke was right about that, but there was a day or days somewhere down these white dusty roads where killing would break out like some violent storm whose destructive power Thomas could not imagine, and where, as he had just learned, his own officers—Paine, Abbott—might kill him if the Rebels didn't. He had not fired his musket since Falmouth and he hoped he would remember how to load the thing, so many steps, and that he wouldn't foul it or burn himself on the heated barrel. Worst of all was the mystery of what he'd do, his behavior, when the fighting began, the blood and confusion and men trying to kill him. Luke knew it of himself but Thomas didn't, and when he thought about it he was afraid.

After roll call they swallowed some hardtack and salt pork standing in quiet huddles in the cool darkness, the campsite now a trampled wasteland of dead campfires, stacked rifles, rolled tents and blankets, knapsacks buckled and ready to go like baggage strewing the floor of some colossal train depot. In the distance downriver the strident braying of mules in the wagon park rose on the air, nervous-sounding, malcontent, as if they too knew there would soon be hell to pay.

"Did you ever see an officer shoot a man?" Thomas said. There were weevils in his hardtack; he sat digging them out with Elisha's pocketknife.

"I did, I'd shoot him back," Rivers said.

"Hell you would," Merriman said.

"I damn sure would," Rivers said.

He had come back from Frederick with a black scab above his left temple. Merriman was unmarked but had lost his forage cap. Both men reeked of alcohol. Neither had slept; they'd been brought back—they and several hundred others—by a regiment of cavalry dispatched by General Meade to scour the city for them. There had been no arrests. Forgive and forget with battle looming.

"I'll put a ball through any sonofabitch shoots you, Tommy," Rivers said.

"Why are we talkin so?" Elisha said. "Tommy'll do his duty. We all will."

"I bout shit my pants first time I seen the elephant," Merriman said.

"I wish you'd shut up," Elisha said.

"Git you a Reb and then it ain't nothin to it," Rivers said. "I got me one right quick at Ball's Bluff, soon's they come out of the woods at us. Near blowed his head off, and I warn't scared no more."

"Them woods was a quarter mile distant," Merriman said. "You couldn't of seen what you hit for the smoke."

"It was when they first come out. There warn't no smoke yet."

"You got your friends all round you," Elisha said. "You can't get scared. Now let's not have no more of this talk, all right?"

The drummer beat assembly again and they formed up by company and marched, in turn, to a commissary wagon, where, on an open place beside the road, rations had been set out on a gum blanket: little mounds of coffee, sugar, and salt pork, more or less equal in size. Corporal Dugan would indicate a pile and then Sergeant Cate, with his back to the blanket, would read a name off the company roll and that man would step forward and claim the pile. Sergeant Holland then gave the man a stack of ten crackers, scooping them out of a wooden hardtack box, and as many packs of cartridges as he needed to bring him up to sixty rounds. They'd been carrying forty rounds and had seen no action but cartridges had gotten wet in the rain and stream crossings and been thrown away, and some had been thrown away too to lighten the load. Sergeant Holland didn't question them about this, not today. He only asked them how many they needed. They came in packs of ten, including caps, and Holland would slap the packs into their open palms and let his hand linger there a moment, as if in benediction. It was first light now, and the men waited for their turn without looking at one another or speaking, and all about them, across the acres and acres of bivouac, it was quiet.

The bridges were clogged with artillery and baggage wagons, and so the men waded the Monocacy, toiling across waist deep with their shoes hung around their necks and their muskets held above their heads. The river bottom was slippery and littered with sharp stones, and they lurched, stumbled, cursed. On the east bank they dried their feet as best they could and fell in and marched on toward Pennsylvania. The roads up here were wet but good, covered for long stretches in crushed stone, and for a while the army made rapid progress, traveling parallel roads, working ever north. The sun was up now and the sky once more a luminous robin's egg blue, and once more cloudless. The smell of their sweat accrued, moved with them.

"How'd Jake get his head broken?" Stackpole asked.

"It was a girl done it," Merriman said. "In a public house. Hit him with a whiskey bottle. She was the owner, I think. I couldn't altogether make it out."

"You were too drunk," Stackpole said.

"I warn't yet. This girl was orderin free drinks for all the boys in blue.

Settin at the end of the bar in a pair a them net stockins. Plump thing, but pretty enough. Strong, too. Said she wanted us to enjoy ourselves fore we met up with Bobby Lee. I think she was a copperhead."

"A copperhead wouldn't give you no free drinks," Elisha said.

"I think she was tryin to get us drunk and muddle us. She said Lee burnt York Pennsylvania to the ground and that Ewell done the same to Harrisburg. They was some boys from the Eighth Ohio in there and they believed her."

"Maybe it's true."

"We'd have heard," Luke said.

"Jake said it was all lies and called her a copperhead. The girl tells Jake to watch his tongue and when she said it the Ohio boys started in on Jake's bare feet. Said he must be a nigger with feet like that and had the Twentieth run out a shoes. Jake give em a good cussin and said he'd whip any of em cared to walk outside with him. The girl told him to pipe down."

"I hope you stood with him," Luke said.

"I kinda did, but I had my mind on fuckin this owner or barmaid, whatever she was. I was tryin not to misplease her."

"Stood against the Ohio boys, I mean."

"I would a done, if they'd of come at him. But they was just laughin. It was the girl that come at him. Told him to stop cussin them boys or she'd throw him and his dirty feet out on the street. Jake called her a copperhead whore, and that's when she hit him. She'd brung the bottle with her down by her side where you couldn't see it. Jake fell off his bar stool and I grabbed him up and drug him outside."

"I'd have used the bottle on her," Luke said.

"We didn't go into town to fight, Luke. Anyways, Jake was all right. He wanted to go back in there a course but I got him calmed down. We found us another groggery right on the same block and there was three boys from the Iron Brigade in there and they was friendly and we took up with em. We drunk some more and one of em said let's find us a brothel, and we did."

"Hope you cleaned Jake up first," Stackpole said.

"They had a washroom at the brothel, made us all go in there. Then a skinny little whore took Jake upstairs feet and all. It was the last of our money. Two dollars a jump, and they took greenbacks. If we hadn't of got them free drinks at the other place, we couldn't of paid it."

Listening to all of this, Elisha thought of Iris. If it hadn't been for her he'd have gone into Frederick with them. He'd have reminded Thomas of his promise and the two of them would have found a brothel and whores who would have fucked them once and sent them on their way and never known their names, and Elisha would have thought that's all there was to it. But he knew different. Iris had shown him. She'd shown him how to touch and be touched, and explained how a girl doesn't come as easy as a man, and that you have to wait for it sometimes. Elisha had never thought about that, a girl coming. Like it just felt good to them, having you inside, and no special moment to it. But there was, and it made perfect sense when Iris told him. She said she didn't come with most of her customers, only the ones who took their time and were good to her, and she led him through it the second time, and said he must always treat his girls so.

He wanted to think about Iris but not talk about her to anyone but Thomas. She was his secret, a soft warm place inside him that was like carrying her with him. He imagined her at the farmstead at Head of the Pond, she was a farm girl herself and would not mind the barn smells or the chickens or the work of cutting hay and riching up the garden soil with dead herring. He would ride to town with her and she would take his arm and they would walk down Main Street, and everyone would take notice.

Elisha Smith. Home from the war, and look what he brung with him.

She's pretty.

Ain't she, though.

Oh yes, ain't she.

And so Elisha passed the time, marching toward Gettysburg.

By noontime the parallel roads had merged into one, bunching the army, compressing it, making the going harder. It was still quite wet and there was little dust, and when you came up over a rise you could see the column stretch away solid to the horizon, like a dark steady-moving river, with here and there a regimental wagon or ambulance swallowed in its midst, and the noncoms out alongside, plodding along disconnected from the dense mass and looking oddly solitary. They marched all day, with halts of not more than five minutes, and by midafternoon the grumbling had commenced.

"Goddamn Hancock, whoever wanted him to run this corps?"

"You did."

"No more I don't."

"Blame the Rebs, boys," said Henry Wilcox. "It's them we're chasin."

"Why? Why don't we just hunker down, let em come to us. Like they done at Fredericksburg."

"Lee ain't as dumb as Burnside, that's why."

"You think Meade's as smart as Lee?"

"Jesus Christ I hope so."

They passed through the little brick town of Mount Pleasant, where again girls fluttered handkerchiefs and women gave them bread and jars of milk as they strode by. They went up a broad green valley through a cherry orchard whose trees dripped clusters of ripe fruit but the officers and noncoms were keeping a close watch on them now, hurrying them along, and there was no opportunity to break rank and help yourself to a handful. The sun fell to the horizon and they kept going, kept passing fields and copses and streams that would have made good stopping places, until they understood that it was not a good campsite they were marching for, but to gain position on the enemy.

"If we're going to fight I guess I'd prefer to get on with it," Thomas said.

"Hell," Merriman said, "Tommy'll outfight us all."

"A scared pup when he got here, and look at him now," Stackpole said.

"You ain't alone in a battle," Elisha said. "That's what you got to remember."

The sun went down, and they marched through the long summer twilight, through the dusk, and the fat moon rose and they legged on through its silver-lemon light and the sculpted shadows of trees and groves and roadside buildings. Conversation had died and there was no sound but the river-like soughing of footsteps, the cowbell clink of canteens and cups, and now and then an oath when a mosquito bit, or some-body's heel was stepped on.

Another brick town, this one named Liberty, and Luke wondered why, liberty from what, for whom. It had gone late now, and the houses were dark, with only an upstairs window lit softly here and there. Halfway through the town, on the lawn in front of a stone church, the brigade band was playing while some dozen soldiers sang "We Are Coming, Father Abraham." You could hear it up ahead, reeds and drums and a fiddle too, and the robust men's voices buoyant above them, afloat on the night, boxed between the two-story brick facades on either side of the street.

> *We are coming, coming, our union to restore,*
> *We are coming, Father Abraham, three hundred*
> *thousand more.*

General Gibbon, their division commander, was sitting on his horse beside the singers, who stood forward of the band. He was leaning with both his gloved hands on the saddle pommel, eyeing the column as it flowed by, and smiling. Colonel Hall sat next to him. The song was sprightly and the men caught its mood and saw the steely Gibbon actu-ally smiling and smiled themselves. Their gait quickened, they fell in step with one another.

"That's Billy McGuinness over there," Merriman said. "Them boys're Nineteenth Mass."

"They sure sing good," Elisha said.

A man and woman had come out onto the roofed porch of the house across the street in bathrobes and slippers.

"Chase them back to Virginia," the man called to them.

"God bless all of you," the woman said.

> *If you look across the hilltops that meet the*
> *northern sky,*
> *Long moving lines of rising dust your vision*
> *may descry . . .*

Then it was behind them, slowly dying, gone by the time they passed the town's last straggling buildings, a second church, a white-clapboard store of some sort with a gallery along its front, an incongruous-looking log house with a trellis laden with roses. They remembered it, though, the surprise of coming on it in that silent sleeping town, the leavening feel of the music in their tired bodies, and the memory went with them down the wearying moonlit road and in some strange way sustained them.

They came to another town some hours later and poured on through it without pause and then, north of it, where both wild and cultivated fields rolled away to the horizon, came the order to halt. Ahead of them in the darkness, as far as they could see, the army was scattering on either side of the road, the solid column suddenly melting, dissolving, the men stumbling this way and that and collapsing in the grass.

The men of the Twentieth stacked their rifles, dropped their knapsacks and rolled blankets, and a good many of them headed for the woodlot bordering the field. The grass was knee high and damp from the rain. The dark woodlot was busy with squatting men, the night air odorous with it.

"Ain't this attractive," McNamara said.

"Oh, if our sweethearts could see us now," Merriman sang out.

Afterward they washed their hands with canteen water, taking turns pouring for one another, and spread their blankets on the stiff grass and sat down and ate some pork and hardtack and drank from their canteens. Rivers had come over and spread his blanket next to Luke's.

"It's gone two o'clock," he said. "Be light soon."

"You ought to put them feet in a museum," McNamara said.

"You ought to suck my ass," Rivers said.

McNamara laughed.

"Won't be long fore I have me some shoes," Rivers said.

"Take shoes off a dead man, would you," McNamara said.

"Goddamn right I would."

"Let's go to sleep, boys," Elisha said.

"We'll fight tomorrow, won't we?" Thomas asked.

"First and Eleventh Corps is up ahead of us, what I hear," Rivers said. "They'll get hit fore we do, looks like."

The night was cool and Thomas lay down on his side next to Luke and tucked his knees behind Luke's and pressed his chest up against Luke's back. Spooning. Rivers lay down on Luke's other side and wriggled in backward against him until Luke was sandwiched between Thomas and Rivers with his face to Rivers's filthy sack coat and breathing his odor, which was earthy and sour with the long day's dust and sweat. It made Luke think of the root cellar under their barn, and he fell asleep to a vision of blanched carrots and celery and luminous white turnips on the cool, damp, hard-packed ebony dirt.

TWO

They lay in those fields all through the following day, wondering why they'd been pushed so hard the night before. That night they built fires, boiled coffee, crumbled their hardtack in it.

"I guess Meade's another dumb sonofabitch like the rest of em," McNamara said.

"They ought to of put Reynolds in charge. You'd see somethin then."

"Him or Hancock, one."

"Give him a chance, boys."

"Yeah, like we give Burnside a chance, and Hooker. You lose a lot of fights givin chances to halfwits."

They moved at dawn and at midmorning passed through Taneytown, Maryland, where people stood along the street and cheered and sang to them. "Tramp! Tramp! Tramp!" and "John Brown's Body." Boys and girls, men and women, their blended voices raucous and celebratory on the humid summer air, as if this were a final homecoming, and the fighting all behind them. Girls, smiling, doled out food from baskets: cheeses, cakes, pies, bread. A black-haired girl in a second-story window blew them kisses.

"I wonder if she'd care to have my address," Merriman said.

"I doubt it," Stackpole said.

"What's the matter, Luke, ain't she pretty enough for you?"

They spoke loudly, shouting through the noise, the hubbub.

"Luke ain't a ladies' man, I don't think."

"When the war's over," Merriman said, "we'll all be ladies' men. We'll be the ones whipped Bobby Lee, boys. Every one a us a hero. Girls won't leave us alone."

They bivouacked that afternoon on a big farm where two north-leading roads intersected, and Lieutenant Paine led Company I out on picket duty. They skirted corn and wheat fields and waded a stream and took up position beside a fallow field that had been planted in winter rye that had overgrown it in a pale green, silklike carpet. On the other side of the field was the trace of a road, and beside it a log cabin with white-blue smoke rising from its brick chimney.

Sergeant Holland led a detail, including Luke and Thomas and Merriman, across the field, which was wonderfully soft and pliant underfoot, to stand post along the road. He sent Rivers and Chase and Delaney forward toward the next woodlot to take first sentinel and the rest of them stacked their rifles and shed their knapsacks and sat down in the sun, in the roadside grass and wildflowers. The log cabin was directly across the road from them, set back a way with a garden plot in front of it, tomatoes and summer squash. A neat stack of wood chunks by the front door. There were no outbuildings visible except a chicken coop and a small and windowless building made of fieldstone.

"Why don't we go over there see what's for dinner," Merriman said.

"We'll have no confiscations," Holland said. "We're in the Union now."

But then the weathered plank door of the cabin swung open and an old Negro woman came out. She wore a brownish cotton dress with petticoats swelling it out. Her head was wrapped in a sky-blue bandanna knotted on her forehead. She came past the tomato garden and across the road, walking with a limp that pulled her sideways with each step. Her skin was a grayish cocoa-brown and drawn tight over the bones in her face and when she came near they could see the crosshatching in her sunken cheeks, the seams in her forehead, the frostlike white in her hair. She understood that Holland was in charge—by his chevrons, perhaps, or by his attitude as he watched her approach, a certain critical sharpness in his eye, a questioning distrust.

"Hello, Dinah," he said.

"You is late," she said.

Holland looked at Merriman and back at the woman. "Late for what?" he said.

"They fightin already."

"Who is?"

"Who you think? Southrons and y'all."

Holland smiled. "And how do you know they're fighting?"

"I hears em."

"Is that a fact?"

"You cain't hear them guns?"

"No I can't."

"They powerful."

Sergeant Holland looked again at Merriman. "Did the First and Eleventh Corps pass through here?"

"Must of done," Merriman said.

"You saw the front half of the army go through," Holland told the woman. "It's them you think you hear."

"I don't think, I knows."

"Crazy old nigger, ain't you," said a private named Roker.

The woman looked at him. "Old ain't crazy," she said. She turned back to Sergeant Holland. "I gots some eatins for y'all," she said.

"Do you," Holland said.

"I knowed you was comin. Gots a heap of em."

"Luke," Holland said. "Thomas. Go see what she's got."

They got up and followed the old woman across the narrow weed-grown road to her cabin. She moved very slowly, patient, bobbing sideways. She'd left the door open. They followed her inside, into the heat and smells of cooking. It was a single room with windows front and back that let in the daylight. There was a split-log floor and a crude pinewood table on which sat a very large pan of warm cornbread. An old cast-iron stove with a bake oven had been set in the fireplace and a stovepipe run up the chimney and on the stove, on a skillet, two slabs of beefsteak sizzled and spat. On a plank counter beside the stove were mixing bowls, earthenware crocks, two more raw steaks on a platter. The woman put on two padded mittens and bent over and pulled a second pan of cornbread from the oven, as large as the first. She set it on the table on a towel and took up a toasting fork and turned the meat over.

Luke and Thomas looked at each other. They looked at the old woman.

"How'd you know we were coming?" Thomas said.

"Southrons up to Chambersburg. They to Gettysburg. You *gots* to come, fore they owns the whole thing. You already late."

"Coming through here, I mean," Thomas said. "Past your house."

"How I know anything? You take this cake out and come back, hear?"

"But all this food," Thomas said.

"Ain't I keep sayin it? I *knowed*. Y'all take that cake fore it gets cold."

Luke used his cuff to slide the hot pan across his arm and lifted it. Thomas picked up the cooler one.

"Y'all come back. Be a smart more."

They went back across the road like waiters with the great pans of yellow bread.

"Do you think she's crazy?" Thomas said.

"I don't know," Luke said.

The men watched them come, sprawled in the tall grasses.

"Well done, lads," Sergeant Holland said.

They laid the pans on the ground, bending the grass over. Sergeant Holland opened his pocketknife and knelt and began cutting the corn-bread into hunks.

"She told us to come back," Luke said.

"Go on, then," Holland said.

The old woman had set out two plates of thick china, white with pale blue rims, and on them the two steaks. Beside each plate a glass tumbler of milk, a fork and knife.

"Set yourselfs," she said.

Thomas looked at Luke. "Maybe we should ask Holland," he said.

"He sent us here, didn't he?" Luke said.

They sat down across from each other and took up the knives and forks. The meat was tough but juicy and rich tasting, and when it went down they could feel that richness in their hungry bellies. They ate quickly, thinking of Sergeant Holland. They took gulps of milk. It was warm and thick and sweet. The woman had put the other two steaks on the skillet. They could smell more cornbread in the oven.

"Are they still fighting?" Thomas said.

"They be fightin till you gets there. It ain't far to go."

"I never was in a fight before," Thomas said.

"I knows that. You a child." She looked at Luke. "You ain't been in no fight neither."

"No," Luke said.

She poked one of the steaks with the fork. "You brothers, ain't you."

"You must have powers," Thomas said.

"I old, that's my powers."

"But to hear shooting all that way off."

"You gots to listen, child."

"I am listening."

The woman put the toasting fork down and moved past them across the room. In the corner was a corroded brass bed, tidily made up, and next to it an old maple chest of drawers whose lacquered finish was worn and peeling. Luke wondered how it had come to this cabin in the middle of nowhere. He wondered how the bed had. The woman leaned down and opened a drawer. She rummaged around, found something, and brought it to the table.

"You take this," she said, and put a plain silver cross, much tarnished, in front of Thomas. "You carry it wif you, it give you luck."

Thomas hesitated.

"Take it," Luke said.

Thomas picked up the cross. It was surprisingly substantial, weighty. It had no string or chain.

"Massa done give it to me day he free me. He say the good Lord wif him now, and wif me too."

"But you should keep it," Thomas said.

"I ain't need it no more."

"But you might."

"No I ain't. I free. Gawn stay free. Y'all gawn whup them Southrons."

"Do you have something for my brother?" Thomas said.

"He ain't a child like you."

A child, Thomas thought, and felt encased in his own youth and inexperience, his blithe nature, inescapable from the time he'd left the Vineyard. He had thought being with Lilac had changed him but it hadn't, or hadn't changed him enough for what lay ahead. He dropped the cross into his coat pocket.

"You boys havin a nice afternoon?" Merriman said in the doorway.

"We're done," Luke said, and pushed his plate back.

"Godamighty," Merriman said. He'd seen the meat.

"You next," the woman told him.

Thomas cut a last piece of meat and forked it into his mouth. He and Luke stood up.

"Set yourself," the woman told Merriman. "You two: take them dishes out and scrub em."

"That ain't necessary on my account," Merriman said. He sat down.

The woman turned the two steaks. They hissed, spat grease.

"You boys better get on back," Merriman said. "Tell Holland I'll be along directly."

"Gots more meats in the springhouse," the woman said.

Thomas looked at her. "How much meat?" he said.

"Gots a half a steer. Better you eats it than the Southrons."

"But where'd you get it?"

"Gets it where I gets it."

"Holland's waitin on you two," Merriman said.

She fed all ten of them. In between they sat beside the road with the bills of their caps pulled low against the sun and discussed whether the old woman was crazy, or a witch, or had just guessed their coming, and whether she could really hear firing to the north. They wondered where she'd acquired half a steer, butchered, and who chopped her firewood, and where her milk came from. They wondered if she owned the land where her cabin sat, and how she'd come by it. No one could make any sense of it, not any sense at all.

"She may be a witch," Merriman said, "but them vittles is real."

"Go take your turn, Rivers," Sergeant Holland said. "And you, Delaney."

"Eat in a nigger cabin," Rivers said. His hair was still blood-matted where the bar girl had hit him with her bottle.

"Go on, Jake," Luke said.

"Hell, I'll go in his place," Merriman said. "Get me another beef-steak."

"That you won't," Sergeant Holland said. He was watching Luke and Rivers, neutral as to the outcome but curious.

"They smell so," Rivers said.

"It's clean in there," Luke said. "She's cleaner than any of us."

"He don't have to go he don't want to."

"He wants to," Luke said.

"Shitgoddamn," Rivers said, and picked himself up and headed across the road.

"You be respectful," Luke called after him.

Rivers nodded and went on across the road behind Delaney to the cabin of the ancient black woman. Delaney told them afterward that he'd drunk his milk down and she'd refilled his glass and he'd thanked her for it. Said he never once looked at her except when her back was turned, but you couldn't call him in any way disrespectful. Ate his beef-steak fat and all, Delaney said.

Then on the other side of the field of winter rye the boy Davis was beating the general. There was a particular urgency in it this time, something peremptory. The men scrambled to their feet and selected their muskets from the two stacks. The three sentinels came at a lope, converging from either side of the cabin. Chase and Tom Jackson came out of the cabin stuffing their bloody steaks into their haversacks. The old woman stepped outside into the shade of the building. She watched them don their knapsacks and shoulder their guns and set out across the field at a half run. Thomas waved to her but she did not wave back. As he jogged over the thick soft rye he reached into his pocket and touched the cross.

Willie Davis had stopped drumming. The men had earlier built a couple of fires and were hastily scattering the charred wood and stamping out the flames. Others were slinging on their haversacks, their knapsacks.

"There's hell to pay, boys," Henry Wilcox said. "They've shot Reynolds."

"The hell they did."

"He's dead, I tell you. A staff officer brung the news. Horse all in a lather. There's a hell of a fight up the road."

"Fall in," Paine said.

"There's a big fight and we're losin it."

"Fall in, goddamn it!"

Sergeant Cate had posted and they formed their line on him. Paine, flushed and sweating and glowering martially, ordered them into column and moved them out at the double quick. They skirted a great cornfield. The ground was worn from their coming and they moved rapidly and in good order.

"Hancock's gone on ahead hell for leather. Left Gibbon in charge of us."

"Ole Gibbon. Hard-ass sonofabitch. He'll be all right."

"I just seen Reynolds a couple a days ago. He was sittin on his horse, eatin a apple."

"Let's make em pay for it, boys."

"Luke," Thomas said. "I have to stop."

"Not now," Luke said.

"I have to."

Luke looked around. "Sergeant Cate!" he said.

Cate was alongside the column some paces back. He trotted forward.

"Thomas has to do his business," Luke said.

"You better hold it, son," Cate said.

"I can't," Thomas said.

They were coming into a low valley where the stream ran. Here and there on the far side, highlighted by the sun, russet cattle grazed. Higher up, in the distance, you could see the encampment.

"All right," Cate said. "Be quick about it."

"Thank you, Sergeant."

Thomas spun out of line toward the cornfield shedding his knapsack. Lieutenant Paine had come up.

"What the hell is this?" he said.

"He's sick, sir," Cate said.

"I don't give a goddamn," Paine said. "Get back in column, Private."

"I'll see to him, sir," Cate said.

"Wipe his ass for him, will you?"

"No sir," Cate said.

The men passing, hurrying along at the double quick, kept their eyes front and gave no sign of hearing them—except for Jake Rivers, who glanced darkly at Paine, at Thomas, at Paine again. Then, quickly, the column was by them, the sibilant footfalls and tinny rattle receding downhill.

"You desert, Chandler, I'll have you *both* shot," Paine said, and turned and followed his company.

"You hear that?" Cate said.

"I won't desert, Sergeant. My word on it."

Cate nodded, shouldering his musket, and hurried on while Thomas plunged in among the rows of corn. He put his musket down and shed his knapsack and haversack and stripped his coat and lowered his pants and voided himself in watery torrents. Sweet relief swept over him. He cleaned up as best he could with handfuls of dry corn leaves. He put on his coat, slung his haversack. The leafy stalks with their clusters of green-dressed corn rose like miniature trees in a thick silent forest. He moved away from the odor of what he'd done and sat down on the dry lumpy red-brown dirt and listened. The column was gone. Crows squawked somewhere. He could feel a lazy scuttling of graybacks on his scalp, a vague itch not worth scratching.

There was a closet under the stairwell of their house in New Bedford and Thomas had liked to let himself in when no one was looking and close the door and sit against the wall in the dark among the coats and boots and umbrellas while life went on beyond the door without him. He would sit there for a long time, just listening—to the voices of his parents, of Luke and Maggie, the girl who'd worked for them before Rose came, and, in summer, with the windows open, to the distant clop of hooves on the cobbled street and the murmur of passing voices. He remembered hearing Luke ask Maggie where he was and sitting still while Luke went all over the house, up and down the stairs, looking for him. Luke had gone out and after a while his mother had come home and asked Maggie where he was and Maggie said she guessed he was outside somewhere and Thomas had known that for as long as he sat there nothing and no one could harm him.

He uncapped his canteen and took several warm swallows. The crows had ceased to cry out and there was perfect silence but Thomas knew it was a lie. *God,* he thought. *Oh God, please help me.* He reached into his pocket and gripped the cross. It was greasy-feeling, like a coin. Its edges bit into the pad of his hand. He stood up, still holding it, and shrugged into his knapsack and picked up his musket and went down the narrow leaf-flagged corridor between rows of corn to the wide and jeopardous world beyond.

THREE

They'd fought all day of July 1 to the north and west of town and in the late afternoon the Federals broke and came boiling through the streets in disorderly retreat, the Confederates pursuing them like dogs on their heels, drawing every drop of blood they could. The Federals came up Carlisle Street, running. The cooler among them would pause to load and fire then whirl and run on, across the Diamond and down Baltimore Street. Charles Will and five of his employees, two white and three Negro, and his two lodgers, a Mr. Phipps from Philadelphia and a Mr. Irons from Lancaster, listened to the din of musketry and shouting and horses' screams sitting on the dirt floor of the cellar of the Globe Inn. You could tell exactly what was happening; the Federals' yells were guttural, husky, desperate, while the Southerners whooped and ululated as if in the delirium of some primal blood sport, as perhaps it had become. There was cannon fire; it tore the air as thunder does and reverberated in the walls of the building and the ground on which they sat.

Just listen to it, Mr. Will said. Another Southern victory.

It could be a tactical retreat, Floyd Wilkes said, and the two other colored boys, Roland and Trig, looked at him sourly. Floyd, since his decision to enlist, had been studying Hardee's Rifle & Light Infantry Tactics. Mr. Hamblin, the master at the colored school, had loaned it to him. Floyd had spoken to Roland and Trig about joining up—they could journey together to Washington, he'd urged—but they'd derided the idea.

I ain't get myself shot for no white folks, Trig said.

It isn't for white folks, Floyd had said. It's for yourself. It's for all Negroes, North and South.

All the niggers? What they done for me?

And so it went. No empathy for their brothers in bondage. No appreciation for the Emancipator, Mr. Lincoln. Godless boys who went with girls—Floyd knew about it—in barns and woodsheds and hayricks, who blasphemed and violated the Sabbath and were not above stealing from their employer. Floyd knew this, too; lumps of sugar, ginger cookies, a biscuit or two. What would fit in their pockets.

A tactical retreat, Floyd? said Mr. Will. A stampede is more like it.

Yes sir, Floyd said.

Mr. Phipps and Mr. Irons looked at each other and shook their heads in mutual sympathy. Phipps was a banker, come to Gettysburg to see Mr. Sebold of the Gettysburg Bank about some monies. Irons was a traveling salesman representing a porcelainware factory in Lancaster. There were two other white people: Lebrun, the chef, and a chambermaid, Etta Dowling. They had served breakfast to the Union generals Buford and Howard and their staffs, and when the fighting had begun far to the west and north—for a long time it had been like a ceaseless crashing of thunder on two horizons—Mr. Will had told them to go about their business. They'd served dinner to Mr. Phipps and Mr. Irons—roast turkey, boiled ham, vegetables, cornbread, apple pie—and then the battle had swept into Gettysburg and Mr. Will had hurried everybody to the cellar.

What are we gonna do, Mr. Will? asked Etta.

Do? said Mr. Will.

We ain't servin supper, are we?

We have two guests, Etta. Would you let them go hungry?

At this rate, remarked Mr. Phipps, we'll all be prisoners of the Confederacy.

Not a bit of it, Mr. Will said. You'll find them entirely congenial. They've enjoyed our hospitality before and will again, by the look of it.

We gawn do business with them Southrons? said Trig.

In the same impartial spirit as we did before, Mr. Will said.

They ain't whup us before.

Oh yes they did. They whipped us all over Virginia. They've been whipping us ever since the war began. One of these days Mr. Lincoln's going to come to his senses and call it off.

I wish he would, said Lebrun, the chef.

He can't, Floyd said. He never would.

None of your sermons, Floyd, said Mr. Will.

Sermons? said Mr. Phipps. What sort of sermons?

Oh, said Mr. Will, lots of abolitionist claptrap. Floyd's an adherent of Frederick Douglass and Sojourner Truth and the like.

The battle was moving south, into the maze of streets and side streets. Horse hooves pounded up Carlisle Street. There was a furious rumble of wagons and artillery and the shouts of drivers at mules and horses. Some stopped on the Diamond, some went on through.

Floyd a stuck-up nigger, Roland said.

He's an idealist, Mr. Will corrected. Nothing wrong with that.

The ignorance, Floyd thought. The ignorance of my own people.

You'd do well, Roland, to develop your mind some, Mr. Will said.

I tries, Mr. Will.

You don't try very hard, that I've noticed. You too, Trig. In some ways Floyd is to be admired.

He give hisself airs, is what I mean, Roland said.

He doesn't mean to, do you, Floyd? Mr. Will said.

No sir, Floyd said, hating himself for his meekness and vowing once more to leave this town forever.

The fighting seemed to have moved well south of the Diamond. Muskets banged in random scatter punctuated by frantic-sounding volleys that surely meant killing. On the Diamond now a drum hammered triumphantly and voices rang out, answering one another.

They've captured your town, Mr. Phipps said.

It's all right, Mr. Will said. They were here before and no one was harmed.

They stripped the goddamn stores, Lebrun said.

You watch your tongue, Mr. Will said.

I was scared half to death, Etta said.

They're honorable men, Mr. Will said. Foraging is permissible in wartime. No army was ever more gallant. However—he smiled drily at Floyd and Trig and Roland—I think it'd be best if you boys stayed here tonight.

That be nice of you, Mr. Will, Roland said.

Southerners are a mite touchy about Negroes, I believe.

They hate us, Floyd said.

Not if you keep your place, Mr. Will said.

I keeps my place, Trig said.

That's debatable, Mr. Wills said joshingly.

I might still go home, Floyd said.

Don't be idiotic, Mr. Will said.

I've a right to, Floyd said.

Good God, Mr. Will said.

You stay here, Floyd, Etta said. Please.

I should milk the cow, he said. She'll be in discomfort.

Won't be no cow, Roland said, them Southrons find her.

I'll hide her then.

Pride, said Mr. Will. It'll only get you in trouble, Floyd Wilkes.

Git you shot, Trig said.

Git you sold down South, Roland said, and then where you be?

They're right, you know, Mr. Will said.

I'll stay the night tonight, Floyd said. I'm obliged, Mr. Will.

They could hear it now and they marched all afternoon toward the rumble of the guns. The sergeants had orders to prod stragglers back into line at bayonet point and the provost guard to shoot anybody who refused to fall in. The sun fell lower. A rattle of musketry could now be heard under the growing boom of artillery. A private named Butters reeled out of line, dropping his musket, and fell to his knees, put his hands to his face and began to sob. Company I was the lead regiment today and Colonel Revere, walking at the head of the column, heard him and came back at a hobbled run with Colonel Macy beside him. Revere dropped to one knee and put his hand on Butters's shoulder.

"What is it, Private?" he said.

"I can't," Butters said. He was shivering violently now and his teeth knocked together. Tears ran down his stubbled face. "I can't," he said. "I can't, I can't, I can't."

Revere looked up past him. "Sergeant Cate," he said.

Cate saluted briefly. Revere stood up.

"Take him into the woods," he said. "Do what you can and leave him if you have to."

"Leave him, sir?" Macy said.

"Leave him," Revere said.

"Up with you, son," Cate said.

He helped Butters to his feet and took his arm and walked him, sobbing, in among the trees and out of sight of the column. Revere moved off, limping, toward the front of the column. Macy spat on the ground, shook his head, and followed.

Thomas was living now as in a languid dream, where time moved slowly and colors were muted and sights and sounds seemed to register belatedly on his consciousness, exotic, fantastical, not real. He did not know, could not remember, when the column had been ordered out of the road and onto the roadside fields, where they tramped across wheat and flourishing corn, cutting a wide avenue of mashed amber and green while on the road, white as bone-dust, advancing ambulances and artillery— the guns yawing and skidding heavily as the drivers whipped the teams along, limbers jouncing, caissons rattling—battled for passage against empty supply wagons and laden ambulances going pell-mell in the other direction, away from the fighting. Along both sides of the road the walking wounded limped and shuffled. Thomas watched it all, his head turned sideways, mesmerized, as he marched. The faces of the wounded were filthy with sweat and dust and black gunpowder. They wore the white crescent of the Eleventh Corps on their caps and Thomas's comrades were quick to note this.

"Goddamn Dutchmen."

"You boys run again, did you?"

Heads were wrapped in blood-soaked bandages. Some leaned on sticks, dragging stiff legs in blood-stiffened trousers. And yet not all of them were visibly injured. A healthy-looking soldier pushed a wounded comrade in a wheelbarrow. The wounded man, his right pant leg wet with blood, lay back with an unlit pipe in his mouth and his eyes closed and his arms folded tight against his chest.

"*Nicht recht,*" he said through clenched teeth, talking, it seemed, to himself. "*Nicht recht, nicht recht.*"

"Where you goin, skulker?"

"Sonofabitch don't even speak American."

"Dutch sonsabitches."

"What happened up there, anyways?"

A red-bearded soldier with a bandage wrapping his thigh waved in the direction of the guns. "Whole goddamn Eleventh Corps is wiped out, boys. Whole First Corps too. The army's fucked, and that ain't no lie. You might as well turn around go home."

"You suck my ass, Dutchman."

"I ain't a Dutchman."

"You goddamn skulkers ought to be shot."

"I ain't a skulker."

Ambulances clattered by rearward, cutting across a hayfield. Thomas wished he could see inside them, under the canvas, wished he could see the terrible wounds.

"Move along," Sergeant Holland said. "Close up, close up."

More fleeing supply wagons, crack of whips, dust boiling up. A mounted officer—dark blue shoulder board, a staff officer—turned his horse sideways in the road and drew his revolver and leveled it at the sweating face of a Negro teamster.

"Clear the road, you black sonofabitch."

Artillery behind him, stretching back into the risen dust.

"Make way, goddamn it."

The Negro sawed the reins and barked *haw* and his mules heaved to the right. The big wagon swung over into the roadside wheat and the artillery came on, horses digging in and straining to get the limbers and cannon moving again, the caissons, the battery wagons.

"We're close, ain't we," Thomas said, when he saw that the Negro would not be shot.

"We won't fight till tomorrow," Elisha said over his shoulder.

"How do you know?"

"It's gettin late, that's how I know. We gonna attack Bobby Lee in the dark?"

"We might do," Stackpole said.

"Meade ain't that uncautious," Merriman said.

"You think that fellow was right about the First Corps gettin wiped out?"

"Hell no. The Iron Brigade wouldn't let it happen. Nor would Hancock."

"Eleventh Corps, that's another matter."

"Close up," Sergeant Cate said. "Close up, there, close up."

They bivouacked after sundown in woods east of a high, steep, thickly wooded hill. North of them the guns had fallen silent and now there was the sporadic crackle of musket fire. Skirmishers, Elisha explained. They'll keep it up all night sometimes. They found water and made coffee and broke their hardtack into it and skimmed the drowned bugs off and drank and ate uncomplainingly. Most had eaten all of their three-day ration of salt pork but few were seriously hungry after the pies, cheeses, sandwiches, and other foods they'd been plied with since entering Maryland. The moon was up, full, and a warm mist had unraveled itself in the woods, suspended among the black trunks in fleecy scarves and ribbons.

"By God I could use some liquor," Rivers said.

"I could too," Willie Davis said.

"You wouldn't know what to do with it."

"Drink the sonofabitch," the boy said, to laughter.

"You scared, Jake?" McNamara said. He held his lighted pipe before his face.

"When was I ever scared?"

"You still got that pistol, Mac?"

"I got it. Be some Rebs wish I didn't."

"I wonder will Lee go for Harrisburg now he's whipped us."

"He ain't whipped us."

"Ask them Dutchmen if he ain't."

"Lee's got more whippin to do fore he can go for Harrisburg," said Henry Wilcox.

"What if he does go for Harrisburg," Thomas said. "Then what?"

"I guess we'd got to chase him," said Tom Jackson.

"You boys ain't learned a thing in two years," Henry said. "Lee don't go for places, he goes for armies. He'll hit us tomorrow hard as hell."

Thomas hugged his knees and stared at the writhing flames. Today, amid the bloody wounded and the chaos of retreat and advance, he'd felt remote, protected, as if a glass jar or bell had descended around him, insulating him from fear, which he imagined beating against the glass, powerless to get at him. He'd thought it would continue to be but now as he listened to the men it had struck again, cold in his gut.

"Listen to them boys wastin balls," Merriman said.

The muskets made hard flat pops in the distance, one here, one there, two or three in quick succession and then, for a while, nothing.

"Why do they do it?" Thomas said.

"It's a kind of a game," Stackpole said. "You don't want em to get comfortable and they don't want you to."

"Will we be on skirmish?" Thomas said.

"In our turn."

"Anybody got a candle?" Wilcox said.

"Henry's gonna write to his wife."

"Don't be gloomy at her, Henry. None a them ahead-a-time good-byes. Makes you look foolish when you outlive the fight."

There were two or three offers of a candle. Henry took a stub from Jackson and moved away into the silvery darkness.

"He's got the glooms, all right," Jackson said.

"He'd be mourned if he was took."

"He won't be took," McNamara said, drawing on his pipe.

Everyone looked at him. There was the soft snap and whisper of the fire. Voices, low, solemn sounding, at a fire nearby.

"All right," said Tom Jackson. "I'll take that for a true prophecy."

"Amen," someone said.

They were quiet another while.

"What's the name of this town up yonder they're fightin over? Anybody know?"

"Gettysburg," Luke said. He'd asked Sergeant Cate. "It lies between York and Chambersburg."

"Well, here we go again. Small little place ain't nobody ever heard of, then Bobby Lee comes along and there's a fight and the whole world knows her name."

"Gettysburg," someone murmured.

They all watched the fire burn.

"By God I could use some liquor," Rivers said.

Thomas and Elisha sat with their backs against the trunk of a white pine tree in the quiet of midnight. In front of them rose the big round tree-clad hill, with the moon looking down from the gun-blue sky to its right. No tents had been pitched. It was too warm for spooning and the men lay among the trees apart from one another with their blankets shrouding them and Elisha thought of the scattered dead at the field hospital at Antietam, the surgeons draping the wounded in their blankets as they died. Campfires still smoked and there were few mosquitoes. Shots still popped in the distance, intermittent now and desultory sounding, as if the deadly game of before had lapsed into something idle, perfunctory.

"Sharpshooters," Elisha said. He spoke very quietly. "They ain't movin around like skirmishers do. Must be a smart chance of em in that town."

Thomas didn't say anything. He could smell days of sweat on Elisha, the dirt on him, the collected dust, and knew that he smelled the same. His coat lay beside him and he reached for it and dug into the right pocket and felt for the cross the old woman had given him. He caressed it with the tips of his fingers.

"Got them scopes long as their gun barrels," Elisha said. "Infernal things. Put a ball between your eyes at half a mile." He unbuttoned his haversack. "Look what I got, Tommy. Been savin it." He lifted out a thick soft slab of something wrapped in newspaper. "It's cherry cake," he said. "Lady give it to me in Taneytown. We'll go halfs on it."

"I ain't hungry," Thomas said.

"You ain't hungry for cherry cake? Here." And he tore the limp wedge in two very gently and lifted a piece into Thomas's cupped hands.

"She was a pretty lady give me this. Wore her hair down long. You didn't see her?"

"I might have."

Elisha brought his cake up with both hands and took a large bite. "Damn that's good," he said, with his mouth full. "Go on have you some, Tommy."

Thomas nodded. He took a bite of cake.

"Lady told me what it was," Elisha said, "or I wouldn't of known. Cherry cake. I never heard of such."

Thomas took another bite. He chewed it slowly, looking out over the body-strewn forest floor. It was open underneath the trees, kept so by wandering cattle like so much woodland down here. On the Vineyard you could hardly move through the woods for the brush and greenbriars.

"Your Rose don't make it?" Elisha said.

"She ain't *our* Rose," Thomas said. The cake was moist and delicious but it didn't matter that it was. He could have eaten it or not, either way.

"I know she ain't," Elisha said.

They ate. Thomas slapped his ear, a mosquito.

"Lord," Elisha said, "I did enjoy her upside-down cake. Warn't it good?"

"Everything was."

"I didn't mean she belonged to you, Tommy."

"I know."

"She don't belong to nobody. Belongs to herself. Way God intended."

They ate. A mosquito whined, did not alight. Behind them someone snored, a sound like the air being raggedly sundered. Elisha pushed the last of his cake into his mouth and bunched the oily newspaper and tossed it aside.

"Tommy."

"What."

"Would you still go see them twins if somethin was to happen to me?"

"Nothing's going to happen to you."

"But if it did. I'd like to know you was gonna see em."

"All right," Thomas said.

"You'd know how to find em. Take Luke with you. You wouldn't have no trouble then."

"I find them, then what?"

"You might speak to Iris for me."

"Tell her what?"

"I don't know. That I died brave, I guess."

"You think you'll die brave," Thomas said.

"Well, I hope I would."

"Shut up about it, will you?"

"I don't mean no offense."

"Shut *up*," Thomas said, and bowed his head and closed his eyes.

Elisha lifted his arm around his shoulders and pulled him against him.

"Don't pay it no mind," he said. "It's just what-iffin. Ain't neither of us gonna get killed. Nor Luke."

Thomas looked up. "I don't know what I'm doing here," he said.

"Don't you worry about yourself," Elisha said. "You're gonna do fine. Matthew's your file partner and me and Luke'll both be in the next file, either side. Mac'll be close by. Joe Merriman too. I keep sayin it: it ain't like you're among strangers. You gonna finish that cake?"

It lay in Thomas's lap, half eaten. "You have it," he said.

Elisha hesitated, then unhooked his arm and took up the cake in both hands. Never in his life had he been full, as the expression went, except on that snowy night at the Chandlers' when Rose had cooked an Indian pudding and the three boys had eaten to their hearts' content, spooning cream onto it, as much as you wanted, and the cream melting into little rivers. Rose watching them, smiling like it was some magical trick they were putting on for her, eating that entire pudding. That was the only time. Like droppin food down a hole, his mother always said.

"I don't know that I'll die brave," Elisha said.

"If you were to die you would," Thomas said.

"You do your best. That's all it is."

They were quiet awhile. A distant crackle of gunfire, then silence.

"Where are you sleeping?" Thomas said.

"Next to you," Elisha said. He licked the crumbs off his fingers and thumb. "I'll get my blankets," he said.

FOUR

They decamped in the dark and marched for an hour, and then there was a long delay, the regiment standing in column for another hour on the Taneytown Road while the darkness paled to first light and officers galloped here and there hollering at one another to do this or that to no visible effect. More regiments arrived, some to wait in column like the Twentieth, some to move on up onto the dark elevations to the north and west. A little before six Colonel Hall rode up and spoke with Colonel Revere, and Revere and his officers turned the regiment and took it up a long ridge slope directly west and posted it here, just shy of the summit, in reserve.

Reserve! It was a reprieve, a deliverance, and Thomas closed his eyes, drank a deep breath of the summer air, cool and sweet at this hour, not yet fouled by the occupancy of an army. The order was passed to lie on their arms, and they laid their guns down in formation and sat or lay down more or less where they wished. The colors remained cased, lying on the ground side by side, at about the middle of the line.

"It don't mean we won't fight," cautioned Elisha, who had seen Thomas take that grateful breath of air. "Not if the Rebs hit here."

"Do you think they will?" Thomas said.

"Well," Elisha said, studying the long sweep of land to the south and west, and the wooded ridge on the other side of the valley, "they got a awful long way to come. I misdoubt they'd even get here, let alone break through."

Luke said nothing, gazing west and south. How peaceful it looked, how bucolic. God was here. In the amber wheat, the tall grass, the fences, orchards, the gem-green trees. Away to the left, just this side of a road that cut diagonally across the valley, stood a red barn and red-brick farmhouse with shade trees and a well. A hawk banked against the sky, coasted down, rose again. God had made it all and would remake it when He had seen justice done here.

"Course," Elisha said, "you never know with Bobby Lee."

They sat, lay, scattered about like breakfast picnickers. Broken clouds layered the sky, filtering the glare of the rising sun. The terrain here was meadowy, wild rye and switchgrass, thistles, Queen Anne's lace, honey-suckle, daisies, wild roses, with frequent iron-gray rocks cropping out, lichen-barnacled and cut with deep fissures. To their right, a little uphill of them, huddled a copse of young oak and chestnut trees, shaped rather like an umbrella, stretching downhill toward a stone wall. The ground beneath it was overrun with brush and brambles, and around it too the hillsides were snarled in brush and scrub.

In front of them, along a stone wall perhaps a hundred yards down the gentle west slope, was the front line, the Seventh Michigan and the Fifty-ninth New York, in the process now of taking down a rail fence that rose above the stone wall and leaning and piling the rails and posts on top of it. The wall was perhaps three feet high, its stones jagged and black, and where it ended, running south, the rail fence went on, and the infantry were busy breaking it too, wrestling posts out of the ground and smashing rails loose with their musket butts, stacking them any way they could for protection.

Then Colonel Revere ordered Companies D and G to their feet and into line and into column, and Captain Patten marched them away, south along the ridge then west into the valley, into the high grass, to make up Colonel Hall's contribution to the skirmish line. Thomas watched them go and breathed thanks that Company I had not been chosen and wondered, irrationally, if Revere knew of him somehow and had spared him for now. The men had left their knapsacks and they marched loose-shouldered and brisk with their guns at right shoulder shift, some stone-faced and some nonchalant, some talking, some even smiling at some remark or drollery.

Thomas stared after them. He'd had a recurrent nightmare when he was a small boy attending the Parker Street School in New Bedford, and this waiting for the fight to begin was like it. In the dream he'd been chosen or had inexplicably volunteered to play piano at the Christmas recital. No one doubted he *could* play it, and the day bore down on him, the moment when he would walk out onto the stage in front of his schoolmates and all their parents and sit down at Miss Price's piano and— what? Admit he was an impostor? Strike the keys and fill the auditorium with discordant nonsense? He didn't know. He didn't know the shape the disaster would take, only that disaster was inevitable.

Elisha was watching him, the pained squint of his eyes and the way he kept passing the back of his hand over his mouth.

"I'd love a wash," he said, "wouldn't you, Tommy?" Sometimes it was the small things that cheered a man or took his mind off the fight that was coming. Talk of baths and food and girls, talk of home.

"I guess I got other things to think about," Thomas said.

"We're a sight, ain't we?" Elisha said, as if he hadn't heard him. There'd been no opportunity to bathe or shave in two days and the cleanshaven all wore a stubble. Elisha's stubble was corn-yellow and his cornsilk mustache was crowding his upper lip.

"We ain't had rations since Monocacy Junction," said Rivers, who had left his file and come over to sit with them. "When ago was that?"

"Two days," Elisha said.

"Feels longer," Rivers said. "I ain't got naught but a couple a crackers left."

"If the wagon don't come up tomorrow I'll share with you, Jake," Elisha said.

"One of us will," Luke said.

"It's kindly thoughts," Rivers said.

The army was still arriving and an hour later the ridge and the land behind it to the east were acrawl with men, wagons, guns, mules, horses. The teams were pulling the guns and caissons up the back side of the ridge from the Taneytown Road, a gentle climb but a long one, over corn and wheat already well trampled, leaving wheel- and hoof-chewed swaths behind them, the swaths crisscrossing and merging with one another, until men and animals and wagons had flattened everything to green and blond carpeting. Ambulances were gathering down along the road, and ammunition wagons. A steady cacophony of hollering and wagon clatter and neighings and mule-brayings and whipcracks, with the white-gold dust billowing up. Officers—Hancock, Gibbon, Hall, Harrow, Webb—passed and repassed along the ridge, followed by their staffs. Orderlies galloped this way and that.

A battery, six guns, went down the west ridge slope toward the enemy and unlimbered on the summit of a gentle rise about halfway to the diagonal road. Rhode Islanders, somebody said. The teams stayed harnessed to their limbers and they cropped the grass, which was so tall they did not need to bend for it. They'd left the caissons on the ridge, behind the copse. Another battery—no one knew from what state—unlimbered on the ridge summit north of the copse.

You could not see the Rebels yet on their mile-distant ridge with its thick cover of trees. Nor could you hear them through the noise and confusion on this side. Now and then would come a flash of sunlight on steel through the trees and you knew they were on the move over there, that some great deployment was under way, and the men commenced to argue again about what Lee would do.

"Could be he'll head straight for Harrisburg and leave us settin here like fools," said Joe Merriman.

"Will you shut up about Harrisburg?" Rivers said. "He ain't goin no damn where after what he done to us yesterday."

"He'll hit one of the flanks," McNamara said. "That's what he does. Jumps you and rolls you up."

"The flanks has got hills on em."

"He'll hit em anyway," McNamara said.

"Safest place to be is right here in the middle," Merriman said.

"By God I wish he would hit us here," Rivers said. "I'd like to see them sonsabitches cross that valley with our batteries on em."

"So would I," Luke said, and they all looked at him.

"Lee ain't that stupid, Luke," McNamara said.

Then two laden pack mules led by Negroes came up the hill and the Negroes unstrapped four boxes of cartridges from the mules' backs, lifted them to the ground, and pried the lids off.

"Twenty more rounds, every man," Lieutenant Paine said. "March!"

They got up and waited in line to help themselves to two more packs of cartridges and caps.

"By Christ," Elisha said. "Eighty rounds."

"Where we gonna carry em all?" Rivers said.

They sat down again in the weeds and grass and opened the packs. Their cartridge boxes were full and they distributed the new cartridges in their haversacks, their coat pockets. They placed the tiny brass caps in their cap boxes.

"I guess Lee ain't goin to Harrisburg," Merriman said.

"This fight ain't over, is it."

"I told you it warn't."

Thomas worked very slowly. It was good to have something to do. He counted ten cartridges into his right coat pocket where his cross was and put the other ten in his left. *I'll use them first,* he thought, *and then the weight will go away.* He inserted the caps, carefully one by one, into their small black-leather box. He wondered how hot they got, and whether they burned your fingers when you removed them. *The gun barrel gets hot,* Elisha said. *You can burn your hand on it,* he said. *Get you a rag or handkerchief or some such.* Thomas opened his haversack and found the cloth bag he'd been using to keep his salt pork in. He put the bag in his right pocket with the cartridges and the cross.

"You boys ready to see the elephant?" It was Delaney, the redheaded Rhode Islander who'd journeyed down from New Bedford with Luke and Thomas all that while ago. Grinning. He was coming back from somewhere down the east side of the ridge.

"Are you?" Luke asked him.

"It's why we come, ain't it?" Delaney said.

"It's only a fool ain't afeard the first time," Rivers said.

"I didn't say I wasn't, did I?" Delaney said.

Midmorning the clouds burned away and a Rebel battery came down out of the woods and unlimbered on the slope directly across from them. Another appeared off to their right, guns and gunners and horses specks in the distance, and after a while an intermittent, almost casual artillery duel began. The Rebels would loose a round at the Rhode Island battery in the field or at the one near the copse, solid shot, bolts and balls. They would scrape the sky in an invisible whistling arc and fall long or short, the bolts hitting the ground with a thud that seemed to check the earth in its turning and burrowing, flinging up dirt and stones and tatters of grass. The cannonballs skipped and bounded, crushing brush and scrub and grass. The Union batteries would answer, the terrific blasts flattening the air along the ridge slope then careering away, echo upon echo, into the distance. Then, as by mutual agreement, there'd be a cessation. Fifteen minutes, thirty, and then one side or the other would send a shot across, and the other would answer it, and neither, yet, quite found the range.

The skirmishing started at about the same time in the high grass out beyond the road. The men hid in the grass and shot at one another from behind trees and fences. The gunshots were loud and reverberant and the smoke rose in lazy drifting puffs. The shooters would dodge from tree to tree and disappear back into the summer grass. The two lines maintained a respectful distance from each other, swaying back and forth but never breaking.

McNamara and Elisha were playing poker through it all. They sat cross-legged, keeping score with percussion caps, each cap representing five pennies. By noon Elisha owed two dollars. Thomas watched them play, but his mind wasn't on it, it was on the guns, the whistling ordnance. Every one seemed to be coming toward them but the men only glanced across at the source of the shot, listened a moment, and went back to what they were doing.

"I just want to get on with it," Rivers said. He was cleaning his musket.

"They ain't gonna hit us here," McNamara said.

"You don't know that," Rivers said. He'd poured some canteen water down his gun barrel and now pushed a torn piece of rag down it with his rammer.

"Come on play a hand, Tommy," Elisha said.

Thomas shook his head.

"It'll relax your mind."

"It'll relax his pocketbook," McNamara said.

Luke looked at him and smiled faintly. He was lying on his side, reading *Wuthering Heights*.

"It's commencin to stink up here, ain't it," Rivers said.

With all the traffic up and down the back slope of the ridge, there was no place to dig sinks and the men had to go where they might, among bushes or high grass and never very far from their position. And there were the horses of the battery north of the copse, and the horses of the Rhode Island battery's caissons not ten rods away, and the leavings of officers' horses, dropped at random.

"It'll stink worse tomorrow," McNamara said.

"I about forget what a privy looks like," Merriman said.

"War ain't for the delicate," McNamara said, laying down four jacks.

"Goddamn shit," Elisha said, and threw in his cards.

"You ought to learn to bluff," McNamara said, and helped himself to a percussion cap from Elisha's pile. "Half the time I beat you I'm bluffin."

"I ain't good at it," Elisha said.

The Rebel battery let fly and the bolt sang in the air and struck a moment later close to the limbers of the battery near the copse, and the horses reared and pawed the air and whinnied frantically and the men cursed and ran to grab their halters and calm them.

"Rebs hit that limber chest you'll hear some cussin," Merriman said.

"I'm surprised they ain't yet."

"The day is young."

"By God I hate this waitin," Rivers said.

"Try to wait quiet," McNamara said.

They saw General Sickles's Third Corps move forward into a peach orchard on its green salient a half mile away above what they would come to know as the Emmitsburg Road. The Peach Orchard, the Emmitsburg Road. The names would become known to them in the coming days and, if not, in a year or two or three, when the histories began to appear. For now they would know them, by name or not, as well as the landmarks and features of their home neighborhoods, and with that same intimacy of remembrance and association. Culp's Hill, Cemetery Hill, Cemetery Ridge, Seminary Ridge (Rebel territory for three days), Little Round

Top, Plum Run, the Devil's Den, the Wheatfield, the Codori farm. In the Peach Orchard, in front of the rows of miniature trees, the Third Corps deployed facing the road. The artillerists unlimbered and you could see it all a half mile away, vivid in the clear tintless light of the high sun—dark blue ranks of men, garish flags, gleaming steel. Their skirmishers were in the fields well beyond the road, their fire a rattle, firecracker-like in the distance. The skirmishers from the Twentieth were down there somewhere.

"Ought to of stayed where they was," Rivers said. "They done left a big hole in our line."

"Dan Sickles knows what he's doin," McNamara said.

"Mac likes Sickles. He don't like Hancock nor Gibbon, but he likes Sickles."

They'd gotten water—there was a good spring down across the Taneytown Road—and built a fire with fence rails and made coffee. McNamara had won three more dollars and Elisha had quit the poker game.

"He likes him cause he shot that man fucked his wife," Merriman said.

"One reason," McNamara said.

"I'd a shot him too," Rivers said.

"You'd a gone to jail if you had," said Stackpole.

"How come Sickles not to?"

"Fancy lawyer got him off."

"Stanton," Luke said, looking up from his book.

"That's right. Abe's number one man."

"Seward's his number one man," Luke said.

"Stanton is," McNamara said. "Seward's a goddamn abolitionist got his head up his ass."

"Don't argue with Luke," Rivers said. "He got more education than all a you put together."

"Just listen at him," Merriman said. "Jake's a abolitionist now."

"No I ain't," Rivers said.

"Have some coffee, Tommy," Elisha said.

Thomas shook his head. "It makes me jumpy," he said. He'd been hearing them talk as if from the distance of being half asleep, apart from it and indifferent to what they were saying. It was idle talk, irrelevant, misplaced. In fact, he wondered how they could talk so lightly, so stupidly, at such a time.

"Ain't you tired?" Elisha said. "Coffee would help."

"I must be, but I don't feel it."

"I don't guess nobody does right now," Elisha said.

"I wonder what's taking so long," Thomas said.

"Lee's up to somethin, all right," said Elisha.

"It took Jackson all day to get in position at Chancellorsville," McNamara said. "He marched them boys clear around our pickets."

"You know how Stanton got Sickles off?" Luke said. He had closed *Wuthering Heights*.

They all looked at him.

"Temporary insanity," Luke said. "Means he was out of his head when he did it."

"Out of his head," Rivers said, "and he got a whole corps under him."

"You just said you'd a done what he done," McNamara said.

"And I would of. But I ain't got a corps under me."

"Wouldn't that be pretty? General Jake Rivers, corps commander," said McNamara.

"The Rebs'd die laughin and the war'd end right there," someone said.

"Who was that fellow Sickles kilt, Luke?" Rivers said.

"Key. Philip Barton Key. His father wrote 'The Star-Spangled Banner.' Wrote the words, that is."

"By God," Rivers said.

"I do wish I knew what Lee was up to," Merriman said.

"Stay here you'll find out," said McNamara.

"Well," Rivers said, "your pa writes a song it don't give you the right to fuck a man's wife."

"Not Sickles's wife," Luke said.

The battle opened far to their south, hidden by woods and by the rocky hill called Little Round Top, musketry so voluminous it was indistinguishable shot from shot and over it like a great blanket the steady thunder of cannon. It began around four o'clock, both sides agreed afterward. Smoke rose, dirty white and darkening, and hung thicker and thicker above the treetops. The noise went on and on, savage and unabating, till you wondered how either side could stand so much fire. Here, the Rebel batteries across the way had ceased their intermittent shooting, and the skirmishing had all shifted south, across the Emmitsburg Road in front of Sickles's men.

"I told you they'd hit our flank," McNamara said.

"Why don't Sickles advance? He's just settin there."

"He advanced far enough, I'd say. Ain't that gap he left already big enough for you?"

Their officers stood in front of them halfway down to the wall, looking off toward the noise and smoke. Abbott and Macy stood companionably together. Macy said something and Abbott shook his head and laughed. Colonel Revere stood apart from all of them, very still, his hand resting on his sword hilt. His Negro servant stood in back of him, chewing a blade of grass and watching where Revere watched. The servant looked worried.

"I'd prefer to fight as listen to it," Rivers said.

"Jake needs a fight," McNamara said, "so's he can get him some shoes."

"Might be I'll get your shoes," Rivers said.

"You'll get you some shoes," McNamara said, "but they ain't gonna be mine."

Luke sat hugging his knees, gazing south. Silent, inscrutable; more than he'd been before he and Thomas had joined up, more than ever.

"What are you thinking?" Thomas said.

"We'll be file partners," Luke said. "I'll be right behind you."

"That isn't what you were thinking."

"Yes it was."

"Matt's my file partner," Thomas said.

"I'll swap with him when it comes to it."

"Paine won't let you."

"Cate will," Luke said.

"Maybe we won't fight after all."

"Listen," Luke said. "It's not our time yet."

"You don't know that."

"Yes I do. God isn't ready to take us yet."

Thomas looked at him. "God?"

"That's right," Luke said.

"What about me, Luke?" Elisha said.

"This is bad luck, this talk," Rivers said.

"Here's what I think," Elisha said. "Rebs pinned me at Antietam, they ain't gonna pin me so soon again. There's a reason God saved me, is what I think." He was thinking of Iris.

"That could be," Luke said.

"It's one a them things you know in your heart," Elisha said.

"I don't," Thomas said.

They were fighting on Little Round Top now, and just the other side of the Peach Orchard. Thomas reached into his pocket, dug around among the paper cartridges, and held the cross.

"It's comin this way, boys," Merriman said.

"It is for a fact."

"By God I wish someone'd look to that gap," Rivers said.

The First Minnesota had been held in reserve all day south of Cemetery Hill, where even shellfire couldn't get them, but then when General Caldwell went forward into the slaughter at the Wheatfield, Colonel Colvill took them up onto the ridge where Caldwell's division had been. There was a reserve battery there under Lieutenant Thomas and the men fell in beside it. It was a ridge only technically at this point, having fallen gradually away from Cemetery Hill to level ground from which the fields ran gently downhill to Plum Run and out beyond it to the Emmitsburg Road and, eventually, up again to Seminary Ridge. They formed up, looking across the broad shallow valley with the dry creekbed meandering through it and some large rocks strewn about and a few trees.

They'd been in position about an hour and had watched in mute dismay as remnants of Sickles's Third Corps came straggling to the rear, many with terrible wounds, and now it looked like the army was getting whipped twice in two days. A man staggered past them with his jaw shot away carrying a piece of it in his hand, teeth and all, and yet on his feet and walking, eyes staring intently ahead, moving with the fixed purpose of a deaf man, with no sound to distract him. Another man came crawling back on his hands and knees with his innards hanging out of him, dragging on the ground. The living dead. Off to the left the fighting raged on but they could not see much of it for the trees and thick smoke of battle. It was noisy, all right.

Then more Rebels came down off Seminary Ridge, a whole brigade, and across the Emmitsburg Road, and that is when the predicament of the First Minnesota and of the entire army became plain. Neither to their right nor their left was there any support. There was a gap in the Union line a quarter mile long and none but this one depleted regiment to fill it. And right then, providentially, General Hancock came riding by, cantering north, trailed by a staff officer. The general looked natty as always in a white shirt with ruffles and his black chin whiskers neatly trimmed, but his pale eyes were blazing. He'd been directing the counterattack against General Barksdale and thought everything was under control and when he saw that dark cloud of Rebels coming toward him on a wide front he thought it was more of General Sickles's men heading for the rear. The sun was low in the sky and smoke overhung the valley and shadows had begun to flood the countryside. Hancock stopped his horse to have a look and with that the Rebels let loose and the air whined and buzzed. The staff officer dropped his reins and sat up with a jerk and slumped forward, and Hancock wheeled his big horse and galloped straight up to Colonel Colvill. Colvill saluted him and Hancock returned it briefly and looked up and down the ridge. He stood up in his stirrups and looked beyond the regiment toward the rear.

God almighty, he said, are you all we've got here?

Yes sir, right now we are, returned Colvill.

Jesus goddamn Christ, Hancock said.

Yes sir, Colvill said.

What regiment are you? said Hancock.

First Minnesota, sir.

Hancock twisted around in his saddle and pointed to the solid mass of Rebels with their bright flags in the air. You see those colors? he said.

Yes sir.

I want you to take them.

I will, sir.

Hancock didn't wait another moment but spurred on to look for more men because there wasn't any way in the world one regiment could stop a brigade. A brigade ran around fifteen hundred men and the First Minnesota what with attrition and casualties was down to two hundred and sixty-two, including officers. The regiment was being sacrificed to buy the little bit of time needed to bring reserves up and so save the army, and they all knew it. Five minutes, Hancock said afterward. They had to give him five minutes or all was lost.

Colonel Colvill ordered them into line. He ordered them to fix bayonets. Then he raised his sword and took them forward at the double-quick. The first Rebel line—it was the Eleventh Alabama—had stopped just the other side of Plum Run and through the smoke their officers could be seen bustling here and there trying to re-form them where they'd gotten out of line during the advance across the valley. The Minnesotans could see the red battle flags and, even in the haze, the glint of the sun off their Enfields.

They advanced about two hundred feet and could see their faces now, and they halted and delivered a volley. The fusillade took down a fair number of the enemy and threw them into some confusion, and before the Rebels could regain their balance Colvill ordered the charge. They were running now, and the hollering began, that drawn-out hurrah that gets stuck in you and becomes a kind of grinding in your throat that goes on and on without you thinking about it and makes your throat ache afterward. The Alabamans had opened up on them and men began to drop, officers too, including Colonel Colvill. The colors went down and someone picked them up and they shot him too and another took them up again. They crashed into the Rebels with bayonets leveled and began slashing and stabbing. The Alabamans turned and ran, leaping over rocks and dodging brush and scrub, back to the relative safety of the second line, another Alabama regiment, with the rest of the brigade massed not many rods behind.

The Minnesotans crossed Plum Run and would have charged them too, but the Rebels had recovered now and opened fire and in a few moments half the regiment was down. They scrambled into the slight depression of the creekbed, where there were some covering thickets, and returned the fire,

but now the Rebel brigade got into line and another one was moving down
on them on their right, firing in enfilade. Dozens more of the Minnesotans,
scores, toppled over or reeled drunkenly, dropping their guns, or sat down
hard—all the ways of falling in battle—and with the Rebels advancing
from two sides, firing as they came, Captain Messick, the last officer left
standing, ordered them to fall back at the double-quick. They got out of
there fast, what was left of them.

What was left was forty-seven men unscathed while all the rest who'd
advanced with Colonel Colvill, two hundred and fifteen, were dead or
wounded. They did not take the Rebel flag, as General Hancock had directed,
but they purchased something much more precious, which was time. Five
minutes, ten. The day was saved, and the Union. Right there. Saved.

They watched the rout of the Third Corps in the dust and smoke and
the battle spread farther north, closer to them, their own army falling
back everywhere along the line, being driven, the smoke getting thicker
and darker till the two armies were ghost armies, shadows, blue and butternut indistinguishable, and you could see the yellow flashes from the
musket barrels spitting fire in the gloom. Colonel Hall sent the Nineteenth Massachusetts and Forty-second New York down into it and they
marched away in column at the double-quick and disappeared into the
haze and noise down where the ridge leveled off. The noise swelled still
louder and you had to raise your voice to be heard above it.

"Ain't I told you about that gap?" Rivers said.

"They ain't broke through or we'd know it," Merriman said.

"That goddamn Sickles, didn't I say it?" Rivers said.

"Shut up," McNamara said.

"You shut up."

"Jake," Luke said.

"I'm finished," Rivers said.

It was evening and they were still fighting, the sun far down the sky
above Seminary Ridge and visible only as a soft shrunken orange-pink
disc through a fog of musket and cannon smoke. Across the valley, in

the smoke and shadows, the Rebel battery woke with a roar and a shell split the darkened air with a shriek and this time someone said *Duck, boys* and the men went flat to the ground. The shell exploded close above them in a spray of white fire and the pieces came singing down and one took Henry Wilcox's leg off.

Luke saw it and seized Thomas's shoulders and pulled his face against his chest and locked an arm around his neck and held him.

"What?" Thomas said, trying to pull away. "What happened, Luke? What *happened?*"

Revere, on his feet, yelled for a stretcher and a percussion shell hit the ground in front of them and exploded in a geyser of earth and stones.

"Wounded! Wounded, goddamn it!"

Tom Jackson had come scrambling over on all fours. He knelt with Revere and took Wilcox's hand. "Rest still, Henry," he said. "Close your eyes."

The Rebel battery across the valley to their right had opened too and the sky keened and a shell burst downhill behind them, and another went off high overhead, and now their own batteries were replying. You had to shout to be heard, and the air was sulfurous and bitter with smoke.

"Wounded!"

The two stretcher bearers, brigade musicians, came running, bent over like hunchbacks. They opened the stretcher and set it down and slid Henry onto it and looked up at Revere.

"He's dead, sir," one of them said.

"No he ain't," Jackson said.

"Get back to your rank," Revere said.

"He ain't dead," Jackson said.

"Get back," Revere said. "*Now.*"

Thomas squirmed and Luke let him go—what was the point, this was only the beginning. Thomas saw Henry and stared a moment, then sank back down and closed his eyes and sucked in a deep breath. A percussion shell struck off to their left and the earth and pebbles flew and came raining down, and the smoke rose and drifted. The stretcher bearers were taking Henry and his leg to the rear. He lay on his back with his arms dangling, hatless, gaping wide-eyed at the smoke-filled sky. His arms danced as they jostled him.

Thomas raised himself and looked again. Luke moved closer and threw an arm around his shoulder, half covering him. "Never mind," he said. "Just never mind, Thomas."

"Rebel bastards," Jackson said. "Rebel sonsabitches."

"We'll make em pay, boys," Rivers said.

"Here they come," Merriman said.

Everyone rose on their elbows to look. Rebel infantry had swept down out of their woods in a line a half mile wide with skirmishers scattered out in front. They came down into the high grass and disappeared, all but their red flags and erect bayonets, moving forward myriad and glinting and eerie in a tight line.

"Steady, boys," Revere said, moving calmly among them. He was the only man of the Twentieth not lying down. "It's not our fight yet. Just lie steady."

A shell exploded midair, shrapnel, and hit somebody over in Company C.

"Wounded!"

There were two Union regiments along the Emmitsburg Road and they began firing at where the bayonets were, at the movement in the grass, and a new layer of fleecy smoke spread across the valley.

"Tommy?" Elisha said, speaking with his face pressed sideways to the grass.

"Henry's dead," Thomas said.

"I know he is. You got to think about somethin else."

"His leg tore right off."

"You hush, now. Don't think on it."

A shell burst to their left and a man yelled hoarsely, somebody in Company A, and Revere called for a stretcher then knelt beside him and placed a hand on his shoulder. Half his right foot had been torn away, the leather brogan severed with the foot.

"Goddamn," the wounded man said, and spat past his shoulder. "Sonofabitch."

"Steady now," Revere said. "You're going to be all right."

Stretcher bearers were there now and they wrapped the mangled foot and lifted the man over and he closed his eyes and folded his arms. A shell exploded somewhere down the back side of the ridge. They carried the wounded man down toward where it had hit and Revere rose and resumed his pacing.

"Why don't you get down, sir?" Macy said.

"I don't think it matters, Colonel, standing or lying."

"Just a suggestion, sir."

Revere wondered what Macy's true feelings were now, and Paine's and Abbott's and the rest of his officers'. It was his abolitionism that had won him the appointment by Governor Andrew as colonel of the Twentieth, surprising everybody—Macy, Abbott, Henry Ropes, and Sumner Paine above all. They said he was unfit for command and should have been gentleman enough to decline the appointment, and when he arrived in Falmouth no officer would speak to him except officially. He had taken his meals alone in his room, waited upon by his servant, Charles, rather than be shunned at the officers' mess. Nights he read Victor Hugo and Sir Walter Scott or wrote letters to his wife while in the room below, Macy's room, the other officers drank whiskey and talked and laughed with a vivacity that Revere thought somewhat forced, a show of blitheness and camaraderie put on with him in mind, to give emphasis to his isolation.

He had not told his wife of his ostracism. He understood it, and he expected to rebut all their complaints when they met the enemy. Nor did he tell Lucretia about the rheumatism that bored into his right hip like an auger, or the fever which he took to be an echo of the malaria he'd contracted during his imprisonment by the Rebels after Ball's Bluff.

Better now, stronger, he had forgone the ambulance when they'd left Monocacy Junction and had walked at the front of the regiment the rest of the way, thinking to blunt their animosity by enduring the long marches with them as well as by his forbearance, his patience, and perhaps he had. They had begun to speak to him unofficially—of the campaign, of the mood of the men—and here was Macy offering solicitude for his safety.

"I'm afraid if I were to lie down I couldn't get up again," he said, smiling.

Macy looked up at him unsmiling, and Revere turned away, regretting the attempt at self-deprecation, at humor, which had clearly gone wide of the mark. I must be myself, he thought.

The Rebel line came past the Codori farm and across the Emmitsburg Road. The grass was more beaten down here and you could see them better. The two blue regiments fell back, stopping to load and fire, falling back, stopping again. The battery near the copse was throwing shells at the Rebel line and the Rhode Island battery down on the field opened with canister. It was all smoke and fire and noise down there, and through it you could hear the random scattered hollers and cries of pain. The Rebels came on through the high grass, and the Union infantry were running now. It was too late to limber up and the artillerists scrambled to rope the guns to the limbers.

"We'd better load, Colonel," Revere said.

Macy jumped up and passed the order, and the men sat up and dug out a cartridge and bit it off and poured the powder and pushed the ball into the muzzle. They drew out their rammers and drove ball and powder home.

"Don't forget the cap," Luke said.

Thomas nodded and fitted a cap onto the nipple with trembling fingers.

A shell went off behind them, and another in the air above them and someone cried out and the stretcher bearers came running without being called. The officers were all on their feet now, watching the Rebel advance. They came on at the double-quick, dim in the smoke, pausing to fire and load, and there was the shrill floating otherworldly cry of the Rebel yell. The Rhode Island artillerists had gotten four guns roped and had left two and here they came, running for it, whipping the teams up the ridge slope. There was a gate in the rail fence and the men who were positioned there swung it open and smashed it with their musket butts, and the artillerists, running, whipping their teams, made for the opening.

The Rebels swarmed past the abandoned guns like a wave. Revere watched four or five of them fall out and turn the teams around and get the two captured guns moving back across the valley. Napoleons. Now they'll be used to kill us, he thought. The Rebel line, two deep, came up the field, yelling, driving Lieutenant Brown's artillerists and the Eighty-second New York and Fifteenth Massachusetts before it. Revere turned to look at his regiment lying on their arms in formation, ready to go

forward in a line of battle if the Rebels got across the wall, and nodded.
They were one of the best regiments in the army and would do whatever
he asked them, and with the thought a sudden pride rose in him, like
love in its strength and sweetness, and he knew he was where he should
be, had to be, and that God had called him to it and would sustain him.
He turned back toward the enemy and out of the high smoke came an
arcing whistle that he could see as well as hear, a black thread raveling
toward him, stopping—he could have sworn—midair, perhaps as high
as a house roof, a black circle now, a sphere, motionless, suspended, and
then it blew.

Macy saw Revere fall and knew he was in command of the regiment
now. Shrapnel: the ball or balls had buried themselves in Revere's lungs
or his stomach or both, tunneling downward; the pain would be terrible
if Revere lived awhile. Macy called for a stretcher and they carried him
off soaked in blood, and his servant followed, weeping openly. He had
picked up Revere's hat, as if it mattered anymore.

The four uncaptured guns of the Rhode Island battery came through
the gateway with the yelling Rebels not far behind them. The men along
the fence and wall opened fire. Two of the teams with their limbers and
roped guns plunged on up the slope and kept coming and the men of the
Twentieth rolled or scrabbled out of the way, the horses lathered and
wild-eyed and skittish as runaways, limbers rattling furiously, the guns
fishtailing on their tow ropes. The cannoneers were powder-blackened,
they looked like minstrels. They stopped the horses on the ridge crest
just behind the regiment. There was nowhere to go and Macy told the
men to lie flat and they did, six feet in front of the guns. The Rebels were
charging the wall now and the two guns behind the Twentieth opened on
them with canister, blowing the air to smithereens.

Thomas lay on his stomach with his shoulder against his brother's,
his face in the thick dry summer-smelling grass, his hands covering his
ears. The cannoneers reloaded—they worked quickly, carrying the shells,
handing them off, swabbing, ramming, adjusting the screws—and the
guns roared again, and each time Thomas felt the air compress against
him and the torrid heat of the muzzle flames on his back. His eyes were

closed and in the darkness he could see Henry Wilcox's stump with its splintered bone and collapsed glistening webs of tendon and muscle, the blood so new looking, so bright red, and he opened his eyes.

Luke was up on his elbows watching the fight at the wall. You couldn't see much for the smoke. Everyone seemed to be yelling, both sides, but no words were discernible in the din of musket fire, the squirts of flame in the dusky smoke. Thomas moved closer to Luke and put his face to his side and smelled the sweat-impregnated wool of his coat and the sweaty earthsmell of his unwashed body. Luke had grown in the last few days, had become a man and unafraid of dying, while Thomas had not. Yes, he had thought screwing Lilac would change everything but it had only made life dearer to him. The guns had quit behind them and so had the Rebel batteries across the valley, though Thomas did not know when that had happened. He listened to the fight raging on at the wall, musketry, cries of pain, officers cursing, and then a chorus of yells went up to their left and Thomas looked and so did everybody and there was a whole division, maybe more, long dark blue lines in perfect order, flags silk-bright in the smoke, sweeping over the low flattened ridge crest like a great tide and downhill toward the enemy. There was General Hancock on his jet-black horse, standing in his stirrups and waving them on with his black slouch hat. *First Corps boys,* somebody shouted, *Rebs'll catch it now.* They deployed along the fence line, firing on the Rebels point-blank, and Thomas knew he would not have to fight today.

FIVE

On her daily rounds on Main, Union, and Water Streets, she was not as bold in her demeanor as before, not so proud. It was not a choice she made but rather an involuntary flinching from the eyes of the white people, a shying from the judgment that had ever stood in their gazes. She could not help it. She hated them for it, and somewhat hated herself. She did not think they knew anything of what had happened to her, it was only that they detected a change, which pleased them. Mr. Daley the druggist had all but ceased his little gallantries, and Mr. Bodfish at Smith, Bodfish, Swift waited on her in the usual dour silence but without the occasional flicker of interest in her, the morose quasi-compliments on her dress or her selection of his meat or farm produce. She still dressed pretty, hat and boots and silk dresses and parasol, and still walked tall and kept her chin high, but she could not quite look at them, and they were heartened by that.

She had not seen Peter Daggett again. She did not know if he'd gone running his mouth about what he'd done. She doubted it. She did not know if Oliver Shiverick had. Shiverick would be the greater braggart, the more accomplished liar. Daggett had refrained from raping her not out of conscience or scruple but because he'd lost his nerve, and Rose knew enough about white men to take it for granted that he would hold this against her and not himself. She watched for him, half wanting to see the coward, to assert herself before him somehow, perhaps remind him what Luke would do to him when he came home. She did not wish to see Oliver Shiverick again. Him there was no frightening, no pushing, no getting around. Him she would leave entirely to Luke.

"Who was it, Rosie?" the doctor said one night at supper.

"Who was what?" she said, though she knew what he was asking.

There was an old chestnut tree on that side of the house and she looked out at it. The evening sun was on it and its leaves shone, glowed in its golden wash. A bird spoke up, robin or cardinal. There was so much beauty in the world and so much peace, but it was a false beauty and a false peace and you could not take refuge in it. The meanness would search you out, even on Martha's Vineyard, with its quiet ways and surface civility. Still, the chestnut tree with the sun on it had never appeared so handsome, and her heart knocked a little bit quicker as she gazed on it and now, slipping down the sky as though off the back of the prevailing southwest wind, riding it all this way, she heard something— heard it in time, she thought, to throw it up as a barrier to the doctor's question.

"They're fighting," she said.

"Who is?"

"North and South," she said. "It's begun."

"What makes you say so?"

"A feeling," she said.

"Then God help us."

"He will."

They were quiet awhile, spooning up her sweet chicken chowder. There were baked oysters and cucumber salad.

"Rosie? Tell me who attacked you."

"We should be thinking of Luke and Thomas now. Sending them a prayer."

"Rose. Please."

Rose looked at him. His worried face, love written all over it. "I most certainly heard you say you wouldn't press me on that," she said.

"I know I did."

"Well, a promise is a promise."

"But I've been thinking," he said.

"You haven't said a word about your supper."

"Didn't I?"

"Those boys come home," she said, "I'll have somebody to cook for. Don't you know I enjoy to cook?" Because his appetite had left him. It had gone quite suddenly, smaller portions, smaller still. Now all he did was pick.

"It's a fine supper," he said.

"You'll waste away, you don't take in more. I wonder if that cough doesn't rub the edge off your appetite."

"Do I not have a right to know?" he said.

She put her spoon down and looked again at the gilded chestnut tree. "You'd go to the constable," she said.

"Why not?"

"I'd get no justice," she said. "I'd be the one at fault."

"Did he molest you, Rose?"

"Yeah he molested me. Took all that good food, threw it in the road. Ate some of it."

"You know what I mean."

"If I said he did, this whole island would turn on me."

"Then it would turn against me too."

"And what good would that do me?"

A smile: wry, weary, injured. "You don't think much of me, do you?"

"You know that's not true," she said.

Again came that noise, that silent thunder. Rose closed her eyes and sent her own prayer down toward where it had come from.

"I do my best," the doctor said. "I know it's not all it could be, but . . ."

"You do fine," Rose said, and thought shut *up*. Shut *up*, shut *up*.

"Let's go back to New Bedford," he said. "Or Boston. You belong in a city, Rose."

"Haven't we been through this?"

"This time I mean it."

"Then they get what they want. They drive me away."

"Does that matter?"

"My pride matters."

"I don't even know what that means, Rose."

No. No you wouldn't. "Anyway, I don't want to do a thing till the boys come home," she said.

"But why?"

"Hush. They're fighting, George. Listen."

"Listen?"

Rose smiled. "I don't mean listen," she said. "I mean *feel*. You can feel it."

"Perhaps I can."

"It's coming," she said. "Day of judgment. Wrath of God."

"God help our boys."

"Our boys are the wrath," Rose said, thinking of Luke.

SIX

There were of course no trains and so Mr. Irons and Mr. Phipps were compelled to stay on at the Globe for as long as the fighting should last, and Mr. Will was glad of it. Also lodging there now were two newspaper correspondents, Mr. Davidson of the Charleston Mercury and Mr. Lathrop of the Richmond Enquirer, who had followed Lee's army up from Fredericksburg. The correspondents kept irregular hours but managed to be present at mealtimes, during which they argued amiably with Irons and Phipps about states' rights, the philosophy of secession, slavery, and the war itself. The two Southerners said that no Yankee army could defeat Lee's and that after the present battle, or the one after it, or the one after that, the North would realize it and sue for peace. Mr. Phipps and Mr. Irons smiled ruefully and granted that it might be so.

But then there's Vicksburg, Mr. Irons said. What happens if we take Vicksburg?

You'll never conquer the South, said Mr. Davidson.

The three youths, Trig and Roland and Floyd, waited table and listened to this talk expressionlessly with their eyes downcast. Trig and Roland didn't think the Northerners could whip General Lee either and it didn't overly trouble them, but Floyd Wilkes listened to the guns on July 2 and knew it was the sound of Lee's army being bloodied as never before. Floyd and the other two slept in the Globe's hot oakwood-smelling attic and did not venture out of doors except to use the backyard privy.

The white employees at the Globe came and went, including Mr. Will, who lived close by on York Street. The only imperative was to stay clear of the southern end of town, where there was incessant if sporadic shooting

between Union sharpshooters on Cemetery Hill and Rebels at upper-story
windows near the edge of town and on Baltimore Street at the corner of
Breckenridge, where they'd heaped up a breastwork of overturned wagons,
logs, timbers, and other debris. There were few citizens about but plenty of
Rebels, cantering horsemen and gaggles of foot soldiers stepping smartly
along with their guns on their shoulders. They were a slovenly lot, long-
haired and unshaven and their uniforms patched and faded and ill fitting.
They lifted their hats to Etta Dowling the chambermaid and wished her
good day and joked that they would say howdy to Abe Lincoln for her when
they caught him. On the whole they behaved decently, especially for such
rough men. True, they'd cleaned out smokehouses and chicken coops and
had requisitioned every last loaf of bread at every bakery, but, as Mr. Will
pointed out, the Northerners would do the same in their place.

Have done, said Mr. Davidson. And worse.

Far worse, said Mr. Lathrop.

They were at supper at the end of the battle's second day. It was very
late, after midnight, in fact. The fighting was finally over, the last spat-
ters of musket fire having died away, the cannon ceasing to boom. Another
stalemate, clearly. Tomorrow hostilities would resume yet again. A three-
day battle, at the least. Mr. Will sat with his guests. Lebrun had made a
beef stew. Floyd and Trig waited on them. They stood by with their hands
clasped behind them, stone-faced. Roland was washing dishes.

Fredericksburg, said Mr. Davidson. Remember?

Your boys in blue, said Lathrop, ransacked that helpless town. Rich or
poor, it didn't matter. Robbed them all.

Not just that, Davidson said. They went on a rampage of destruction.
Fine furnishings smashed and thrown out of windows. Family portraits
defaced. It was wanton.

They broke pianos, Lathrop said. Strewed the pieces about the streets.

They were unhappy, Mr. Will said, after the whipping you gave them.

Davidson smiled grimly at the memory. Marye's Heights. He wore a
mustache, golden brown, and his hair fell about his shoulders. Floyd won-
dered why he wasn't in the army.

That in no way excuses it, Davidson said.

I agree, said Mr. Will.

Floyd, watching discreetly, saw Mr. Phipps and Mr. Irons look at each other. Mr. Irons shrugged. Mr. Phipps sawed a chunk of beef in two and put it in his mouth.

The Confederacy, Lathrop said, does not make war on civilians. It does not make war on women. It might interest you gentlemen to know that General Lee put out a general order just last week, stipulating that very thing. Said he didn't want our army to repeat the atrocities of our enemies. Wasn't that the phrase, Edward?

It was, Davidson said.

What atrocities? Mr. Irons asked.

Why, all over the South, Davidson said.

Poor Virginia, Lathrop said. She's been laid waste.

General Lee won't allow such behavior up here, Davidson said.

Mr. Irons turned with his fork in his hand and looked at Trig and Floyd. Floyd met his eye and Irons smiled a slight enigmatic smile and turned back to his plate.

No right-thinking person can help but admire General Lee, Mr. Will said.

You sound partial to him, Mr. Phipps said.

He's a fine and gallant man, said Mr. Will.

And yet I heard you were for abolition. That you're a Republican, in fact.

Mr. Will smiled charitably. You have me confused with David Wills, the attorney, here in town. Wills, with an ess. A friend of President Lincoln's. A fool, in my opinion. Dessert, gentlemen?

He nodded at Floyd and Trig and they came forward to clear away the crockery. It was then that the two Confederate generals, Ewell and Early, walked in, their little pack of aides spilling in behind them.

I do hope, General Early said, we ain't too late for some supper.

It was after eleven and they were still fighting over on Culp's Hill. No artillery now, just the banging of rifled muskets continuing their deadly work in the dark. The shots would erupt in dense clusters, a furious rattle, then break off to a scatter. Closer by, on Cemetery Hill, the sharpshooters potted away at Rebels in the town, and the Rebels shot back at them.

"We're holdin," Elisha said.

"The Twelfth Corps," Merriman said. "They're good boys."

"Maybe Lee ain't so smart after all," McNamara said, "tryin to take them hills in the dark."

Another rise in volume, hundreds of muskets exploding at once. They could see the smoke float skyward above Culp's Hill, slow, diaphanous.

"I wonder will Lee quit if we hold em," Elisha said.

"Lee didn't come up here to quit," McNamara said.

They were on the front line now, along the remains of the rail fence. Macy had ordered them forward sometime after eight o'clock. It would be their turn, if the Rebels struck here again. No more watching. To their left was the Nineteenth Maine. To their right was the Seventh Michigan. The round moon bathed the trampled valley with its scattered trees and crippled fences and dead and wounded men, who lay everywhere, in a random ghastly strew. All across the field the cries of these wounded, their groans and pleas for water, knelled discordant and broken in the moon-tinged air. Stretcher bearers with lanterns were venturing down as far as the Emmitsburg Road to retrieve them, and there was a steady traffic up the long slope and through the line and over the ridge and down.

Thomas looked out on it in silence. The moon shone brighter than he ever remembered it. It painted the treetops, the rocks, the dead bodies, the rooftops of the Codori farm. Trees and fence posts cast ink-black shadows. There were dead Union men down near the road and many dead Rebels. There were dead Rebels directly in front of the rail fence and the stone wall that ran north from it. Most of them lay on their backs with their arms outflung and their knees bent slightly and their mouths and eyes open, and in their sprawled and operatic positions they seemed to be striking poses in the moonlight. Their uniforms appeared colorless and their foreheads glowed white above their beards and powder-blackened cheeks. Down the field, where the Rhode Island battery had been, three horses lay in various states of mutilation. A leg sheared off at the haunch, an abdomen ripped open. Dead men and horses were not yet odorous but the air was impregnated with the smell of the long day's human and animal leavings and Thomas wished a wind would come up and blow the smell away.

"I wonder will somebody write to Henry's wife," Merriman said.

"Stonewall will. He loved Henry like a brother," said Stackpole.

They were sitting in the scraggy grass and weeds, the ground all littered with the torn scraps of paper cartridges. Their guns lay unloaded along the ruin of the fence, pointed west toward the enemy.

"Henry said it'd happen, didn't he?" Merriman said.

"That was just talk," Luke said.

"It was true talk, wasn't it?"

"Wish we could do somethin for him," Elisha said.

"Remember him," Luke said. "That's what you can do."

"Remember him kindly," Stackpole said.

"It ain't no other way with Henry," Elisha said.

The order had come that no fires be built—there were Rebel skirmishers west of the Emmitsburg Road—so they could not make coffee, though many had none left anyway. For supper they ate the last of their hardtack. Elisha and Luke shared a cracker each with Rivers.

"Why don't you write his wife, Luke," Merriman said. "Or you, Tommy. You boys'd write a good one."

"I ain't writing her," Thomas said.

"Cheer up, Tommy. You seen the elephant and lived to tell about it."

"I don't think that counts, getting shelled," Thomas said.

"Ask Henry if it counts," Rivers said. "Ask Colonel Revere."

"Maybe we ought to pony up some money, send it to his widow," Stackpole said.

"Maybe we ought to get paid first," McNamara said.

"I didn't say do it tonight," Stackpole said.

Sergeant Cate came down the slope with his musket riding his shoulder, gripping it by the barrel and letting the gun rest there, comfortable. When they saw him, Sergeant Holland and Corporal Dugan came from someplace over toward the copse.

"At ease," Cate said, before the men could scramble up. He nodded to Holland and Dugan.

"We're holdin em over yonder, ain't we, Sarge?" Merriman said.

"Holdin em good," Cate said. "You boys hear about Sickles?"

"Heard he fucked up good. Saw it, too."

"Got his leg shot off," Cate said.

Silence. The men all looked at the ground.

"He gonna live?" said Corporal Dugan.

"He might do. He lit up a cigar whilst they were carryin him to the rear. Smoked it, too."

"Why I like him," McNamara said.

"If we do hold them hills what happens?" someone asked.

"I think Meade intends to set here," Cate said. "Let Lee hit us again. The corps commanders are all down that little white farmhouse, talkin about it."

Another silence. The muskets kept up their chatter on Culp's Hill but it seemed to be less busy over there. More men, farther down the fence, got up and came over to listen to Cate.

"First thing tomorrow," Cate said, "you boys get the rest of this fence down, pile it up good."

"They ain't much left to get down, Sarge."

"Get it all down," Cate said. "Pile the rails where they'll stop a ball."

"They gonna hit us here, Sarge?"

"They already done," Rivers said.

"That wasn't anything," Cate said. "A brigade. It was an after-thought. It was our flanks got hit hard. The thinking is, they hit our right, they hit our left, now they'll hit our center with everything they have. The center would be here and along the stone wall yonder. Almost as far over as that hill with the cemetery on it. If it's so, you boys'll be in the thick of it."

Another silence. Someone cleared his throat and spat.

"We could use some shovels," McNamara said.

"I'll see to it," Cate said.

"And rations," Rivers said. "Our bread bags is empty, Sarge."

"Commissary wagon'll be up tomorrow," Cate said.

"Tomorrow when?"

"When it gets here," Cate said.

The shooting was dying away on Culp's Hill. Everyone looked in that direction. You could not see the hill from here, just the lazy rifle smoke rising off it.

"They ain't took the hill or you'd hear em yellin."

"They're done, then. Our whole line has held."

More shots rang out, but they were solitary, diminishing, a final punctuation.

"You boys get some rest," Cate said. "Be hell to pay tomorrow."

"Sergeant?" Merriman said. "They bury Henry Wilcox?"

"Not yet," Cate said.

"Revere?"

"He's alive yet."

"He won't live," McNamara said. "Got a damn shrapnel ball in his guts."

"No, he won't," Cate said.

Fireflies were winking across the slanted and rolling fields. The men did not know what time it was, but the moon had moved over toward Seminary Ridge and the night was well along. Some of them had gone out and picked up the guns and cartridge boxes of the dead and brought them back to use against the Rebels tomorrow. Luke had gone with McNamara and Elisha. He could not help staring at the dead men. Their glazed astonished eyes, mouths open in surprise. As if death had been the last thing they'd expected. Their blood had dried solid and black and already abdominal swelling had begun. He thought of his mother's body in the parlor in New Bedford, pale and peaceful, holding a bouquet of white flowers on her stomach. There was death, and there was killing. Henry Wilcox's leg had come off and he'd died in a few minutes, barely time to comprehend the fact. Luke remembered Henry's arms dangling off the stretcher so dead and useless. There was blood on the trampled grass in places where no bodies lay. In some places the grass had been soaked in it. They'd brought back three or four muskets each, Enfields, cradling them in their arms, and laid them at intervals along the fence line.

Skirmishing had recommenced along the Emmitsburg Road but it was sporadic, more dutiful than malign, as if the men on both sides were putting off the real killing until tomorrow. The sharpshooters on Cemetery Hill fired too but only intermittently. The regiments along the fence and the stone wall began to spread their blankets and gradually the murmur of conversation subsided all along the line, and the men slept where they would fight tomorrow. Musket barrels shone in the moonlight beside them and where the grass was beaten down flat you could see used caps lying about, tiny and glittering, and the mothlike scraps of torn cartridges. The fireflies sparked, drifted. Luke and Thomas and Elisha had laid their rubber blankets some way back from the fence. They pulled their shoes off, their coats, and wrapped themselves in their red wool blankets and sat looking across the valley. The Rebel campfires still glowed in the woods on Seminary Ridge, but weakly.

"This is it, isn't it?" Thomas said.

"What is?" Luke said.

"We're going to see the elephant."

"You seen it," Elisha said.

"Not like we're going to see it tomorrow."

"Maybe," Elisha said, "but you don't know. They almost broke through on the left. Could be they'll try it again."

"You heard what Cate said."

"Yeah I heard him. Now let's get some sleep."

"I can't," Thomas said.

"Well I can." Elisha lay down on his side and pulled his blanket up over his shoulder and drew his knees up. Luke and Thomas sat looking out. A Union skirmisher on the near side of the road fired a lone shot that went unanswered. With the grass so beaten down, the skirmishers hid themselves in the little swales and in the shadows of trees and any scrub that was left.

"What do you think they're doing at home now?" Thomas said.

"Sleeping. What the hell you think?"

"There are no mosquitoes. Isn't that funny?"

"Maybe all the smoke keeps them at home."

Thomas nodded. "Rose might be awake," he said. "She's awake a good deal. I hear her moving around."

Luke looked at him. "She worries, I guess. Has a lot on her mind."

"You're asleep. You don't hear it."

"I guess I don't."

They sat awhile. Silence on Cemetery Hill, silence along the Emmitsburg Road.

Thomas turned and looked down at Elisha. "Elisha?" he said.

"Let him sleep," Luke said.

"Listen, Luke. He wants me to go see Iris if he gets killed. I said I would."

"Go all the way to Virginia?"

"If I get killed, could you do it?"

"You're not going to get killed."

"But if I do."

Luke shrugged. "All right."

"You could mention me to Lilac."

"I'd have to, wouldn't I."

"I don't know what you'd tell her," Thomas said.

"That you loved her."

"I didn't, though. I liked her."

"I'm not going to go all the way down there just to say, 'Thomas liked you.'"

"All right. Tell her I loved her. And tell Iris Elisha loved her. Which he did. Does, I mean."

"He thinks he does."

"What's the difference?"

"The one's a mistake, the other isn't."

"Why can't real love be a mistake?"

"If it's a mistake it isn't real love."

"That's a bunch of shit."

"All right, it's a bunch of shit. Can we go to sleep?"

"Is there anyone you want me to speak to?"

"I don't think so."

"Mariah?"

"Will you quit it about Mariah?"

"Why?"

"Because I don't give a goddamn about Mariah."

"You used to."

"So?"

"You screwed her."

"I didn't either."

Luke didn't say anything. He sat with his arms wrapping his knees, looking out. A stretcher team came up the slope from far down the field. The two bearers moved slowly and with difficulty over the rough ground. A third man led the way carrying a lantern, which swung this way and that, its soft yellow light dancing on the moon-silvered ground. They came through the gateway and went up the slope. The wounded man had been shot in the stomach. A Reb. "Susan," he said. The voice was parched, stretched thin. "Susan. Oh God, Susan."

Luke and Thomas looked at each other and did not speak. It was no longer new to them. Abdominal wounds, imploded blood-welling holes in shoulders. Mangled legs. They took the man up the ridge and down the other side.

"Who did you screw, if it wasn't Mariah?"

Luke didn't answer him.

"Tell me, Luke."

Thomas looked at him in the moonlight. His black beard was three days old. It made him look older, harder. God help the Rebels tomorrow, Thomas thought, with an odd mixture of pride and aversion.

"Tell me," he said again.

Luke didn't move or speak but Thomas knew he was going to. He was gathering it up in his mind to tell because he, Thomas, had insisted, and because Luke had begun to see that if he died tomorrow and didn't tell it, it would be lost forever. So Thomas waited. Silence now, everywhere; on the two hills to the north, along the Emmitsburg Road, on Little Round Top to the south. The wounded had all been retrieved, or at least had ceased to groan and cry out. The air was cool, breathless, fetid. Luke, blanket-draped and hugging his knees, drew a deep breath.

"Rose," he said.

"Rose?"

"Yeah."

"Not our Rose," Thomas said.

Luke did not look at him. He nodded.

"Rose Miranda?" Thomas said.

"*Yes.*"

"You liar."

Luke didn't answer.

"You goddamn liar."

Elisha woke and raised himself on his elbow. "What is it?" he said.

"He says he screwed Rose," Thomas said.

"Lower your voice," Luke said.

"Rose?" Elisha said.

"You bastard," Thomas said.

Elisha looked up at the two of them and tried to make sense of it.

"I had a feeling you'd take it hard," Luke said.

"You're a bastard," Thomas said.

"It's why I didn't tell you," Luke said.

"Goddamn you," Thomas said.

"Tommy," Elisha said.

"Don't defend him, Elisha."

"I ain't."

"You go to hell, Luke. Rose, too. You both go to hell and rot."

Thomas sprang to his feet, bringing his wool blanket. He bunched the blanket under his arm and went down the slope past the men asleep on their blankets and over the collapsed rails and out onto the field, among the fireflies and the dead. He sat down with his back to them, wrapped in his blanket like some stolid speechless Indian. There was a dead Rebel sprawled facedown not ten feet from him.

"Oh Lord," Elisha said. He'd sat up with his blanket around him. "Is it true?"

"Yes."

"You oughtn't to of told him, Luke."

"He made me. What the hell is he so angry about?"

"You knew he would be."

"Not like this I didn't."

"You don't see it, do you?"

"See what?"

Thomas sat perfectly still, his back to them, his red blanket glazed silver-gray by the moon.

"Maybe he thinks of her like you do," Elisha said.

Luke looked at him.

"I did myself, a little bit," Elisha said.

"That's foolishness and you know it."

"It ain't neither. She was just that pretty. And she sung so pretty. Cooked good. Smart as a book, too. I hadn't met no one like her. I still ain't."

"I thought you loved that girl in Virginia," Luke said.

"And I do," Elisha said. "But she ain't no Rose, Luke."

"Well," Luke said, "I love Rose. I lay down with her for that. Nothing else."

"I guess she's sweet on you too."

"She is, or she wouldn't have lain with me."

Elisha turned, eyed him a moment, then looked front again. "You're somethin, ain't you." It was spoken somberly, without envy or sarcasm.

"You can't help who you love," Luke said.

"I guess not. I love a whore."

"Don't say that," Luke said.

"It's the plain truth."

"She isn't a real whore," Luke said.

"I don't mind. It's the war that done it. And I don't expect nobody high as Rose, I don't care what color."

"But you loved her," Luke said.

"I thought of it, anyways. I was too young to of done it, I guess."

Luke nodded. It was wrong, what he'd said to Thomas a little while ago. Thomas and Elisha had as much right to love her as Luke did. *You can't help who you love.* That was the whole of it. Rose, Iris. Choice had nothing to do with it.

A shot broke the stillness down near the road, its echo careering up the valley.

"It ain't but a few hours till dawn," Elisha said.

"Go talk to Thomas," Luke said. "Bring him back. He has to get some sleep."

"I know he does. I didn't say it blunt to him, but I guess we'll see hard fightin tomorrow. Lee ain't gonna try them hills again except for a diversion."

"Go talk to him," Luke said.

"Ain't that for you to do?" Elisha said.

"He won't listen to me," Luke said.

Elisha brought up a sigh. "All right, then," he said.

"Tommy."

Thomas didn't look at him, didn't show he'd heard him. He gazed at Seminary Ridge, dark in its tree cover with the remains of the Rebel campfires glinting through. The dead Rebel beside him slept with his face to the ground, one knee cocked beside him. Tomorrow more of the enemy would be here, swarming the fence line, the stone wall. Deafening ceaseless crack of muskets. There'd be so much blood on this ground. . . .

"You got to get some sleep, Tommy."

Elisha sat down beside him with his long legs stretched out.

"He made a slut out of her," Thomas said.

"Don't talk so."

"He did. They're both sluts."

They were quiet awhile. A Rebel skirmisher fired from the shadows of the Codori farm and skirmishers answered, three quick bangs and then silence.

"Did you know about it?" Thomas said.

"How was I gonna know about it all the way down to Virginia?"

"I mean did Luke tell you."

"Course not."

"I ain't going home after the war," Thomas said. "I don't want to see her again."

"Don't talk foolish."

"Luke can go home and fuck her all the rest of his life."

"It don't make her a slut because she done Luke. It don't make Luke one neither. I'd of done her if I could."

"You wouldn't."

"I would. And so would you."

"You don't know anything, Elisha."

"I know you ain't admittin the truth, like Luke just done."

"What truth?"

"The whole of it. I'll do mine: I wonder would I of enlisted if I hadn't of knowed Rose Miranda. I wonder if you would of, or Luke. Even Peleg Davenport. He talked of her, you know."

"What of it?" Thomas said.

"She give us somethin to fight for. Made us see. Not by preachin, I don't mean. Just by who she was."

"We were abolitionists before we ever knew Rose."

"You warn't but a little shaver when she come."

"So what."

"Come on get some sleep, Tommy. It might go hard on us tomorrow."

"I thought you said it wouldn't."

"Well it might. And you don't want to go into a fight with anger in your heart. You was to die, it'd always be there."

"There's nothing when you die."

"We won't know till it happens, I guess."

"Ain't you the wise one tonight," Thomas said.

"Come get some sleep."

"I hope we do fight tomorrow," Thomas said.

"We'll be like to."

"The sonsabitches killed Colonel Revere," Thomas said. "They killed Henry Wilcox."

Elisha looked at him. His young unshaven face glowed white in the moonlight, like he had a fever on him.

"Slavery sonsabitches," Thomas said. "If they come straight across, we could kill a smart of them, couldn't we?"

"I'd say so."

"Cate says they will. Says they'll come straight at us."

"You come on now, Tommy. Luke'll worry you don't come. He won't sleep hisself till you do."

"I'll come when I'm ready," Thomas said.

SEVEN

A man could get right to the ticklish spot on your heart if you were one type of girl, and if you were the other type he never could. That was all there was, two types, the one and the other. Rose guessed there were more of the first type than the second, which was a good thing for the human race, though the second type did produce their share of babies. If you were the first type, a man could make you smile when you didn't want to give even that much away just yet. He could, if he appreciated you, spark a light in your eye that you could feel spread out across your face, changing its shape, and for the better. It didn't mean love, except rarely, was what Rose believed. You'd go your separate ways and the feeling would wither away quicker than a flower out of water. That was the difference. With love it didn't wither but instead grew the way fire can run up the walls of a house. You couldn't save the house, and you couldn't save yourself, even if you wanted to.

Rose was the first type of girl.

Mariah Look was the second.

"That girl loves herself, is what I think," Rose said one night at supper.

It was getting dark and in the smokelike autumn dusk you could see the shriveled copper leaves of the big chestnut tree, which seemed to retain some of the departed aureate light. A fire whispered on the dining room hearth. Luke had just turned eighteen and begun his final year at the Centre Street School, and now he was sparking Mariah.

"Is that fair?" the doctor said.

"I know what I know," Rose said.

"You never even met her," Luke said.

He'd grown to man size, and so quickly that she'd missed it while it was happening. He'd added some bulk, certainly, over the summer, always out of doors, rambling the shore to bathe or catch eels and crabs in Lagoon Pond, cutting the winter's firewood in one or another of the West Chop woodlots, helping farmers get their hay in for a few cents a day, not for the money but the healthful labor, the exercise. Walking behind the reaper in the broiling sun, gathering sheaves. He was tireless at it, much valued by the men he worked for. The sun browned his face and his big hands and narrowed his deepset eyes. He wore his black hair long and careless. If you didn't know you'd have thought him hard-looking. Dangerous.

"I see her in town," Rose said. "She takes no notice of me."

"Well, you've never been introduced," Luke said.

"She knows very well who I am."

It was just that Rose didn't want to see Luke make a poor choice for himself when he could have any girl he wanted.

"She doesn't speak to me either," Thomas said.

"She does so," Luke said.

"She *nods* to me," Thomas said.

"You're a pup, that's why," Luke said.

Thomas was still only fifteen. He'd shot up tall but thin, delicately constructed. The sun didn't brown and harden him the way it did Luke. If it didn't roast him pink it gave him a gingery tan that faded in a matter of days. Or so it seemed, looking back. He'd spent hours this summer, on good sunny days, trying to teach himself to play the piano. Rose had taught him the scales and how to read music. He would bang away, but it was very clear he had no aptitude. Poor Thomas. Smart as a steel trap, but what would he find to do with all those brains?

"Perhaps," the doctor said, "she's shy."

"Haughty, is what I call it," Rose said.

"Is she an abolitionist?" Thomas said.

They all looked at him. Rose smiled a quiet sideways smile.

"I'm sure she is," Luke said.

"I ain't," Rose said.

"Why don't you ask her?" Thomas said.

"Why don't you mind your own business," Luke said.

"Sam Look seems like a decent sort," the doctor said. "I'd be surprised if he weren't a Lincoln man."

"I'm sure he is," Luke said.

"I ain't."

Luke aimed a look at her, hard but not angry. He was bent over his food and eyeing her like that, stern, like she was a sister talking up impertinent to him. Rose smiled.

"Sit up, Luke," the doctor said.

Luke did. He smirked. He wasn't in love with the girl. He might have thought so, but he wasn't.

"Why don't you invite her to Sunday dinner?" the doctor said.

Luke thought about it. "All right," he said.

"Means I eat in the kitchen," Rose said.

The doctor put his fork down. "Really, Rose," he said. "You're demonizing the poor girl."

"She would *not* want you to eat in the kitchen," Luke said.

"She wouldn't have any choice, would she, Father?" Thomas said.

Rose smiled. "Invite her next Sunday," she said.

"One of these Sundays," Luke said, making it clear he wasn't going to be pushed.

Quilting parties. Taffy pulls. Singalongs at the Seamen's Bethel. They played charades and the bishop's hat and proverbs and other silliness. After the games came the forfeits resulting from them: kiss the hand of everyone in the room, girls and boys both, kiss everybody blindfolded, make a fool of yourself standing on a chair in the pose of a Greek statue. There had been no parlor games in Rose's girlhood and she couldn't see any value in them until Luke explained it to her.

She could not quite pinpoint when he'd taken up visiting her at night in her bedroom while Thomas and the doctor slept. It had begun, Rose could only suppose, the night Joseph Ruffin, the runaway Georgia slave, came to the house. Luke came into her room, leaving the others downstairs, and sat down in the dark uninvited, and the precedent had been set, the privilege established. Give a man an inch and he takes a mile, even a fine boy like Luke. But then she was to blame too, it was improper and she knew it and could have put an end to it by forbidding it. But she did not, she let it go on and even kissed his face from her bed that time after he'd whipped those two boys who'd slandered her and the doctor, Peter Daggett and the Howland boy.

The gatherings with their music and parlor games and forfeits were held Saturday nights, and afterward, if it was late and Thomas and the doctor were asleep, Luke would come to her. *Highly* improper, oh yes, but she did enjoy his company, his earnestness and the way he worked at clarifying everything to himself as well as her. He would go to his own room first and take off his shoes. Later she learned he was deceiving Thomas by laying feather pillows in his bed in a huddle and covering them with his blankets. He could not have guessed what would eventually happen—Rose was sure of this—but the success of the ruse was one more step leading to it. He would tiptoe out and quietly close the bedroom door. He would tap on her door and she'd rise noiselessly and put on her robe but no slippers and let him in and close the door.

"I wonder you children can't think of anything better to do," she said. "Play some cards. Walk out and look at the moon. Harvest moon's coming soon."

"I know it's all stupid," Luke said, "but it's the only way you can see a girl."

"You think so," Rose said.

They had to speak not quite in a whisper but very softly, their voices for no one but each other, husky in the absolute stillness of the hour.

"It's the only way to kiss her, then," Luke said.

"Depends on the girl. And anyway, that ain't kissing."

"How do you know?"

"I just do."

"How?"

"I been kissed," she said.

"By whom?"

"Never you mind."

She sat close to the fireplace clutching her robe around her. She'd thrown a couple of logs on the fire and they were blazing up now and throwing some warmth. Luke sat on the floor, propped back on his hands, lit buttery by the flames. His gaze would shift from the fire to Rose's bare crossed ankles, and she made no effort to cover them.

"You invite this girl to Sunday dinner and I'll see you get left alone with her in the parlor. Then you try your luck."

The clock in the hall downstairs whirred and struck and kept striking, on up to midnight.

"Bedtime," Rose said.

But Luke was studying over what she'd said. "Try my luck at kissing her," he said.

"It's what you want, isn't it?"

"It isn't a crime, is it?"

"Honey, of course it isn't," she said.

He wanted more, if he was any way normal. Eighteen years and fullgrown. After the policeman had raped her, Rose had lost the itch between her legs in the same way she'd lost her taste for spirits the first time they'd made her sick. A man on top of her, liquor in her belly—she'd had all she wanted of either. But then the memory loses its fearful grip on you, and you reflect on it and reason tells you that men and liquor don't always have to be that way. That they never have to, if you're careful, and lucky. And one night Rose took a drink of some huckleberry brandy a girl named Anita Pires had smuggled into the orphanage, and it brought on the sweet feeling of floating, of being outside yourself where the world can't touch or hurt you, and she had not been sick. It had taken much longer, a full year, before she could look at a boy and see him separate from what that man had done to her in the carriage shed. It was a wonder she liked boys, but she did like them. You couldn't help the type of girl you were.

"Remember something," Rose said. "Girls want to do those things just as much as boys do. It's only that they aren't allowed to. Or they think they aren't supposed to want it."

Luke thought about this, gazing into the fire. Rose wondered if white boys were stupider about such matters than colored boys and Portuguese but decided it was upbringing, not race.

"Her father's strict with her," Luke said.

Mr. Look owned the soap manufactory on the waterfront near Union Wharf. Toilet soap, hard and soft soap. Rose bought it at the drugstore,

and at C. M. Vincent's. The Looks were well-to-do, not wealthy. They
were Methodists. Went to church every Sunday.

"You ask her about abolition yet?" Rose said.

"I haven't had a chance."

"A chance? Oh please."

"I haven't. We're always in a group."

"Well, what do they talk about at those singalongs and whatnots?"

"Nothing much."

"Not the war? Not Abe Lincoln? Not abolition?"

"What did you talk about when you were seventeen?"

"Boys and other foolishness. Put the fire screen up and go to bed."

He pushed himself up off the floor, slow but obedient, and she knew
you only had to mention it to a boy like him, a man like him, and he'd let
you alone. Wouldn't ever force himself on a girl.

Before they left New Bedford the doctor had taken her and the two boys
to hear Frederick Douglass speak and Rose had fallen in love with him.
That it was love she'd never doubted. They'd sat quite near him in the
auditorium and before a half hour was out, love had come pouring into
her heart and settled there. He was the most handsome man she'd ever
seen. Soft deep womanish eyes, womanish cupid's-bow mouth, but a
man's big shoulders and strong cheekbones and fine mess of hair, and
a man's bold stride and bearing. And that voice! Rich as music, solid as
thunder in his chest. *Slavery is the enemy of all mankind, and all man-*
kind should be made acquainted with its character. I have seen women,
with their frantic children surrounding them, tied to a post and lashed till
their blood covered their garments. . . . Rose forgot where she was. She
forgot the doctor sitting beside her. She forgot Luke and Thomas.

It was the moment, belated, when she saw slavery in all its illogic and
evil. If this man, smart as any college professor and beautiful to look
at, could be a slave, then where was the sense in it? Be a slave because
your skin was brown? She'd known it before in an abstract and lazy
sort of way without ever dwelling on it. The South was so far away, the
slaves, and what could a body do about it anyway? It was the way the
world was made. But after thirty minutes listening to Frederick Doug-

lass, Rose's love-drunk heart woke to another emotion just as powerful. Indignation. Wrath. Rose was Cape Verdean and not African, but if she went down South and the slave sellers got hold of her, they'd put her in chains just the same. She'd be sold, worked, whipped, kept poor and ignorant, and all because of her color. And now a thought crossed her mind: how did she know her father wasn't African? An escaped slave, or the son of slaves? He'd gone away or died, her mother never said which, and by the time Rose was of an age to be truly curious, her mother was dead too, and there was no one in the world—no kin that Rose knew of, no friends—who could tell her. They'd never been married, Rose knew that. Miranda had been her mother's name. Rose had always assumed she was Cape Verdean on both sides, but that might not be so. And the mere possibility hardened her further against what was being done to all those thousands of Africans on the plantations. Could be she had blood kin down there. They were her brethren anyway, all of them, made so by the color of their skin.

I'm an abolitionist, Rose thought, and it made her proud. It gave her a role in the world, gave her a certain value. Not the fact that she'd chosen to be one, but rather the other way around. It had chosen her, taking hold of her like a hunger, a driving force, as consuming, she would discover, as love could be.

She did not meet Frederick Douglass. She did not speak to him. He concluded his speech and came down from the stage and the audience crowded around him and the doctor stayed back, and of course the boys did too. They were very young, Thomas barely chest high to an adult. Rose remained with them reluctantly, her gaze fixed on Mr. Douglass, who spoke animatedly, smiling, throwing his massive head back in laughter. They were hardly twenty feet from him but Rose could not hear what he was saying, only that beautiful voice, smooth, timbrous, *large,* and everyone else, white people and colored, as ordinary in his orbit as buzzing insects. Rose stood rooted, watching him, and his gaze shifted and found her standing there. He stopped speaking. Eyed her. Smiled.

We must hurry home, the doctor said, and when Rose looked again, Mr. Douglass was reimmersed in conversation, looking into the eye of the man before him, nodding. Come along, Rose, the doctor said. He was right, of course; his wife was very ill and the nurse would be wanting to go home herself, but Rose knew as she left the building, holding Thomas by the hand, that behind her was a chance she would never have again. A door to another life and another world closing forever. And so few doors, worlds, open to a colored girl: she'd known that before tonight, how could she not?

She could only guess, fantasize, the what-wasn't. She was his wife, touring the country with him, standing beside him through the triumphs and indignities—ignorant bumpkins throwing cabbages and eggs at him, hitting her too. She would stand tall through it, would not duck or flinch. She was his confidante, his lover. Then the doctor mentioned that Mr. Douglass was married, and the dream had to be revised. Rose knew about living in sin, the goings-on at Brook Farm and the Oneida Community. Then—Rose questioned him—the doctor said that Mrs. Douglass was illiterate and did not accompany Mr. Douglass on his travels and in fact seemed indifferent to his cause. All right, then. There was divorce. Rose had heard of that, too. In fantasy anything can happen. She read *My Bondage and My Freedom* and heard him speaking it to her, telling her—just her—his story. The doctor brought home *Uncle Tom's Cabin* and she read it hungrily and with mounting rage and kept it by her bed and reread the more lurid passages and thought of Mr. Douglass the while. She went on loving Frederick Douglass for a long time. Why, she wondered, did people marry so wrong?

Her father brought Mariah in their chaise in a gentle snowfall in the Christmas season. The snow fell slow and feathery and had dusted the hood of the chaise and the backs of Sam Look's horses on the short ride. Luke stood at the parlor window and watched Mr. Look wrap the reins and get down and come around and help Mariah to the ground. She wore a fur-and-velvet jacket and a toque that cupped her head snugly, as a child's hat might.

"Father," Luke called, and heard him come up the hall, clearing his throat.

Mariah took her father's arm and they came through the gate, which swept the snow back when Mr. Look opened it. Luke moved into the hall as his father threw open the front door. Thomas had come too. Rose, in her apron, crept out of the kitchen into the dining room and listened at the doorway.

"Merry Christmas, Sam."

"Same to you, George."

"Merry Christmas," Luke said.

"Mariah," the doctor said. "Welcome. Luke, take her coat."

A pause as Luke did. Some stamping of feet.

"I hear you're going to Harvard, Luke," Mr. Look said.

"Yes sir, if I pass the entrance exam."

"Admirable. What would be your line of study?"

"I'd like to go on with my Greek and Latin. Maybe medicine. I don't know."

"Greek and Latin," Mr. Look said. "You've got a smart boy here, don't you."

Rose listened. Nothing so far from Mariah.

"Terrible news from Virginia," the doctor said.

"No surprise," Mr. Look said. "We can't win this war and we might as well face it."

"Young Peleg Davenport was killed," the doctor said. "I don't know if you heard."

Silence.

"No," Mr. Look said, "I didn't."

"He died in that terrible charge."

"Well, he died for nothing."

Good, Rose thought. *What I expected.* She stepped into the hall and went toward them, wiping her hands on her apron.

"Rose," the doctor said, "you know Sam Look."

Mr. Look still wore his snow-dusted frock coat and held his hat in his hand. He met her eye and she would remember, with satisfaction, the startle in his face, a kind of disorientation. The effect she so often had on white men. She smiled, kept coming, and extended her hand. Mr. Look took it uncertainly, with just the slightest hesitation.

"And this is Mariah," the doctor said.

"Mariah and I know each other," Rose said.

Mariah brought her gaze up and spoke for the first time. "We've not actually been *introduced,*" she said.

"Well, now you are," the doctor said brightly.

Mariah smiled faintly and looked at Luke. Her gaze was jade-green and languid, speculative, veiled. Luke was watching her, and Rose knew it didn't matter what she said or thought or how stupid she was. Not now, anyway. Not for a while. Her hair was gathered back of her head like a plump hank of spun gold. She had a bigger bosom than Rose did and a waist cinched in just as small as hers. She wore pointy kid boots with tassels that swung and danced just below the hem of her Christmas-green hoop skirt. Silver ear bobs set with rubies. There's men, Rose thought, who'd pay money to take her home and never touch her if she didn't want them to. Just to own her, like some gorgeous pet.

"What time shall I call for her?" Mr. Look said.

"Stay and have a glass of wine," the doctor said. "A bit of wassail."

"Another time, thank you."

"Three o'clock then," the doctor said.

"No wassail for you, Mariah," Mr. Look said.

Mariah smiled cryptically. She shook her pretty head. Mr. Look sneaked a look at Rose and she caught him and smiled and he looked away quickly. Mariah had looked at her that once, and not again.

"Thank you, Mr. Look," Luke said.

"Not at all, my boy," Sam Look said.

She'd been determined to put on an out-of-the-ordinary dinner, without knowing exactly why. In another week would come the effort of Christmas dinner and here she was spending Saturday night and all of Sunday morning cooking for a nose-in-the-air white girl who had yet to speak to her in the street. Feeding wood chunks into the Monarch, barking at Luke and Thomas to keep the woodbox full. The kitchen hot as July.

She roasted a ham. Turnips, yams, spiced apple rings from the root cellar. Mashed potatoes. Biscuits. Two pitchers of sweet cider, sweating-cold from a night in the icebox. And then: sugar cookies *and* sponge cake filled with her huckleberry jam and covered with buttercream icing.

Thomas sat at the kitchen table eating a buttered biscuit and watching her as she made everything ready. She opened the oven and leaned into its hot breath and drew out the ham, sizzling in its juices. She set it down and closed the oven door and brushed a wiry coil of hair back from her damp forehead. The doctor had gone into the back parlor with his newspapers. There was a fire going in there. Luke had taken Mariah into the front parlor to show her the Christmas tree and they had not reappeared, though the room was without heat.

"Do you think he's kissing her?" Thomas said.

"If she lets him he is."

"Why wouldn't she?"

"She might not approve."

"Why not?"

"Some girls are like that."

She lifted the heavy pot of boiled potatoes and poured the hot water out and dumped the potatoes into an earthenware bowl.

"I wonder," Rose said, "what she thinks about slavery."

"Ask her," Thomas said.

"She might resent it, me being colored."

"All the more reason to ask her."

"Why don't you ask her?" Rose said.

"Luke'll tan me if I do."

"Luke's probably wondering himself."

"I bet he knows," Thomas said.

"I don't think so. You ask her, you'll be doing him a favor." She spooned butter out of the crock, let the potatoes melt it. She got a pitcher of cider out of the icebox. "Go call them to table while I mash these things," she said.

Mariah surveyed the table, the place settings and chairs, and Rose could see her counting them in her head. She finished counting and looked at Rose with those hooded eyes and a smile tugged her mouth over. The cook, a Negro, sitting at the family table. Would wonders never cease. *A plantation down South,* Rose thought. *She'd fit right in. Slaves waitin on her hand and foot.* Luke held a chair for her and she sat down with a rustle of petticoats and bone crinoline. Rose took her place at the head of the table opposite the doctor and Mariah observed it and then looked thoughtfully out at the falling snow.

"Would you like some cider?" Luke said.

"Yes, please," Mariah said, and slyly met his eye.

"You've surpassed yourself, Rosie," the doctor said.

He carved and the plates went around with their slabs of ham. The bowls of vegetables were passed from hand to hand. Mariah helped herself to small portions and kept her eyes downcast. Rose watched her. The bowls completed their circuit and everyone fell to eating.

"Did you know Peleg Davenport?" Rose said.

Mariah seemed to think it over. "Not well," she said.

"He brought a runaway slave to our house," Thomas said. "Off the *Lizzie Freeman*. Does she know about that, Luke?"

"Will you shut up?" Luke said.

"It doesn't matter anymore," the doctor said. "The Fugitive Slave Act is a dead letter."

"There was talk," Mariah said. She had paused with her fork halfway up. She sat straight but with a slight forward tilt, and you could not but notice the grace of her neck, its slenderness, its smoothness. "I didn't entirely believe it," she said.

"Why ever not?" Rose said.

"I just didn't. I suppose because it went against the law."

"It was a bad law," the doctor said. "We didn't feel bound by it."

"I wonder nobody stopped you," Mariah said.

"We're strong for abolition," Thomas said.

Mariah smiled her cryptic smile. "I know," she said.

"Are you?" Thomas said.

"Thomas," the doctor said, "this is not an inquisition."

"I just don't know what would *become* of the Negroes if we freed them," Mariah said.

"Honey," Rose said, "they done *been* freed. It's called the Emancipation Proclamation."

"But they aren't free, in fact."

"A lot of them are. Haven't you heard 'Kingdom Coming'? 'Say, darkies, have you seen the massa with the mustache on his face?'"

"No, I've not," Mariah said.

"'Go along the road sometime this mornin like he going to leave the place,'" Rose said.

"I've not heard it."

"Rose is up on all the war songs," the doctor said.

"That ain't a war song," Rose said, "that's a freedom song. *Isn't*, I mean."

"I'm thinking about enlisting," Luke said.

Rose would remember the moment forever. The snow sifting down through the bare limbs of the chestnut tree, a low fire on the hearth, the ham on the table, the bowls of vegetables, the white biscuits. They had not lit a lamp and the waning daylight was spare and colorless, a thin gray twilight. At the time it annoyed her slightly, as diverting attention from Mariah's views on slavery. Nonviews, Rose called them. But afterward she saw that it was Luke's intention to do so. Draw the fire onto himself.

"Good God," the doctor said.

"Why not?" Luke said.

"You're but eighteen."

"They take them at eighteen," Luke said.

"What put this idea in your head?" the doctor said.

"He wants to fight slavery," Thomas said. "I do too."

"Don't you even think about it," his father said.

"Why not?" Thomas said.

"They won't take you at sixteen, that's why not," Luke said.

"They took Elisha."

"It's different now."

"I'll lie about my age."

"Be quiet," Luke said.

"Who would like some more ham?" the doctor said, and picked up the carving knife.

"The boys would," Rose said.

"Mariah?"

"No thank you."

"You're going to Harvard this fall," the doctor said, carving. "After that, we'll see."

"If Elisha can do it," Luke said, "I can." He passed his empty plate.

"It isn't a question of *can*," the doctor said.

"Should, then. Why should Elisha go and not me?"

"Father says the war will be over by the end of the summer," Mariah said.

"What do *you* say?" Rose said.

"I think he's right," Mariah said. "I think you'd be wasting your time, Luke."

"The more reason to hurry," Luke said.

"We'll talk no more about it," the doctor said. "Thomas, pass your plate. And let's get those vegetables moving again. Rosie, you're a miracle."

"Ain't she the beatenest cook?" Thomas said.

"Yes she is," Mariah said, smiling her smile.

She did not get him alone until Wednesday afternoon, when Thomas went sledding with a crowd of boys—and girls—on Manter Hill. Thomas, who stuck to her like a burr these days. Can I help you with the dishes, Rosie? Do you need a load of wood? Will you help me with my lessons? You're so good at figures! He would sit at the kitchen table through the dimming afternoons while she cooked the supper, at his lessons or reading by the light of an oil lamp till she worried about him, living his life indoors and without friends, it seemed. Luke often stayed on after school let out; Mr. Pease was helping him bone up on his Latin and Greek for the Harvard entrance examination. Or he would come home and drop his pile of schoolbooks and eat a hermit or some gingerbread and set out on a solitary ramble on West Chop or up the hill toward North Tisbury, restless, craving movement as if it were a potion he needed, a tonic, as perhaps it was. He would come back a couple of hours later with his cheeks burned cold and ruddy and his union suit damp underneath his layers of clothes and Rose would heat water for him and he would fill the tub and drag it outside—outside, in the cold and dark!—and take his bath. It's good for the blood, he said. Oh? Rose said. We'll come out there one night, find you frozen solid in a tub of ice. But the doctor said it wouldn't hurt him if he didn't linger.

On that Wednesday afternoon he came straight home from school and Rose said that the supper was all prepared and asked him if she could go with him on his walk. Luke looked at her, surprised. He smiled, as if the idea were humorous.

"Think you can keep up with me?" he said.

"I said walk, not race," she said.

The temperature had not risen above freezing and the blanket of Sunday's snow still covered the roadways, grooved in parallel and criss-crossing lines by the wagon traffic, and coated fence rails and rooftops. They went down Drummer Lane and north on Main, into the country, where the road went down close to the water and wandered its way north out West Chop. It was cold and the sky was iron-gray, but there was no feel of more snow coming. Rose had tied a scarf under her chin and put her Leghorn hat on over it.

"You've been avoiding me," she said.

He looked at her. "I wouldn't do that," he said.

"You an awful busy man, then."

"Not that busy."

There were sheep fields uphill from them, and, to their right, across the dunes and marsh grass, they could see the still, slate-gray water, and the mainland lying low and indistinct in the distance.

"You don't want to talk about her," Rose said.

"Who?"

"That pigeon of yours."

"I will, if you can leave off insulting her."

They passed the Chase farmstead, the house crouched large and driftwood-gray against the gray sky.

"Did you kiss her?"

Luke didn't answer.

"Right," she said. "It isn't my business."

Luke said nothing.

"I won't ask again," Rose said.

They walked awhile. The feathery snow crunched underfoot where it wasn't trampled down.

"I asked her and she said no," Luke said.

Rose looked at him beside her and smiled. "You asked her?"

"I thought I ought to."

"Honey, never ask a girl can you kiss her."

"Why not?"

"Lots of reasons."

"What if you try and she doesn't want you to?"

"She'll let you know."

"Stick a hatpin in me," Luke said.

"That's one way," Rose said.

They walked on. Rose thought of taking his arm, thought how natural it would be.

"She said you oughtn't to kiss until you're engaged," Luke said.

"There's some think so."

"What do you think?"

"I didn't have anyone to teach me the rules," Rose said. "Except the orphanage, of course. Those matrons, you look at a boy wrong they'd strap you."

"How'd you court, then?"

"Sneak out a window at night. And then there were picnics with the Catholic orphanage. Out at Rocky Point. There was a good-looking boy named Anthony used to spark me. Portuguese boy. More colored than white. There were a lot of children to keep track of, it wasn't hard to get away behind a big rock or up into some woods."

"He kissed you."

"Kissing ain't a sin."

"What else he do?"

"Never you mind."

"I bet I know."

"We were talking about Mariah, I thought."

Luke nodded.

"Go on," Rose said.

"She lets me kiss her at forfeits is what I don't understand," Luke said.

"I told you: that ain't kissing."

Luke made no answer to this and as if by wordless agreement they slowed and then stopped walking. In front of them the road sloped gently down and ascended to the knob of land where the lighthouse stood on its bluff. Rose looked at him and he at her and neither of them spoke or smiled.

"Rose?" he said.

"What."

He shifted his gaze finally and looked out toward the water. A schooner was passing, six masts, making toward Woods Hole or perhaps New Bedford. You could not feel a breath of wind yet her sails were full and she slid briskly over the smooth, bright-gray, slick-looking water.

"What?" Rose said.

Luke shook his head. "Nothing," he said.

"Nothing?"

"I forget," Luke said.

Rose smiled. The moment was gone but not gone, fixed in both their memories as a kiss would have been but without the weight of one. They walked comfortably on, content with what had just happened, unfinished though it was.

"We won't talk about her anymore," Rose said.

"I don't mind talking about her."

"I hope you don't expect to win her by enlisting."

"Not likely. Her father's dead against the war."

"Copperhead."

"Just about. He questions me and I don't say much. I don't argue with him. Is that wrong of me?"

"You aren't courting the father."

"I could stand up for abolition, all the same."

"Stand up to the daughter."

"Mariah's all right. I told her about Joseph. About his scars. She agreed it was a terrible evil."

"It'd be an evil without the whippings and the scars."

"I know that," Luke said.

"Does she?"

"I think so. She's coming around."

"Her daddy might not like that."

"Her daddy can go jump in a lake."

Rose smiled. *Good,* she thought. *That's good.* They were walking slowly now, and again she thought of taking his arm. The schooner moved smoothly out ahead of them.

"Rosie?"

"What, sugar."

"Should I enlist?"

"Lord, honey. I can't tell you that."

"Mariah said it'd be stupid. She says the war's lost."

"You know better than that," Rose said.

"I feel guilty sitting it out."

"There's time yet," Rose said.

"Not if we lose another big battle."

"You'll do what's right," she said, nudging him toward it against the will of her own heart, partly, at least, to spite Mariah Look.

Then, in the early spring, Mariah jilted him. That's how stupid she was. Even Rose was surprised.

"She said I preached too much," Luke told her. "Said she was tired of talking about the war."

"You ought to have known not to push like that."

"I was trying to make her see the light."

"Some can't see it," Rose said, "and some don't want to. Ones that don't want to are the worst of all."

It was after supper and dark, and they were walking out on William Street, just the two of them, because Thomas had gone to bed with a sore throat. Let's take a walk, Rose had said, seizing the opportunity. She'd invited the doctor for form's sake, knowing he'd decline.

April had arrived and the night was balmy and moist and the tree frogs were singing noisily in all the low wet places and ponds, their shrill jingling chorus afloat on the night. A little piece of the moon squinted down at them and the stars were dulled to tarnished silver by the soft heavy air. Rose had known enough to let Luke alone about Mariah for the better part of a week. His pride had made him icy, even with her. Thomas said he spoke to Mariah in school civilly but only when he had to, and did not look at her when she recited.

"She still have *Uncle Tom's Cabin*?"

"I guess."

"Well, you better get it back."

"I'll get Thomas to ask her."

"Thomas?"

"I don't talk to her anymore."

"Don't talk to her to ask for something that's not hers?"

"I wouldn't ask her for a drink of water in the desert."

Rose laughed. The laugh buckled her over. She straightened up and now the sheer happiness of spring and the peepers' song surged up through her and she took Luke's arm without thinking. He stopped for a split second and she could feel his heart miss a beat, and then they were moving again, and it was done, and fine with both of them.

"It's *my* damn book," she said.

"*Rosie,*" he said, smiling. He'd never heard her curse.

"I bet she didn't even read it," she said.

"I don't think so," Luke said.

He was over her. No one else would believe that, such was Mariah's beauty. She'd thrown him over and both convention and common sense said he pined for her and would for a good long time. Luke didn't care what they thought, another thing to love in him.

"I should have known I couldn't change her," Luke said.

"You can't blame her for her upbringing," Rose said, in a forgiving mood now.

They'd passed the last of the bone-white Greek-style houses and William Street had petered out in a footpath that bent west to skirt a woodlot with a field on the other side where Luke had gathered hay last summer. She kept his arm in the curve of her ungloved hand. She could feel the warmth of it through his jacket. She could feel its sinew.

"You should only love people who believe as you do," Luke said.

"It's a sight easier." She thought for a moment of Frederick Douglass and his illiterate wife, never at his side in his fiery orations.

They walked on, slow. The bare trees cast faint shadows over the beaten footpath.

"I'm definitely going to enlist," he said.

"Luke. Don't do it just to show that girl."

"She'd disdain me if I didn't, and she'd be right. You can't preach abolition and then sit home."

Rose didn't say anything.

"If you were a man you'd go," Luke said.

"I've often thought so."

"I know you would. And you'd think less of me if I didn't."

"That's not true."

"It is, even if you don't know it."

"What would I do if you left?" she said.

"You'd . . ." He looked at her walking beside him and Rose could feel her heart racing and knew his was too. She gave his arm a gentle tug, stopping him in the treeshade.

"We should go back," she said. "Doctor'll be missing us."

"I don't want to go back," he said.

"I don't either."

They stood looking at each other. The peepers sang somewhere off beyond the woods. Sleighbells. She stepped against him and put her arms around him. He was big, solid. A man. She had never held a man, just thin weedy boys. Luke wrapped his arms about her, tentative at first, and looked at her hard, wanting to make sure this was more than just some of her devilment. She smiled and laid her face against his chest and Luke pulled her in and held her.

"Rosie," he said.

"Don't talk, sugar. Just close your eyes."

He closed them and she rose to kiss him.

"That's right, honey," she whispered, after a time. "That's just right."

The kissing was established, and they could not get enough of it. They kissed in the hall, the kitchen, the two parlors, anywhere there was a closed door or a couple of rooms between them and Thomas and the doctor. Luke, who had always been an early riser, was downstairs before her in the predawn, and they kissed in the kitchen by lamplight, the big house silent around them, as if it were empty and all theirs. They kissed in the umber dusk of the barn at candle lighting, Luke being quick these days to help Rose put Nancy up, and vice versa, Rose as quick to follow Luke out, an indiscretion neither Thomas nor the doctor seemed to notice. The kisses there were brief, stolen, and the close sweetish hay- and dung-smelling air and the nearness of the horse gave them an almost criminal excitement, like sacrilege.

"We're going to get caught at this," Rose said one evening in the barn, where they could at least talk out loud.

"I don't care if we do," Luke said.

"Which means I have to do the caring for both of us."

"They'll know sooner or later," he said.

"Not yet, sugar. It'd make terrible trouble, you hear me?"

Luke shrugged, still holding her.

"Promise me, Luke."

"All right," he said.

It advanced, and now Luke was running a hand deep down her back, and only her crinoline stopped it from continuing down her hip, her backside. In the front parlor one afternoon—the doctor was at work and Thomas out somewhere—he turned her around, very gently, and cupped her breasts in his hands and kissed her neck. They stood that way for many minutes, Luke hefting each one gently, caressing them, studying the feel of them, till Rose finally stepped away and turned, smiling, to kiss him in the usual way. Now what? she thought. But then came Chancellorsville, the answer to her question occurring all those miles away at about the same time she was asking it.

The *Monohansett* brought news of the disaster on her Saturday run from New Bedford. Mr. Daley was ready with it when Rose went into the drugstore for rose water and soap, and an order of salicylic acid for the doctor. Mr. Bradley's house girl, Bridget Moynahan, was waiting at the counter with her basket on her arm. Rose came in cheerful, then saw Mr. Daley's clouded expression as he glanced at her and wondered for a moment if he'd gotten wind of Luke sparking her, had spoken to some busybody who had seen them hugging.

"Rose," he said, "did you hear?" And she knew she and Luke were safe. Bridget Moynahan eyed her sourly.

"What?" she said, her heart falling anyway. The war. Another battle lost.

"Hooker's been whipped to a fare-thee-well. Place called Chancellorsville. They got around us and dang near wiped out the whole army."

"How?" Rose said.

"Well . . ."

"*How?*"

"Rose, I don't *know*. That infernal Jackson. Caught us asleep, apparently."

"It's a judgment," Bridget Moynahan said. She spoke with a brogue; she'd been born over in Ireland.

"Bridget's brother was lost at Antietam," Mr. Daley explained. "He was in the Twenty-eighth Massachusetts."

"I'm sorry for it," Rose said.

"His blood's on Mr. Lincoln's hands," Bridget said.

"I'd say it was on General Lee's," Rose said.

"Now, now," Mr. Daley soothed. Rose knew he sided with her.

"They're only defending their country," Bridget said. She had a pinched face, sharp little nose, pale freckles. Rose felt sorry for her but not sorry enough to keep quiet.

"It's *our* country," she said.

"Please," Mr. Daley said.

"He was but nineteen," Bridget said.

Rose turned away, leaned her stiff springy crinoline against the counter, and looked out through the polished display window into the sunny street. The ice wagon went by, paint-faded, boxy, lumbering, Mr. Swenson sitting bunch-shouldered in the shade of its flat roof. There were nurses in Washington, D.C., and even, she'd heard, on battlefields, but not colored ones. There were no Negroes in the Sanitary Commission. You had to be a soldier if you were going to aid the cause, they were willing enough to spill colored blood, though not side by side with the white men. I ought to have been born a man, Rose thought, only half joking to herself. The ice truck rattled on, the mare's hooves thumping dully, rousing the yellow dust. Rose thought of Luke, what he'd most certainly do now, and when the surly Irish girl had paid and gone, she unfolded her list and pretended to read—baking soda, one bottle; vinegar, a bottle; alum; a hair sponge—guessing, hoping, that it was the right size. She read rose water and lavender soap and salicylic acid for the doctor.

"Another year of this," Mr. Daley said, wrapping her purchases, "and they'll turn Lincoln out of office."

"It won't keep up," Rose said.

Mr. Daley leaned over with a pencil to tot up the amount.

"It can't," Rose said.

Mr. Daley shrugged, smiled weakly, and slid the bill toward her. Rose opened her silk purse, hating General Lee anew and all the slavers, every last one.

Dinner that day was funereal. Deep-dish apple pie, but no one had an appetite for it.

"God*damn* them," Luke said.

"Luke Chandler," his father said.

"I don't care," Luke said, bent low over his food.

"Maybe it wasn't as bad as everyone is saying," Thomas said.

"Maybe it was worse," Luke said.

"I don't understand it," the doctor said. "Hooker seemed so able. Fighting Joe."

"An abolitionist, wasn't he, Father?" Thomas said.

"So they said."

"I'm enlisting," Luke said. "Before summer."

Silence. They all sat motionless, waiting for Luke to say more if he would. Not even the doctor would oppose it now. Especially not the doctor. Rose's heart filled: with love, with sadness. There *was* some good in the world. This family. Luke. Others.

"There goes Rosie," Thomas said, always the one to call attention.

Rose smiled, weeping, and dabbed at her eyes with her napkin.

"He hasn't even left yet," Thomas said.

"I know that, sugar."

Thomas put his elbow on the table and rested his head on his hand and with the other hand slowly forked up a bite of pie. Sulking.

"Sit up, Thomas," the doctor said.

Thomas removed his elbow and slouched back in his chair. "Maybe I'll go too," he said.

"Maybe you won't," the doctor said.

"I want to fight those damn Rebels as much as Luke does."

"If I hear one more curse at this table . . ." the doctor said.

"Honey," Rose said, leaning to take Thomas's hand, "how'm I going to get along with both my boys gone?"

Thomas shrugged, still sulky.

"You wait your turn," Luke said.

"War'll be over," Thomas said.

"No it won't," the doctor said.

"Come to me tonight," she said in the kitchen, whispering.

"When?"

"When you can. Wake me if I'm asleep. Be very quiet."

He looked at her. Nodded.

"You mustn't wake Thomas. You mustn't come if he's awake."

"He won't be. He'll . . ."

"Hush, and go on out of here now."

She soaked the little sponge in vinegar and inserted it and blew out the lamp and got into bed. The sponge seemed to fit all right and there was no more than a slight tingle, not unpleasant, from the vinegar. She heard the hall clock strike eleven and sometime later Luke touched her awake and sat down, heavy, on the bed. He was clothed, shirt and trousers, but shoeless.

"You sure Thomas is asleep?" were her first words.

Luke nodded. The moon was up and she could see him in its thin colorless light. He told her about his trick with the pillows. Rose smiled.

"You devil," she whispered.

She reached up with her bare arm, stroked his hair.

"Lock the door."

He got up, padded to the door and set the catch on the latch, and came back to the bed. She put her hand on his leg and now he saw that her shoulder was bare.

"There was something happened to me one time I need to tell you about," she said, still in that even whisper. They would always whisper in this bed, would have to.

He listened to her tell about the policeman when she was sixteen with his head bowed, frowning darkly.

"Dirty bastard," he said when she was done.

"It's over," she said, "long ago."

"I'll find him and kill him."

"I don't want that. Just want you to know. And that it was my only time."

"I thought that boy at the orphanage. Anthony."

"We got intimate, but not that intimate."

"What does that mean?"

"Means I know a few things."

"I don't know much," Luke said.

"You have to take your clothes off, did you know that?"

He smiled. "So do you."

"They're off."

He looked at her arm, her shoulder.

"You gonna sit there all night?" she said.

His hand shook as he worked his shirt buttons. He had never undressed in front of anyone save Thomas and he understood now what an act of trust it was. He looked around for a place to put his shirt and chose the rocking chair, which was by the bedside table, and hung the shirt over its back. He glanced at Rose. She was watching him. He drew a deep audible breath and unbuttoned his trousers and stepped out of them and hung them on the rocker back. He sat down and removed his socks. He hesitated with a hand on either side of his briefs then slid them down without looking at her. He dropped them on the chair and still did not look at her as he approached the bed. She made room for him and he would remember, first of all, how warm she was, and how like the peaceful thrilling scent of wisteria was the fragrance of her skin. He took her gingerly in his arms and felt the rapid delirious throb of his own heart. It started with a kiss, he knew that, at least. The difference was, the whole body was in play, the kiss just one point of contact, sensation. It went on awhile. Kissing, touching. He felt her all over and slid himself against her and she took his hand finally and directed him.

"Like this?" he said. Whispering it.

"Yes."

"All right?"

"That's good, honey. That's just right."

"Oh Rosie. You're so beautiful."

"That's good, Luke. Oh God."

"You're so beautiful."

Oh God, she breathed. *Oh Lord. . . .*

Afterward she stole downstairs in her robe as silent as a prairie Indian among enemies and let herself out the kitchen door to the backyard and removed the sponge and douched with an alum and baking soda solution under the eye of the spring moon. There was no wind and the air smelled wonderfully of lilac and wet grass. All those little babies, she thought, washing right out of her. Half-white half-black babies. A pale-skinned Negro was in the middle, not a member of either race, and in Rose's experience white people were even more disdainful of them than if they were of darkest ebony, as if the white part were something stolen, an act of Negro effrontery. She would have to think about it if Luke ever wanted to give her a baby. She straightened and let her robe down. There was a wooden bucket of well water by the kitchen door and she rinsed her hands in it and crept back inside and up the giving, creaking stairs and down the hall to her room. She got into the bed and Luke pulled her gently against him.

"I can't again, honey. I haven't got the sponge in."

"Just for a minute."

"That's how babies get made. Man say, Just for a minute."

"I won't be able to sleep."

"Yes you will. Close your eyes."

"Why?"

"Close your eyes, Luke."

Her hands caressing him were like the wings of a bird and the pleasure finally so intense he felt he'd choke on it. And then the slow drift back to his corporeal self and the canopy bed and Rose beside him, up on her elbow, naked and lovely in the faint light of the sky in the windows, whispering to him.

"I wanted to tell you one more thing."

"All right." He put his hand on her shoulder, ran it down her warm silk-smooth back and over the hard curve of her hip.

"I never undressed for Anthony, nor any other boy. Not completely. Not like this."

"It doesn't matter," he whispered.

"Does to me."

"I guess it does to me, too."

"I know," she said. "Reason I didn't do it."

Maybe, then, it was Luke she'd been waiting for all these years. Or not waiting: she couldn't remember not loving him as she did now, as if the boy had stood in all these years for the man he would become. A colored girl needed a protector in this world, sad but true; Luke had signed on for that a long time ago, and she'd loved him for it more even than she'd realized. Black and white together, though: her heart misgave her. The evil of the world would seek them out, stalk them to their doorstep. Where would they go? Where live? She couldn't find it in any dream, as she had dreamed a life with Frederick Douglass. The war helped, in its perverse way: who could think beyond it?

She could not but feel guilty in deceiving Thomas and the doctor. She owed them better, she knew that, but knew also the hurt it would do them to know what was going on, and in this very house. It was clear to her that Thomas felt toward her as Luke did, but in an unformed, half-conscious, childish sort of way, not yet brought to ripeness by desire or jealousy. That would change, Rose knew by instinct, should Thomas learn she was lying down with Luke, and perhaps with any man.

As for the doctor, for a long time she'd seen the longing in his kindly face, but so leavened by courtesy, etiquette, pure decency, that it seemed as much fatherly as it did carnal, a harmless stretching of his affection for her. He would tolerate her taking a husband, a lover, but not his own son. It would be a betrayal, Luke sneaking in to take what he, Dr. Chandler, would not attempt, for honor's sake. If she would love Luke, and there was no question of that, she had no choice but to deceive.

"Act natural with me," she told him, walking beside him on the road to the lighthouse on a Sunday afternoon. Her parasol on her shoulder, Kashmir shawl, white gloves.

"This is natural," Luke said, and stopped, turned her gently and kissed her.

Rose returned the kiss then stepped back out of his embrace. "If you can't behave," she said, "I won't walk out with you."

"Who's looking?" Luke said, gesturing at the green fields, the woods uphill to the west. It was a breezy day; the Sound was pastel blue and scalloped with whitecaps.

"Just takes one person," she said, "and the whole town'll know."

"So what?" he said. They were walking again.

"I'm older than you, is bad enough. But a colored girl? Luke Chandler and a nigger? You got any idea how hard it would go on both of us?"

"I'd have to set a few people straight, I guess."

"You can't set the whole island straight."

"One at a time I can."

She took his arm in spite of herself.

"I'm going to marry you, Rosie. The world'll just have to—" He broke off, looked at her.

"If you'll have me, I mean."

Rose did not know what to say. Her heart filled, swelled. Yes, yes, but where would they go, where live in peace? A city maybe: teeming, too busy to notice or bother them. Europe, perhaps. Why not?

"I'll have you, honey," she said.

"When I'm back from the war."

"You're going to Harvard when you get back from the war."

"Maybe."

"Oh yes you are. Be a doctor. A lawyer. I need nice things, you know."

"Will you wait?"

"Unless I find someone better." Smiling airily, her chin in the air.

"I'll kill him."

"Don't talk so, Luke. There's enough killing in this world."

"When, exactly, are you going to enlist?" Thomas said at supper one night.

It wasn't a friendly question. The two boys had been sharp with each other for some days now. Rose, worried about it, would step out onto the front porch when they left for school and watch them go down William Street with their belted stacks of books slung over their shoulders, walking side by side but apart from each other, neither speaking. Some deep, unformed suspicion was rubbing at Thomas. Luke said he slept hard, never heard him go in and out, but maybe his heart heard. Rose would watch them out of sight, hoping either one would turn and say something to the other, but neither did.

"He'll enlist when school lets out," the doctor said.

"That's not until June," Thomas said.

"I know when it is," Luke said.

"I thought you were anxious to get down there."

"For God's sake, Thomas," the doctor said.

Rose put her hand on Thomas's arm, which always had the desired effect. "Honey, there'll be plenty of war left for your brother."

"Not if Lee whips us again," Thomas said. He left his arm under Rose's hand.

"Let's enjoy Luke while he's still here," Rose said, throwing her lover a smile. *My lover. My man.*

"Enjoy him," Thomas said. "Right."

Rose looked out the window. The great chestnut tree seemed sheathed in sunlight, leaves like dark green feathers. The days were so long now. She pulled her hand back from Thomas's arm.

"Thomas," the doctor said.

"Yes, Father."

"Suppose something were to happen to Luke. Suppose he didn't come home."

"Don't speak of it," Rose blurted.

Luke looked at her, then down at his plate.

"I want Thomas to grow up," the doctor said. "These are dire times, Thomas. We all must do our part."

"You already said I can't enlist," Thomas said.

"There are other ways," the doctor said.

"Like what?"

"Pulling together," the doctor said. "Enduring."

"Be twice as much work around here for you and me," Rose said. "We'll be bound to help each other, you're going to have to attend to me, hear?"

Thomas shrugged. "I hear."

"He's too busy," Luke said, "sparking Clarissa Parker."

Thomas screwed his mouth over in annoyance.

"Clarissa Parker?" Rose said. "Pretty little girl wears those pretty ribbons in her hair?"

"I'm not sparking her," Thomas said.

"You talk to her a lot," Luke said.

"I talk to Billy King too. Am I sparking him?"

Rose smiled at the two of them. This was better.

"You two will always be brothers," she said.

"Unfortunately," Luke said, but not meanly, and it drew the tug of a smirk from Thomas.

"I want to lie down with you and never get up."

"There's more to loving, sugar."

"I know that, Rosie."

"We can always find some dark place to lie down in. It's the days I worry about."

"I'll marry you and it won't matter."

"It will to some," she said.

"The hell with them," Luke said.

"You might not want such a life," she said.

"You might not either," he said.

"Oh yes I will," she said, and rolled toward him, and it was some time before they spoke again.

Then the *Gazette* came out shouting Colonel Macy's appeal and Luke had to answer it, school be damned. Even the doctor knew he did. The newspapers were carted over from Edgartown in the late afternoon and the doctor, leafing through his copy in the front parlor while supper cooked, fastened on Macy's notice, and after a long moment put the paper down and stared out into the lilac evening on William Street. The birds still twittered and the faintest of breezes rustled the leaves of the shade trees. The doctor looked out, sitting stock still with his chin in his hand.

Rose called them all to supper. The doctor was quiet at the table.

"You feeling unwell?" Rose asked him.

He managed an abstracted melancholy smile. "Just tired," he said.

Thomas, too, was quiet, broody. Luke and Rose looked at each other.

"Father," Luke said, "do you know what the ablative absolute is?" He was still studying his Latin and Greek twice a week with Mr. Pease, though the Harvard entrance exam was not until midsummer, when he'd most certainly be gone.

"I recollect it, yes," the doctor said.

"I have it cold," Luke said.

Rose wondered if enlistment was so much on his mind anymore. The two of them living each daytime as mere interval, as time to be gotten through, to be filled as usefully as possible. Studying Greek and Latin was one way. Their lives' true essence, the point of everything, began when Luke came into her bed, the one or two hours of the twenty-four that really counted. She had told Luke that there's more to love than lying down together, but she also believed—she was quite sure—that the joy and abandonment they found together in the dark were rare between a man and woman. That most couples settled for far less.

"I guess you haven't heard," Thomas said.

"Heard what?" Luke said.

"There's an officer at the Mansion House. Army of the Potomac. He's wanting recruits. I was to town today. Everybody's talking of it."

It was a dagger of ice, slid into the small of Rose's back. The cold met her spine, froze it.

"What regiment?" Luke said. "I don't want to go out West. I want to fight Lee."

"The Twentieth Massachusetts," the doctor said. "Elisha Smith's regiment. It's in today's newspaper. I thought I'd wait till tomorrow to mention it."

Luke cast a pensive look out the window.

"Well," Thomas said, "that regiment ain't out West, by a sight."

"Thomas," said the doctor wearily, "will you speak—"

"I'll go down there first thing tomorrow," Luke said.

"You don't have to, Luke," the doctor said. "Not yet."

"I'm either going to enlist or I'm not, Father."

The doctor nodded glumly. "You're right," he said.

That night Rose clung to him and he to her, and she could feel the heaviness of her own heart against the warm solid wall of his chest.

"It's my fault," she whispered. "I come into this family, turn you all into fire-breathers."

"You don't think we'd have been so anyway?"

"Honey, I don't know."

"Well we would."

"Not like you are."

"We would, Rosie. We *would*."

"Easy for me. Preach abolition, curse General Lee, and never get shot at."

"If you were a man you'd be long gone in one of those colored regiments. I wouldn't want to be the Rebel got in your way."

"Maybe I'm just talk, Luke."

"Bosh," Luke said.

"Well. At least I'm not selfish. Selfish'd be keeping you home."

At breakfast she set the platter down in front of him and, the room being empty, kissed his cheek and touched the back of his neck. The doctor had gone out in the carryall to bring another baby into the world. It was nine o'clock and Thomas had not appeared but this was not unusual on a Saturday. Luke's stomach was fluttery and he had no appetite—a weakness, he thought—and with effort downed two eggs, a slab of ham, a buttered biscuit, and a glass of buttermilk. He got up from the table and stood in the kitchen doorway with his plate and tumbler watching Rose, who was washing dishes with her back to him, humming "Swing Low, Sweet Chariot." He looked at her waist, at the graceful sway of her hips in the ballooning hoop skirt. She sensed him there and turned with a sudsy coffee cup in one hand, the wet soapy rag in the other, and smiled at him sadly.

"Rosie," he said.

"Put them on the table," she said.

He looked at the kitchen table, confused, then remembered the plate and glass in his hands and set them down.

"Rose."

Rose rolled her eyes ceilingward, *Thomas*. Luke nodded and stayed where he was. "I said I was going to enlist, so I guess I'd better go do it," he said.

"Don't you go get drunk afterwards," she said. "That's what boys do when they enlist."

"How would you know?" He was feeling steadier now, calmer.

"I know boys, that's how."

"Miss Know Everything." He smiled.

"Know a *few* things."

"You know a smart of them," Luke said. It made him feel horny, talking like that. He shook the thought off and turned.

"Luke," she said, stopping him. He turned back, waited.

"I love you, honey."

And he knew that if there'd been any boy left in him it was gone now, turned to memory by those brief half-whispered words. He instantly felt the weight of them, the obligation to be worthy. Now. Forever.

"I love you too," he said.

Again that smile. Tears in her eyes. "You go on now. Tell Father Abraham you're coming."

"I damn sure will," he said.

Thomas caught him halfway down Drummer Lane. He'd been awake and dressed all this time, watching out the bedroom window.

"Hey," Luke greeted him, walking.

"I'm coming too," Thomas said.

"Fine," Luke said.

"No. I'm enlisting."

Luke stopped, stopping Thomas. The two of them alone in the cool arbor of the lane.

"Don't try to stop me," Thomas said.

"I'll kick your ass," Luke said.

"If I don't enlist now, I'll go to New Bedford and do it. Wouldn't you rather have me with you?"

"You're too young."

"I'll lie."

"Jesus Christ," Luke said.

"Please, Luke."

"Father won't ever forgive me."

"You don't control what I do."

"Do you understand we could get killed down there?"

"That question's so stupid I won't answer it."

"You'll be fighting. Killing people."

"Good."

"Living hard. Marching. Eating stale bread."

"Good."

"Jesus Christ." Luke shook his head slowly. He leaned and spat. "I'll tell Father what you're planning."

"Snitch," Thomas said.

"I don't care."

"They can't watch me twenty-four hours. I'll go to New Bedford, I swear it. It'll be on your head if I end up out West, Mississippi or Vicksburg or some such place."

"Vicksburg's *in* Mississippi, you stupid bastard."

"I guess I'll find out, won't I. Say hello to Elisha for me." He turned uphill, began walking.

"Goddamn it," Luke said, and Thomas heard the surrender in it and stopped. "You want to be a fool, be one."

Thomas remained facing up the lane, poised there, as if he needed to think about it. He gave it a moment, then shrugged and turned and came back down.

"If I get in trouble over this," Luke said, "I'll tan you worse than Father ever did."

"Father never tanned me at all. You either."

"Well, you're going to find out what it's like, you don't put this all on yourself."

"It is on me," Thomas said. "I *want* them to know it. I want Rose to."

"See that she does," Luke said, and they did not speak again until they reached the Mansion House, where Lieutenant Macy of the Twentieth was waiting for them in the sunny lobby.

"Good God," Rose said. "What were you *thinking*?"

It was directed at Luke, though she was looking at both boys, standing side by side, equal in height but in so little else as yet, Rose kneeling in her flower garden among the dame's rocket, in a house dress, no crinoline, squinting up at them with a hand shielding her eyes. Thomas smiling like the cat with the canary in his belly.

"I meant all along to join up," he said.

"I'd have had to whip him to stop him," Luke said.

"Then you should have."

"He'd have gone anyway, to another regiment. Sneaked a boat to New Bedford."

"I'd have brought him home by the ear if he'd tried it."

"I ain't a damn baby," Thomas said.

"Oh sugar," Rose said, softening. "Of course you aren't." It was her fault, no one else's. Her ceaseless talk of Lee and Jackson and Davis, praying their destruction out loud. How many girls, in all of history, had sent boys off to war?

"This way we can be together," Thomas said. "Look out for each other."

What have I done? Rose thought again. This sweet boy, never felt hatred in his heart, never felt pure anger.

"The colonel said it's the best regiment in the army. The Bloody Twentieth, they call it."

"Shut up, Thomas."

"You shut up."

"It's no secret, Luke," she said. "I didn't think it was a croquet club."

"I tried to stop him. I did, truly."

"No one could stop me," Thomas said. "Is there any breakfast left?"

Rose nodded, put her trowel down, and got up off her knees.

"Let him do for himself," Luke said.

"Hush," Rose told him.

The doctor only smiled his defeated smile when he heard. The delivery had been a protracted one, the afternoon nearly gone by the time he came traipsing in through the kitchen door with his black bag. The boys were at the kitchen table shelling peas. Rose was at work on an upside-down cake. It was her intention to feed them their favorite foods in the short time they had left. Upside-down cake, sponge cake, fried chicken, all the biscuits they could eat.

"You aren't going to tan me, are you, Father?" Thomas said.

"When did he ever tan you?" Rose said.

The doctor set his bag down and went to the sink to draw some cistern water.

"It wouldn't be a bad idea to tan the both of you," Rose said.

Thomas was trying to hold in a smile. Enlisting had gone to his head like corn liquor. He'd been about town most of the day, telling every chum he had. Clarissa Parker, apparently, had been greatly sobered.

"Who'll put Nancy up for me?" the doctor said.

"Not me," Thomas said.

"You're going to be a soldier," Luke said, "you better get over being afraid of a horse."

"I'm not afraid of her," Thomas said.

"Luke," Rose said, and gestured toward the door, the barn, with a toss of her head.

Luke scowled at Thomas and got up. The doctor was in the doorway to the dining room, on the way to his office.

"I think a bottle of wine tonight, Rose," he said.

"Hurrah," Thomas said.

Luke eyed him a moment, then went out to stable Nancy.

They had a week, and afterward Rose would wonder how she and Luke escaped detection, reckless as they were. The answer, if it wasn't pure luck, was the utter innocence of Thomas and the doctor, the impregnability of their imaginations. In their heart of hearts they might have wished to lie down with Rose themselves, but they'd have considered it a kind of blasphemy to say or even think it, much less attempt such an assault on the fabric of the family. Luke, they had no doubt, felt the same.

It gave him and Rose a certain freedom. Thomas was jealous but unsuspecting when Luke and Rose drove to Lake Tashmoo to enjoy a picnic. (He took her in the bed of the carryall, lifting her skirt; the air was heavy and very warm and she thought *fornication,* a word laden with godlessness and sweat and satiety, and embraced it. That other side of the coin of love.) They could stroll to the harbor after supper was over and the dishes done without drawing suspicion on themselves, they could take walks in the afternoon.

Thomas did not ask to come but made his own demands of her: to go eeling with him one afternoon in Lagoon Pond, to sit in the kitchen while she worked and ask his childish questions—Would she write to him and send him hermits and cookies when he was in the army? How can you tell when a girl is sweet on you? Would Negroes be as cruel to white people as white people were to them if the situation were reversed and the Negroes ran the country?—and to listen to her admonitions to expect a little homesickness at first and not let it make him blue, to keep his teeth clean, not to mind it if the older men joshed him some.

And so she balanced them, brother and brother, loving each as hard as a girl can love but with a different kind of love, so that on either side it could flow freely. She would wonder, growing thoughtful, if she loved the doctor as hard as she did his sons and thought not, unless gratitude and pity counted. And maybe they did. Wasn't gratitude love? Certainly she would never leave, never abandon him, so long as Luke and Thomas were away at war. Some things the heart will not allow.

"What'll happen to us?" she said, whispering to Luke one night in the dark, when the future seemed to stretch out like a wasteland or wilderness peopled only by her enemies, and which she would surely walk alone. *She loved him to desperation.* . . . It was a line from a book, Emily Brontë, George Eliot, Lord Byron, Mrs. Stowe, somebody. She wondered how they knew the feeling.

"Hush," Luke said. "Nothing will."

"If I was to lose you, honey . . ."

"You won't."

"You'll be careful."

"Sure I will."

"And then we'll tell them," she said, only half believing it. "When we're all together again."

"You bet we will."

"But how?" she said. "How tell them?"

"Just do it, right out plain," he said. Said, "You hush now and stop your fretting."

"There are different positions," she said another time, another worry shaping itself. "I read them in a book. Saw some pictures."

"What book?"

"On married life. A girl had it at the orphanage. Stole it somewhere, I guess. Said if you get tired of the one position you can liven it up a little."

"I'm not tired of it."

"When I'm old and gray you will be," she said. She did not know how much older than Luke she was. Three years? Four? "Be wantin that book then, keep you interested."

"Never," he said.

They lay awhile, alone with their thoughts but not alone. The big elm sighed in the moonless night beyond the open window. *Never.* Well maybe not. Maybe you could will a future for yourself. Rose relaxed, smiled invisibly in the darkness.

"Then we could try now," she said, "seeing I've no reason to hold back."

"Be fine with me," he said.

"Let's see what I can remember," she said, and put a hand on his shoulder to move him.

"He's so proud of himself," she said, walking the West Chop road. "Let him be proud, will you? It's only a few more days."

"I wonder if he didn't do it to impress Clarissa Parker."

"It's why most boys do it. And the girls egg them on. Send them off with kisses to Bull Run and Fredericksburg. And I'm no different."

"Maybe you credit yourself too much."

"I hope so," she said.

The day was bright but the wind had circled around and now blew from the northeast, raw and nattering, like the dry northeaster on a clear winter's day.

"Well, someone has got to fight this war," Luke said.

"I know that, honey. You get mopey when it's your own that's going."

"Maybe there won't be any more Fredericksburgs or Chancellorsvilles."

"There'll be dying," she said. The wind caught at her, tore at her straw hat. She gathered her shawl tighter around her. "Lord this wind's mean. Let's go home, Luke."

"Thomas'll be there."

"Please, honey. Let's just go home."

He stayed till dawn on their last night. They had fallen asleep sometime after midnight, had woken and loved and slept again. He had taken her once more at first light, sleepily and gently, and she held him and wetted his shoulder with her tears.

"Why you going now, honey? Why not wait?" Irrational, her heart talking.

"It's too late. We signed our names."

"Why'd I let you? In God's name why did I?"

Then Thomas got up. They could hear him moving around, selecting his clothes, pulling them on. They lay still. Thomas put his shoes on and went quietly to the door and let himself out. They held their breaths. He went along the hallway, creeping, the floor planks shifting with faint creaks under his weight. He went past Rose's door and down the stairs.

"Go. Go *now*."

Luke rolled off the bed and gathered his clothes against his chest and went naked out into the hall. He closed the door noiselessly—he had oiled the hinges of both bedroom doors when all of this began—and crept into his room and sat down and listened. Nothing. Thomas was at the other end of the house. Luke threw his covers back and removed the pillows and crawled into the bed and lay on his back with his heart pumping, listening. There was no sound but the whistlings of the birds. His heart slowed. He closed his eyes and rolled onto his stomach and slept.

She did not look at Luke, afraid of what would happen if their eyes met. There was nothing she could do for either boy now but feed them and so she did, on corned beef and fried potatoes and biscuits and blueberry pie swimming in thick cream. Thomas ate hungrily, boyishly; Luke ate abstractedly, thinking ahead to Virginia. The doctor sat down and drank a cup of coffee and did not eat. The dining room, which got the evening sun, was now shadowy, cool. It was a breathless and beautiful early-summer day on Martha's Vineyard.

"Rose," the doctor said, "sit a minute."

She'd been bustling back and forth to the kitchen, bringing more coffee, more buttermilk, more biscuits, trying to outrun sorrow by keeping busy. She'd hardly slept and her head was light and her eyes dry and gritty and her limbs heavy.

"Got biscuits to put in the oven," she said.

"We don't need any more," Thomas said.

"Thought I'd wrap some up to take with you."

"Sit," the doctor said.

Rose hesitated, reflexively wiping her hands on her apron, then sat down. The doctor bowed his head and extended a hand toward each son.

"Let us pray," he said.

They all looked at him.

"Pray?" Luke said.

"*Think*, then," the doctor said. "Let us think of each other, and of time gone and time to come."

They joined hands on the table, Luke with Rose's right hand in his, Thomas with her left. They lowered their heads. The hall clock tick-tocked hollowly in the silence. The birds warbled distantly. Luke held her hand tight. *I haven't forgotten you,* his grip said. Rose returned the pressure. She closed her eyes.

"Let us give thanks," the doctor said. "To each other, and *for* each other."

They sat. Time grew, stretched itself. A minute. Another. Praying was wishing and Rose wished for the annihilation of the Confederacy and Luke's safe return. She tried to imagine for the millionth time what would happen and could see only more of this illicit love, more deception, Luke no more capable of hurting the doctor than she was. She had never been to Boston or New York City and could not picture them, or herself living there. Her mind returned to the war and she asked the God she'd never believed in to spare Thomas too. Beyond that she did not know what to pray for. She did not know what was possible.

"May we all be together at this table again," the doctor said.

Silence. Thomas relaxed his grip and looked up.

"Amen," Rose said.

"Amen," said both boys. Luke gave her hand another squeeze and released it.

The doctor cast a smile of chagrin and love at all of them and coughed drily into his fist.

There was no crowd to see them off, and there were no speeches. It was a school day, and no children were there; midmorning and the sun rested high on a high, hard-blue sky. The *Monohansett* towered over them, throwing its blocky shadow over the wharf, breaths of steam rising from her stack. A smell of tar, of sea mud and weed and fish scales from the fish market, against whose weathered-shingle wall a gutted swordfish hung by its tail. Some of the passengers were aboard the steamer already. They stood along the rail, leaning on their elbows, looking down at the four of them, at the others waiting to board. Luke and Thomas had removed their coats.

"Thank you for the money, Father," Luke said.

"The idea is to hold on to it. Save it for some exigency that might arise."

"Like what?" Thomas said.

"That's for you to decide," the doctor said.

"Watch out someone doesn't steal it," Rose said, tearful.

Luke looked past them, out past the Chop, his gaze far away. Looking to Virginia, to the work to be done there. He seemed very calm. Rose felt a spasm of resentment, of jealousy—of the war, the cause, his regiment. He wasn't hers anymore, not all of him.

"Don't weep, Rosie," Thomas said.

"I'm not," she said, and wiped her cheeks with the back of her wrist.

The steamer's whistle blew. People began picking up their satchels, their valises, and moving toward the gangway.

"Oh dear," the doctor said.

"Good-bye, Father," Thomas said. "Good-bye, Rosie."

She hugged him hard, felt his bones collapse in against her. "You be a good boy," she said. "Look out for your brother, hear?"

Her eyes were full, her vision blurred, when she turned to Luke. She hugged him as if she would squeeze the breath out of him. She could smell the lye in his clean shirt and vest, and the clean summery tang of his skin. She held him as long as she dared, then stepped back, looked up at him through her tears.

"Good-bye, Rosie."

"Let's *go*," yelled the agent at the top of the gangway.

The boys leaned and picked up their valises. They fished their tickets out of their coat pockets.

"Bless both of you," the doctor said.

"Bless you, Father," Thomas said.

He turned and trudged up the tilted gangway carrying his valise, his coat hung over his other arm. Luke, right behind him, handed his ticket to the agent and looked back and blew Rose a kiss. She returned it and he nodded and disappeared through the hatchway. A few moments later the boys appeared at the rail above them, Rose's last view of them, slouched forward side by side in their white linen shirts and black vests and cravats, hatless, Thomas grinning like a boy on a holiday excursion, Luke gazing down unsmiling, a hardness setting in already, a readiness for what he had to do. The whistle blew again and they dragged the gangway in and cast off. The engine clanked and rumbled to life, the big wheel stirred ponderously and began to turn, shedding streams of water, and the *Monohansett* shuddered backward, clear of the wharf. Thomas waved as they slipped away, still grinning. Luke raised a hand, nodded. The steamer paused, spewing black smoke now, then lurched forward, steadying herself, gaining speed, gliding, her clank and rumble dying across the wide empty dark blue Sound, her smokeplume smearing the azure sky, until she was a chalk-white toy in the distance, and Rose and the doctor were alone.

EIGHT

General Early, said Mr. Will. You are welcome. And this would be . . . ?

General Ewell, Ewell answered.

A pleasure, sir.

General Early took his hat off and slapped it against his leg, knocking the dust out of it. The two generals and their staffs were stained head to foot with the dust and smoke of battle. They looked stiff, dead tired, fought out. They removed their soiled sweat-darkened gauntlets. They unbuckled their swordbelts and went back into the hall to hang them. They peeled off their heavy coats and hung them too and came on into the dining room, General Ewell stumping on a wooden leg. Floyd counted four aides. Majors. He knew that General Early had dined here when the Rebels had come six days ago, but he, Floyd, had been hiding under the McCurdys' front porch and had been spared witnessing it or being compelled to wait on such swine. He had never seen a Rebel general in the flesh and the sight turned his insides simultaneously cold with fright and white-hot with anger, the two emotions warring with each other, creating a nervous eruptive confusion of thoughts and resolves. He had been obsequious to white men almost as bad as these, but the indignity of skulking under a white man's porch, of lying for hours near his own urine had shamed and hardened him.

Mr. Will rose to his feet, smiling menially, menially ducking his head. This is Mr. Davidson, he said, of—

I know Mr. Davidson, General Early said, and I know this other newspaper sonofabitch.

General Ewell smiled faintly at General Early's roguish language. He was bald on the dome of his head, with black side-whiskers and a wiry mustache and beard that jutted off his chin tuftlike. The officers all wore Confederate-gray vests with gold buttons.

And Mr. Phipps. And Mr. Irons.

Yankees, observed General Early.

We were just leaving, Irons said, scraping his chair back.

No need, said General Ewell.

Mr. Phipps stood up too. Mr. Will looked at the two generals, smiling uneasily. He looked at Irons and Phipps. Mr. Phipps wiped his mouth with his linen napkin and dropped it on the table with a disdainful flick of his wrist.

Don't aggravate them, Henry, Irons said.

I'd heed that advice I was you, General Early said. We been aggravated by Yankees more than is agreeable today.

You boys, Mr. Will said quickly, addressing Trig and Floyd, hustle these dishes away. Floyd, see what's left of the stew. Light the stove. One of you might have to run down the street and fetch Lebrun back.

Mr. Phipps and Mr. Irons were moving toward the hall stairs. They went slowly, strolling with their hands in their pockets, taking their time, another artful show of disdain.

Seat yourselves, gentlemen, Mr. Will said. I wonder, in a pinch, if you could abide ham and eggs. Tonight's supper—

Ham and eggs would be fine, said General Ewell.

And some wine, General Early said.

Floyd and Trig, each with a tray, were stacking the dirty dishes. The Rebels were choosing chairs, sitting down around the oblong table. The two newspapermen, Davidson and Lathrop, remained seated.

Mr. Will, may I please speak with you? Floyd said.

You get this table cleared, Mr. Will said.

Both big oval trays were fully laden and Floyd and Trig bore them, raised high on the palm of one hand, down the hall to the kitchen, where Roland was busy washing dishes in a tub of warm soapy water and rinsing them under the cistern pump. Floyd and Trig set the heavy trays down on the pinewood table.

Guess who out there now? Trig said.

General Lee, Roland said.

You almost right, Trig said.

We can't wait on these people, Floyd said.

They looked at him, Roland turning with his hands in the gray water. What people? he said.

Jubal Early, Floyd said. Richard Ewell. They're the enemy. Slavery men.

I ain't no slave, Roland said.

You could be one. Any of us could.

But I ain't. And I got a good job and do intend on keepin it.

Mr. Will pay us good, Trig said. You got to member that, Floyd.

Mr. Will came in looking vexed. The table needs setting, he said. How much stew is left?

Mr. Will, Floyd said, I'd prefer to wash dishes than to wait table.

Mr. Will was looking into the kettle that had contained the beef stew. He stopped, the lid in midair. Not tonight, Floyd, he said.

Not what? Floyd said.

Abolition. Slavery. We all have a job to do.

I said I'd wash dishes, Floyd said.

Mr. Will brought up a steamy sigh. Run and fetch Lebrun, he said. Then we'll talk about it.

Mr. Will—

Please, Floyd. We have to feed these people. They're our guests.

Would you feed Napoleon if he came in here? Would you feed Genghis Khan?

Fetch Lebrun please.

They gonna eat anyhow, Roland said.

Trig said, You think he be safe, Mr. Will?

It's two blocks away, Mr. Will said. Roland, you go down to the cellar, get a couple of bottles of Bordeaux wine. Can you read Bordeaux?

Yes sir.

Trig, you get that table set.

Yes sir.

Floyd, if you meet anyone, tell them you work at the Globe and that Generals Ewell and Early are on the premises.

I'm not afraid, Floyd said.

That's good, Mr. Will said. Throw some kindling in the stove, Trig.

Floyd went down the spacious hallway past the hung coats and belts and weapons, the scabbarded swords and holsters, past the darkened lobby and out onto Race Horse Alley and down the alley to Carlisle Street. A fat moon hung in the sky and by its light he could see the debris of the Union retreat of two days ago. The road was peppered too with torn paper cartridges, some of them skittering around windblown and others squashed flat, ground into the dirt. A putrid smell, like rotten eggs, hung in the summer air. Up on the Diamond someone was playing. "Aura Lea." The fiddler was inexpert or perhaps the fiddle makeshift, primitive, but the melody even so was a doleful lonesome sound, and Floyd felt its sweet yearning touch his heart like a cool finger.

There was lamplight inside the rococo little railroad station and the side door was propped open and now Floyd smelled gangrene and blood and heard the cries and groans of the wounded. A hospital, Rebel surgeons at work. The bloodsmell was strong, metallic. Floyd hurried on without attempting to look inside. He crossed the railroad tracks, pulling his moonshadow along beside him.

Lebrun lived on the first floor of a boardinghouse a block beyond the tracks. The building was unlit but open. Enough moonlight filtered into the hallway to see by and Floyd tapped on Lebrun's door and was surprised by a sullen grunt within. Floyd cracked the door open and put his head in and smelled whiskey. The room was tiny, a cell, with a window looking out into the side yard, the window shut against insects, trapping the sour whiskey vapor. Floyd went all the way in. Lebrun was sitting on the bed with the open bottle held loosely between his knees. He was a thickset man and his pale jowly face looked haggard and distressed in the moonlight. He had not taken off his clothes, even his vest.

Shit, he said, recognizing Floyd in the milky darkness.

Mr. Will wants you. We have some guests want dinner.

What time is it? Lebrun said.

Rebel officers. Early and Ewell.

That bastard Early was in before, Lebrun said. He lifted the bottle, tilted it up, and drank. I dislike cookin for such, he said.

That's up to you, Floyd said.

No it isn't. I got a daughter, did you know that, Floyd?

Of course I know it.

Floyd wondered how drunk Lebrun was, how able. He badly needed a shave. He looked like a derelict, a bloated mendicant.

Lives up to Mummasberg.

I know.

Studies piano. I got to pay for it. Pay for her dresses. Her goddamn sheet music. Everything. He brought the bottle up, took a final swig, set the bottle on the nightstand, and corked it. How many is it to cook for? he said.

Six.

Shit.

You don't have to cook for those people.

What did I just finish saying? Lebrun said.

You're a free man, Floyd said. Just like me.

He loved the sound of that. A free man. Freedom. The anger of before had entered his bloodstream—calming rather than exciting or agitating him, like liquid iron running in him. He was beginning to understand how the great insurrectionists—Toussaint Louverture, Nat Turner, John Brown— went about their fell business so coolly.

Tell em I'll be along direct, Lebrun said, ignoring Floyd's try at rabble-rousing. I best tidy up or Will'll pitch a fit.

Suit yourself, Floyd said.

He went back down the hallway and let himself out into the rotten-egg-smelling night and closed the door quietly behind him. The smell was dead horses, he realized. The armies would leave the horses where they lay. The mules. Lord what a stink they'd make. The men, he supposed, would all be under the ground. Hundreds of them. Thousands.

There were three men, soldiers with muskets, on the station platform. Infantry. Floyd had not seen them previously, did not know if they'd been there, back in the shadows. They did not appear to be wounded. They stood easily, musket stocks resting on the ground, as if waiting for a train. Two of them wore beards.

Who goes there? one of them said.

Floyd glanced at him and did not answer. He came across the railroad tracks.

It's a nigger, one of them said.

Smile, so's we can see you, boy.

Hey. I ast you a question.

Floyd kept walking. Calm. The blood rising in him angry but calm.

I wonder is he a runaway.

He's a uppity sumbitch, whichever.

Hey. Nigger.

The voices were following him. Floyd stopped, turned. Lebrun had not come out. The three Rebels sauntered up with their muskets shouldered. One of them, the clean-shaven one, was a sergeant, the chevrons on his right arm a bleached-out yellow.

What's your business, boy? he said.

Floyd shrugged. Nothing, he said.

Nothin? What's that monkey suit you wearin? He meant Floyd's ochre waiter's jacket.

I work at the Globe Inn, Floyd said.

Sir. I work at the Globe Inn, SIR.

I work at the Globe Inn, Floyd said again.

Say what? The Rebel sergeant unshouldered his musket and held it low across his body with both hands.

I work at the Globe Inn, Floyd said, and the sergeant clubbed him with an upward swipe of his gunbutt so sudden and deft and vicious he must have practiced it often, an oblique cutting blow, Floyd going down sideways, the side of his head flashing hot-white, the ground leaping to meet him.

He might have blacked out for a few seconds, he didn't know. The night seemed to have darkened but he could dimly see the legs of the three men, their shabby brogans. The side of his head was a sheet of pain. He touched himself above the ear: blood in his hair.

Let's get on back, the sergeant said.

Ain't you gawn ask him again, Sarge?

Let's just get on back, the sergeant said.

Lebrun was coming up the hill.

Evenin sir, one of the Rebels said.

Lebrun didn't answer. The Rebels passed him and went on down the short hill to the railroad station. Floyd had climbed to his feet. Wobbly, the world whirling him around. His head throbbed, compressing rhythmically.

Ah Jesus, Lebrun said.

I wouldn't say "sir," Floyd said.

Didn't what?

Call them "sir." They could kill me I wouldn't do it.

Ah Jesus, Floyd.

Lebrun took Floyd's arm and they went up Carlisle and along Race Horse Alley to the Globe. Lebrun steered him into the unlighted lobby and Floyd fell into a soft chair. He was still dizzy and the throb seemed to have worked in deeper. He touched the side of his head and his hand came away wet with blood. Lebrun disappeared. Floyd could hear the Rebels across the hall, their voices weary, bitter-sounding. The words were distinct but he could not put them together as sentences, could not make sense of them.

Mr. Will spoke brightly to them from the doorway—Dinner in ten minutes, gentlemen!—then came into the lobby and went down on one knee in front of Floyd and put a clean white towel in his hand. Floyd put the towel to his bleeding head.

You'd better go see Doc Duffy, Mr. Will said.

I want a gun, Floyd said. A pistol.

Mr. Will stood up. He took a step backward.

No more groveling, Floyd said. No more. His voice seemed to come from deep in his throat, thick and sluggish. He knew he sounded drunk.

I can't spare anyone, Mr. Will said. You'll have to walk yourself to Duffy's.

All right, Floyd said.

Mr. Will nodded, satisfied with the response. He went to the door. No more talk of guns, Floyd, he said.

All right, Floyd said.

Mr. Will nodded again and was gone. Floyd sat in the dark awhile with the towel pressed to his wound, soaking up the steady leak of blood. He could hear them going back and forth between the kitchen and dining room, Roland and Trig, the eager mincing footsteps of Mr. Will. The food arrived; the Rebels' voices rose, lightened. A cork popped, more wine. The tap and clink of cutlery. Mr. Will in the dining room, taking a glass of wine with his guests, no doubt. Floyd gripped the armrests and pushed himself to his feet.

He stood a moment. His head felt empty, nothing in it but the leaden throb. Blood loss, but there wasn't anything he could do about that. He went slowly, carefully, to the doorway. The hallway was empty. The Rebels' coats and swordbelts hung along the wall opposite the lobby. Floyd crept across, still holding the towel to his head.

I am not unsympathetic to your cause, Mr. Will was saying.

You'll take Confederate money then, General Ewell said.

Floyd could picture Mr. Will's smile: a twinkle. When it comes to that, he said, I'm a thorough Yankee.

The Rebels conceded a grudging laugh. They'd paid in greenbacks last time and Mr. Will was confident they would again.

That there's damn good wine, General Early said.

The swordbelts hung from wooden pegs next to each gold-braid-ornamented coat. A thin holster on each belt. The holsters were buttoned shut. Floyd chose one of the generals', he did not know which one, and tucked the blood-soggy towel under his arm and unbuttoned the holster and slid the heavy revolver clear. He'd studied weaponry in catalogues and manuals and knew it for a Colt Walker forty-four caliber. He opened the black leather cartridge box and found two sealed packets, six loads to a packet, and took out both of them and dropped them into the right pocket of his ochre jacket. He turned, stealthy, as Roland came out of the kitchen with a tray loaded with two platters of fried potatoes and onions.

Floyd froze with the big Colt in his hand, muzzle tilted down toward the carpet. Roland froze too and stared at him. His gaze, unafraid but dumbstruck and vaguely sorrowing, went to the gun, then back to Floyd's face and the blood-welling gash on his temple. Floyd stood, arrested in midstep, waiting. Roland glanced toward the dining room and again at Floyd, truly mournful now, then wheeled about quickly and carried the tray back into the kitchen.

Floyd turned, staggered, righted himself. His head was pounding, a dull reverberant beat that obscured the voices in the dining room. He dropped the bloody towel without knowing it and scuffed out into the moonlight with the preposterous concussion-hatched idea that he would work his way around behind the Rebel lines counterclockwise to the Union Army and join the fight tomorrow, turning Jubal Early's own revolver, or General Ewell's, which would be equally satisfying, on the Rebels.

In the hour before dawn broke, all three boys dreamed of the Vineyard. Their dreams were similar and perhaps—who can know?—in some cases identical, like visions passed from one to the other. In the summer dreams, a hawk wheeled lazily on the empty blue sky, rugosa roses stood green and lush in the sand, trimmed with white or magenta flowers, and someone—Rose? Mr. Pease the schoolmaster?—said, They flower twice, you know. Early summer and late. There was crabbing from a rowboat in Lagoon Pond—or was it among the rocks below the light-house on West Chop?—lowering chicken necks tied to a fish line, the big bluecrabs coming up hugging the meat with both spiny claws, gnawing on it so obsessively they did not notice what was happening until they were dangling midair above a bucket. First one claw would release and after a moment the other, and the crab fell into the metal bucket with a brittle clatter. Crabs are so stupid! It made you smile. A fish at least had to be hooked. And now a flotilla of sailing ships swarmed down the Sound in the smoky southwest wind, the golden smoky light of a summer afternoon, sloops and schooners, all hurrying somewhere in concert, their bellying sails a slightly dingy canvas-white but tinted gold by the sun—hundreds of ships, thousands, making hard for what? Where? No one knew.

The winter dreams had food in them and the aromas of food. Roasts, biscuits, pies. Elisha dreamed of Indian pudding. He dreamed of upside-down cake and Rose. Rose not at the Chandlers' but at Head of the Pond on a lamplit evening, Rose seated at the cloth-covered dining table watching him eat, smiling across at him with her head propped on her hand, Rose come to live with them, to stay with them always.

Luke dreamed of her, and so did Thomas. In Luke's dream, they were kissing. He wanted to lie down with her but she said no, Mariah Look will arrive at any moment, and Luke cursed Mariah and went on kissing Rose, the kisses voluptuous and sweet-tasting but not enough, Rose leaning back from him, smiling, finding humor in the situation. Later, sweetheart, she said. Later, I promise. While in Thomas's dream Rose was leaving to join the Union Army—enlisting!—standing on Union Wharf in a hoop skirt and shawl and straw hat but with an Enfield rifle on her shoulder, Thomas and his father pleading with her not to go but

Luke on her side, saying she must, the war would be lost if she did not. Thomas started to explain to her the difference between the Enfield and the Springfield but Rose wasn't listening. I don't know how to work this thing, she said, unshouldering her musket. Don't tell her, Luke, Thomas said. *Don't tell her.*

Elisha woke first of the three. There was fighting again on Culp's Hill. Cannon fire, musketry, the familiar semidistant din of battle. The dawn sunless, color-bled. Elisha lay beside Luke, close to the half-wrecked rail fence. Thomas had come in finally from his sulk, silent, ignoring them, and had laid his blanket some rods up the slope from his brother. Elisha threw off his wool blanket, got up, looked around, and pissed where he stood. It didn't matter anymore, the air poisonous with the droppings of men and animals, the fly-swarmed viscera and torn flesh of dead horses, the gases of human bodies. Elisha had smelled it on other fields but never this bad. He buttoned up and sat down on his gum blanket. He was very hungry.

The skirmishers were coming to life along the Emmitsburg Road, crawling and slithering in the bent grasses, the ditches, appearing and vanishing among the roadside trees and bushes, the heavy humid air muffling their shots, encumbering the lazy drifts of white smoke. Men were waking along the ridge, sitting, standing, wandering around looking for a place to do their business. Uphill, on the ridge crest, some officers had built a fire, and Elisha could smell their boiling coffee. He yawned. He wished he had some coffee at least.

Jake Rivers came down the line, in full uniform already, sack coat and forage cap. Still shoeless: Elisha wondered if he even noticed anymore. He squatted on his haunches. His mustache hung on either side of his mouth and he wore a three- or four-day beard. His hair was snarled and crusted where the bottle had hit him and his uniform dirtier even than Elisha's. He nodded to Elisha and eyed Luke's sleeping face.

"You hear aught of rations?" Elisha said softly.

"Hell," Rivers said, and leaned and spat.

"What's that mean?" Elisha said.

"It means I ain't."

Luke opened his eyes and heard the fighting and sat up and looked back in the direction of Culp's Hill.

"It's all right," Elisha said. "We're holdin."

"What's Tommy doin up yonder?" Rivers said.

"He's put out," Elisha said.

"Who at?" Rivers said.

"Me," Luke said.

"It ain't nothin," Elisha said.

Thomas was awake now. He rose on his elbows and looked at them.

"Come on down here, Tommy," Rivers said.

Thomas only looked at him, thin face both sleepy and crabbed. He uncovered himself and got up and went toward the copse, looking for some privacy.

"What come between you?" Rivers said.

Elisha looked at Luke. Luke shrugged, granting permission.

"They're sweet on the same girl," Elisha said.

Rivers, still squatting, sat down and hugged his knees. "She's sweet on Luke, I guess," he said.

"Tommy only just found it out," Elisha said.

"She a pretty one, Luke?"

"Her name's Rose," Luke said, "and I'd say it fits her."

"Yella hair?"

Elisha squinted at the copse, suddenly detached, as if the question did not concern or interest him.

"Black hair," Luke said.

"Them's pretty too," Rivers said. "Got that nice white skin."

"Her skin's not white," Luke said.

"Ain't it?" River said.

"She's colored, Jake."

"Say again?"

"She's colored."

"She ain't either," Rivers said.

"Dark as any slave," Luke said.

Rivers bit his lip and gazed out toward the tree-hooded ridge where the Rebs were camped, to the haze-veiled purple-gray mountains far beyond.

"I've heard of such," he said.

"You'd like her," Luke said.

"I might do, I guess."

"I've known her a long time. So has Thomas. So has Elisha."

Elisha eyed the copse, listening soberly to all of this.

"She don't smell, I imagine," Rivers said.

"Does Rose smell, Elisha?" Luke said.

Elisha smiled. "If she does, I'd like a sniff of it," he said.

Rivers shook his head slowly. "I don't know what to think no more," he said.

Luke leaned forward, laid a hand on Rivers's arm, the soiled sleeve of his coat, gripped it, and let go. Rivers met his eye, grateful, and looked down.

"I ain't educated, Luke," he said.

Luke smiled. "Paine's educated, and who's the better man?" he said.

"Jake is," Elisha said. He'd come all the way into it now.

Rivers's face softened. "You boys are full a shit," he said.

"No we ain't," Elisha said.

Thomas came back from the copse and donned his coat and hat and stood looking out over the valley, where, if Sergeant Cate was right, the Rebels would come in strength with the intention of hitting the Union center and puncturing it—break it and keep on going, all the way to Washington. The sky was still low and dirty white. Far to the south, a Rebel battery came across the Emmitsburg Road single file, guns and caissons, and up onto the silk-green eminence of the Peach Orchard with its shot-torn little trees and stopped, gun by gun, and unlimbered, the men moving unhurried to unhitch the guns and turn them while others lifted the ammunition chests down then led the teams back a short distance and parked the limbers. The caissons stood back of them, hooked to their limbers, the teams remaining in harness. Another battery, six or eight more guns, percolated across the road and went into line below the orchard.

Luke, in his coat now, his cap, came up the slope and stood shoulder to shoulder with Thomas.

"It's warm," he said.

Thomas nodded.

"There'll be a detail going down to that spring to fill the canteens. Make sure they get yours."

Thomas didn't answer.

"Did you hear me?" Luke said.

"I heard you."

"Thomas. Listen."

"I ain't going home," Thomas said.

"None of us are."

"After the war, I mean."

"Don't talk nonsense."

"I ain't. And I ain't your file partner today either."

Luke looked at him. "I'm sorry to hear it," he said.

The noise on Culp's Hill rose, dense musket fire and a chorus of yells, and you knew the Rebels were on the move, boiling up the steep hill through the woods, the Twelfth Corps boys up there pouring it on them.

"The Rebs don't give up, do they," Luke said.

"Why'd you do it, Luke?"

Luke watched the skirmishing, the puffs of smoke, down along the road. "I love her," he said.

"That ain't what I mean."

"Will you stop saying 'ain't'?"

"You shamed her. Made a slut out of her."

"It isn't that way if you love someone."

"Why didn't you wait? Do it properly."

"On account of the war, I guess." Luke wondered if that was true.

"Wars make good excuses, don't they," Thomas said.

"I might not see her again."

"You'll see her. But I ain't going home and that's all there is to it."

They stood side by side, unspeaking. The fighting loudened on Culp's Hill, a terrific chorus of gunshots, crescendoing. Luke imagined the minnie balls thunking into tree trunks, splintering limbs, whistling through leaves.

"You going to be able to fight today?" Luke said.

"Watch me," Thomas said.

Luke looked at his brother. Something had been extinguished in his face. The angel in it.

"Thomas," Luke said again.

But then Sergeant Cate came down the hill carrying a shovel. "Roll call," he said.

They followed him, wordless, not looking at each other. The regiment fell in and the sergeants took the roll. No one had disappeared in the night. There was only the one shovel and Cate handed it to John McNamara and told him to use it and pass it on.

"Where's our rations at, Sarge?" Rivers said.

"We're waiting on them," Cate said.

"We ain't been served in three days."

"I know that," Cate said, and moved down the line, gesturing men toward the fence.

They swarmed it, pulling the last standing posts over by the sheer force of their numbers. They piled the rails in a flattened zigzag, a knee-high snake fence. McNamara scraped and hacked out a trough with the shovel, piling dirt and fist-sized stones in front of it, along the fence line. He passed the shovel on, and it went along the line from hand to hand, company to company, until the trough ran the length of their position. To their right the Seventh Michigan were digging in with their metal dishes and cups, scraping and gouging and cursing the inefficiency; Cate took the shovel from the last man and offered it to a lieutenant of the Seventh, who took it and thanked him.

The overcast receded upward, lightened, but still roofed the heat in, the humidity. The color bearers uncased the flags and worked the flagstaffs down into the ground till they stood more or less erect, the big bright flags drooping in the sultry air. The men sat down beside their knapsacks, their rolled blankets, their muskets. Everyone begrimed from digging and laved in sweat. They watched Seminary Ridge, from which Rebel batteries were continuing to emerge, unhurried, methodical, gun after gun after gun coming down out of the woods and into line, the line lengthening, creeping north, on and on, more cannon than had ever been arrayed against this army or, they felt sure, any other.

"By God," Rivers said.

"How many do you reckon it is?"

"A hundert."

"More."

"They'll hit us here, then. For sure they will."

"Fore they do they'll shoot the hell out of us."

Thomas stared at the guns, crouched like malign snouted insects. The land they stood on was slightly downtilted, pale yellow-green, trampled after yesterday. The cannon muzzles were aligned perfectly, running in a great arc. Some had a coppery gleam of bronze in them. Thomas had not learned which guns were which—Napoleons, Parrotts, and so on— but he knew the different ways they could maim and kill you. Solid shot, shell, canister.

"Are you all right?" Luke said.

"Stop asking me that."

"Tommy's in a fightin mood," McNamara said.

"Rebel bastards," Thomas said.

"We gonna sit here and let em shoot the hell out of us, Sarge?" Merriman said.

Cate, walking the line, paused and cast a long look at the guns. "You want to charge em?"

"No, I wouldn't care to."

"Where's our rations, Sarge?"

"We're waitin on em."

"It's them nigger drivers," McNamara said. "Seen the guns and got scared."

"They can't see the guns where they are. No more can General Meade."

"Meade knows where they're at."

"He better."

"This isn't your file, Private," Cate said.

"I'm just settin with these boys," Rivers said.

"You get where you belong when the fight starts."

"I intend to," Rivers said.

Cate strolled on. Luke dug *Wuthering Heights* out of his knapsack. McNamara lay down on his back and pulled his cap over his eyes.

Thomas gazed out at the perfect line of Rebel cannon. The skirmishers shot at one another down along the road, keeping busy. There was a new outbreak of musketry on Culp's Hill.

"They don't hold that hill," Merriman said, "it ain't gonna matter what happens here."

"They'll hold it," Luke said, reading. *Mr. Hindley came home to the funeral; and—a thing that amazed us, and set the neighbors gossiping right and left . . .*

"You're the big expert, ain't you," McNamara said from under his cap.

. . . he brought a wife with him.

"He thinks he is," Thomas said.

Luke stopped reading and looked at his brother. Thomas was gazing stonily out across the valley. Rebel batteries still trickling down into line.

"Luke's right," Elisha said. "Them boys'll hold that hill come whatever."

"They got to, that's all," Merriman said.

"And stop this damn bickerin," Elisha said. "Pretty soon we'll be needin each other. Them guns ain't the half of it."

There was a silence.

"By God I'm hungry," Rivers said.

They did not have watches and could not hear the steeple clocks in the town, and so could only guess at the hour. Nine o'clock? Ten? It was hard to say with no sun. There was occasional fire now from the Rebel batteries, very intermittent, almost casual, a shell whistling overhead and letting go midair behind the ridge, a bolt making the dirt and grass jump harmlessly down in front of them. As if the Rebels were amusing themselves, firing not to hit anything so much as to make noise, to relieve the monotony of waiting. There were Union batteries placed at intervals along Cemetery Ridge and on the anchoring hills, Cemetery Hill and Little Round Top, and they answered in the same sporadic fashion, nobody taking much notice until a shell, from the Rhode Island battery on the ridge behind the Twentieth, went wrong and killed Lieutenant Ropes of Company K.

Shrapnel. A bad fuse. Lieutenant Ropes was lying on his side, reading *Little Dorrit*. The shell exploded above him and sent a piece through his back and out his stomach. Someone hollered, a corporal, and Macy and Abbott came running, yelling for a stretcher. They knelt down and Abbott took Ropes's hand. More officers gathered. The artillerists came down the hill, shaking their heads at what they'd done.

"Dumb sonsabitches," McNamara said.

"It warn't their fault," Elisha said.

The stretcher bearers came over the brow of the ridge at a run. They looked at Macy and he shook his head: Ropes was gone. They put the stretcher down, no longer in any hurry, and lifted him onto it very gingerly. His eyes were open and he seemed to be smiling. His coat front was soaked in blood.

"Harvard College man, wasn't he," Stackpole said, after a decent interval.

"Been a lot a them. Putnam, Holmes."

"Hallowell."

"Revere was a Harvard."

"Who makes them goddamn shells, that's whose fault it is," Rivers said.

"It was a accident," Elisha said.

"A accident at the goddamn factory."

"It's done," Elisha said. "Let it lie."

Mr. Heathcliff has just honoured me with a call. About seven days ago he sent me a brace of grouse—the last of the season. Scoundrel! He is not altogether guiltless in this illness of mine; and that I had a great mind to tell him.

There was a small fight going on in the valley to their right, concealed by the low hump of land that hid the town from them, and hid the Rebel guns in that direction. Brisk rifle fire, no more than a company involved on either side. Word came that the Rebels had gotten into a barn that stood uncomfortably close and the Unions were trying to dislodge them. The Rebel artillery got into it, ripping the sky with shot and shells, and then the Unions rushed the barn, took it and fired it, and the smoke rose into the pale sky, black, thick, and kept rising.

Their rations had still not come.

Then the firing stopped on Culp's Hill. There was a final burst, the shots coming myriad and with a sudden fresh intensity, as if two new armies had been thrown in, and then a rapid decline, thinning, dwindling to erratic exchanges and finally lone shots, sullen sounding, griping. The men on Cemetery Ridge all looked at one another. They gazed out toward the wooded hill, where the white smoke already was clearing off.

"Praise the Lord," Merriman said.

"Didn't I say it about them Twelfth Corps boys?"

Rivers lifted his starved face and squinted at the sky. "By God look at that," he said.

The sun was burning away the overcast. In moments the fields had brightened to that summery gold-green. South Mountain was a soft cool blue in the distance, with a bank of spun-fleece clouds piled above it. The air would be clean on the mountain, it would be sweet to breathe.

"It's a sign," Merriman said.

"Sign you're gonna be thirsty," McNamara said.

"There you go again with the bickerin," Elisha said.

"Listen at Elisha," McNamara said. "Thinks he's a sergeant now givin out orders."

"I'm only sayin do your bickerin with the Rebs," Elisha said.

"Shut up, boys," someone said, "the brass is comin."

It was Meade himself, his staff strung along behind him, traveling slowly south along the ridge crest. Hancock was up there now, near the Rhode Island battery that had killed Ropes. So were Gibbon and several others. Meade reined up and spoke to Hancock and Gibbon. He was ugly, all right, beady-eyed in his spectacles, craggy, his beard prematurely salt-and-peppered. Hancock looked like a warrior beside him— never mind the starched shirt and collar—well built and erect on his black stallion, head held high, eyes quick and watchful and burning. They talked for a few minutes, then Hancock and Gibbon saluted and Meade returned it and rode on.

"I wonder what that was."

"It was Meade tellin em we held that hill."

"I could of told em that."

It was suddenly very quiet. The skirmishers had hunkered down out of sight and the batteries on both sides had gone silent. Smoke still rose from the burning barn, twisting slowly skyward and hooking north toward the town, and Thomas watched it and wished it could blow this way and overwhelm the fecal-smelling air and kill the clouds of flies above the dead horses.

Hancock and Gibbon had ridden partway down the slope and were talking with the brigade commanders Hall and Harrow, and with Macy and Abbott and officers from the Michigan and New York regiments that were in line on either side of the Twentieth. Negro servants attended some of them and the black men stood by listening to Hancock with their heads tilted attentively, as if his words were meant for them, too. Hancock said something and smiled, and the officers on the ground grinned back at him but the Negroes did not. General Gibbon sat aloof, gazing out at the Rebel guns.

"What do you think they're sayin?"

"Nothin."

"Ain't nothin *to* say. Rebs gonna blow us all to hell and if there's aught left hit us with two, three divisions."

"It's gonna be bad up here, whatever."

The conference broke up. Hancock and Gibbon rode on south and the line officers scattered to their regiments. Lieutenant Paine came down and walked the length of his company, nodding coolly but not uncordially at the men, as if noting, affirming, that they were ready.

The sun floated up toward high noon and the heat built. Men who had held on to their shelter tents fixed their bayonets and rammed them into the ground and stretched the shelter halves over the rifle butts to form canopies against the beating sun, the ridge now resembling a shantytown of white-roofed huts. Luke, still reading *Wuthering Heights,* crowded in with Rivers and Merriman, Thomas with Elisha and McNamara. Across the way, Rebel artillerists moved about the guns, checking elevations, swabbing muzzles, lugging ammunition chests forward. The silence held, Sabbath-like. A bird warbled in the copse. Bees wandered the air over the beaten-down grasses, indifferent to the swollen bodies. You could hear the bees, their drowsy humming, it was so quiet. It made Elisha think of the fields at Head of the Pond and how the clover would come up at this time of year, sprouting amongst the seed grasses, and he would break off a leaf and chew it, and how juicy it was, with a semi-sweetness like some tart green fruit.

"Play me some poker, Elisha," McNamara said.

"You ought to get rid a them cards," Rivers said, leaning out and speaking past Elisha. "You don't want em on you you get kilt. Cards is the Devil's tool."

"I didn't know you was a God fearer," McNamara said.

"I am before a fight," Rivers said.

"God has better things to worry about," Luke said, reading. *His abode at the Heights was an oppression past explaining. I felt that God had forsaken the stray sheep there to its own wicked wanderings, and an evil beast prowled between it and the fold, waiting his time to spring and destroy.*

"I ain't in the mood for cards," Elisha said.

"Better'n just settin here," McNamara said.

"I ain't in the mood."

"Tell you what," Merriman said, looking out, "them fences down yonder are gonna play hell with em." He was sitting with his legs tucked tailor fashion, studying the situation. Post-and-board fences ran along either side of the Emmitsburg Road. Rebel skirmishers had flattened them to the south, near the Codori farm, but farther on the fences still stood. "They got to knock em down or come over em, and either one they'll catch hell."

"They're definitely coming, aren't they?" Thomas said.

"Sure they are."

"I'll play," Thomas said.

"You oughtn't to, Tommy," Rivers said.

At that moment, the sun having slipped just down from high noon, the first shell was fired. It came from over by the Peach Orchard, the echo careering out, the shell tracing a shrieking arc above the valley, over their heads, exploding behind them down the back side of the ridge, where a horse whinnied shrilly, whether of fright or pain they didn't know. No one moved. The echo died away and another gun went off, another keening shell that burst somewhere behind the copse, and as the men scrambled to pull down their makeshift tents, the bending mile-long line of Rebel cannon exploded all at once and the world, in an instant, was a bedlam of thunder, flame, smoke, and whistling iron and steel.

They snatched up their muskets and scrambled on all fours into the shallow trench they'd dug and lay packed against one another in the terrific heat. The cannonade built to an incessant roar that overspread the valley and ridge like some deafening biblical inferno, while through it shot and shells whistled, screeched, whined, hissed, the shells bursting with the savage crack of lightning, the shot concussing the ground, throwing clods and gravel into the air.

Thomas and Elisha lay huddled close to the little breastwork of dirt facing each other. Rivers lay behind Luke, curled against him, the knob of his skull pressing between Luke's shoulder blades, Luke hugging *Wuthering Heights* to his chest. Everyone was sweating profusely, warmed not just by the sun but by the heat of their packed bodies. Thomas and Elisha were inches apart but did not speak against the noise. Thomas's eyes were not round with fear as Elisha had expected but flat, cold, evasive. Elisha began to wonder if Thomas would ever forgive his brother and thought how such enmity, if it persisted, could poison both their lives.

There was no air now, only sound, noise, and you breathed it, warm in the lungs, scented bitterly with sulfur. The ground shook. The sky darkened and the sun shrank to a pink disc in a midday dusk, like its weakened self at sundown. A limber was hit somewhere nearby; the ammunition chest exploded and the horses screamed loud enough to be heard through it all. A shell burst overhead and Macy ran down the line with Abbott behind him, and they knew someone in the regiment had been hit. Elisha looked at Thomas's hard-set perspiring face and wished the fight was over and he could speak to him. Have one of their heart-to-hearts like they used to, about girls and screwing and marrying Negroes. Get it all straightened out. It was good talking to Tommy, like being in a room where you're always comfortable and happy. *It ain't Luke's fault. It ain't nobody's. Even now I'd lay down with her I had the chance and so would you. It's a big fight here and it ain't no tellin what could happen to any one of us, so . . .*

You couldn't see Seminary Ridge now for the smoke. You couldn't see the Rebel batteries, just the spurts of flame up and down the line. The Union guns had not answered yet and the huddled infantrymen were cursing their own batteries and twisting around and sending them hateful looks, but Elisha knew that General Hunt was saving his ammunition to rake the Rebel infantry when they came across the valley. *It ain't no call to get angry, them gunners is catchin hell same as everybody. Catchin it worse, maybe.*

In the obscuring smoke the Rebel gunners were beginning to overshoot, raining ordnance on the reserve lines on the ridge crest and down the back side, where Meade's headquarters were, the ambulances and wagons, the provost guard, the stretcher bearers, the various servants. Playing hell all the way down to the Taneytown Road. It was safer here, on the front line. Elisha rolled over, looked back and saw the shellbursts. A bolt or ball took the limb off a big tree in the copse, and it fell with a silent crash. A saddled horse with a front leg shot off at the knee galloped along the ridge three-legged, moving brisk and purposeful with its legstump swinging tendrils of blood this way and that. Elisha closed his eyes to the sight and huddled back down facing Thomas.

Then Union cannon began answering—Hancock had ridden the line and ordered the battery commanders to commence firing, larding the order with curses and blasphemy. The muzzle-spat flames gave the Rebel gunners a target and they began finding the range of the ridge crest. A shell exploded in front of the Rhode Island battery and cut a private's arm off and sheared away the top of another man's head. He dropped like a marionette whose strings have been cut and his head spilled its blood and gore and wasn't a human head anymore. All along the ridge crest limber chests were blowing, horses were going down, floundering and kicking in their harnesses. Cannonballs smashed guns, exploded limbers, took the legs off men and horses. *By God,* Elisha thought. There'd never been shooting like this. It was like the end of the world. He looked at Thomas and Tommy gave him a wry look, almost a smile.

Colonel Hall came by, strolling, smoking a cigar. He nodded at Elisha, at Thomas. Smiled and walked on. The Nineteenth Mass. were on the ridge crest in reserve where the Twentieth had been yesterday, hugging the ground, the same brave boys who'd fought so hard down the slope yesterday when Sickles was routed, and a bolt struck the ground and tunneled under them, pitching a man like a rag doll ten feet in the air head over heels, unmarked and stone dead when he landed.

Then Hancock appeared in the dirty roiling smoke, mounted, with three officers trailing him, one carrying the headquarters flag. His horse was skittish, dancing in place and chucking its head up and down, but Hancock reined it in hard, made it go slow through the smoke and pandemonium. The men rolled over, half rose. A percussion shell landed behind him, blowing a geyser of dirt and stones into the air, and Hancock looked casually back over his shoulder and again at the men and smiled. Luke saw it, and he sat up and raised his cap and gave a hoarse guttural cheer that he could feel, scraping his throat, but not hear. Rivers sat up and did the same, and Merriman, and it spread down the line until they could hear their collective selves, a growl, not sullen or admonitory but lusty, brash, affirming. Hancock, reining in that jittering horse, smiled a little wider and lifted his own black slouch hat in return.

Thomas had given himself to it, roaring like a man with the bloodlust on him, but Elisha joined in with half his heart, strangely oppressed by the sight of Hancock sitting on his horse where he could be blown apart or decapitated at any moment. *Go on, General,* he wanted to say. *Ride on fore you're killed.* Because what good would it do? Where was the sense in it? Reynolds killed already. Colonel Revere, Henry Wilcox. Elisha could see Henry like he was here beside him, the bushy mustache, eyes with that soft-dark melancholy in them. Henry was dead but he wasn't, not completely. Something of him remained, was still here. Hancock gave the stallion a nudge with his spur and let up on the rein and his staff followed him south toward the lower ground, still picking their way along in stately deliberation. The men put their caps back on and got down again.

The smoke grew denser, more opaque; thick as a Martha's Vineyard fog but not fuzzy like fog, nor in any way still and peaceful. The boys had never seen a forest fire but the smoke was like the smoke of one, as if all the woods hereabout were burning. Another limber blew and Elisha thought of the suffering horses and his mind flew back to Iris and the safety of that candlelit room where he did her on the four-poster bed. He wondered what she was doing at this moment, and if she'd heard there was a big fight going on in Pennsylvania. She would know he was in it and would always wonder if he survived it—unless he went back down to Virginia and showed himself to her. *I never seen a thing like it, Iris. It was like the end of the world in the Bible. After a while you could smell the horses that was hit. Their entrails. But you don't want to think about that.* He thought of the three times he did her, each one different because he was getting the hang of it by the end, and how she'd put him under her the third time and ridden him, and her tangly hair falling forward and Iris smiling down at him as she rocked on him. She'd said it would take him longer the third time and it did. *Lord I got to go back there.*

A shell exploded overhead; Elisha heard a chorus of yells and knew men had been hit in the middle of the line, and did not rise up to look. "Wounded! Wounded!" Macy, leaping to his feet, hollering uselessly, his voice lost in the noise and no stretcher bearers this side of the ridge. A private in Company G whose name Elisha did not know sat up and peeled his coat back. He'd been opened up above his right hip and the coat stuck to it, and he grimaced as the coat came away. Macy knelt beside him and looked back over his shoulder up the hill. A red bloom was spreading on the wounded man's white shirt. He bunched his sack coat and pressed it to his side with both hands and sat there with his legs splayed out, cupping the coat against himself, and hung his head in utter resignation. Another man was crawling like a baby up the slope with the bone gleaming white in his thigh. Macy looked at him and let him go.

It went on, but nobody who lived it had much sense of time. An hour? Two? An hour and forty-five minutes, Hancock said later. Toward the end the Union guns, clearly on somebody's order, went silent battery by battery, beginning on Cemetery Hill and working south. The Rhode Island battery had quit long ago, perforce. Only two guns remained serviceable and there weren't enough men left to work even the two. Limbers were being brought up to pull them to the rear. The cease-fire spread down the Union line to the guns on Little Round Top. The Rebel guns were quitting too. They did not stop all at once as they'd begun, but piece by piece, in decrescendo, their thunder diminishing in constancy and volume, becoming irregular, fitful, dying, until here and there down the long line a lone cannon would go off, stubborn, as if its crew must have the last word, do one more bit of damage. A gun boomed, a fuse shell that went off prematurely and flung its shrapnel harmlessly into the field short of the line, and it was over, and the smoky fields and hills were locked in the deepest silence the men had ever heard.

They stirred and looked at one another and did not speak, strangely self-conscious of their own voices. Almost reluctantly—as if time would begin again the moment they put themselves in motion—they stood up, stretched, drank from their canteens, unbuttoned, pissed. The bloody powder-grimed artillerists roused themselves and set to work swabbing out the muzzles, lugging ammunition forward, cutting the harnesses of dead horses. There was the creak and rattle of new guns coming up, new caissons, and the raised voices of the artillerists, the sounds carrying clear and oddly melodious in the immense stillness. Stretcher bearers came down the slope and began taking away the dead and wounded. The man with the hole in his side had lain down and they bore him away. Elisha could not tell if he was dead. The Nantucketer Chase went to the rear leg-shot, using his musket as a crutch. A light breeze was blowing now and the smoke slid slowly westward, evaporated, was gone, and the world was clear and bright again under the sun. The sun had moved over. Three o'clock, you'd have said.

"Could have been worse," Rivers said.

"Depends where you were settin," Elisha said.

Their own voices were loud in their ears, seemed to reverberate inside their skulls.

"They're coming, aren't they?" Thomas said.

"Hell yes they're comin," Merriman said.

"They'll catch hell doin it."

"Load up, men," Lieutenant Paine said.

The order was being given all along the line. Ramrods glinted and there was a great racket of clashing, scraping steel. They loaded the Rebel Enfields they'd collected in the field the night before.

"Leave your rammer out," Elisha said. He stuck his ramrod in the ground and Luke and Thomas did the same. They scraped hollows in the mounded dirt and opened their cartridge boxes and filled the hollows with cartridges.

"Get to your file, Rivers," Sergeant Cate said.

"Couldn't I stay here?" Rivers said.

"What's this?" Paine said, hands clasped behind him, sword swaying as he walked.

"Just some talk, sir," Cate said.

Paine smiled. There was a feverish light in his eyes, but he was otherwise collected, patient in the way a cat is patient, awaiting the moment. "'We few,'" he said. "'We happy few, we band of brothers.'"

"Yes sir," Cate said.

Paine moved on.

"I ain't a brother to that sonofabitch," Rivers said.

"What was it?" Elisha said.

"Shakespeare," Luke said. "*King Henry the Fifth*. The night before the battle of Agincourt."

"Kings fought in them days, didn't they," said Rivers.

"That one did," Luke said.

"It's a nice thought, all of us brothers," Elisha said.

The battlesmoke was gone but the burning barn still sent a rope of black smoke into the sky, the breeze tugging at it, breaking it apart. The silence held, as oppressive now in its way as the heat. McNamara bit the end off a cartridge and threw the ball away. He poured the powder into his palm and spat in it and with two fingers painted a shiny jet-black smear down each stubbled cheek. He blackened the bridge of his nose.

"That ain't gonna scare nobody," Rivers said.

"It's scarin the piss outa me," Merriman said. "You look like a goddamn Injun."

"That's what I want to," McNamara said. "Go on, Tommy. Put the war paint on."

"You'll be dirty enough without that," Elisha said.

But Thomas tore a cartridge and painted a V on either cheek. Luke shook his head.

"What of it?" Thomas said.

"Nothing," Luke said.

A flock of birds crossed the sky to the north, arrowing west, in the direction Lee had come. They sailed over Seminary Ridge and disappeared.

"By God it's quiet," Rivers said.

"Maybe they ain't comin."

"They're comin."

"Our Father, who art in Heaven . . ."

Someone down the line, maybe from Company H, was on his knees with his head bowed. Colonel Hall had come up on foot, moving north.

He had just spoken to the New Yorkers to their left. He waited for the prayer to be over, his bearded face pallid, fatigued, dysentery-ravaged. The men of the Twentieth got up. They bunched in to listen to him.

"We'll be firing by regiment," he said, "so never mind what those men on either side of you are doing. You listen to Colonel Macy. He'll tell you when and how." He looked down the silent debris-strewn valley, unbuttoned his holster. He drew his pistol and looked at it thoughtfully. He rammed it back down in its holster.

"Boys," he said, "we have got to win this fight, and the first goddamn man I see running or sneaking I'll blow him to hell. Just stand to it, boys, and give em hell. You see me running, shoot me on the spot. Blow my goddamn brains out."

He raked them with narrowed eyes, nodded, spat, and moved on north to give the speech to the Seventh Michigan. The men of the Twentieth looked at one another.

"He meant it about shootin him," Merriman said.

"He's a good one, ain't he."

"Ain't nobody in *this* regiment gonna run."

Colonel Macy was addressing them now. "We'll fire by volleys. You new men, you know how that works."

"Yes sir."

"Yes sir."

"We're going to let them get close, about two hundred yards, so don't be anxious. Aim low. And mind you don't shoot your own skirmishers." He dug into the breast pocket of his coat and brought out his timepiece. He opened it, eyed it a long moment, snapped it shut and repocketed it. "We're going to give them Fredericksburg, men. Get even with the bastards."

They nodded, murmured agreement, and moved to the rifle pit, the breastwork and rails where they would be fighting, and crouched or sat. Jake Rivers went with Luke and not to his own place in line, though Sergeant Cate had spoken to him about that. The sun had moved over a little farther. It was still very hot.

"Sir?" Luke said.

"What?" Lieutenant Paine had come by again. He stood with his hands behind him, squinting out across the valley.

"Do you know any more of that speech? St. Crispin's Day, sir."

Paine glanced at Luke and resumed his perusal of the distant ridge. "A bit," he said.

"Could you give it to us, sir?"

Paine gazed out from under his hat brim. He drew in a breath and lifted his voice. "'He that sheds his blood with me shall be my brother,'" he said. Others turned, stared up at him.

"'Gentlemen in England now abed shall think themselves accursed they were not here, and hold their manhood cheap while any speak that fought with us upon St. Crispin's Day.'"

Silence. Up behind them the battery commander hollered an order. They'd brought a new battery up.

"Thank you, sir," Luke said. For the moment he almost liked Paine.

"Do your duty, Private," Paine said, and moved on.

"What day did he say?" Stackpole said.

"St. Crispin's," Luke said. "A saint's day. That's not the point, though."

"I see the point," Stackpole said.

"I still ain't his brother," Rivers said.

"Today you are," Luke said.

"I ain't," Rivers said, and then, rising to his feet, "Party's startin, boys."

They were coming now, emerging from the woods all along Seminary Ridge. Skirmishers first, strung out like beads on a string, and behind them the first battle line, stretching solid and innumerable from south of the Codori farm, disappearing in low ground behind the farm buildings and visible again as far north as you could see, moving unhurried and silent, like a dun-brown phantom army whose only corporeality were its blood-red battle flags and glinting bayonets, still tiny in the distance. They came on down the gentle incline, past their own guns, flowing around them like water, and now a second line emerged from those pregnant woods, and still you could not hear them, could not hear a sound anywhere.

NINE

Lieutenant Cushing looked like a girl. Alonzo Cushing. Many said so, but never rancorously. He was that fair, that frail-looking, and he kept himself cleanshaven. He had a girlish bee-stung mouth but firmset, not change-able and pouty like a girl's. He was cheerful and never got the blues. Jokes and profanity around the campfire made him smile, but it was an odd quiet smile and you could not tell what his actual thoughts might be. He was twenty-two, a New York boy, town called Fredonia. West Point, class of 'sixty-one, and he never spoke of abolition, for or against, and no one knew where he stood on it, or if he stood at all. You could get nothing out of him but that mild cryptic smile, and the fellows never pressed him because some of them would have been disappointed either way. He was very popu-lar with the men who served under him.

His battery was on the ridge crest north of the copse and the Rebels shot it all to hell during the cannonade. They blew up limbers and caissons, knocked out four of his guns, killed almost all the horses—the ground was strewn with their gut-spilling carcasses—and of the forty-eight men under his command, well over half were wounded or killed, including Private Donahue, whose legs had been taken off by shrapnel and who had asked them to kill him and then shot himself with his own revolver when they would not.

Cushing had been hit in the groin. He could not walk without lean-ing on Sergeant Fuger, moving at a halting bent-over limp holding him-self together with his left hand, the hand blood-steeped and cradling what looked like bloody ground meat. In the lull after the guns went silent Ser-geant Fuger told him to get to the rear but he said no, he wanted to go talk to General Webb, whose brigade was posted along the stone wall below what was left of their battery, which was two guns. Using Sergeant Fuger as his crutch, he hobbled down to where the general was standing with two of his regimental officers.

Sir . . .

Get yourself to the rear, Lieutenant.

I want to bring my guns down nearer the wall.

Get your goddamn self to the rear, son.

He won't go, sir, Sergeant Fuger said. He spoke with a German accent. He'd come over ten years ago and had fought Indians out West.

Let me bring those guns down, Cushing said. Soon's they cross that road I can give em an awful time of it.

With two guns? Webb said.

Canister, sir.

The general looked at Cushing's wound. It was like an opening in him where his insides would all slither out if Cushing let go with his left hand. It occurred to Webb that the boy would never be intimate with a woman even if he didn't die here, and he wondered if Cushing had thought of that.

All right, then, Webb said. Permission granted.

Sir? We'll need help. I thought the Nineteenth Massachusetts . . .

Tell Colonel Devereux to pick you out some volunteers.

Yes sir.

There'd been a low jungle of brush and scrub on this side of the copse as well as in front of it, but the men had cut it down and the guns were light, three-inch ordnance rifles, and they rolled over the slash, rope-dragged, bumping and tilting this way and that while Cushing stood watching, leaning on Sergeant Fuger. They lugged the limber chests down and piled canister beside each gun. Cushing leaned on a private named Dunne while Sergeant Fuger adjusted the elevations. And so they waited for the assault, Sergeant Fuger still serving as Cushing's crutch, and the blood running in a sheet down the inside of his leg.

They could hear them now, the rustle of their footfalls, the clinks of their accouterments like a multitude of cowbells in all that stillness. They crouched or lay belly-down behind the breastwork and watched them come. The two battle lines, each comprising two ranks advancing shoulder to shoulder in perfect synchrony, were well apart, as ocean wave follows ocean wave, with here and there a solitary mounted officer in front, the horse moving sedate and leisurely, as if on parade. Behind both lines came the file closers, dotting the landscape like the skirmishers. The blood-colored flags flattened out fitful and lazy in what breeze there was. Bayonets gleamed by the thousands, bright slivers in perfect slant alignment.

"Route step," someone muttered. "What's Lee thinkin?"

"I prefer they'd hurry."

"Why?"

"So's to get on with it."

"By Jesus look at em all."

"The Lord is my shepherd . . ." Someone else praying now, it sounded like Butters, whose nerve had failed him on the road in Maryland.

"Steady, men," Macy said, walking the line. "Steady, now. Steady."

"He maketh me to lie down in green pastures. He restoreth my soul . . ."

"When it comes, aim low, boys," said Sergeant Cate.

"I can hear em breathin."

"The hell you can."

"Listen. You hear that?"

"Aim low, boys. And knock those colors down."

"I wish they'd make some noise."

"It ain't natural, is it."

"Yea, though I walk through the valley . . ."

Luke uncapped his canteen, took a drink of warm water. Dry mouth, dry hands. Musket at half cock, cartridges piled in front of him, ramrod lancing the ground, handy beside him. Elisha had said to mind you didn't forget to replace the cap each time or you'd fill your gunbarrel full of unfired charges. Luke took another drink—there'd be time afterward to refill his canteen or maybe it wouldn't matter, but he didn't really believe that—and thought of Rose and her garden and how dewy it was in the morning, and Rose drawing water from the backyard well, the wooden bucket bumping the wall as it came up and the creak of the winch and the strength in Rose's brown arms and the feel of her naked in bed, warm and brown and incredibly soft against him. The God he'd found in Virginia was looking down on all of this and would not let him die today because He had more work for him, though Luke didn't know what it was unless it was just Rose, white and black marrying, proof of something, a triumph over the illogic of race hate. He knew anyway that he wasn't going to study medicine, had known it for some time. There was too much else to do, a whole country to be remade when the war was over.

John McNamara loaded his picked-up revolver, leaving the top chamber empty, stuck it in his belt, and opined to himself that it was time for the Union batteries to open on the bastards. Jake Rivers squinted out at the enemy and thought of a country church he'd seen somewhere, white-clapboard, and imagined himself wearing Sunday clothes, a vest, nice black shoes, sitting quiet in a varnished pew while the organ played pretty songs, and perhaps Luke would be there, and he, Jake, bathed and cleanshaven and smelling of lye soap, as Luke was. Maybe Luke's nigger sweetheart would be there too, right there in a white man's church and pretty as a flower, a dark red rose, and he, Jake, sitting alongside of her like some goddamn abolitionist and not saying a word about it, acting the gentleman for once in his life.

Luke was still thinking of her. He'd wanted to have an ambrotype made of her to bring along with him, but she said there was too much finality in that, too much separation, the image supplanting his memories of her. I want you to hold on to *me,* she said, not some picture of me. She also said, jokingly, that an ambrotype would take the edge off his wanting her, but Luke knew that wasn't true and wondered if Rose knew it. There was a place over in Cottage City that made them but Rose deflected the idea, evaded it with a light remark and a smile.

"You all right, Tommy?" Elisha said.

"God look at em all," Thomas said. The old fear was creeping back, like some cold growth up his stomach wall. He felt suddenly embarrassed by the black smears on his cheeks, felt mocked by them.

"We'll stop em," Elisha said, but he had his doubts, the Rebels came on so quiet and deliberate and steady, like they and not God had designed this day, and they had the power to implement it in their own leisurely fashion.

"Them goddamn batteries ought to open," McNamara said.

"Why don't they?" Rivers said.

"Our Father," Elisha said, "who art in Heaven." He looked at Thomas. "Pray with me, Tommy." But Thomas was watching the Rebels and seemed not to hear him. "It does help," Elisha said. The Rebel skirmish line had advanced near the Emmitsburg Road, where the Union skirmishers had been waiting all this time, and shots broke out, fracturing the quiet. Elisha again bowed his head. "Hallowed be thy name."

"There is no God," Thomas said, and the bitter truth hardened him again, checked the creeping fear.

"This ain't no time to talk so," Rivers said.

"I don't care," Thomas said, watching the Rebs. "I don't *care*."

"Thomas," Luke said, "listen to me."

But then the artillery opened from Cemetery Hill, and then from Little Round Top, and then from the ridge north of the copse, and the Rebel guns answered, and the terrific noise took over again, and the men quit talking but continued to watch the Rebel infantry sweeping slowly toward them in their two solid waves.

Remember that day with the snow? How Luke stood up to them boys was bein disrespectful to Rose and then I slept at your house and she fed us so good, Indian puddin and whatnot, you remember that, Thomas? I didn't want to go home. I never told you that part of it, did I? I wished the snow would of fallen all night and all the next day and it'd took us a week to dig out. They'd of needed me on the farm and I knew that but I still wished it would of snowed some more. That was one of my best times, that night with the snow. Was it for you, Tommy?

"Tommy?" Elisha said.

Thomas looked at him. "What."

"Was it for you?" They had to shout to be heard.

"Was what?"

A shell screeched above them, burst down behind the ridge. The Union batteries were tearing gaps in the Rebel lines now, and as soon as they did the Rebs dressed their ranks, tightening in shoulder to shoulder, the lines beginning to shorten.

"They're dressin," Merriman said. "Jesus."

"Goddamn fools, ain't they," Rivers said.

"Was what?" Thomas asked Elisha again, through the din.

Elisha wondered if he'd dozed off and dreamed talking to Thomas. It spooked him; he wondered what was happening to him.

"Will you at least look at me?" Luke said.

"Make it up with him, Tommy," Rivers said. "This here's your brother."

"Not anymore," Thomas said, for he knew that the anger of last night and this morning, the hatred he'd felt, could liberate him from cowardice and need and all the things that had made him a boy.

"That's wicked, Tommy," Rivers said.

"He don't mean it," Elisha said. He was beginning to feel disoriented, as if the world were fragmenting, coming apart like a picture puzzle.

"Surely goodness and mercy will follow me . . ."

The guns pounded the air, smoke rolled down the valley. To the south, partially hidden behind the Codori farm, the Rebels had stopped. Officers rode up and down flaunting their swords like flashing wands and the battle lines dressed again and came on at the left oblique, parade-ground perfect, slantwise across the valley, through the Codori farm, across the Emmitsburg Road. The guns on Little Round Top could not miss now. Shells landing in their midst flipped men into the air in sprays of dirt, tossed hats, rifles, severed limbs. Flags went down, came up again. Behind them now lay their dead and badly wounded, while the walking wounded limped and shuffled back the way they'd come through the sea of smoke. Hundreds of them, and more hundreds.

It began to look like half their army had been shot away. The rest came on, the lines wavering now, breaking apart here and there as men stopped to pull down some remaining lengths of fence or separated to go around a rock or a tree and stayed separated. The batteries on the ridge were firing shotgun blasts of canister now, the Rebels going down in bunches.

The Union skirmishers had been giving way from the time the Rebels approached the road and of a sudden they were running. They disappeared behind the long flattened hump of ground that now hid the Rebel left; a moment, and over the crest they came, pell-mell up the long uneven slope at a lopsided run with their muskets weighting them sideways, their haste and abandon comical somehow. They came in panting, dripping sweat, leaping the breastwork like deer, and threw themselves on the ground. Men from the Twentieth, from the Nineteenth, some Michigan men, all mixed together.

"By God there's a smart of em."

"Half of em's kilt, ain't they?"

"Never mind that. There's a smart of em left and they mean business. They kilt Eddie Vogelman, you boys know him?"

"Sonsabitches!"

"They got plenty of us and no mistake."

"The Lord is my shepherd, I shall not want," began Butters again.

"Ain't we heard that one already?" McNamara said.

"Shut up, Mac."

"He leadeth me beside the still waters . . ."

"Steady, men. Steady, now."

The Rebels descended into the swale where the skirmishers had vanished, the two solid lines disappearing by increments, legs and shoulders and heads. It was a final respite and everyone knew it. Elisha spent it thinking of Iris and vowing to leave the army the day his three years were up no matter what and go down there and work that land for her and Lilac, war or no war. They couldn't see anything to their right because of the rise of ground, but there was heavy firing now, and yelling, hoarse and savage, and they knew the Rebels were advancing on the stone wall. There was a battery south of the copse now, maybe six guns, about halfway down the slope to the stone wall. Luke looked over and saw them ramming in tin cans of canister.

"Stand," Macy said, and Abbott and Paine and the other officers echoed it.

"Stand, boys."

"On your feet and ready to give em hell."

They scrambled up and formed their two ranks, file partner behind file partner's right shoulder. Luke's heart beat furiously but his mind was empty now and he knew only this smoky valley and its relentless din and his brother beside him.

"Thomas," he said, and stretched his hand out sideways. Thomas looked at it, and after a moment took it. He returned the pressure, then tried to free himself, but Luke gripped his brother's hand and would not let go, and Thomas acquiesced, passive but not unwilling, the two

of them standing with their hands joined, watching the low flat curve of
land that hid the Rebels.

"This is what we came for, Tommy," Luke said, and wondered when
he'd started saying *Tommy.*

"I know," Thomas said.

"Let's give em hell, shall we?"

"All right," Thomas said.

"Surely goodness and mercy . . ."

"Here they are, boys!"

The ground seemed to exhale them, so close you could read the murder in their shaggy battle-hardened faces, something between fright and
rage, something dark and volatile. On they came, at the double-quick at
last, and Colonel Macy gave the order, *Ready,* and the muskets came up
glinting, cocked, *Aim,* and the men sighted down them. Luke squinted
down his gunbarrel past Jake Rivers's puny shoulder at pumping knees
in shapeless trousers of dull brown or colorless gray or blue denim, stolen from some Pennsylvania farmer, skinny Rebel knees, slavery sonsabitches, and the ire broke over him again. Macy said *Fire* and the volley
blew the air to bits and the Rebel line shuddered to a stop, staggered
as by a blast of wind, men toppling like chess pieces this way and that.
Luke could not tell, in all that smoke and slaughter, if he'd hit anybody.
He had not felt the gun kick his shoulder. He glanced at Thomas, who
had lowered his smoking rifle, slow, and was staring out as if perplexed
at what he saw.

"Load!" Luke said, *"load,"* but there was firing now all along the line,
to their right and to their left, Hall's entire brigade, and now Thomas
couldn't hear him, or Luke hear himself. He bit a cartridge, spat the
paper, poured the charge, rammed it, remembering to replace the cap.
Seeing him, Thomas did the same but in that slow dreamy way, as if
he could not quite remember what he was doing here. The Rebels were
firing back and there was the insect music of minnie balls in the air,
now a beelike hum, now a mosquito whine, sometimes a whistle, like
the winter wind at night. The Rebels were shooting high for the most
part, but here and there a man went down and everyone got low, kneeling and even lying prone with their guns laid across the piled dirt and
rails, rolling over to reload, then back on their stomachs to fire. Luke

knelt and loaded and fired, loaded and fired, tasting the bitter powder on his tongue. The Rebels kept falling, but there was so much shooting you couldn't tell if it was your ball or another's that dropped a man, or if he'd been hit by three or four minnies at once. The smoke thickened, the Rebels becoming shadow-like in its swirl.

They could not hear Macy or any human voice, but they didn't need to be told to fire at will. The lines that had come up out of the swale in perfect order were disintegrating. Some of those men had taken cover in low places or behind granite outcroppings and were shooting steadily and doggedly, but the main body, in pieces, was drifting to the right, as you would tack across a beating wind instead of plunging straight into it, biting cartridges, pouring, working their rammers, firing as they went. Luke, kneeling, picked a man out, a dim scarecrow with his wrists protruding from his coat, and shot at his knees and saw not him but a man beyond him throw his arms in the air as if in surrender and pitch forward on his face. Thomas was on his stomach with his gun resting across the breastwork. Rivers and Merriman and McNamara and Elisha, lying or kneeling, fired and reloaded with a practiced deadly rapidity, fired and reloaded, fired and reloaded. It was an Elisha that Luke could not have imagined; sweet boy's face gone narrow-eyed and rigid under its grime of powder, the mild blue light in those eyes blanched steely, colorless. McNamara was yelling, whether to himself or at the Rebels Luke didn't know, the words lost in the din. Over to the left a Union regiment had swung out perpendicular and was enfilading the Rebels—Luke could make out musket coughs of smoke, stabs of flame—and that, too, was pushing them north, hurrying them. Flags went down, rose again. Men staggered, fell. A mounted officer was shot off his horse.

And then it seemed to be over. The Rebels were swarming straight north now, in seeming haste and disorder. A scattering of them remained, nestled down sniper fashion, but their fire was intermittent, occasional, as if they were waiting to see how things would go before they would agree to fight any harder. Luke rammed a ball home and fitted on a new cap, but suddenly there was no one out there to shoot at except the sheltered Rebels, who were doing no damage at the moment and might even have given up. In front of the fence line, stretching away downhill to the Emmitsburg Road, a new harvest of dead and writhing wounded.

"Fredericksburg!" someone shouted at the Rebels, the dead and living both.

"Fredericksburg, you sonsabitches!"

A Rebel downfield fired and missed. Luke did not return it but many did, the balls kicking up little sprays of earth and dust and shreds of grass.

"Fredericksburg, you secesh bastard!"

"Thomas," Luke said.

"I'm all right," Thomas said. He was still lying prone. He let his head fall forward on his arm and hid himself.

"God*damn,*" Luke said happily.

"Put that gun on half cock fore you kill somebody," Elisha said.

Luke let the hammer down.

"I got me six or seven of em," Rivers said. "You?"

"I don't know," Elisha said.

"Joe?" Rivers said.

"Got a officer," Merriman said.

But the battle over on the right was getting louder. The rising ground hid most of it and anyway you could not see much through the smoke, but the battery uphill from the stone wall had opened, and the Rebel batteries had begun to concentrate on the copse, fuse shells bursting in midair blooms of white fire, and the musket fire was turning nonstop and deafening. Luke looked at Elisha and at Rivers and knew the fight wasn't over. No: Colonel Hall, specter-like in the smoke, was yelling in Macy's ear and Macy nodding, nodding, then spinning away to find Abbott, who stood close to where the two regimental flags were planted atilt in the ground, to yell in Abbott's ear. Abbott threw him a quick salute and took off at a run toward the right end of the line, yelling an order that no one could hear, the men rising, staring at him uncomprehending until he pointed with his sword and with his left hand took Sergeant Cate by the arm and thrust him in that direction, toward the copse. Cate stumbled, caught himself, turned, and swung his arm, Abbott still pointing, frantic, with his sword, and the truth swept the regiment, spreading down the line like wildfire, and they scrambled up and shouldered their guns and went at a swarming double-quick, all order lost, all consonance, to stem the Rebel breakthrough.

Cushing's two guns opened up on them after they crossed the road and scythed wide gaps in their line. The Rebels dressed on their colors, dressed and dressed again, and swept up close to the wall still massed, and that is when the Seventy-first Pennsylvania ran for it. They came shinning up the slope, color bearers included, right through Cushing's battery.

Cushing stood his ground. He and Sergeant Fuger and the rest of them. They got another round off and Cushing yelled something inaudible and in that moment the back of his head let go in a spray of bone and brains, the minnie having found the bull's-eye of his open mouth. He fell forward on his knees and Sergeant Fuger caught him. He let him down gently, dead already. The Rebels were just the other side of the wall. Fuger, gesturing, ordered them to reload the number four gun with triple canister. The Rebels came over the wall, following General Armistead, and Fuger nodded and the explosion rent the air and blew a hole in them, flinging them every which way. But they closed up and came yelling up the slope, and that long shelving plot of ground became a slaughterhouse.

The Twentieth's rush toward the copse was, quickly, a stampede. Thomas was bumped, jostled, nearly knocked down, his musket nearly knocked off his shoulder. The color bearer, Sergeant Curtis, had taken up the national flag and a corporal whose name he didn't know—Company D, he thought—was carrying the regimental colors. Luke looked back, saw that Thomas was right behind him, and took off, leading the charge, it seemed, with Abbott and Paine—where was Macy?—and the two flags close behind them, opening out sharp-hued in the smoke. Thomas began to run, keeping his eye on Luke. Luke looked back, found him, and ran on.

"Luke!" Thomas shouted. "Elisha!"

He could not hear himself. A shell went off in the air ahead of him and another on the ground, percussion, chucking a couple of men in the air head over heels, and in the smoke and flying debris Thomas lost sight of Luke. The Seventh Michigan were still in position, shooting at Rebels out in the field; an officer was yelling at them, moving down the line and taking other officers by the shoulder and pointing with his sword. Some understood and leapt up and joined the rush north while others stayed in line, prone or kneeling. Minnies hissed and buzzed, men fell as they ran, others tripping over them, cursing.

"Elisha! Luke!"

The stone wall began and there were dead Rebels on this side of it, dozens, shot pointblank by canister, gore-soaked and hideous. The cannoneers had roped the guns and were pulling them back up the slope. Thomas looked at the bodies. He went on, searching right and left for Luke. Ahead all was smoke and confusion and now, at last, Thomas heard the Rebel yell—how, in all that noise?—liquid and shrill, cold on the skin. He could not see McNamara or Rivers or Merriman, just the two flags moving deeper into the sulfurous smoke, the gunfire, the exploding shells.

"Luke!"

There were Rebels in the copse: it was infested with them. The colors drifted toward it up the gentle slope, drawing along this army turned mob in a dark blue enveloping wave, and Thomas ran after them, figuring that's where Luke would be, at the front of the charge. The national flag stopped abruptly, teetered and fell, and Thomas, running, saw Sergeant Curtis up ahead, stretched out motionless on his stomach. Someone had dropped his musket and was lifting the flag: Elisha, so filthy with dust and black powder Thomas almost didn't recognize him. Elisha paused to measure the big flag's weight, to find the right grip on the flagstaff, hands wide apart, Thomas thinking *Don't Elisha don't* and Elisha, satisfied, moving again through the smoke, yelling, Thomas at his side, advancing uphill toward the copse, whose shade spat musketfire, threw out more smoke. Men stumbling, falling.

"Where's Luke?" Thomas shouted. His throat was parched.

Elisha stopped and looked at him as if surprised to find Thomas here. Men surged past them, loading as they went; Matthew Stackpole went by and McNamara, reloading, hollering voicelessly. Rebel minnies buzzed, sang, made the air hum.

"Where's Luke?"

A shell went off behind them; they ducked and dirt and gravel rained down on them.

"Luke! Where's Luke?"

Elisha shook his head, he couldn't hear Thomas, and started forward, and was hit.

The ball staggered him; he went limp, knees buckling, and let go of the flag, collapsing forward. Thomas fell to his knees and helped him over onto his back. The wound was under his arm, a hole the size of a dime, dark as red wine. Thomas looked around, saw McNamara send a minnie into the copse. The flag was aloft again but Thomas could not see who carried it. There was no help anywhere, not stretcher nor ambulance, and Thomas remembered the cloth bag he'd pocketed for when his gunbarrel heated and which he hadn't needed yet. He dug it out, pushed it into the hole with his index finger, and felt the warm blood steep it. Elisha was looking up at him wryly, as if some huge joke had been played on the two of them that they might have foreseen and avoided.

"Don't move," Thomas said—Elisha couldn't hear him, Thomas couldn't hear himself—"I'll go find—"

Someone was yelling in his ear, Sergeant Holland. He grabbed Thomas by the arm as you would a child who doesn't get up when you tell him and hauled him to his feet. He picked up Thomas's musket and thrust it at him and Thomas took it mechanically and Holland yelled something Thomas couldn't hear. Men were crowding the copse, firing into it. A shell went off above it, blasting a limb off a tree. Holland yelled again and shoved Thomas forward, and he went.

The colors were moving north between the copse and the wall. It was up there the Rebels had broken through. Thomas chose the copse, where the nearest fighting was, guessing Luke had gone there. Sergeant Holland had stopped harrying him and shouldered his musket and run on, following the colors.

Elisha stared at the sky, which was a clear clean blue, the smoke all gone, the sky like a Vineyard sky on a July morning. He was looking for something, he did not know or could not remember what but it was there, he knew it was, knew he would find it by and by, and he smiled, knowing it, and knowing that the battle was far away and that he was done with it.

Thomas had cocked his gun and reshouldered it and he went on up the rising ground. The air vibrated with minnies and he realized or perhaps remembered that there were Rebels not only ahead of him but out in the field still, in the slash and behind rocks, keeping up a stubborn and well-aimed fire. A man in front of him was knocked sideways, arms flailing as he went down. And here was Paine, dead on his back, bullet-riddled, one foot gone, the stump gnawed-looking, as if an animal had done this to him. Paine, Elisha. *Not Elisha no the hole in him so small and clean no brains blown out no guts showing* . . .

The men had fought their way into the copse and at its verge Thomas leveled his musket and stepped inside a smoky forest night where the men crouched in the thickets firing at Rebels massed low and indistinct not five rods away, the noise so loud now it hugged the skull, compressed it. A netherworld, a sulfurous hell. Thomas could not see Luke, there was no hope of it in such smoke, in such confusion. *His eyes were open and the wound so small* but he must find Luke and keep him safe somehow and he moved closer, kicking through the brush, and saw McNamara. Mac was standing half protected by a tree. He took aim deliberately and squeezed a round off, the gun jumping backward against his shoulder and Mac, almost in the same moment, letting it swing down vertical, holding it by its leather sling, biting a cartridge in what seemed like the same motion. A shell exploded in the treetops, flinging shrapnel through the leaves, piercing a man in the back, another in the shoulder, lopping the arm off, the man sitting down, eyes open, staring. Leaves fluttered down, a drizzle of twigs. Mac glanced up then went on reloading.

"Where's Luke?" Thomas said, loud in his ear.

Mac, replacing the cap, the musket halfway up, paused and looked at him. Face laved in black-dyed sweat, eyes bloodshot.

"Luke," Thomas said. "Luke!"

Mac shook his head ambiguously. He hadn't heard the question or he didn't know or he had no time for anything right now but killing. Thomas went on, moving from tree to tree, and did not think of being hit, nor fear it. As if he'd seen the future out beyond all of this darkness, a place sunlit and tranquil and familiar. But he must find Luke and take him there too. He dropped to his hands and knees and crawled forward, dragging his musket, working toward the left. He could see no one he recognized and thought he must be among another regiment. A shell sputtered and let go and everyone ducked or flattened themselves on the ground but no one was hit. Thomas rose on one knee. A scrap of daylight between trees, gray as broth, and a Rebel silhouetted against it, ramming a ball home. Thomas brought his musket up and fired and, to his great surprise, the Rebel spun, lithe as a dancer, and fell to the ground.

Luke had been hit in the thigh. A hard pinch, like a bee sting. Yellow-jacket, hornet: vicious. He dropped his musket and stumbled and someone caught him and kept him from falling. It was Rivers.

"Sonofa*bitch*," Luke said.

Rivers said something but Luke couldn't hear it. He tried to put weight on that left leg and found he could, with some difficulty. The ball had gone through, blood was running down his leg on both sides, and Luke thanked God it hadn't struck a bone. He took a step, limping, and Rivers let go of him. He looked around for his gun and Rivers held him as he bent down and retrieved it. Again Rivers spoke, inaudible, and jerked his thumb toward the rear.

"Where's Thomas?" Luke said.

Again Rivers jerked his thumb toward the rear.

"Where's Thomas?"

The regiment was rushing the copse and the scrub and brush between it and the stone wall. Luke looked around for Thomas and could not see him. He cursed and shouldered his gun and hobbled on with Rivers beside him. They came to the dead Rebels uphill of the stone wall; Luke looked at the few blue-clad corpses mixed in and did not see Thomas. He was losing blood fast, but he told himself it would clot up by and by and he must find Thomas. He hobbled on with Rivers beside him. A shell exploded up ahead, throwing two men high off the ground. Minnies from down the field stitched the air, whining and humming, and Rivers said *goddamnshit* and pitched forward, breaking the fall with both hands and rolling onto his back, mouthing savage curses.

Luke stopped. Rivers had been hit in the side, just above the hip. Luke knew he should go on—hadn't every superior from Macy to Sergeant Cate drummed that into their heads?—but his head felt light and a short rest, he thought, would do him good. He lowered himself to the ground, using his gun as a crutch, and, when he found it hurt too much to kneel, pivoted gingerly and sat down beside Rivers.

It felt good not to be standing. The thigh was burning now as if a candle flame had been touched to it, and his pant leg was blood-soaked and plastered to the leg and he wondered if an artery had been hit. *Father would know.* Rivers tried to sit up—he wanted to look at his wound— but only grimaced and lay back down. Luke put his hand on Jake's chest and looked uphill and yelled *Wounded!* and could not hear himself. The men were at the copse now, shooting into it, and fighting in the brushy ground between copse and stone wall.

"Wounded!"

Rivers closed his eyes. His face was knotted in pain, or was it anger? The ball must have pierced his stomach. *Father would know.* A surgeon would have to remove it, but it was probably too late anyway. *Father would . . .* Luke's head seemed to be detaching itself, floating. His thigh was filling with that burning pain, as if the ball had not exited but was there, molten, red-hot, expanding. The blood still ran down copiously and felt strangely cold on his skin.

He did not want to leave Jake but there was something he needed to do and he found his musket and prepared to raise himself on it. Jake had shut his eyes tight and was baring his teeth, a badger snarling at his enemies to the end. "I have to go," Luke said, but could not remember why. The blood was seeping steadily out of Rivers and the ground was drinking it. Jake spoke, cursing, and felt beside him and took a handful of grass and tore it. Terrific gunfire in the copse and beyond it, shells bursting, smoke getting thicker. "I have to go," Luke said, or perhaps only thought it, and pulled himself up on his rifle crutch. *I'll ask Father he'll know.* He stood there, swaying slightly, trying to remember what it was he needed to do.

Luke needn't have worried about him. Thomas was fighting well now. All fear had left him—when had that happened?—and he moved among the humming minnie balls and bursting shells with the fatalism of the veteran fighter who knows one is going to get you or it isn't and the best way to avoid death may be to walk right through it. North of the copse the stone wall jogged in to form a corner or right angle, and it was here the Rebels had broken through. They'd fought their way into the trees and up the slope alongside them, and if there could be worse killing than what went on in those twenty minutes or however long it was, Thomas did not want to see it. He'd stayed in the copse when the Rebels had been pushed out of it and had shot a man hardly a rod away in the back, between the shoulder blades, and another in the stomach, and had seen that one stagger back and fall as if he'd been punched. McNamara had plunged into the thick of it with his revolver, shooting men point-blank and finally disappearing in the melee. The struggle went on awhile and by degrees the Rebels gave way, melting back down the incline and over the stone wall, what was left of them.

When the last ones scrambled back over the wall, Thomas came out of the copse and resumed looking for Luke, but not as before, he was not calling his name anymore. The ground was strewn thick with men and horses and broken limbers and crippled guns, and as the smoke drifted off you began to smell the tinny smell of blood, the sweetish fishy stench of horse guts, and already, as if they'd been waiting underfoot all this time, flies were gathering above the maimed and belly-opened horses and over the pools of blood coagulating in the sun.

Thomas moved from body to body across that tilted scrubby field, and with each passing moment his heart grew colder. He saw a face sheared off to the bone by a shell fragment but the man's hair had been yellow, he wasn't Luke. He saw a man, not Luke, who'd been shot in the eye at close range and the skin burned from his face by the muzzle flame. He saw men who'd been clubbed to death by muskets swung like giant base ball bats. He saw a skull broken in like an eggshell and beside it the bloody rock that had done it, and still none of them was Luke.

At the stone wall some of the men were sending volleys after the Rebels, while others only stood watching them go. In the field out front, as the firing abated, Rebels began to rise up from hiding, with their hands in the air, and the Union men climbed over the wall with their muskets leveled and went down to bring them in as prisoners. Thomas watched it a moment then searched the copse with a dread certainty growing in the pit of his stomach. He expected an officer to notice him and order him into line, but none did. He was out of the copse now, working his way methodically south. He found quite a few men of the Twentieth.

The Rhode Islander Delaney, who had joshed them about seeing the elephant, dead. Men from other companies, dead and wounded. A shell exploded in the copse but he didn't duck or look for signs of another coming, because he knew he would live for as long as it took him to find Luke and probably much, much longer.

He was one of Kemper's men, took all those casualties trying to get at the Yankee line going across at the left oblique. The Yankee batteries had given them holy hell and then when the shooting began the most of them had veered off left like they might find it easier going over there but he, Private Jesse Pollard, had drifted over only far enough to find a snug place to lie down in, a little dip in the brushy slopeside about four rods from the stone fence with a nice flattish gray rock to lay his Enfield across. The Yankees would rise up from behind the fence to fire and Jesse would shoot at them. He shot at the officers walking up and down and got him one.

Then the boys broke through over on the left and the Yankees forgot about this sector, though there were plenty of boys pouring it into them like Jesse was doing, and went running to lend a hand and with the land elevated beyond the wall and them running across it in such numbers it was like ducks in a shooting gallery. Shooting in this deliberate fashion and hardly drawing any fire—it's different in a charge, defending or attacking, time speeds up and you load and fire like a machine and can't tell half the time what you're hitting or not hitting—Jesse was able to think about why he was killing these fellows and take satisfaction from it.

A friend of his in the regiment, Wilbur Jeffers, had given him a letter he'd taken off a dead Yankee after Fredericksburg when the Yankees had given up and gone back across the river. The Yankee's name was Wm—how he'd signed it—Barker and he was writing, it could be seen, to his brother back home. It was a short letter, hasty. We are to attack them tomorrow, wrote Wm Barker. Many will be slain & I am as likely to fall as anyone. But I am content to take whatever is to come. Shd I be slain you will be the eldest left & I doubt not you will fill my place. On you will fall the delightful task of maintaining Father's & Aunt Charlotte's declining yrs. You will be kind to Walter & Abbey. Forget my faults & forgive. Good bye & God bless you.

What you aim to do with this? Jesse said, handing the letter back to Wilbur Jeffers.

Keep it for a souvenir, I guess, Wilbur said.

That ain't right.

No?

We should send it on. You got the envelope?

Right here.

Wm Barker, it turned out, hailed from Brattleboro, Vermont.

We'll add a little something, Jesse said, for their edification. Let em know what we think of all this trouble they've brung down on us.

You write it, Jess, Wilbur said.

I'd be pleased to.

The paper was good foolscap, lined, and the envelope bore the stamp of their Christian Commission—Christian? Jesse could puke—and there was room enough at the bottom of the page for Jesse to write, in big bold letters: THIS LETTER WAS FOUND ON THE BODY OF A MAN SAC- RIFICED BY THE LINCOLN GOVERNMENT IN ITS UNPATRIOTIC, UNHOLY & HELLISH CRUSADE AGAINST A PEOPLE STRUGGLING FOR THEIR RIGHTS UNDER THE CONSTITUTION. IT IS A SAD FATE TO FALL IN AN INGLORIOUS CAUSE.

Ain't that a mite severe? Wilbur said.

What do you call this war? Jesse said.

Severe, Wilbur said.

And who begun it? Jesse said.

He had resealed the envelope with wax and given it to the regimental chaplain without saying what he'd done and the chaplain had said he'd get it across to a Yankee chaplain for mailing. That was some months ago and Jesse had spent many idle moments wondering if the letter had found Wm Barker's kin in Brattleboro, Vermont, and if so whether it had stung their Yankee arrogance, had caused them some hurt and regret. Because there could be no Christian forgiveness anymore, there was only payment to be wrung from the enemy and all their kin, in blood and tears, and Jesse hoped he'd wrung those ones good.

He shot a skinny little Yankee, looked like a rat from this distance, and when he was reloaded a bigger fellow, broad-shouldered, was plunked down beside him on the bloody ground and even in the smoke Jesse could see his left leg shining like it had been painted red. The little fellow was dead meat or would be soon and the other would lose the leg or bleed to death. Jesse shot at a mounted officer higher up the ridge and missed, and when he looked again the big Yankee was on his feet and Jesse shook his head, a snake'll bite you if you don't kill it all the way, and sighted just below the Yankee's ear and finished him.

He found Elisha still on his back but with one arm flung out, knees wide apart and bent slightly. He was staring at the sky but his eyes were glassy and vacant. Thomas knelt and his chin went to his chest and he closed his eyes and was alone with his grief. He'd known it, yes he had, oh yes: had known that little coin-sized wound was a deep, deep hole and that Elisha's sweet young life was running from it faster than the blood was, much faster, to take to the swirled discolored air. Thomas drew in a lungful of that air, breathing the lingering essence of Elisha. He closed his friend's eyes with a light touch of his index finger and spoke to him. I have to leave you, he said. I have to find Luke.

The Rebels were streaming back across the valley, not quite in panic but as quick as they could go, short of it. The batteries on both sides were still firing, the sky a canopy of screeching noise and shellbursts. But the canopy seemed higher somehow than before, the threat seemed diminished. The Rebel gunners were aiming high again and their shells exploding down behind the ridge as before. Thomas stood up—a shell whistled directly above him and on over the ridge—he didn't glance up or flinch—and continued working his way south, moving from body to body until he found Luke and Rivers.

He found them on ground they'd watered with their blood and fell to his knees as if he'd been shot himself. Elisha. Luke. *Both of them. Oh God both of them.* Luke had been shot in the head and his brains scattered. He'd been shot in the leg. The leg had bled amply and had no doubt been hit before the head shot killed him. Thomas looked at his face, trying not to see the mess on one side of his head. Luke's eyes were open. He looked surprised and a little angry. His leg wound would have been bad enough and maybe fatal and Thomas wondered how long he'd suffered with it. He felt Luke's presence and wished to speak to him but did not know what to

say. He pushed himself to his feet and went down the slope and found a
Seventh Michigan blanket among the debris along the wall, thinking *both
of them both* and brought it back weeping and covered Luke with it and
knew Luke was grateful. He wanted something else and Thomas knew
what it was. Rivers's eyes were closed and his lips retracted in a hideous
smile and Thomas went back down to the wall and found another blanket and covered him, too. Then he sat down and wept himself dry, wept
his heart empty, his head bowed, his hand to his face, the very portrait of
human grief. When he was done at last he put his hand on Luke's breast
under the blanket and spoke to him as he had to Elisha. He told him it
didn't matter about Rose and that he was sorry for his anger. I wish you
could see this, Thomas said, watching the fleeing Rebels. Guns on Cemetery Hill and Little Round Top were dropping shells among them, but
they were so dispersed you could not kill more than one at a time. We
whipped the sonsabitches, Thomas told Luke. Gave em holy hell.

Thomas sat there. He'd run out of things to say. He could feel the
dried tears, sticky on his face. Tears and gunpowder. The sun was well
down the sky, a luminous red-orange disc through the smoke. There
was cheering to the north, moving this way. An officer was riding south
along the line, cantering smartly, two aides following him. It was General Hays. All three of them were dragging Rebel flags on the ground
behind them. The men stood up, raised rifles in the air, cheered. Some
of them tossed their hats up. Thomas watched them. His hand still on
the wool blanket over Luke's breast, the body still warm through it. He
knew something now: Death is selective. It seems random but is not. It
has its own inevitability, its own terrible logic, and Luke's conviction
that he could not be killed today had been childish. He could be. He was.
Death had marked him, had been waiting.

"Tommy."

It was Joe Merriman. The Twentieth's new color bearers were following Captain Abbott back to their position. Both flags torn, tattered.
Thomas wondered vaguely and without caring what had happened to
Colonel Macy. Merriman squatted down on his haunches and laid his
rifle down. Abbott looked up and saw the two of them but didn't say
anything. Merriman looked at the two covered bodies and at Thomas's
hand on Luke.

"That there Luke?"

Thomas nodded.

"I'm sorry, Tommy," Merriman said.

"I went into those trees looking for him. He was right here all the time. I must have passed right by him."

"You seen Jake?" Merriman said.

The cannons were still answering one another across the valley but it was dwindling. Rebel shells were still tearing up the back side of the ridge. General Hays and the two others had loped on in the direction of Little Round Top. The Twentieth's color guard had planted the flags in their old position by the dirt-and-rail breastwork. Captain Abbott stood with his arms folded, watching the Rebels recede beyond the Emmitsburg Road.

"Tommy," Merriman said. "Where's Jake?"

"This is Jake," Thomas said.

"Ah, God," Merriman said. "Ah shit."

"They died together," Thomas said.

"Ah, God."

"Elisha's dead too."

"I seen him," Merriman said.

"He was carrying the colors," Thomas said.

Merriman looked at him. "What the hell for?"

"He picked them up. The national flag. The sergeant carrying them was hit and Elisha was right beside him. He never hesitated."

"By God," Merriman said.

"Delaney's dead."

"I seen him, too. I couldn't see Jake, why I thought he might of made it."

"And Paine," Thomas said.

"I seen him get hit. I was right with him. Shrapnel took his foot off. He's layin there, gets up on one arm, got his sword in the other hand, wavin it, and they shot him all to hell. I hear Macy's wounded. I believe we lost half the regiment, dead or wounded."

"Why is everyone so goddamn happy?" Thomas said.

Merriman leaned sideways and spat. "We whipped em, is why. We whipped Bobby Lee. Saved the Union, Tommy. Saved it right here. Today."

Thomas bowed his head and was weeping again. Not child tears, nothing in them of bafflement or self-pity, not anymore, not ever again. Merriman laid a hand on his shoulder. Thomas wiped his eyes. I've got to stop this, he thought.

"I know it don't help much," Merriman said, "but it's worse when you lose the fight besides. Ball's Bluff. Fredericksburg. All them dead boys, just wasted."

Thomas looked up, blinked the last tears away.

"Look at em run," Merriman said.

Across the valley, in the thinning smoke, the last of the Rebels were scurrying antlike for the trees on Seminary Ridge. The Union guns had stopped shelling them but they ran anyway, fearful perhaps of sharpshooters, indifferent to discipline and dignity. The thick woods swallowed them and nothing remained of the retreat but the wounded—walking, limping, crawling.

"You boys havin yourselves a picnic?" It was Sergeant Cate, striding up with his rifle on his shoulder.

Merriman stood up but Thomas did not.

"His brother's kilt," Merriman said. "Him and Jake Rivers. Died alongside of each other."

Cate looked at Luke's blanketed body. He looked at Thomas. "I'm sorry, son," he said. "And I'm sorry about Private Smith."

"They was like brothers," Merriman said.

"I know that," Cate said.

A Rebel gun went off near the Peach Orchard and the echo caromed away into silence.

"I'm going to put him in for a battlefield promotion," Cate said. "For taking up the colors."

"Thank you," Thomas said.

"Don't thank me," Cate said.

"I imagine Luke died just as brave," Merriman said.

"I imagine he did," Cate said.

"I'd as soon sit here awhile, if I might," Thomas said.

"That'd be fine, Tommy," Cate said.

TEN

The smoke was gone as if it had never been—even the barn had burned itself out—and as the long day waned the western mountains were softest blue. John McNamara had stepped over the breastwork and gone down the slope and sat on a flat rock, chewing some hardtack and looking out toward the mountains. The commissary wagon had come up finally but the men had forgotten how hungry they were and there'd been little elation. They'd formed up around sundown and the first sergeants had called the rolls, and almost every company had lost nearly half its men dead or wounded. Stackpole and Merriman and a few of the others remembered when the regiment had numbered better than eight hundred, and now they were not much more than a hundred fifty.

McNamara sat with his back to them as still as a feature of the landscape, as Thomas had sat last night and in about the same place, although it was hard to tell, the land had been so transformed. The fields were worn as flat as a fairground and their topography muddled by the acres of dead bodies and half-dead wounded, mostly Rebels, and a vast debris of muskets, ramrods, forage caps, cap boxes, cartridge boxes, blankets, canteens. Men had ventured out to rob the bodies and in their rummagings had thrown away playing cards, Bibles, suspenders, toothbrushes, ambrotypes, writing paper, socks, underwear. And everywhere, on both sides of the line, was a rubbish of torn cartridges and brass caps. McNamara had found Elisha, hunting for him as Thomas had hunted Luke, and covered him with a shelter half.

"Mac's heart's broken," Stackpole said.

"He ain't as hard as he seems," Merriman said.

Their voices were overloud, as deaf people speak who cannot hear themselves. Otherwise it was very quiet but for the scattered cries and groans of the unretrieved wounded. Skirmishers had gone out but were leaving one another be, and who could blame them?

"Mac always had one friend," Merriman said. "Remember Peleg Davenport?"

"From Martha's Vineyard," Stackpole said. "Like Elisha."

"Davenport was a good un," Tom Jackson said.

They'd made coffee. The shipment of hardtack was good for once and they'd crumbled their crackers into their hot coffee and spooned up the pieces, no bugs to pick out. The salt pork was stringy and some of it rancid, and a few of the men had broiled a slice over the open fires, but most had pitched theirs away. Perhaps the fight had shrunk everybody's appetite, or perhaps the smells, ever more pervasive and foul, made eating difficult.

"Hard to believe they're gone," Stackpole said.

"They ain't gone," Jackson said.

The wounded were the first concern—the ones who might be saved, at least—and the ambulances and stretcher bearers had been bringing them in for a couple of hours. With the shelling stopped the ambulances could move about freely. The wounded, including Rebels, were being doctored in farmhouses down back of the ridge, and already Colonel Hall had sent a man from each company—not two, they were stretched too thin now—to help with burying the amputated limbs.

"You feelin unwell, Willie?" Merriman said.

"I got a kind of a earache," the drummer boy said.

He'd been sent to the rear both days to assist the stretcher bearers and today a shellburst had narrowly missed killing or maiming him. There was blood on his sleeve and he was as begrimed as any of the men.

"Could be you got your eardrum broke," Jackson told him.

"No he ain't," Merriman said. "It'll pass, Willie. You ain't alone, believe me."

"I seen em bring Wilcox down," Willie said. "His leg come off the stretcher and one a them band musicians . . ."

"Don't talk of it," Merriman said.

They drank their coffee. Incredibly, fireflies had begun to wink in the dusk. Somewhere down the field a wounded Rebel called for his mother.

"I wish they'd tend to that sonofabitch."

"They will."

"Jake Rivers'd be cussin him. Tellin him to shut up."

"Jake'd be complainin about this air. By God it stinks, he'd say."

"Had a delicate nose, cept when it come to himself."

"He wasn't a bad fellow," Stackpole said.

"None of em was."

"We paid dear today, didn't we?"

Thomas drank the last of his bitter coffee, swallowing too the dregs of hardtack. He shook out the cup and attached it to his belt and without speaking stepped up onto the dirt breastwork and over the piled rails. The rails had been gashed and splintered by minnie balls. No one said anything. Thomas went down to McNamara and sat beside him as Elisha had sat beside him, Thomas, last night. He thought with a spasm of shame and regret of his petulance and knew it was because he'd loved Rose, as Elisha had said, and how childish and inadequate that love had been.

"The boys are worried about you," Thomas said.

"The boys can suck my ass," McNamara said.

Thomas touched the cross in his pocket. He had remembered it only after he'd come down from sitting with Luke and gotten into line. It had ridden forgotten in his pocket through everything and he'd wanted to throw it away, hurl it as far as he could, but he remembered the old woman and did not. He was glad now that he hadn't.

"You don't want some coffee?" Thomas said.

"I did, I'd make it."

They sat awhile. The moon was rising, full again but softened, made paler by a thickening woolen sky. The valley, so starkly moonlit last night, was dark and its horrors blurred and indistinct.

"You and your niggers," McNamara said. "You. Luke. Elisha. You had enough of em now?"

Ma, the Rebel said. *Ma. Please.*

"Poor bastard," Thomas said.

"No one invited him here," McNamara said. "You had enough of em?"

Thomas looked at him. His eyes were dark, narrowed. No tears in them, only ire and bitterness. There was heat in him, while Thomas's grief was cold and quiet.

"Cate said Macy lost a hand," Thomas said.

McNamara said nothing.

"He said Hancock was wounded," Thomas said.

"Hancock?"

"He'll be all right, Cate said."

They sat awhile looking out over the valley. The air smokeless, clear, rank.

"Tommy."

"What."

"What'd you let him pick that flag up for?"

"How was I to stop him?"

"I'd of knocked him down if I had to."

"I could get shot for that."

"It ain't a requirement to pick up the colors."

"He wanted to do it."

"Stupid sonofabitch, wasn't he."

"No," Thomas said.

Ma. Ma, it's . . . An ambulance came rattling up from the direction of the Codori farm, its lantern swinging side to side. It did not stop for the wounded Rebel.

"Let's bury them, Mac."

"Bury who?"

"Luke. Elisha. I don't want them in a burial pit."

McNamara thought awhile. "What'd you mean to dig with?"

"Maybe we can find that shovel was around yesterday."

"Ain't likely."

"Bayonets, then," Thomas said.

"Bayonets," McNamara said. "Might as well use a damn kitchen knife."

"I intend to do it, Mac," Thomas said, rising.

But McNamara stopped him, a strong hand on his arm. "Tomorrow," he said. "First light."

"I don't want them to lie all night."

"Ain't nothin gonna happen to em where they're at. Let em sleep."

Sleep. Thomas wondered if it was in any way like sleeping.

"Where were you gonna find a lantern at?" Mac said.

"Don't need a lantern."

"Yes you do. And we're more like to find a shovel in the morning."

Thomas didn't say anything. He was beginning to realize how tired he was. A kind of stupefaction setting in.

"You'll be more ready for it in the morning," Mac said. "I will be too."

"Will Cate be all right with it?"

"We do it in the morning he will."

All right," Thomas said. *Sleep. Let them sleep.*

ELEVEN

It rained in the night, showers, and Thomas slept through them and dreamed of Luke and Elisha in the house on William Street and was sure they were alive after all, and that it had all been a misunderstanding. Then McNamara kicked him gently awake and he smelled the fetid stinking air and knew they were dead and what he had to do now, this minute, before the army got stirring. It was sunrise or earlier, but you couldn't tell which, because the sky was steel-gray in the east and the world all dank and color-bled in the half-light, and even the summer leaves were a flat and cheerless green. There was no shooting between pickets and no sign of the Rebels save a battery here and there just this side of the trees on Seminary Ridge. Thomas threw off his sodden blanket. McNamara had two shovels. He dropped one at Thomas's feet. He was not wearing his sack coat. His white shirt was yellow with sweat and age. His unshaven face did not look dirty so much as scorched by fire.

Thomas sat up and put on his shoes. He reached for his sack coat, then changed his mind and left it. Up and down the line the men slept like the dead. The rain had doused the fires. McNamara and Thomas went along the ridge carrying their shovels and McNamara said he'd found them at the little whitewashed farmhouse down the hill where Meade had been staying. The place had been shelled good and was a field hospital now with a hole in its roof. There were dead horses in the yard and some fresh graves, and hogs were busy eating out the horses' guts and rooting at the graves. One hog was feeding on a human arm it had found or maybe dug up. There was no guard posted and Mac had helped himself to the shovels, which were leaning against the barn wall.

"What was your plan," McNamara said, "bury em alongside of each other?"

Thomas shook his head. "Where they fell," he said.

"They're like to be dug up later, buried proper."

"I know," Thomas said.

Luke and Rivers lay side by side under the blankets as Thomas had left them. "I might as well do Jake, too," Thomas said.

"Do the whole regiment, why don't you. It won't take but a month."

"I might want to look at Elisha one more time," Thomas said.

"I wouldn't," McNamara said.

"I might want to."

McNamara shrugged and trudged on toward Elisha, whom he'd covered yesterday with his shelter half. Thomas broke the ground with his shovel and carved his first spadeful. It was hard work but he was equal to it now, sinewy and lung-strong from marching, his hands hardened from constant use out of doors. The soil was woven with roots and cluttered with stones and with rocks as big as melons. He had to stab at it, stab and hack, to cut the roots and loosen it. He had to pry the rocks from their lodgments and kneel down and lift them out. The black earth had a cool peaty smell, a relief against the stink of the humid air. McNamara was digging some ten rods away, and it was only now that Thomas saw what near neighbors Luke and Elisha had been in dying. And the copse: how close it was, really. Not much more than a stone's throw, but a mile away yesterday through the smoke and shellfire and men dying.

He'd gone down a couple of feet and was laved in sweat when Captain Abbott, in command of the regiment after Macy's wounding, came down the slope. He was alone. He was eating what looked like a slice of hoe cake and Thomas eyed it as he climbed up out of the half dug grave and saluted.

"At ease," Abbott said. He was wearing a forage cap. Another of the Harvard men: a bland disdain lurking in the well-made, still-boyish face—for bad breeding, ignorance, abolition. "Who's this?" he said, looking down.

"My brother, sir. Private Luke Chandler."

"Have you permission?"

Thomas took off his cap. He wiped his forehead with the back of his wrist. "No sir," he said.

Abbott nodded. He tore off a bite of hoe cake and looked at McNamara, who had dug down thigh deep and was keeping an eye on them as he worked.

"That other one's Private Elisha Smith," Thomas said. "That's Private McNamara burying him."

"The boy who took up the colors. Company I."

"Yes sir."

"He's Corporal Smith now."

"Yes sir."

"You're one of those Martha's Vineyard boys," Abbott said.

"Yes sir."

"Lincoln men," Abbott said. "Colonel Macy has mentioned you."

"Yes sir."

"Want to free all the niggers, do you."

"Sir?"

"What."

"My brother's dead, sir."

"Quite right. I apologize, Private . . . ?"

"Chandler, sir."

"Chandler. Yes."

"There were only the two of us."

"I'm sorry."

"I'd like to get on with this," Thomas said.

"Permission granted."

"Thank you sir," Thomas said, and took the long step down into Luke's grave.

Elisha still lay under the shelter half.

"Don't look at him," McNamara said.

"I've seen worse," Thomas said. "I've seen everything."

"He's changed since yesterday."

Reveille had been drummed and the men were moving about and fires were smoking and there was the mutter of voices up and down the line.

Thomas looked down at the dirty white shelter half with its row of black buttons while McNamara waited.

"I'll write his family," Thomas said. "I could mention you if you like."

"And say what?"

"Whatever you tell me."

"I guess you'll think a somethin."

And write Father and Rose. And say what?

"You gonna look at him?" Mac said.

"I guess I won't," Thomas said.

Nor did he look again at Luke, but buried him wrapped in the blanket. Over both graves they arranged the rocks and stones they'd dug up to make a cross, working silently together on their knees. And then it was done, and Mac came back and they stood by Luke's grave.

"You want to speak some words?" McNamara said.

"I don't know what there is left to say."

"I guess they know what we're thinkin."

"I don't know what they know," Thomas said.

"Maybe nothin."

"Maybe. We going to bury Jake?"

"There ain't time to bury Jake, even if I wanted to."

"I hate to leave him."

"He'll get buried," McNamara said.

They left the shovels for someone else to use and went slowly back toward what was left of their regiment. Here and there, somehow, fires had been started. They wavered feebly, guttered, sent up clouds of white smoke.

"Mac," Thomas said, and put a hand on his arm, stopping him.

He looked at Thomas. Eyes hard and luminous as bright coal. Mac was a killer but there was sorrow in those eyes too, and it was old sorrow, maybe as old as the man himself.

"When they charged us yesterday, I aimed high," Thomas said.

McNamara stared at him. "Say again?"

"I aimed high on purpose. I didn't want to shoot anybody."

"What the hell you talkin about?"

"I couldn't. It didn't matter who they were."

"They're tryin to kill you, that's who they are."

"I know. But listen. We got into the trees and I had a clear shot at one and I did it again. I aimed high."

"Tommy. While you was aimin high he was tryin to kill one a your own."

"He didn't, though. He fell. I thought I'd hit him by mistake but I couldn't have. Someone else shot him right at that same moment."

McNamara watched him. Those savage stricken eyes.

"I realize that now," Thomas said, "but I thought I'd killed him and I was glad."

He stopped, looked out across the valley. The Rebel batteries were limbering. There was still no musket fire but it was light enough now to see their pickets, spread out and crouched in semi-concealment out beyond the Emmitsburg Road.

"I hit two more, on purpose," he said. "Killed them, and was glad I did."

McNamara was looking at him strangely now. His eyes softening a little. "It ain't hard," he said.

"Don't tell the boys," Thomas said. "That I aimed high, I mean."

McNamara gave him the small sideways curve of a smile. "The boys won't mind," he said.

They went down across the wet flattened debris-littered fields in column, a miniature company under the command now of Captain Abbott. The Fifteenth Massachusetts also sent a company, and the Seventh Michigan, three truncated dark blue snakes wending down across the valley at a weary route step. The smell of the dead had gotten worse if that was possible; a stench of putrefaction that swarmed in your lungs and leached down to knead your stomach with every breath you took. Abdomens of the dead of two days ago were so swollen that their pants and coats hugged them like skin and buttons were letting go and the faces of the men lying belly down were as black as Negroes' faces from the blood gathered in them. The men on their backs were as pale as wax and their chests and bellies puffed out like air balloons. There were hundreds of dead and the corpses nearly all barefoot, either dying so or robbed of their shoes. There were some wounded too from yesterday. Some of them had tied handkerchiefs or rags torn from their shirts to their ramrods and stuck the rammers in the ground, tiny white flags of surrender and supplication. Almost all the wounded were Rebels and the men spoke to them variously as they passed.

How's it feel, you Rebel bastard?

Fredericksburg, you bastard.

Never mind him. You hold on, friend, we won't leave you die.

We got good surgeons in our army, Reb.

Good surgeons? said a Union soldier. What army you talkin about?

Abbott took Company I down along the line of a destroyed rail fence that ran east and west toward the Emmitsburg Road and then across the fence line at the left oblique to the red barn and redbrick Codori farmhouse with their shade trees and well, which had been drunk dry by the Rebels. No one fired on them. As if the wet weather were unsuitable for fighting. The Rebel pickets were quite a way west of the Emmitsburg Road and if there was to be any fighting today it would be on Seminary Ridge and the Rebels on the defensive this time, but no one thought there would be.

Abbott sent pickets out across the road, the men moving cautiously at trail arms about twenty feet apart with Sergeant Holland behind them. The previous skirmishers were deployed along the road and now they formed up and went back up the long gentle slope in column and still no shots were fired.

There had been Rebel wounded in the barn and the dirt floor was bloody in places and there were mounds of blood-soaked hay and bloody rags and bandages and articles of clothing. It would rain later and they would shelter in the barn but now the bloodsmell and flies drove them out and they built a fire in the barnyard with planks ripped from a stall and made coffee. The farmhouse had not been badly used but the Rebels had been through it and opened drawers and closets and of course taken every last thing there was to eat. No one blamed them for that. Captain Abbott walked through the house then sat down on a ladderback chair in the front dooryard and opened a book. A Rebel skirmisher fired a shot from way up near the tree line and was twice answered, and the quiet settled in again. Later there was some skirmish fire, avid little pops, far off to the north.

The rain began at noon. It came down hard and sudden out of the low lightless sky, dousing the fire and sending the men running to the blood-

smelling barn, the sergeants and corporals joining Captain Abbott in the
farmhouse. It rained all afternoon and on into the night, and the pickets
hooded themselves in their gum blankets and covered up their muskets and
sat silent and huddled with no thought of fighting. The skirmishing to the
north had ended long ago and in fact Lee's army had begun to decamp,
supply trains and ambulances and Negro prisoners first, with their cav-
alry escorts, leading the way slowly back to Virginia.

The Rebel infantry abandoned their line around one in the morning of
July 5. Thomas Chandler, on sentinel about halfway up between the
Emmitsburg Road and the trees on Seminary Ridge, heard them start.
He heard the drumrolls and shouted commands and the rain-dulled
clinks of the thousands of pieces of equipment and weaponry and, in
time, the vague insistent soughing of the columns moving out, which
might have been wind and rain but was not. The Rebel pickets, scattered
in concealment uphill near the edge of the woods, were of course the last
to leave. You couldn't see them in the dark and rain, but you knew they
were there, you heard a muffled voice or some coughing, or sensed shadowy movement, and when Thomas realized they were gone he wondered
if he'd fallen asleep and missed their leaving.

"Mac," Thomas said, after another hour had crawled by. "They're
gone."

It was still raining. The night blackness was thinning to a broth-gray
rain-washed dawn.

"I know." McNamara was off to his right, dimly visible now.

"Let's go on up there," Thomas said, "see if they're gone all the
way."

"Get shot, you mean."

"There's no one in those trees," Thomas said. "The infantry's been
gone hours."

"Might be some pickets yet," Mac said.

"There's nothing," Thomas said.

The men on outpost were within calling distance and Thomas hollered down to Sergeant Cate. He asked if they could go on up to the
woods and look around and Sergeant Cate said they could and that he'd

bring his detail along behind and that the rest of the company would likely follow.

"Hey," Thomas said. "Jimmy."

Jimmy Wells was the third sentinel, to his left. Wells had joined the regiment right after Chancellorsville and this had been his first battle too.

"We're going to move up a ways, post those woods," Thomas said.

"I heard you," Wells said.

They moved up the slope and into the trees with their muskets at half cock. The rain whispered in the leaves and freshened the air but even so the smells of the three-day camp assaulted them suddenly, as if the woods contained and held them intact. They could see the rain-soaked ashes and char of the Rebel campfires and the charred stubs of fence rails that had been laid across them. Here and there lay an overturned hardtack box that had been somebody's seat by the fire. In the ashes too were the bone fragments of cattle and fowl, appropriated from the rich farms hereabout.

"Rebs eat better'n we do," McNamara growled.

They went on, disappearing and reappearing to each other in the semidarkness among the trees, past more dead fires, more litter. Here and there a tree limb obstructed the way, brought down by a shell or bolt, leaves silver-bottomed in the gloom. All danger was gone and there was an illicit-feeling pleasure in walking here, as in entering a room or house that isn't yours and poking about, making yourself free of the place. The Rebels had been here by the thousands, all through these woods. They'd lived here three days. Had told their stories around their fires. Had laughed, cussed. Quietly, late at night, while most slept, a certain few had confided in one another—about their sweethearts, perhaps, or their hopes for after the war. On the battle's final day they'd formed up here and come down off the ridge in mile-long waves and thousands of them had died, and Thomas had killed two of them.

They went on down the long gentle slope that was the back side of Seminary Ridge. It had been lived on, too, and been torn and gouged when the Union batteries had fired long. There were dead horses here, wrecked caissons and limbers and commissary wagons. The air malignant with horse rot. Below them now, in a low broad expanse of open land, a large farm with generous shade trees, chalk-white barn and house, the house gabled, with a gallery and a whitewashed chimney bracketing it at either end. The three of them stopped, still well apart, and waited. Silence, except for the rain. They looked at one another, nodded, and went on, stepping through a narrow winding brook. The pasture and fields of corn and wheat running north and west were all trafficked flat, rail fences pulled down or vanished.

"The Rebs done a job on this place, ain't they," McNamara said.

"Well, we done the same to them," said Jimmy Wells.

The three of them stood in the house yard, hooded in their gum blankets. There'd been campfires here, and there was litter, but less of it than on the ridge.

"A general quartered here, I bet," Wells said.

"Maybe it was Lee," McNamara said.

"Could of been."

"I wonder what Lee thinks of us now," Thomas said. He thought of Rose, and how she hated Lee. He had not written them yet, there'd been no chance. *Tonight I must. Tonight* . . .

"Thinks we're some tough sonsabitches," McNamara said.

"You think Lee cusses?" Wells said.

"Cusses?" McNamara said. "Lee's God, ain't you heard?"

A chicken clucked in the big empty barn, silencing the three of them. It clucked again.

"My Lord," Wells said, and they were off, clutching their blankets, running, seized by a mutual release and giddiness.

"I ain't had real food in a week!"

"I ain't either!"

"How we gonna cook her?"

"Hell, right in that farmhouse!"

The barn door was wide open. The bay was a long high cavern with stalls on either side and the loft above the middle. They stopped, let their eyes adjust, listened for the chicken and heard instead a human sound, part groan and part sigh but broken, stuttering.

"Reb," McNamara said, and shed his blanket and cocked his Enfield.

"He's hurt," Thomas said, and cocked his gun and advanced toward the sound, which came from a stall halfway down.

"You be careful," Mac said.

"Hey," Thomas said. "We ain't going to hurt you."

He listened. "Ah," the man said. "Ah. Oh God."

The stall door was half open.

"Watch it, Tommy," Mac said behind him.

Thomas laid his gun across the half door and swung it slowly in till he saw the young black man lying on his back on a bed of bloody straw.

"What's there?" Mac said.

"Jesus God," Thomas said, and caught himself on the doorpost.

"What?" Mac said.

"Oh my Jesus," Thomas said.

A Rebel detail had found Floyd Wilkes before dawn, going to fill their canteens in the stream called Willoughby Run. It was as far as Floyd had gotten in two nights of traveling. He could not move by day and had spent July 3 hiding in the woods south of the Chambersburg Pike, where hostilities had begun on the first day, as attested to by the many rotted bloated bodies, both Rebel and Union. Here, down near the Run, where he could at least slake his thirst, Floyd had listened to the great battle he had hoped to join with his purloined Rebel Colt revolver. Shoot Rebels with a Rebel gun, just one and he'd be happy. He'd gone on after dark—the fighting had ended early this day—working his way south along the Run to some woods west of the Schliemann farm. The rain was coming down in earnest now. He was weak from hunger and fatigue and blood loss and had stopped to rest, and it was here, curled up under some viburnum with the rain dripping down on him, that he had heard the Rebel retreat. He'd slept awhile, his first real sleep since stealing away from the Globe Inn, but the rain soon woke him. He'd discarded his yellow waiter's jacket—no garment could be more conspicuous—and was drenched to the skin. He'd lain in the rain awhile, then gone to the stream to drink.

Hell fire, said one of the Rebels. What we got here?

Floyd was on his knees, bent to the stream, drinking. He had thought Lee's army were all gone. A rear guard, skirmishers, had not occurred to him. The Rebels had appeared suddenly out of the woods, dark shapes cloaked in capes or blankets and wearing slouch hats. One of them raised a lantern.

Well I'm a sumbitch. Git up, boy.

Floyd pushed himself to his feet and felt a momentary dizziness. There were seven or eight of them, pathetic things, ragged and skinny and hirsute in the dingy lantern light, carrying their muskets carelessly by their sides.

By Jesus, one of them said. *He'd noticed the revolver. Without his jacket the pistol was plainly visible stuck in Floyd's belt.*

The Rebel with the lantern set it down and they all raised their guns and Floyd's last thought—he was wrong, it wasn't his last—was that he would be shot seven or eight times in the chest. He drew the revolver and cocked it and fired at the middle Rebel and the gun jumped in his grip and the ball went high.

Their muskets weren't loaded. They were bluffing. The pistol shot was a sharp sound in the rain with barely an echo. There was a moment of mutual hesitation—Floyd steeling himself to be cut in half by musket fire, the Rebels in blank astonishment that a Negro would fire on them—and then someone yelled *Sumbitch!* and they rushed at Floyd, who fired again and shot one's hat off. They bowled him over, half in the cold water, and punched and kicked him until their corporal told them to quit and said they would bring the murdering nigger to Sergeant Waring and see what he suggested. They dragged Floyd to his feet. The hatless Rebel was gingerly touching his scalp.

I'm a shoot you, nigger, he said.

You hurt? the corporal said.

Another inch I would a been. Look at this fuckin hat.

Nigger cain't shoot worth a shit, I'll say that.

That ain't the goddamn point.

I know it ain't.

I'm a kill you, boy. I'm a cut your balls off.

Look at him. Someone already give him a good wallop.

Ain't no wonder, he goes around shootin at white men.

Someone had picked up the revolver. *This here's Confederate issue,* he said.

Cain't be.

Why it is. Nigger stole this off a officer.

You goin back to Virginia, boy.

He ain't gawn get that far.

You gawn learn you a lesson, boy.

They bound Floyd's wrists behind him with his own leather belt and marched him through the rain, shoving him when he lagged, supporting him under the arms when he weakened, keeping him erect, to the edge of the woods above the Schliemann farm, where a company of Rebel skirmishers was trying to keep a fire going under a tree. They were crouched around it, covered like old women, crones, in their blankets. Floyd's head wound had begun to burn again but it seemed distant, it had somehow lost its power to discomfit him very much. It was sleep he wanted, sleep would solve everything. He looked at the white farm buildings, visible in the darkness, envisioned the Schliemanns asleep in their beds, fat profane Mr. Schliemann, who drove a hard bargain with the Gettysburg merchants but was a decent man, Floyd believed, and would surely not let this continue. The Rebels were talking.

Stole this here sidearm off a officer.

Tried to shoot Higgins in the head. Shot a hole right through his hat.

All right. Y'all take him to that barn down yonder and dispose of him.

Dispose of him how?

Use that pistol you took off him. Was a nigger come at some boys in the Fifty-third Georgia with a knife and them boys bayoneted the sonofabitch. We cain't have it. Knives or pistols, whichever. We just cain't have it.

These niggers up North is dangerous.

Go on take him down there. Teach him a lesson.

He cain't barely walk.

Well, carry him.

This was good. Mr. Schliemann would wake up. He'd once threatened a man with a pitchfork, according to Mr. Will. Some dispute over a cow. He would throw these Rebels off his property and they wouldn't shoot him, Mr. Schliemann. Not a white man. They were moving again, Floyd half asleep, the burn on his scalp forgotten. The ground leveled off and Floyd noticed a rocking chair lying on its side in the dark, the rain, and came to his senses sufficiently to know that the Schliemanns had fled days ago, as had everyone south and west of town. Of course they were gone, Floyd could picture it, the provident farmer driving his milk cows and hogs with a switch, Mrs. Schliemann and their sundry children in the carryall, which

*no doubt was laden too with valuables. There would be no rescue. Floyd
was going to die, and to his surprise there was no terror in it and hardly
any sadness, for it seemed to have happened already, his death and whatever pain preceded it, and he was now watching or perhaps remembering
it, from the everlasting safety across the River.*

Thomas uncocked his musket and leaned it against the wall. In the last
three days he had seen men killed and half killed, had seen them blown
apart and decapitated and dismembered, but nothing as bad as this.
The Negro lay on his back. He had been stripped naked and his face
was bruised and swollen and disfigured. His legs were spread and drawn
partway up, and with one hand he was holding himself together where
his genitals had been. His clothes had been flung in a corner. Thomas
knelt. The Negro looked at him. There was a terrific smell of blood. The
Negro lifted his free hand, it quavered like a leaf, and Thomas took it.

"Water," Thomas said. "Do you want some water."

Floyd Wilkes nodded. Thomas unshouldered his canteen, still holding his hand.

"By *God*," McNamara said behind Thomas.

Jimmy Wells was there too, speechless. Thomas uncapped his canteen and tilted it to Floyd's mouth. He seemed unable to swallow. The
water filled his mouth and spilled over. Wells had turned back into the
barn bay and was vomiting.

"By God," McNamara said again, quietly this time.

"You rest easy," Thomas said. He capped his canteen and set it down.
"You're safe now. The Rebels are gone. We whipped them."

Floyd closed his eyes and gave a barely perceptible nod. He swallowed
a groan. Thomas looked back over his shoulder. McNamara was gone.
Thomas reached into his coat pocket and dug out the cross. He disen-
gaged his other hand from the black man's and placed the cross on his
palm, and closed his fingers around it. He was watching Thomas, following him with his eyes. He kept his fist closed around the little cross
but seemed oblivious of it. His breathing had become more rapid and
shallow.

"I'm coming back," Thomas said. "You rest easy."

Wells had finished vomiting—yellow gouts of hardtack—and was spitting the grainy residue. McNamara stood in the wide barn doorway looking out into the rain. Wells spat a final time and followed Thomas to where Mac stood. The rain pattered down. It fluttered on the barn roof.

"Ain't nothin we can do for him," Wells said. "He'll bleed to death in a hour." McNamara stood motionless and silent.

"Looks like they took a saw to em," Wells said. He shook his head and spat again. "I wouldn't do a hog that way."

"Shut up," McNamara said.

"What'd I say?"

"Just shut up."

"Mac," Thomas said, "what did you do with that pistol?"

McNamara looked at him.

"What did you do with it?" Thomas said.

"It's in my bread bag."

"You got any loads?"

"Two," Mac said.

"Give it here," Thomas said.

"Wait a minute," Wells said.

McNamara unbuckled his haversack and brought out the Remington, wrapped in some cotton cloth to protect it against crumbs and coffee grains and sugar and whatnot. He unswaddled the gun.

"Let's don't mess in it," Wells said. "It ain't our problem."

Thomas turned on him. "What do you want to do, Jimmy? Tell me."

"Leave him be."

"Goddamn if I will."

"The boys on post'll be along any minute," Wells said. "Let Cate figure it out."

"The hell with that," Thomas said. He opened his hand and McNamara laid the revolver in it. He lifted the hammer and turned the cylinder so that a cartridge would rotate into the chamber and cocked the gun.

"Come on help me, Mac," he said.

McNamara nodded and the two of them went toward the stall where the dying man lay. Thomas hid the revolver by his side and they went into the stall. He knelt again beside Floyd, who opened his eyes. He was still gripping the cross. McNamara dropped to his knees on his other side.

"Take his hand, Mac."

McNamara did. Floyd closed his eyes and began to pant, and each short shallow breath seemed to send a spasm of pain down through him. He was sweating hard. McNamara looked at Thomas.

"Help is coming," Thomas said. "A surgeon. We'll take you home. To your family."

He put his hand very gently over Floyd's's eyes and brought the heavy gun around. His hand shook slightly but he angled the muzzle under Floyd's chin without touching him and McNamara nodded and leaned away and the clap of the explosion swallowed the three of them and went skimming along the barn walls and careering roofward, the echo reiterating itself until it found the open door and was gone.

McNamara already had risen and lurched out of the stall. Floyd had died with his eyes closed and although the ball had blown a hole in the top of his skull, his face, at least, was peaceful. Thomas got up, holding the revolver. His knees were unsteady but they held. He did not look again at the dead man, or for the cross.

McNamara was sitting on the dirt floor with his back against a stall door and one knee cocked. Wells was standing where Mac had been before, watching the rain come down.

"Your gun," Thomas said, offering it butt-first.

"Keep it," Mac said.

"I don't want it," Thomas said.

"No more do I. I should never of picked it up."

"We had to do that, Mac."

"He'd of been dead soon. Jimmy was right."

"Not soon enough."

"What're you gonna tell Cate?"

"The truth."

McNamara nodded. "You go on, let me set a minute."

Wells was looking back at the two of them. He watched Thomas come toward him, bringing his gum blanket and the Remington.

"You want this?" he said.

"Not me," Wells said.

Thomas took it by the muzzle and flung it high and far, end over end, into the rain.

"Mac feelin sickly?"

"He'll be all right."

"Poor fella. I wonder what he done."

"What difference does it make?"

"Maybe he was one a theirs. Tried to run away."

"I don't think so."

"Well he must of done somethin."

Thomas didn't answer.

"I wonder where that hen's at," Wells said.

Sergeant Cate's outpost detail emerged from the woods on Seminary Ridge, moving in skirmish formation in their blanket-cloaks, twenty feet apart, weapons at trail arms. McNamara had gotten up and joined Thomas and Wells in the doorway.

"Funny we ain't heard her again," Wells said.

McNamara looked at him and didn't say anything.

"He's talking about the hen," Thomas said.

"I know what he's talkin about," Mac said.

They watched the skirmishers come on.

"It won't always be like this," Thomas said.

"What won't?" Wells said.

"Shut up, Jimmy," Mac said.

"Everything," Thomas said, and pulled his blanket up over his head and shouldered his musket and went out into the rain.

The light was better now and more debris visible in the yard; utensils from the farmhouse kitchen, a sodden feather pillow, oil lamps lying overturned and their glass chimneys lost or broken. A rocking chair lying on its side. The skirmishers drifted closer together, abandoning their formation, and began looking around the farmyard. Joe Merriman picked up a book and opened it and someone called to him, asking if it was lewd, and Merriman smiled and said no and tossed the book aside. It's spoilt anyways, he said. Sergeant Cate stood looking at the big farmhouse, appraising, as if he were thinking of buying it.

"Well, Tommy," he said.

"Rebels are gone," Thomas said.

"What is it, then?" Cate said.

McNamara stood beside him as Thomas told it, with his head bowed, motionless as before. Several of the men had gone into the farmhouse and Jimmy Wells had followed them.

"I'll have a look," Cate said.

"You might not want to," Thomas said.

"You're right about that," Cate said over his shoulder.

They followed him into the barn, out of the rain, and pointed him to the stall where the dead man lay. Cate stood in the doorway and stared at the body and did not speak. Then he turned, abrupt, and walked away.

"Shall we bury him?" Thomas said.

Cate stopped, looked down at the hard bare dirt and thought. "He'll have family," he said, "might want to bury him proper."

"I don't think they'd want to see him," Thomas said.

Cate thought some more. "All right," he said. "I'll order a burial detail."

"I'll do it," Thomas said.

"You've had enough of it, Tommy," Cate said.

"I'd feel better to bury him," Thomas said. "Mac'll help me."

"Wait a minute," McNamara said.

"Mac?" Cate said.

"Mac," Thomas said. "We have to finish it."

"What the hell you think we done?"

"We owe him, Mac."

"Ah Christ," McNamara said, assenting. "Ah shit."

"You might look in his pockets," Cate said. "Find something with his name on it."

First they searched the farmhouse, downstairs and up, tracking it with their muddy brogans, till they found a feather quilt of good quality. They found shovels in a lean-to shed. Wells had spread the story, and the men watched in silence as they took the quilt into the barn.

"It'll be ugly work in this rain," Mac said.

"I know."

"We could put him right here."

Thomas stopped. "Would you want that for yourself?"

"I wouldn't care and neither won't he."

"He should lie under the fresh air," Thomas said. "Under the rain. Under the sun. That's what I'd want and so would you."

"Christ, Tommy."

"I'll never ask you again. I swear it."

"You do, I won't listen."

The smell of blood and intestines had grown stronger. The flies had found him and the sound of them turned Thomas's stomach. The dead right hand cradled the cross—tenderly, it seemed. They lowered the quilt over the body, trying not to look at it, knelt and bundled it, scooping the severed privates.

"Let's check his clothes," Thomas said.

His shirt was of good muslin and his trousers linen and Thomas wondered if he was a servant in a wealthy household and how he'd gotten here. The Rebels had taken his shoes. There were no papers in any of his pockets. There was no pocketbook. His shirt and pants had collected dirt and mud: the young black man had been on the run, hiding out. They searched every pocket and left the clothes where they'd found them. They lifted him between them under his arms and knees, accustomed now to the ponderous weight of the dead, and carried Floyd Wilkes out into the rain, around the barn and out onto the field west of it. They laid him down, stripped their coats and equipment, and began wordlessly to dig, cutting the matted grasses with their shovel blades, prying out hunks of black topsoil. The rain soaked their shirts and ran cool down the backs of their necks. After a while Joe Merriman appeared, and then Wells, hooded in their gum blankets.

"By Christ it's wet," Merriman said.

"Where's you boys' guns?" Wells said.

McNamara paused in his shoveling and looked at him. He shook his head and went back to work. They'd left their muskets and their knapsacks in the barn.

"They don't need a gun," Merriman said, "they got you to protect em."

Abner Riggs, the Nantucketer, had come out. He looked at the shrouded body. "You done the right thing, Chandler," he said.

Again McNamara stopped shoveling. He straightened. "Shut up," he said.

"You got hearin trouble?" Riggs said. "I said he done the right thing."

"You want to talk," McNamara said, "get the hell gone."

"Mac," Thomas said. He'd paused too. "Let it go," he said.

"Let *what* go?" Riggs said.

"Damn if you boys ain't actin like we lost the fight stead a won it," Wells said.

McNamara had resumed digging. His shovel cut into the earth with a wet slicing sound.

"You boys have done a lot a diggin," Merriman said. "Whyn't you let me take a turn."

McNamara worked on as if he hadn't heard him. Thomas straightened, looked up at Merriman, who dropped his musket and gum blanket and began shedding his haversack and various belts. He peeled off his coat and dropped it. Thomas stepped up out of the oblong hole—they'd gone down a couple of feet—and Merriman took the shovel and stepped sideways down into the grave.

"Gimme your shovel, Mac," Jimmy Wells said, unshouldering his haversack.

McNamara ignored him.

"Give it to him," Thomas said.

Mac straightened slowly, drew a breath.

"Just gimme the goddamn thing," Wells said, and took off his coat.

More men had come out onto the field. Sergeant Cate. Tom Jackson. McNamara stepped up and Wells took the shovel from him. The men stood in a half-circle and watched him and Merriman dig.

The rain slanted down. It fell all over the county. Lee's army moved south through it, the long winding columns of men and guns and mule-drawn wagons, the dispirited cavalry, the coffles of black men on their way to auction. It soaked the infantry to the skin and pattered noisily on wagon canvas, muting the groans and curses of the wounded.

It rinsed the dead on McPherson's Ridge and Culp's Hill and in the Wheatfield and the Peach Orchard. It washed the blood from the boulders of Little Round Top and Devil's Den, and from the arms and legs the surgeons were still chucking out of the windows of farmhouses in the valley and along the Taneytown Road. It fell on the rows of wounded in the yard of the Frey farm and the Swisher farm and the Leister House, and those inside, packed wall-to-wall in house and barn, heard its delicious whisper and wished they could drink it.

Merriman and Wells stopped five feet down.

"Tommy?" Merriman said.

"Good," Thomas said.

The diggers tossed their shovels and climbed out, stained from head to toe with red-brown dirt. Thomas and McNamara twisted the ends of the quilt and lifted Floyd Wilkes, slung between them as if in a hammock, and lowered him into the grave and dropped him. He landed with a cushioned thud and his right hand protruded from the quilt, the cross gone, the hand lying palm up, fingers curled loosely, relaxed. It was copper-brown and shapely as a woman's hand, gentle, and Thomas wondered what skills it had possessed. The young man had had an intelligent face.

"Tommy?" Merriman said, offering the shovel.

McNamara had already taken the shovel from Wells. Thomas took the other one from Merriman and he and McNamara looked at each other.

"Okay?" Thomas said.

"Okay," Mac said, and they sank their shovels and began the quick work of filling in the grave.

Epilogue

GETTYSBURG, 1922

———

"I've come a good number of times," said Thomas Chandler, talkative in his old age. "I couldn't count how many. Well, yes I could, but I won't take the trouble. First time was 'seventy-four. My wife came with me every time, while she was alive. She died in 'eleven. My children have all come, one time or another, and my grandchildren. I came alone once. One thing I won't do: come on the anniversary. Not on any account. I don't like the crowds and the hoopla, and I've no wish to see any Southern veterans."

"Why is that, sir?" the black man asked.

"Don't call me 'sir,'" Thomas said.

"You an old gentleman. Got to show respect."

"I'm no older than you are."

"You don't think so."

"No I don't."

"You say you were in this battle?"

"Do you doubt me?"

"I don't doubt you. Point is, I wasn't but five years old then. If you weren't older'n that, they in trouble."

"I was sixteen."

The stranger turned and regarded Thomas's craggy hatless profile. He now had his father's deep-set squint but had not lost his hair as George Chandler had by the time he was forty. Thomas's was a mane, white, thick, backswept from his narrow forehead. He was a spindly old man of some considerable height, with a bent walk.

403

"Sixteen," said the Negro.

"That's all I was," Thomas said.

It was a warm, clear September afternoon. Thomas and the Negro were sitting side by side some twenty yards uphill of the mounted puddingstone boulder that stands at the center of the position the Twentieth Massachusetts occupied on July 3, 1863, before Captain Abbott led them, gesticulating like a man out of his wits, to the copse. The boulder and plaque were—are—a monument to the officers and enlisted men who died here, or received their mortal wounds.

Revere.

Ropes.

Paine.

Henry Wilcox.

Jake Rivers.

Elisha.

Luke.

I had a brother who was killed at Gettysburg. Or: *No, I wasn't an only child. I had a brother who . . .* How many times in all these years had he said that? *Dear Father & Rose. You will have heard of our great victory here wh'ch augurs victory for our Cause but with it comes news of the worst kind & I must tell you bluntly for there is no way to sugar it.*

"Sixteen is mighty young to get your ass shot at," the Negro said.

Thomas looked at him.

"Excuse my French," he said.

He had come along Hancock Avenue, gimping on a cane, a heavy-set and comfortable-looking man with iron-gray hair, in a tweed suit with vest and necktie, a derby hat, smiling at the fine weather, it seemed, as he went along the ridge. Thomas, happening to look back from his seat on the bottle-green September grass—park grass now, weedless and kempt—had waved to him, and the man had waved back and one thing had led to another, and here they were.

"Where'd you fight at?" the Negro said.

"Right here. We were in line down where that boulder is. You can still see where we dug a trench."

"I know that trench."

"And those trees," Thomas said. "We all ran there after the Rebels broke through at the Angle."

"You were at Pickett's Charge, then."

"In the thick of it."

"Give them Southrons hell, didn't you."

"A good deal of it. Funny thing was, we didn't know who Pickett *was*. Hadn't ever heard of him. The brass had, I suppose, but not the enlisted men."

"You heard of Lee, I bet."

"Lee. Longstreet. Ewell. Pickett wasn't that high up. The charge wasn't his idea."

"Be Lee's."

"They ought to call it Lee's Charge. Put the blame where it belongs." *Lee's God, ain't you heard?* McNamara had said that, *Lee's God,* and Thomas and Jimmy Wells had laughed, feeling good about everything in spite of the rain and all the dead, Luke dead and Elisha, feeling as good as possible at such a time, and then they'd gone into the barn.

"What blame?" the Negro said. "Pickett's Charge supposed to be a great thing."

"You wouldn't think that if you were in it."

"I *don't* think it. Lot of folks do, though."

"They don't know how stupid it was. Men going down four, five at a time when a bolt or shell hit just right. And then the rifle fire they took. Thick as hail."

"I know all about it," the Negro said.

They sat, propped on their hands with Thomas's coat and the Negro's cane laid beside them, gazing out over the valley. Except for the railroad tracks, it looked much as it had when Thomas had first seen it in the dawn of July 2, before the second day's fighting had begun, the green and amber-green fields, the oasis-like clumps of trees, the thick concealing woods on Seminary Ridge. Bucolic. Sylvan. In this clear air South Mountain was a liquid indigo, and Thomas remembered how cool it had looked, how inviting. Oh, to be there, and out of all of this.

"My brother fought here too," Thomas said. "He was killed."

"For that I'm sorry."

"My best friend was killed too. He was like a brother to me."

"That's some bad luck, all right."

Thomas turned, pointed. "My brother died right over there. Elisha—that was my friend—died just beyond, a hundred feet or so."

The Negro turned, looked politely to where Thomas had pointed.

"My brother's buried up there in the National Cemetery," Thomas said. "Elisha's family had him brought home. I thought he should have stayed here, been buried next to Luke. But they'd stopped believing in the war, if they ever did. They said they didn't want Elisha to have anything more to do with it. I didn't get home till the war was over, and it was too late to argue with them. Maybe I wouldn't have argued anyway. They were farm people. I don't even know if they believed in abolition."

"But you did."

"I did indeed. And so did Elisha."

"What do you believe now?"

Thomas thought a moment.

"Maybe it ain't my business," the Negro said.

Thomas turned, looked up toward the copse for his daughter. She had not come back yet, or had wandered off somewhere, waiting for him to finish sitting. She'd hired a car and driver at Plank's Garage and she and Thomas had visited Luke's grave while the driver waited. She'd left Thomas there, he needed some time alone with Luke, and gone back to town to browse in the antique stores, leaving him to walk from the Cemetery, still an easy enough stroll, past the souvenir shop and the whitewashed Bryan farmhouse, where General Hays's men had repulsed Pettigrew's North Carolinians, and out along the ridge on Hancock Avenue. She'd told him to bring his Chesterfield and he had, though the air was so warm and kind that even his seersucker jacket felt unnecessary. He raised his head and breathed deep and thought of the air on those hot days in 'sixty-three. The smells! Worse every day, you could not describe them, and he thought, *No one will ever know.* It was like this every time he came back, the loneliness of remembering, but he came anyway because of Luke. Because he could not visit Luke's grave or this low green ridge with its tasteless monuments and statues without feeling his brother's presence, nor escape the idea that Luke—whatever he was now, spirit, wraith, untethered soul, noiseless echo of himself—knew that he, Thomas, was here.

"What's your name, sir?" Thomas said.

"Now you're sirrin *me*," the black man said.

"Getting even," Thomas said.

"Cept I don't mind, myself."

"All right. I'll call you sir, you call me Tom, or Thomas. Thomas Chandler."

The other smiled. The smile a broad curve in his jowly chin. "Ephraim Carter," he said. "Live right here in Gettysburg and always did. Pleased to meet you." He offered his hand and Thomas took it.

"I live on Martha's Vineyard," he said. "Which I bet you've not heard of."

"No I ain't."

"Pretty little island off Massachusetts. Quiet."

"Quiet," said Ephraim Carter. "You had enough noise in the war, I guess."

"That's about the size of it."

Lee's God, ain't you heard? He was back there again, the deserted debris-strewn farm, the slanting rain, the hay-smelling barn, the dying man. He and Mac and Jimmy Wells. Mac spoke of it but once or twice afterward but it preyed on him, made him gloomier than ever. *He wasn't right in the head,* the mill foreman said. *It was the war that done it, if you ask me.* McNamara had fallen off a New Bedford streetcar, drunk, and died under its wheels in 1880. Thomas had seen it in the *Evening Standard* and had arrived in time for the burial. *You're the doctor from the Vineyard. He used to talk about you, sir. How you came through the war together. Gettysburg. The Wilderness. Cold Harbor. By Jesus you saw a lot. And never a scratch on either one a you, John said. Said you saved his life once or twice.*

I never saved his life, Thomas said.

"You ain't answered my question," Ephraim said.

"What question?"

"I asked you what you believed in and instead you asked me my name. But I guess it ain't my business."

"What do you believe in?" Thomas said.

"I asked you first."

"All right. I believe same as I believed in 'sixty-three."

"We ain't slaves anymore."

"So?"

"So now what?"

"Full equality. A nation conceived in liberty and dedicated to the proposition that all men are created equal."

"Father Abraham," Ephraim said.

"He was a great man," Thomas said.

"Some'll say that."

"Won't you?"

"Know what my nephew says? Says Father Abraham was full a shit. Excuse my French."

"Maybe," Thomas said, "your nephew is full of shit."

Ephraim smiled. "He goes along with that Marcus Garvey, you know about him?"

"What's his name?" Thomas said.

"I just said it. Marcus Garvey."

"Your nephew, I mean."

"Moses. We like them Bible names."

"My brother had a Bible name."

"You do too."

"That's true."

"We Bible fools, ain't we."

"My brother was one of the bravest men I ever knew," Thomas said.

"Moses ain't a shrinkin violet. He was in the war. Over there in France."

"I'm glad he survived it," Thomas said.

"He's educated, too, which I ain't, as you can see. I did all right, though. Worked for the railroad. The B&O, the Pennsy. Made Pullman porter, saw a lot a the world. Saw Boston, New York. Saw Montreal Canada. Got a nice pension now. I ain't worked in ten years and don't need to. I tell Moses, say, I hope you do as good on a education as I done without one. Moses' daddy too. He's on the railroad now."

"Who told him Lincoln was full of shit? Marcus Garvey?"

"He tell hisself, I guess. Or studied it out of a book. He down to Howard University this very minute. You comfortable settin here?"

"What does Moses think of General Howard?"

"Who?"

"General Oliver Howard, the one they named the university after. An abolitionist. Fought here at Gettysburg."

"I don't know what he thinks, but if the man's white he prob'ly don't like him. You comfortable?"

"Yes."

"My legs get cramped up."

"Well, move them."

"Believe I will." Ephraim shifted, drew a leg up, then straightened it again, and did the same with the other leg. "I don't know why they don't put benches here. It's a park, ain't it?"

"There's too much junk here already," Thomas said.

He turned, looked again for Rose. They had traveled yesterday. Rose had joined him on the train in the Pennsylvania Station in New York City, and they'd changed in Baltimore and ridden the train to Gettysburg and walked up the hill to the hotel on the square. A long day. Thomas had slept late this morning.

A young woman, not Rose, went by, walking a collie dog on a leash. A motorcar had stopped on Hancock Avenue and four people, men and women, had gotten out and were examining the copse, which was girdled now by a wrought-iron fence. It had shrunk over the years, or so it seemed, an innocuous stand of trees in a park, cleared of the slash and brush underneath. No one could imagine, looking at it now, the hell it had been.

"Moses joined up in 'eighteen," Ephraim said. "Went to fight for freedom, just like you done. Big surprise was, they put all the colored boys separate. Ain't good enough to fight alongside white boys, same as your war. Couldn't go inside the YMCA canteen cept at certain times. Had separate latrines. Segregation, everywhere you look. He come home pissed off, I'll tell you. Said it couldn't be no worse in Germany. Said he was a fool to fight for this country."

"I don't defend that," Thomas said.

"I know you don't. We're talkin about Father Abraham, what he done for us."

"He freed the slaves," Thomas said, "and we made it stick. Right here. And then the Wilderness. Other terrible places."

"Didn't cure segregation, though."

"It did some."

"Didn't cure lynchings."

"No," Thomas had to say.

Across the valley, where Pickett's men had come out of the woods, a group of what looked like schoolchildren was gathered around a park guide or teacher. *The lord is my shepherd, I shall not want.* The sweat running off them as they crouched, waiting, the shallow pit they'd dug turning to mud. Macy and Abbott pacing with their drawn swords. *Steady, boys.* Macy had gone home without his left hand. Abbott had been killed in the Wilderness.

"Do you know," Ephraim said, "that colored folks can't eat at most every restaurant in this town? Gettysburg, Pennsylvania, and colored folks can't walk into a place and have a meal. Can't even get a haircut most places."

Thomas said nothing. He hadn't known. Had not been paying attention.

"Can't spend the night anyplace. Use to be a lot a colored folks come out here, wanted to see where they got their freedom. See where Ole Abe give his speech. They don't come no more. Moses is disgusted. Say he don't care about Lincoln, Pickett, any of em."

"Then why do you come?" Thomas said.

"Come where?"

"Here. Cemetery Ridge."

"Well, sir. I done read where somethin like six thousand Southrons were kilt here in just that one charge."

"Killed or wounded," Thomas said, "but wounded didn't mean you lived. There was tetanus. Staph."

"You want to hear or don't you?"

"Go on."

"It was a judgment on em. I take it personal, and I'll tell you why. My momma and daddy took us outta here just before the Southrons come in the first time. All the colored people were leavin. They were over to Chambersburg—the Southrons, I mean—and we hear how they're catchin colored folks and takin em for slaves. Some say, Well that's just runaways, but there's others say they're takin everybody, don't matter, and they was, for a fact. Takin everybody got black skin. My momma and daddy they threw us in the wagon and we went out Carlisle Street a good long ways and hid out in the woods and waited. Lived under the wagon, built a fire at night cook our food. Was a white family out there let us use their well, I will say that. Us children, we purely enjoyed it.

"But my one brother, see, he was growed and didn't go with us. Name was Thomas, by the way, same as you. Was workin for a white farmer name Watson, I believe it was, and Watson hid him in the barn loft when the Southron riders come through. What I heard, anyways. I ain't but five years old at the time, understand. Southrons found him, I do know that. Story says Mr. Watson tried to face em down, save Thomas, and maybe he did, but he ain't saved him. Southrons took him, and we ain't ever seen him again.

"So I enjoy to come here, think about all them Southrons got shot down, blown up, legs shot off em. A place of judgment, this is."

Thomas's heart had woken and was knocking against the thin wall of his chest. He had told no one of the mutilated Negro, had kept it even from Clarissa, a locked door inside him that he wouldn't or couldn't open to her, he did not know why. He had never gone to Seminary Ridge on any return to Gettysburg, nor west of the ridge, where the white barn had stood and perhaps still did.

"What did your brother look like?" Thomas said.

"Was a long time ago."

"Think."

Ephraim looked at him, the smile shrewd now. "Why you askin?"

Thomas shrugged and looked out over the valley. The schoolchildren were still there. "Just curious," he said.

"Just curious."

"Did any others disappear? Negroes, I mean."

"There was a deal of em from Chambersburg. That's where most were took. From here I know of two got took and never come back.

Thomas. Old woman name Sara. Was a boy name Floyd Wilkes disappeared durin the battle. Took or killed, nobody ever knew."

"Floyd Wilkes," Thomas said.

"His momma was what you might call famous around here," Ephraim said. "A prostitute, I'll say it right out. Kinda crazy, time I knew her, but folks say she was made so when her son was took or killed, whichever. She didn't have no others, you see. Folks treated her kind, what I always heard. Even white folks. Some of em, that is."

"What did Floyd Wilkes look like?"

"Lord, I don't know. What're you after, Thomas?"

"Nothing," Thomas said.

Ephraim looked at him, smiling his smile. "Now that's the first lie you told me."

Thomas looked out at Seminary Ridge. At South Mountain. He had not told Clarissa about Lilac and Iris either, another locked door, nor had he gone back to Virginia to speak to Iris, as he'd promised Elisha he would. For a while he'd intended to but then he was courting Clarissa and then they were married and he couldn't go back without telling her why and he probably couldn't have gone if he had told her.

"I think I found Floyd Wilkes the day after the battle," he said.

Ephraim was studying him.

"In a barn," Thomas said.

"Found him dead," Ephraim said.

Thomas gazed out at the sunlit landscape. The Peach Orchard was an orchard still. Cattle grazed, Holsteins, west of the Codori farm and the Emmitsburg Road.

"Yes," he said.

"Southrons done it."

"Yes."

Ephraim nodded. The smile had left his face, sunshine giving way to overcast. "Why you think it was Floyd Wilkes?" he said.

"He wasn't dressed like a farmhand. Had a nice white shirt. Nice trousers. He had nice hands. Soft."

"It wasn't my brother, then," Ephraim said.

"There were no papers on him," Thomas said. "There was no way to know who he was. So we buried him. Me and some others from my company."

He came home on a late-summer evening with darkness falling early, down the gangway in the sea-smelling dusk onto Union Wharf, where the scattered people looked at him in his faded uniform, knapsack riding his back with the rolled wool blanket on top of it, a small valise in his hand. Some he knew but they failed to recognize him in the poor light, were stumped too by his increased height and leanness, the hollows in his face, the hardening in it. A soldier, but who? There weren't that many from the Vineyard. Thomas ignored their stares and went up Union Street and right on Main, past Daley's Drugstore and Thomas Bradley & Sons and the linden tree and the fountain, and up the dark lilac corridor of Drummer Lane.

A lamp was burning in the front parlor. She was expecting him one of these nights. Thomas climbed the front steps and paused with his hand on the doorknob and closed his eyes and drew a deep breath. His heart was so full it hurt. He opened the door, quiet, and stepped inside, and the familiar smell of the house, cedar and lamp oil and rainy days, came so sudden and strong he nearly staggered.

A lamp burned on the hall table, across from the big mirror. At the end of the hall the kitchen doorway was a square of welcoming amber light. Thomas set down the valise. He unshouldered his knapsack.

Oh, Lord, Rose said, silhouetted in the kitchen doorway, a housedress, no hoop, the curves all her own.

Rosie, he said.

They met halfway. She was weeping by the time they did. She smelled of rosewater, and exotic bloom. She smelled of home and safety and a happiness he would never know again. She clung to him and cried and he held her, rocked her.

Don't cry, he said.

It's happy crying, she said. She leaned back in his arms. Look at you, she said. My Lord.

She took his arm then and led him into the kitchen, and he began to hear the great silence that tenanted the house now, the emptiness. He sat down at the table and took off his forage cap and looked at it. It was stained and shapeless and faded, its lid still emblazoned with the white Second Corps trefoil. It was over, and now what? He had no idea.

Hungry? Rose said.

I guess so.

Got plenty of food. Got cold bean pudding. Cold chicken, fried the way you like it.

Do you have any whiskey?

I do, she said, but I only use it special occasions now.

Well, Thomas said, if this occasion ain't special I don't know one that is.

She smiled. You lose your grammar at the war? she said.

I lost everything, he said. Get the whiskey, Rosie.

The bottle stood in the corner hutch. Rose knelt and retrieved it. She dusted it and set it in front of Thomas. She fetched out a pair of tumblers and sat down.

Your father gave me a talking-to, she said. Said if I kept on I'd reach a point where I couldn't stop, even if I wanted to. Wrung a kind of promise from me: special occasions. I'd gotten worse, you see, after Luke was taken. When your father went, I thought, Well I'll just keep to that promise. Not set here alone and drunk in this big empty house. Anyway, I'd found it was makin me fat.

Thomas looked at her and smiled. He uncorked the bottle and poured and they touched glasses and drank. The whiskey went down strong and its burn touched his aching heart and he put his hands to his face and wept into them.

Oh, sugar, Rose said, and took both his hands in hers. Her eyes in the soft lamplight were tear-swollen, the gentle arcs of her cheeks wet and shining.

I wish I could have been here when he went, Thomas said.

Of course you do.

We were outside of Petersburg by the time I got your letter. He'd been dead three weeks.

I know all that.

He stopped writing after Luke died.

He couldn't. His heart just kind of shriveled up. By the time he died he'd about stopped seeing patients. I'm surprised he lasted as long as he did.

You had to manage everything, didn't you?

Most everything. Your aunt Martha came over for a few days, but she mainly avoided me. She thought your father and I had improper relations. That tired old story.

Thomas tasted his whiskey again. There were no more tears. He had few to give anymore. Rose raised her glass and drank.

Clarissa Parker asks about you, she said. She came to the funeral service, and you know what else? She came calling afterwards. She and the Smiths. Only ones.

I wrote to them, Thomas said.

They were obliged to you, Rose said.

He died very bravely.

I know.

Thomas looked at his battle-toughened hands on the table. Rosie, he said.

She looked at him and knew. He wouldn't have had to say it.

I know about you and Luke.

She bowed her head. Contrite, waiting for the blow to fall.

It's all right, Thomas said. I was angry at first but it was only jealousy. We were all in love with you. Me. Father. Elisha, too. He told me so the night before he died.

Rose was weeping again, head bowed, a sorrowing black Madonna. Don't, she said.

It wasn't your fault, Thomas said.

She blotted her tears with the back of her pretty hand. Luke should have written me he told you, she said.

It was the same night. Everything came out.

Rose came forward in her chair and hugged herself. Don't tell me any more, she said.

All right.

Not one more thing.

I won't.

They both drank. Thomas was getting pleasantly woozy. A liking for spirits had developed in him rapidly after Gettysburg, but there'd been little liquor to be had in the last years of the war because Virginia had been so thoroughly ransacked. You'd go into a plantation house and find the furniture half gone, wainscoting stripped for burning, wine cellars and liquor closets bare. Now and then Hancock would order a ration of commissary whiskey, but it was only a teaspoon.

You found him in the morning, Thomas said.

He'd gotten up in the night. I didn't hear him. Dr. Nevin said he might have felt a brief pain but hardly anything.

Where did it happen?

Rose looked away. I don't think I'm going to tell you that. You have to live in this house.

Thomas shrugged. He hadn't thought about where he would live. What about you? he said.

This isn't the place for me, she said.

It might be.

No, she said. You're old enough to understand that now. I said I'd wait for you and I did, but I have to leave.

Because of Luke, he said.

There's too much memory here. And the way people look at me. The old suspicions, the coldness. The mean gossip.

Where will you go? Thomas said.

Depends how brave I am.

Thomas nodded. Let's have another drink of this good whiskey, he said.

"How old would she be, Daddy?"

"I don't know," Thomas said.

"Eighty?"

"I suppose."

Ephraim dug a watch out of his vest pocket. "I believe it's time for me to step on," he said. "My Lucy'll be missin me."

"We could give you a ride," Rose said.

"I enjoy to walk," Ephraim said.

"We wouldn't mind," Rose said.

"I know you wouldn't, honey."

He leaned forward, rolled onto his knees, and pulled himself to his feet on his cane. "Gettin cooler," he said.

Thomas got up more nimbly. Rose popped to her feet in the smooth springy way of an acrobat.

"Good-bye, Ephraim," she said.

"Good-bye, Missy."

They shook hands. Ephraim turned and shook Thomas's hand. "You come back you look me up," he said. "Ephraim Carter. Live on Queen Street. Be pleased to invite you in for supper."

"I'd be pleased too," Thomas said.

"Bring this bold lady. I'd enjoy to put her and my nephew in a argument, no holds barred. See how it all turn out when the smoke cleared off."

"I'd bet on Rose," Thomas said.

"Think I would too," Ephraim said.

He smiled, touched the brim of his derby, turned, and limped heavily down the incline on his cane. He stepped sideways across the grassy declivity that had been the Twentieth's rifle pit and went bobbing along the edge of the field where so much blood had been shed, then disappeared behind the rise that ran obliquely up to the copse.

"Nice fellow," Thomas said.

"Were you really arguing?"

"Not really."

"The Civil War didn't solve everything," Rose said. "We all know that. Put your coat on, Daddy."

He did, though he felt no need to, and she took his arm and they moved up the slope to the car waiting on Hancock Avenue. The driver was behind the wheel, reading a newspaper and smoking a cigarette.

"Tell him to meet us at the cemetery gatehouse," Thomas said.

"It's late," Rose said. "You're tired."

"I want to walk, Rosie."

She let go of his arm and went around and spoke to the driver, who nodded and threw his cigarette away and started the car. The afternoon had waned and the car's harsh grind and thrum broke across the stillness. The driver made a U-turn, veering onto the grass, and drove away. The two couples who'd been looking at the copse had also left in their automobile.

"I wonder if I'll come back here again," Thomas said. They were walking again, strolling, Rose on his arm. The sun was above South Mountain now, its light turning an oily gold. Autumn light.

"Why on earth wouldn't you?" Rose said.

"Maybe it's time to let the past alone. To let it lie."

They were nearing the copse. The ground rose gently toward it. Three granite monuments, like outsized tombstones, stood in haphazard-seeming arrangement near the wrought-iron fence, marking, supposedly, the ultimate positions of the Fifteenth, Nineteenth, and Twentieth Massachusetts Regiments but with little relation to the chaotic reality. Who knew where anyone had been? Everywhere. Anywhere. Thomas could not even be sure any longer where, exactly, on this park lawn they'd buried Luke and Elisha.

"I'll always come back with you," Rose said, "if that's what you're worried about."

"It's not," Thomas said.

"And then there's Uncle Luke to think about. He'd miss you."

"Maybe I should have brought him home," Thomas said.

"He *is* home," Rose said.

They went on past the copse and the long flat incline above the Angle, where Thomas had killed his first Rebel. Miasma of gunsmoke, noise like a drawn-out endless thunderclap, men falling every which way, shells ripping the sky apart.

"It was so terrible here," Thomas said.

"Not anymore," Rose said.

She looked at her father and he at her, and they went on, slowly, toward the darkening cemetery.

"Not anymore," Rose said again, and Thomas listened to the stillness of the hills and fields and cobbled town, and knew she was right.